METAL ANGELS

PART FOUR

BY

D K GIRL

So here we are, Mikie.

It's been a long while.

And I don't miss you any less.

Kira - 59

Kira fought to stay awake, each slide of her lids harsh as sandpaper against her eyeballs. The hum of the car engine an out of tune lullaby.

'How you feeling?' Leona sat with knees bent, bare feet on the backseat. The top of her tattered lime-green tracksuit was pulled over her knees, creating serious fake boobs. A regular B-grade Dolly Parton.

'Like someone just fucked me over,' Kira said. 'In a way I definitely didn't pay for.'

Sober as a judge, but her words slurred through lips that barely had the energy to pull apart from one another. Thinking hurt.

Hell, everything did. Her skin hot and irritated, like she'd been out sunbaking with lashings of coconut oil. Kira's metal hand rested on the stringless bow she'd taken from the penthouse, now cradled in her lap. It had remained in a contracted state, little bigger than a ruler, and she didn't dare play around with it, in case she found the 'go full size and poke someone in the eye' button. When Clara had pointed it their way at the penthouse the bow had definitely been longer, like Clara's body length long. And the chick was no short-ass.

'Well, you fucked them right back.' Damn if Witchy Parton didn't sound the teeniest bit proud. 'You both did.' Leona nodded at Bradley, curled up between them on the seat like an oversized piece of strange candy, candy that breathed in big gulping breaths. 'It was quite the display.'

'What was with him?' Kira jerked her chin towards the lizard and grimaced. Quick movement equalled bad hurty stuff. 'Did you know he could . . . do that . . . dragon shit?' She kind of hissed it, hoping to keep Tweedledee and Tweedledum riding up front, out of the loop. Right now, Jared and Brian were arguing over which way was the quickest to the airport.

Leona gave Kira a big dose of disapproving-mother face. At least, Kira assumed mothers could look like that. She didn't have a comparison.

'What Bradley did was in no way "shit",' Leona said. 'And no, I was not aware of that particular ability. He has always had a very strong link with the Maiden, but there was no hint of this before. But then, much is not as it was before.'

Cue dramatic shift of gaze to Kira's metal arm. Bug, meet microscope. 'Righto. Settle down. No need for extra drama. Got plenty of that right now, thanks.' Kira rubbed at her knee. Shit. Sunburn goddamn everywhere.

'Indeed. And I believe we are seeing just the beginnings of it.' Leona's gaze, tracing over every inch of Kira's face, was almost as uncomfortable as her sensitive skin.

'Why are you looking at me like that?'

'You are only slightly duller than him now.'

'It doesn't seem like the right time for insults.'

Leona surprised her with a gentle smile. 'I know you are frightened, Kira. And well you ought to be. Your sister, and the visitors she aids, have messed with things they shouldn't have. Brought to us a bright one, the likes of which this Earth has not seen for thousands of years. An ancient soul, built by the gods themselves. I understand the source of Azrael's power, but yours . . .' her gaze moved to the lizard, 'and the suddenness of the Maiden's own gain in strength, well they are both wonderful mysteries.'

Kira let out her breath between pursed lips. She didn't want to think about Blake the world-destroying sister right now. She didn't want to glow or gleam or do anything but get in a cool bath and have someone wash her back for her. Her train of thought moved from baths to showers to its logical conclusion: Nina. Where the hell had she and Rossiter ended up?

The lights up ahead flicked to red, but Brian hit the gas and shot through the intersection.

'Jesus!' Kira cried, bracing herself against the back of his seat. 'Are you fucking insane?'

'Sorry, sorry!' he cried. 'I was listening and got distracted.'

So much for keeping the conversation on the down low.

'Well, let's not add getting arrested to the list,' Kira said. ''Cause one of us in this car is wanted for murder.'

Brian stared at her in the rearview mirror, eyes bugging. 'Murder? Holy fuck, what –'

'Forget it.' Kira slumped against her seat. 'Sweet Christ, I need a drink.'

Jared hunched forward, scrabbling around in the footwell before brandishing a beer bottle. 'Do you want one of these?'

He handed it to her, that glorious bottle of golden fuck-it-all juice. It was within snatching distance when Leona shattered the dream. She grabbed the bottle and dumped it into her own footwell.

'Last thing you need is inebriation, young lady. No telling what could happen,' Leona sniffed.

'I could tell you what I'd like to happen.' Kira pasted on the best glare she could manage, even though it stung like hell where her skin wrinkled.

'I'm trying to help you.' Leona released her knees from captivity, letting the tracksuit jacket slide free.

'Don't need it.'

'Bullshit.'

One point to the witch. Kira kept up the glare for another couple of seconds, then let it slide, turning to stare out the window. The metal running up her neck pinched hard where it met flesh just below her earlobe. She bit down on her lip, hoping Leona hadn't noticed the jerk of her shoulders. Dumb stupid witch and her sudden niceness. What was with that? Leona was wrong, too. About Kira being frightened. Wrong! Not frightened – goddamn terrified. Of pretty much everything. Like this car ride. And being hurt again the way Tamas had hurt her. Of seeing Blake again. Of not seeing Blake again. Kira tapped a fingernail against her metal wrist. The sound that came back wasn't what you'd expect; it wasn't tinny or metallic in any way. More like tapping marble. It had always been like that. The armadillo had always been something strange. Alien. But a part of her, nonetheless. Not usually something to be frightened of.

Leona leaned forward, brushing her fingers against Jared's blond strands. He flinched, turning to stare at her. 'You all right?'

'Thought I saw something caught in there.' Leona smiled. 'Sorry.'

But not sorry enough to stop. Only this time it was Brian's turn. For someone who appeared to be about a thousand years old,

Leona could move. She scooted right up close to the sleeping lizard and reached for Brian's red curls. In her other hand, she clutched the beer bottle. It was open and sloshing golden amber onto the faux black leather seat as she leaned forward.

'Thought I saw something there, too.' Leona's smile was back, but in a too chipper kind of way. Obviously fake. 'Sorry, boys.'

Kira expected some kind of reply, an 'it's okay, crazy lady' at the very least. But there was nothing. They turned back in their seats and locked eyes on the road. Leona settled back with a smug smile on her face. 'That will make things easier for the moment. Keep them focused on a single task.'

'What did you do to them?' Kira said. 'And what are you doing with the rest of the beer?'

The answer to question two came immediately. The witch shoved it between her legs, right up high next to her lime velour-encased lady garden.

'If you're that desperate, feel free.' She waved her hands over the open bottle.

Kira considered it as the scent of hops played at her nostrils. She needed dullness, something to deaden the roar of her body. Something to push back the memory of being goddamn tortured.

She swallowed. 'Pass.'

'Thought so,' Leona said. 'I've just refocused the boys' attention on the task at hand rather than the conversation in the back seat. Thought it would be good for us to chat. We should talk about what happened back there, with Tamas.'

Nope. No, we shouldn't. Kira shook her head. Leona touched her fingers to Kira's thigh. A gentle enough touch but the skin-to-skin contact flared through Kira like acid. Way too close a sensation to what Tamas had inflicted. All at once, a shit storm of memory dumped itself on her. Fuck, it hurt. So much.

'Shit, don't touch me.' Kira pressed against the door. 'Don't touch me.'

'Sorry.' Leona held up her hands in surrender. 'Sorry, love. Kira, take a deep breath. It's all right. Are you listening to me? It's all right. Hey, Kira.'

It wasn't all right. So very not all right. The attack swept up through her core, a rising beast of panic. Her flesh hand shook. Her throat wasn't being fair about letting enough oxygen in, and if Kira had had a heart capable of racing, it would be doing the minute mile right now. She couldn't hang this one on Az. This monster was all hers. A panic attack hadn't haunted her for a long while, but the anxiety had been a constant asshole in the beginning. That first year after waking up with metal parts had sucked severe ass.

Now the claws dug in again, dragging her thoughts to the edge of an inky abyss where fear festered, thick and mucky. Where the fuck was all the air in this car? Kira tried to wind down the window, but it took more coordination than she could get out of her limbs. The pressure at the back of her eyes stepped up a notch, parts of her skull trying to nudge their way free. Dampness spilled down her cheeks. The world was blurry. Fuck. She was going blind. The abyss was taking her –

'Kira.' The sharpness of Leona's voice snapped her back into the car and into the warmth of the seat beneath her. Leona held her metal hand. When had that happened? 'Love, I'm right here. Now take a breath before you pop a lung.'

'I can't see . . . I can't see properly,' Kira said. A three-year-old had hijacked her voice, making it wheedle and crack.

'You're just crying. It's tears. Now look at me, love. Take a breath.'

Fingertips, gentle against her chin. Kira blinked. Once, twice, a million times. Leona drifted into focus. A terrible fake tan had never looked so good. The abyss shrank away. Kira wiped at her face, too rough with the metal, scratching at the skin beneath her eyes. But the sting was welcome. She was back. On solid ground. Out of the freak-out panic zone. Leona cupped her hand to Kira's cheek. No zinging pain. Her skull jigsaw had slotted all its pieces back into place.

'You with me?' the witch said, soft as melted butter.

Kira nodded. 'I don't know what to do. What I'm doing . . . what any of this . . . what's happening to me . . .' The words dissolved on her tongue.

There were flecks of black in Leona's brown eyes. Really quite pretty. 'I've seen the balls of steel you have, Kira. You're going to be all right. And you are not alone. Understand me?'

Kira leaned into Leona's hand. The witch shouldn't get used to it, but Kira was going with the touchy-feely thing in this moment. A feathery touch at her knee drew her gaze. Bradley perched there, black eyes watchful. He let out a couple of bleats, as soft and gentle as Leona's words.

Kira sat back, pulling away from Leona. Kodak moment was over. Snotty nose to deal with. Jacket sleeve would fix that and give Kira a chance to hide for a second, too. Fuck, so embarrassing. Losing it. Perry was the only one who had ever seen her turn feral like that. Christ, she missed him.

Brian eased the car into a right turn, both he and Jared keeping their eyes locked on the road. Neither of them had so much as glanced in the rearview mirror. Whatever focus Leona had incanted on their asses was working just fine. Kira sniffed, sucking back an uncomfortable amount of snot. They were driving through an industrial area. Hulking great warehouses loomed on either side of the road. Deserted at this time of night. Morning? Who the fuck knew. She was just about to ask one of the zombie drivers when Bradley sprang from where he still rested on Kira's knee and launched himself up at the window, splatting flat against it like one of those sticky toys Kira had had as a kid. But the lizard was better value than the shit rubber version. He shifted back and forth across the window, little padded feet acting as suction pads to hold him there.

'Okay. Is that normal?' Kira said.

'Stop!' Leona shouted. 'Pull in over there. Now.' She gestured towards a steel-grey warehouse to the right. Stark-white lights stood sentinel high up on poles, blazing down on two giant piles of tyres. Brian swerved and slammed on the brakes, nearly shoving them all through the front window. Leona was piling out of the car before it had come to a complete stop.

'Vail!' she shouted. 'Vail, where are you, boy?''

'Vail?' Kira swung open her door, collecting a reptilian passenger as she jumped out, Bradley scrambling up the armadillo to sit on her shoulder. 'He's here?'

He fucking well shouldn't be. Kid could barely wipe his own butt last time she'd seen him. Bradley chirped. From the corner of her eye, Kira could make out the bobbing of his head. Yes. The lizard was telling her yes. Hell, this week just kept getting better. Something dark and large shifted behind the pile of rubber to their right. Leona dashed towards it, her short, jack-hammered strides managing to make her look half-chicken. She didn't seem to notice her bare feet on the gravel. Jared and Brian stayed put, the quizzical scrunch of their faces suggesting they weren't entirely sure why. Kira turned back to the bolting witch. The shape behind the pile shuffled out towards them. It was large, all right. And feathery.

'Anzu?' Kira frowned. The beast was in full oversized-rooster mode and limping noticeably. As was Vail, who used Anzu as a giant walking stick. 'What the hell are you doing –'

Her mouth snapped closed as a third figure emerged from behind the pile. It was like a goddamn clown car back there. And this clown was totally unexpected. Miss Happiness herself. Greta, the flame-haired nonfriendly from the farm. Leona drew up just short of where Vail stood with his arms already raised to greet her. She dug her hands into her hips, and his smile slipped. 'Leona?'

'So, you're all right then.' Leona ground her heel into the gravel.

'Yes.' Vail nodded. 'And you?'

'I'm fine.'

'Oh, he's in so much shit.' Kira whispered to Bradley. The lizard responded with a shrill chirp, then leapt from her shoulder, stumpy legs held wide, soaring like a sugar-glider across the short distance to where Vail stood.

'Bradley.' Vail's smile went back to full high beam. He cupped his hands, and the lizard landed on his palms like a pro. 'It's good to see you, little guy.'

'Are we done with the greetings?' Greta stood by Anzu's side. The beast looked exhausted, his sides heaving, wing tips pressed to the ground to keep him steady.

'Hello to you, too,' Kira said. 'Guess William didn't teach you –'

'Kira,' Leona hissed.

'What?'

'He's dead.' Greta hurled the words at Kira like a monkey flinging shit. 'Your sister's people killed him. And would have killed me too if Will hadn't made me run like a fucking scared little girl. So just shut your big, foul mouth and listen, you stupid bitch.'

Kira raised her hands. 'Sorry . . . I'm really sorry about William. Seemed like a good guy. But for the record, they are not Blake's people.' The panic attack was still too raw to start thinking about Tamas again so soon, but Kira breathed through the flutterings. They needed to know. Blake didn't do this. Not this part anyway. 'My sister had nothing to do with what happened back there. Tamas . . .' Breathe, swallow, don't puke. Kira glanced at Leona, then to Vail. 'She didn't fucking kill anyone. And they are hurting her. Tamas told me.'

Vail's expression grew pained, as though he wanted to burst into tears at the news. If he'd looked like shit back at Nina's, he looked like hell now. The bruising on his face had deepened a shade, a green-violet spreading up to his temple and disappearing behind the blunt fringe. The jeans he wore were clearly a size too big, and the long-sleeved shirt was one of Nina's. A pastel-pink floral number.

'I'm so sorry, Kira.' And there was no doubt he was. What was inside that kid? The soul of a saint? 'This is all really messed up.

And it doesn't get better anytime soon.' He paused. 'Kira, I need to give you something.'

'Tell me it's a one-way ticket to somewhere other than here and we are friends for life.'

'I wish I could.' Vail edged forward, and Anzu, the living walking stick, moved with him.

'What's going on, boy?' Leona frowned so hard her eyes were narrow slits. 'There's something . . . not right about you. What have you done?'

Kira joined the frown-fest. Greta was with Vail, and seeing as there was no way she could have found Nina's place without Nina, then that meant one thing. 'You went back to the farm?'

Vail's sheepish glance at his feet told her the answer. 'I had to.'

'Bullshit. You had to stay in bed and watch cartoons.' Kira stopped. That was sounding way too mum-like. Did mums get this damn knot in their guts when the kids went wild? 'Why did you go back, Vail?'

'She called to me.' Vail shuffled his feet, flicking a quick look towards Leona before turning his attention back to Kira. He sucked at being a rebellious teen.

'Who called you, Vail?' Leona's voice sank down low on the spectrum. Mumma-witch was pissed. 'You look like you should be on a funeral pyre.'

Mumma was subtle.

'Back off, all of you,' Greta said. 'The Maiden. She called him. Called to me, too. Vail, just give Kira the damn stone.'

Leona's wide-eyed, gob-smacked expression was priceless. And, on another occasion, would have been hilarious. 'The Maiden called you? You heard her voice?'

'Not exactly, it wasn't like that. I just knew I needed to get back to the farm.' Vail's eyes hadn't left Kira, which was beginning to make her uneasy. 'She wanted me to go to the farmhouse. To find Greta.' He and the feathery crutch, Anzu, made their way past Leona and straight up to Kira. Vail reached for Kira's flesh hand, grasping it tightly. He pulled it to his stomach. Give the boy a burger or seven, his gut was concave.

'Dude, wanna tell me what's going on?' Kira laughed, but nerves jangled through the sound.

A rosie glow mingled with the bruising on his face. 'I'm sorry. This is what I was instructed to do. I had to swallow it.'

Kira was too exhausted for this shit. The breeze made the skin on the back of her hand and her face ache. 'You swallowed a stone?'

'The mea stone?' Leona may as well have squawked. Close enough. 'Why in the Maiden's name would you do that?'

'It was her idea, Leona.' Vail's pitch stepped up a notch. Bright and way too perky. 'She showed Greta where the stone was –'

Greta dug her thumbs into her belt – all that was missing was a cowboy hat and some spurs. 'I was doing what William told me, running. But I only got to the bottom of the hill before it hit me. I had to go back. Needed to look under the fridge, like my life depended on it.'

'The mea stone had rolled under the fridge at the farm, can you believe it?' Vail certainly didn't seem to. 'I mean, something as powerful as that. Just rolled under the fridge like a bad penny . . .' His hand went to his cheek, touching the coin embedded there.

Leona whistled. 'By all the Maiden's laces. These are odd and wonderous times indeed.'

Kira cleared her throat. Her hand was still pressed to Vail's stomach, and the moment was getting awkward. 'Do we have to wait till you poop it out, or what?'

'No.' Vail did a weird thing with his lips, sucking and chewing on them at the same time. 'I need to . . . to, ah, to –'

'Oh for crying out loud.' Greta stormed over to join them. 'He needs to kiss you. The stone will do the rest. We had to carry it in a way that it couldn't be detected. And, apparently, the kid's gut falls into that category. Seeing as little boy wonder here has only one foot in the land of the living, maybe he's good for storage. Who knew a half zombie would be so handy? Well, apparently the Maiden did. Hence, we are here.' She let out a small sigh. 'Shit, I'm sorry. I didn't mean to sound . . .'

'Like an asshole?' Kira said. 'Big fail on that one.'

Vail wasn't a big guy, but now he seemed even smaller, hammered down a foot by Greta's words. And it did something to Kira's already fucked-up insides.

'Come here, Vail.' She grabbed his shirt collar and pulled him close. He gasped and she cut off the sound with a press of her lips to his. Being slightly taller than he was, she hunched forward so Vail wouldn't have to teeter on tiptoes. Kira touched her tongue against his pressed lips, trying to burrow through. It took the kid a second, but then he relaxed. Lips opening, tongues meeting, and heads tilting to get the right angle. Not bad. Not bad at all. Vail leaned into her, his chest against her. She could actually feel the pounding of his heart as their kiss deepened. Kira took control of the kiss, pressing her hand to the back of his head, digging her fingers into his hair. The heat beneath her skin evaporated, and the relief was a gush of pure heaven. Vail made a small sound, a gasp against her mouth, and wrapped his arm around her middle, leaning in. The coin in his forearm pressed against her ribs. Kira's metal hand slipped from the back of his neck and moved to cup his cheek.

Jesus Christ, she needed to back off, pull away. It was Vail for crying out loud. Technically, this was gross. But, oh god, it felt too good. Good like a hot bath after a day's skiing. Good like that perfect pill at your favourite gig. She was whole again, not cracked and chipped and aching. Vail retched, coughing into her mouth and slaughtering the moment.

Their teeth clacked together as Vail's body jerked. Kira's eyes widened. Hard as she tried to pull away, it wasn't happening. There might as well have been magnets in their fillings for all the good it did. Vail's legs buckled and Kira had to cradle him to stop them both from collapsing. He heaved, gasping, hands grasping her forearms with the grip of a titan. Fuck, he was going to throw up in her mouth. Shit. Balls. Shit. He jerked, and something warm and unpleasant rushed into her mouth. Any second now, Kira was going to be doing the same damn thing. A hard pellet shot into Kira's mouth, slamming hard against the back of her throat. She gagged and finally the lock between them broke. Vail staggered back and Kira lost her balance, slamming down onto her backside. But none of that mattered. She was choking. A great lump was forcing its way down her throat, blocking off her air. She clawed at her throat. Vail and Leona were both speaking at her, their words jumbled into one. Making no sense. Heaviness weighted her chest. She pressed her hands there. Unyielding metal greeted the touch of her fingertips. All the way across her chest, down over her breasts, only giving way to flesh at the base of her ribcage. The realisation sucked what little air she could find into oblivion. The armadillo was on the move again. Head spinning, Kira clawed at her shirt, trying to tear at the material, but Leona and Vail held her back, telling her it was going to be okay. Bullshit. She was going full metal. Screaming was a great idea. Breathing was better. And she couldn't do either. Black blotches filled her vision. Any second now she would be out cold.

Swallow. Faster. Harder. Get the damn stone down. Just finish it. Eyes bugging and watering, Kira leaned into Leona, letting the witch sit her upright, as though she were in some labour from hell. Someone was banging hard on her back. Someone else pulled her hair back from where it hung across her face. Her baby stone didn't want to go the last few inches, and the world was getting woozy. Shadowy. And why all the whispering? So many voices in her ears. Or was it one?

Kira squeezed her eyes shut, but it made no difference. Still there. Pssting in her ears. A few words grew clearer. Gain? Gay? What the fuck?

Gaia.

A single word. The stone pushed farther down and it was over. Kira rocked onto her knees, saliva running from the corners of her mouth. The air pouring into her lungs.

'Fuck,' she gasped, 'me.'

'I'm so sorry. I'm so sorry.' Vail was a fluttering, apologetic butterfly at her side. 'I had no idea it would be like that.'

'What happened? Did she speak to you?' Leona peered at her. 'Anything?'

Kira sat back on her heels. She lifted her shirt. Not a dream. A fucking nightmare. The metal covered her front like a chest plate. Her surgery scar, and the blue butterfly tattoo now buried beneath a layer of Telteriun, as were her tits, now two nippleless bumps. Good thing she'd gone bra-commando – yet another reason to love

Nina's boobs, her bras way too big for Kira. There were super-faint etchings over the surface of the metal that reached all the way down to her belly-button. Kira stared down at herself, waiting for the panic. But there was an odd numbness. Not unpleasant. It was the buzz after a few drinks, where everything took a little longer to sink in and things were easier to brush off.

Greta stepped in way too close, peering at her. 'Well, that's new,' she said quietly.

Kira watched Greta trace a finger over her stomach but didn't move to push her away. The touch reached her senses, and it wasn't entirely unpleasant. All the synapses were firing the same message. *This feels nice.* Greta's focus was on the symbols embedded in the metal. Symbols that hadn't been there until about two seconds ago. Cut into the surface of a metal Blake had once told her was damn near impossible to cut. Telteriun was like melting chromium and diamonds together. And apparently chromium plus diamonds equalled crazy tough. Blake had bitched about how long it was taking to develop tools in the Facility that could deal with it.

Kira smooshed her wrist against the side of her cheek, wiping saliva away. Why the hell didn't she feel like freaking out? Her body hummed. It didn't burn or sting. It hummed. The armadillo was eating her alive, and it didn't bother her.

'What is that?' Leona leaned in alongside Greta. They both stared at Kira's new metal belly and its engravings as if they were inspecting a new car. Vail stayed at Kira's shoulders. So did Bradley.

The lizard hadn't budged an inch, not even during the lip-lock session.

'It's Sumerian, cuneiform script.' Greta frowned. 'The Sumerians invented one of the earliest forms of writing.'

'Thanks for the history lesson,' Kira said to the navel gazers. 'But what does it say, and why is it all fucking over me?'

Greta lifted her hand from Kira's hip and shook her head. 'I can't read it. It's an ancient language. But it looks like the same couple of symbols repeated, over and over.'

Vail reached out his hand to help her to her feet, but Kira didn't move to take it. Her body still hummed. Not as strongly as before, but nice and comfy. Still enough to take a second for the outside world to sink in, which meant it took a while for the word to travel from Kira's brain to her mouth.

'Gaia,' she said.

Vail lowered his hand, tired eyes brightening. 'What did you say?'

'She said Gaia.' Greta took her sweet time pronouncing each word, as if saying them too fast would send them scattering. 'Why did you say that name, Kira?'

'It's a name? It was . . . in my head . . . when I sucked back on the stone . . .' Kira shifted her ass against the rough surface beneath it. 'Okay, why is everyone fucking goggle-eyed right now?'

Leona stared at the inscription with all the fervour of a mouse staring at cheese, a ludicrously wide smile parting her thin lips. 'The Maiden was once known by another name. The ancient Greeks were the first to worship Her, and they called her Gaia. The goddess of the Earth.'

Tamas - 60

Tamas stood just outside the shrine, alone in the Orientation Room save for Cym, the Syranian medic. The Waters, a gushing flow of liquid that emitted an odd high pitch, made the only sound in the domed room. Normally something Tamas enjoyed for the way it masked the constant screech in his own ears. But at this moment, even the divine Waters irritated him. He tapped his toe incessantly against the concrete floor, unable to keep himself still.

'How long until they arrive?' Tamas flung out the request, not bothering to turn and look at Cym, who kept a respectful distance. There was a noticeable pause before he answered, likely because Tamas had asked the same question about five minutes earlier.

'Fifteen minutes, sir,' Cym said.

So far as the Syranians went, Cym wasn't unpleasant. He didn't have the haughty air of Parator and Seder and Gren, he wasn't pathetic and easily led like Eron, nor was he domineering like Bel and the captain. He was the most likely of the Syranians to pass for human, having somehow convinced the captain that cutting and colouring his hair would enable greater cooperation from those he worked with on a daily basis. The alien could doctor, too. He'd played a part in patching Tamas up after the Meld. In another life, and if Tamas had been looking for one, Cym might have been an affable acquaintance. But just as the Waters no longer soothed, Cym's presence grated on Tamas's heightened senses.

'There has been no further issue?' Tamas gave up the toe tapping and took up pacing instead.

'No, sir.' Honey smooth, Cym clasped his long fingers behind his back. 'There have been no further issues. A containment cell has been readied on level nine, as instructed, for Azrael's arrival.'

Tamas spun round, mouth engaged to put an end to the ridiculous name Blake had given the gallu, but catching himself before his eagerness to ridicule Blake saw him reveal the creature's true identity. The goddess wanted the wild man's presence hidden from the Syranians. And from their god, Lahar. This great secret was one She had bestowed upon Tamas alone, tasking him with finding the god-slayer and returning him to Her.

A grin pulled at his lips. He had done that. Done all that She'd asked of him. And there had been that unexpected bonus. Kira's agonised screams still rang in his head, oddly comforting. As he'd stared down at her, her veins bulging and body contorting beneath the agony he inflicted on her, Captain Nex had delivered the news that Dumuzi had been located. It was truly the perfect moment. And the day only got better. Enkidu—Azrael— had come to them, had literally thrown himself at them, making Kira's 'interrogation' all the more satisfying by its pointlessness. The bond Tamas assumed existed between her and Enkidu proved far less steely than imagined. The god-slayer had not galloped to her rescue. Kira was no Gilgamesh after all. Laughter edged up Tamas's throat, threatening to bubble free. His attempt to halt it resulted in an odd cough. How on Earth had he ever thought that piece of patched-together trash so large and frightening?

'Is everything all right, sir?' Cym said.

Dumuzi was located. Enkidu was contained. Both were en route to the Facility. Kira was probably quite dead, or near enough. Everything was damn near perfect. Tamas stifled the one prickle of discontent that plagued him. With Enkidu returned, he supposed that Blake's usefulness had all but evaporated.

'Wonderful, actually.' Tamas returned to his pacing, each heavy footfall stomping down on the ridiculous notion that he might miss Blake when she was gone. 'Fifteen minutes, you said?'

Utter contentment would surely come when Enkidu was safely ensconced in the cell.

'Yes, sir.' Cym nodded in a slow, controlled way. 'Though closer to twelve now, I suspect.'

Tamas tugged at the collar of his jumper, the beige wool far too warm. Sweat beaded on his top lip. Layering himself with too much clothing whenever he was around the Syranians had become unconscious habit. The bulk helped to alleviate that feeling of being hopelessly physically inadequate around the statuesque aliens. Tamas wiped at his lip with his sleeve. Screw it. He pulled the jumper over his head. He was the Messenger. He would land the blow that would imprison a goddess of war. Tamas intended to do it without damp armpits.

'I need to send a message to New Weston,' he said.

'Right now, sir?'

'Right now. There is something that needs doing.'

His pace – and his heart rate – quickened as he strode across the Orientation Room. It wasn't every day you issued an order to have someone executed. In fact, it was his first day. Tamas took a deep breath, holding it as he crossed the room. Surely Kira was already dead. She sure hadn't been the picture of health when he'd left her covered in her own vomit, with eyes sunk into her head and veins that looked fit to burst. With his gaze fixed on the floor, Tamas walked straight out through the main doors and almost collided with a man about to enter.

'My apologies.' The black-bearded man tipped his head, eyes lowering. Tamas recognised him as Reuben's temporary replacement. The name escaped him, and he searched for a name tag, finding it at a broad, thick waist. Boyd Pesola.

'What is it?' Tamas said.

'Sir, the incoming packages have touched down.'

The clench of tension at Tamas's gut eased, but only a fraction. 'Do you not think I'm aware of their progress? That message hardly required a personal delivery.'

Pesola leaned forward, his voice lowered. 'Sir, we have lost contact with the location at New Weston.'

The evenly delivered words drummed into Tamas, and his already pounding heart tried to dig its way out of his ribs. 'Lost contact?'

The man nodded. 'They last heard from Clara about twenty minutes ago. We've been trying to reestablish communications, but there've been issues. At our end as well as there. Power surges that keep tripping –'

'I don't give a shit about your issues. Tell them to stop trying and to just damn well do it. Get eyes on the ground there, immediately.' His voice echoed off the high ceiling, giving it a far greater gravitas than Tamas could usually manage. 'Neither the witch or the girl leave that place unless they are in body bags. Do you understand me?'

All too well, if the man's quick intake of breath were an indicator. Reuben wouldn't have needed the direction to begin with. He would have understood without conversation what must happen. An ache played at the backs of Tamas's eyes.

After a too-long pause, Boyd Pesola nodded.

'Yes, yes. Of course, sir.'

The man – whose stocky frame suggested he had none of Reuben's dedication to exercise – scampered down the hallway as though the Precon itself was on his tail.

'Wait.' Tamas stepped out into the hall and past the two guards who stood at either side of the Orientation Room door. 'Blake Beckworth has been secured on level nine, correct?'

The fleeing man halted but did not draw closer. He nodded. 'Yes, sir.'

'Increase security on that level. Are any of the cells on level eleven salvageable?'

'One of them, maybe . . . if we did some work –'

'Then do it. Go.'

Tamas activated the release for the doors, staring at them even after they had closed, blocking the man from his sight. Gut instinct, paranoia, whatever it was, the urge to keep Blake close hooked in its claws and wouldn't let up. Not until he had eyes on Kira's dead body.

'Kira and the witch are being held at New Weston, are they not?' Cym called out. 'Do you believe we have cause for concern?'

Tamas ground his teeth. Sweat again lined his lip, only this time it was not due to excessive heat. 'I believe we can never be too cautious.' He was being ridiculous. Surely. Kira couldn't have anything to do with the loss of comms. This was a technical issue, nothing more. Besides, even if the witch had somehow escaped her cell, and gotten to Kira, they were hours from here. Why then were his nerves paining him, as though echoes of the utukku coursed through him? On edge. Alert. Sensing danger. Tamas cursed under his breath.

From where he stood at the bottom of the three short steps leading up to the shrine, he had a clear view of the totems carved into the ceiling: the Precon, the Syranian god Lahar's totem, a ratlike creature of their world; and the goddess Ereshkigal's more familiar Arabian wolf, with its dish-wide eyes and claws that extended double the length of its paws. Tamas's blood churned a little faster in his veins. His goddess. His mistress. And he had served Her well. Nothing could hinder that.

Nothing would.

The minutes stretched on, pulled to within an inch more than Tamas could stand. Captain Nex and his precious cargo may have landed, but it took time for them to make their way here, down into the depths of the Facility. Tamas scratched at a patch of skin at his elbow until blood seeped beneath his nails. And still no word came from Pesola that New Weston had been reached.

Finally, Captain Nex strode into the Orientation Room, followed by a procession of the Syranian god-soldiers with their respective gallu. Eron was at the centre of the parade, all willowy six-feet-four of him, his silver-white hair pulled back in a tight bun, not a single strand out of place. His face was clear, as though he'd had his make-up done before striding into the room, and his heavy, determined pace contrasted vastly with his usual light, almost hesitant stride. Tamas's gaze fell to the bundle Eron nursed. A tiny naked arm, fist balled, punched at the arched Orientation Room ceiling. Perhaps, Tamas mused, Dumuzi already sensed what approached.

'Give the child to me.' Tamas stepped forward, stopping Eron midstride. The Syranian wavered, glancing at his captain. 'Eron, perhaps you misheard me?'

'No, Messenger.' Eron still wore his contact lenses, and his now sky-blue eyes did not leave Tamas's face as he offered up the white-wrapped bundle. 'It is done. Dumuzi resides in this child.'

'It is not done, it has just begun,' Tamas whispered.

Babies were lighter than he expected, or perhaps it was just this one, gaunt as it was, with hollows beneath each cheekbone. Its eyes were closed, giving no hint of what lay beneath the surface. Such a feather-light, inconsequential thing, yet more important than anything Tamas had ever set eyes upon. It was hard to imagine it would survive the ritual he was about to begin. Dumuzi's true soul lay buried beneath thousands of lives. And each needed to be peeled away, like the proverbial onion – or those Russian babushka dolls – until all that remained was the immortal seed at the core. Tamas moved, but his eyes did not leave the child as he relished the press of it in his arms.

'Azrael has been delivered to level nine?' Tamas strode past the captain, headed for the steps of the shrine.

The Syranian leader nodded and raised his hand, as if intending to touch the child, but withdrew it at the last moment. 'He sustained damage, but Agar is priority. I have had Weylen tend to the gallu.'

'Damage?' Tamas paused, incredulity wrinkling his face.

The captain shifted his gaze towards Eron, who lowered his head. 'It took some effort to subdue Azrael. Agar used considerable force during the recovery, and it punctured a section of the gallu's carapace.'

More was said but the words grew faint, distant. And unimportant. Tamas laid the baby in the natural – but rough – indentation at the top of the petrified stump at the heart of the shrine. The relic had been brought from Iraq by his mother and father. In another, far greater, time this tree's roots had burrowed into the soil beneath Ereshkigal's temple. Perhaps Dumuzi had himself sat beneath the grand branches that must have grown from it.

Tamas pulled back the wrap covering the child who wore only a nappy and a flimsy white singlet that contrasted the deep golden-brown hue of its skin. A shade that matched Tamas's own. But the child didn't take well to the sudden icy cold of the shrine. Wrinkles appeared in the tiny face, and a high-pitched cry launched from barely formed lungs. It hammered at his ears and Tamas staggered back. His senses flamed, skin prickling. But the discomfort couldn't be blamed on the infant. These were early warning signals he knew all too well.

The goddess approached.

The walls of the shrine brightened, a violet hue edging in to join with the emerald glow. The downward flow of the Waters slowed, coming almost to a standstill before commencing again in the opposite direction, rushing up the walls, sucking in towards the goddess's totem on the ceiling. The wolf's head was directly over the stump. Directly over the distressed child. Every drop of fluid gathered over the wolf totem, and the animal grew out from the flat plane of glass it had been carved into. Tamas's smile broke out again, despite the hammering his body was taking. His brain inflated against his skull as the goddess drove Herself into Her Messenger.

Her wolf eased out of its glass prison, dropping down onto slender fluid legs to land beside the child, whose puerile screams reached a new pitch as the beast touched a watery nose to its cheek. Ereshkigal's totem dwarfed both the stump and the child. Its shoulders were level with Tamas's chest, its great head double that of his own. He'd rarely seen the goddess in this form. Twice only. And both of those times had been when his mother was Messenger. Ereshkigal had grown more clandestine over the years as Her plan took shape. And to use this form siphoned more of Her strength, more of Her energy and time, leaving Her vulnerable to those who might watch Her in Kur.

Evidently She did not feel vulnerable now.

Now we shall see what is brought to my altar.

The wolf bared its teeth, glistening fangs that resembled ice shards. In a swift movement, it clamped its translucent jaw around the child's torso. Immediately, the cries ceased. Tiny blue eyes widened, and a pink mouth gaped. Over as quickly as it had begun, the liquid wolf released the child and edged back.

You've done well. It will begin, She whispered. The gentlest She'd ever been with him. A lump filled his throat. *My sister's eyes are turned, focused on another war front of my making. This is the time. Let our battle here commence. The cleanse can begin.*

Tamas's guts clenched, muscles contracting with hard spasms. His spine locked, jerking him backwards in an uncomfortable arch.

Enkidu. You have brought him to me.

'Yes.' Tamas strained to get the words out. 'En…Azrael is here.'

Her pleasure ran through him. Thick as honey in his veins. *You have done well, Messenger. Soon, the great powers of your ancestors will reside within you, released by my touch. Do not fail me now.*

The Waters rained down. Tamas dropped to his knees, grateful tears falling, hidden by the icy droplets that covered him. And he wished for only one more thing in this pristine moment. That his mother could have witnessed this. And understood, finally, that she had been so terribly wrong about him all along.

Blake - 61

The heightened heart rate that had concerned the nurse, and escaped Blake's notice, made itself very known now. The pattern of beats was erratic, their thuds hollowing her chest. Blake leaned against the glass wall, using it as a prop to keep her on her bare feet. She did not recall when her boots had been taken from her. Though the coolness of the concrete was soothing against her soles, she knew she would not have given consent to have the purple steel-caps removed. The gift from Kira had so rarely left her feet, worn every day Blake worked on the carapaces. Weylen had found this amusing and intriguing. According to the assistant, the boots were 'not really Blake's style'. Though what that style might have been eluded Blake entirely.

She traced her toes along a crack in the concrete at the base of the glass.

Lying on her back and staring up at the ceiling had grown increasingly unbearable. But getting herself vertical had almost caused loss of consciousness. Her surroundings swayed, much as they would have if she had been on a ship. Blake tugged at the cord that connected the IV drip to her wrist, and the stand holding the bag of revitalising liquid rolled across the concrete, coming to rest against her. Sweat coated her armpits, lips, and underneath her breasts. Her own odour was thick in the confined space of the level nine cell. Coming most strongly from the bandages covering her sewn-up palm.

'Perry.' She kept her head lowered so the movement of her lips was not evident to the camera that perched high on the wall in the outer corridor. Ever watchful. No one had been posted to stand guard in the containment area. Blake was alone in the cells. She was not even certain anyone watched her through the cameras, and if they did, then they would likely assume fever or infection, or both, had rendered her delusional. She had always paid scant attention to how those around her regarded her. But with Blake's work responsible for some of the Facility's biggest-earning patents, and her disinterest in forming any social bonds with fellow employees, Kira insisted the employees held her in a certain awe.

'Everyone loves a rich, weird-ass genius who isn't terrible looking, B. You've nailed it.' Kira's voice drifted up from the narrow crack in the concrete floor, and Blake smiled. Not alone. She was not alone.

'If you could see me now, Kira, you might reassess. I look quite terrible, I believe.' Blake pressed her hands to her mouth, knocking her forehead against the glass. 'No. No. No.'

Not Kira. Not Kira.

Her sister was far, far from here.

Where you have killed her. Kira is dead. Again. The venom poured into her, rich and sharp against her skull.

'Stop. Just stop!' Blake shouted, her warm breath reflecting off the glass barrier that held her firmly prisoner. She pressed the heel of her palms hard against her eyes. The viper – that sadistic inner voice that spewed vitriol – hadn't taunted her for a while. In fact, not since Perry had . . . appeared. Formed in her mind? Blake dug her palms in harder, to the point of discomfort, but the darkness seemed to aid her in keeping track of what was reality, and what were the delusions of a traumatised mind. Perhaps this wasn't the viper at all. It was a reasonable assumption that between the toxins of the Waters, the poison embedded in the splinter in her wrist, and sheer exhaustion, Blake simply approached insanity.

Every corner of her mind was crammed with thoughts of Kira. And of what Blake had asked of her.

Everything.

Live, when she should have died. Run with a burden that was not hers to carry. And now they were going to use Blake to hurt Kira. Hurt her for what Blake had asked her to do.

'Good times.' Kira's voice rose from the crack, buzzing at Blake's ears.

She lowered her hands, blinking at the brightness of the cell. 'I'm not listening to you.'

You never did. Did you, Blake? Didn't listen to her, didn't see her. Too busy gorging yourself here.

'Piss off.'

Blake grabbed the IV stand and focused on dragging one foot in front of the other, back to where she could lie on the firm bed and stare again at the ceiling. Maybe attempt to swallow at least one mouthful of the stone-cold mashed potatoes that had been sent to her. As though eating were something she was capable of. But the distraction might send the viper back down into the pit.

Blake paused, letting her fingers play against the metal column the IV hung from. The tips of her fingers on the arm that held the embedded splinter had gone quite numb. If Cym had managed to add some of the Waters to the saline drip meant to hydrate her, she couldn't tell.

'Just a little longer,' she muttered. 'We just need to wait, until we are sure that she's not here.'

We?

'Shit.' Blake glanced back at the crack in the concrete. 'I'm not going to be sane enough to blow them all to hell.'

Blow whom to hell?

Blake jerked forward, an instinctive move to escape the voice at her back. The IV stand toppled forward, crashing onto the ground, tugging at the needle but not enough to dislodge it from her arm. Blake dropped to her knees, attempting to increase the slack on the translucent tubing that connected her to the fallen stand.

'Perry?' Blake unhooked the saline pouch and cradled it against her belly. Not as satisfying as a hot water bottle, but just clutching something hard enough to stop the ridiculous trembling in her hands was good enough. The Starpoints shifted beneath her skin but she held firm. 'Is that you?'

Her already burdened heart crept up its pace, and a sob, barely formed and rapidly extinguished, fled up her throat. 'Perry.' Keeping her head lowered, allowing the unkempt strands of her loosened hair to cover her gaze, Blake scanned the room and found what she was looking for. He stood there, most of him little more than a white haze, but the features of his face clear enough.

Hallucination, delusion, or something else, the return of the familiar face poked at raw, tender places inside her. Taking a breath suddenly became a mammoth effort.

Blake? Perry's watery image speared through the bed, his lower legs lost in the shadows beneath the structure. *Oh man, I'm back. I did it. Thought I was lost out there for a minute.* He made no discernible move – all at once, he was just closer. *Blake, are you okay?*

'Yes.' Talking to ghosts. Hearing her sister in a crack in the concrete. Joints on fire, explosives buried in her flesh and extremities going numb. 'I'm fine. Where have you been?'

Blake wiped at her eyes, finding them moist. Stinging. The fever. That's all it was. The sudden reappearance of Perry had nothing to do with the flow of tears.

You're not going to believe this, it was insane.

'Try me.' Blake rocked on her haunches, just for good measure. If curious eyes were watching her via the camera, let them believe what she was beginning to suspect. Blake Beckworth was losing her mind.

When you . . . yelled at me . . . well, I dunno, I just kind of freaked. Next minute I knew, I was back at the pub. Right there. It's all closed up . . . I guess they are wondering where I am . . .

The anxiety in his tone caused his image to flicker. The man required reassurance, that was clear enough even for Blake to see. But it would take up too much valuable time.

'You can move about in the world beyond the Facility?' Blake asked her knees, lips brushing her black linen pants. Once black. Now a patchwork of ugly marks and stains.

Seems so. But Blake –

'How far can you go? Can you control it?'

I don't know . . . I just –

'How did you get back here? Think, Perry.' Blake pressed the IV bag between her chest and raised knees. The fluid strained against the plastic.

Blake, I don't know how I did it, Perry pushed back, the anxiety replaced with anger. *Nothing's clear out there. There's just light. There's no shadows, just light, different shades, different sizes, like everything is caught in the glow of a nuclear blast. It's so weird. There's voices, sounds . . . I was scared. So fucking scared. I wanted to go home —*

'And you ended up at the pub?'

Perry drifted into the adjoining cell, his features blurring as he moved. *Yes.*

'So how did you get back here? How did you find me?' Blake's blouse was soaked through, but she didn't release the bag. Her eyes fixed on the crack in the concrete. The silence drew out far too long. 'Perry?'

He still stood in the next cell. His image vibrated, as though he stood on a surface gripped by a tremour.

'Perry, how did you find me?' Her teeth clacked so hard, Blake bit her tongue as she spoke.

Something pulls me back. It's dragging me back. It's so bright here. This place is the sun. And a black hole at the same time. Pulling at me. I don't really know how I got to you, I just wanted to see you. Because you're the only one who sees me. The vibrations increased to the point where Perry lost his humanoid form altogether. He was a haze, nothing more. *I don't like being invisible, Blake. I don't understand what's happening to me —*

Blake dug her teeth into the cut on her tongue. 'Dead. You are dead, Perry.'

Perry's image rushed into perfect clarity. A lens finding focus. And the sheer and naked horror that took prisoner of his expression threw Blake back into a jagged memory. Kira had worn that very same look when she'd awoken to her new limb. And her new reality.

The viper raised its head, reaching up through Blake's devastated body. *Always meddling. Fixing things that should stay broken. Taking things that are not yours to take. You broke them all, Technician. Destroyer of—*

The scream slammed its way out of her chest. She hunched forward, desperate to hold it back. Crush it down. The seam at the top of the IV bag tore open, and the fluid flowed down her arms, bitterly cold against feverish flesh. The ice froze her vocal cords. Buried the scream. Left her panting. Sucking in air that thinned as it made its way into her lungs.

'It's all gone, Perry. For all of us, what we had, it's gone. And I don't know what is here instead. I don't know. I'm sorry, I'm so sorry.' Blake curled up the hand that held the Starpoints, and the pain almost felled her. 'They want to use me . . . they think they can use me, that I'll help them fix the damage, repair their monsters . . . be the bait to trap Kira. They are so wrong. I'm going to bring this all down. Can you find Kira, Perry? Find her, make sure she is far from here. Her and Azrael. They don't have them.' Blake laughed and her ribs ached. 'She did it, Perry. She fucking well did it. I asked her to run, to hide, and she did it. They think she'll do what they say because of me?' She banged her splintered wrist against the concrete, sure and steady blows that sent fiery bolts up her arm. 'Idiots. Kira hates me. She hates me. I didn't save her. Making her live, wasn't saving her. Living and saving. Very different. Very different.'

Blake, stop. Listen.

'I won't stop.' Perhaps, if she could break her wrist, the shard of bone would spear the splinter clear of her skin.

Blake. Perry's voice boomed in her skull. *Someone is coming. Something is coming . . .*

Blake raised her hand. She had broken skin at her wrist, and blood ran in a thick crimson line down over where the splinter remained embedded in bruised skin.

Oh god. Perry shifted and moved out of her peripheral vision. *Oh god, he's so . . . so bright. It's hard to focus. Blake, look up. Look. It's that guy who was with Kira at the pub. I took them to the airport.*

She jerked her head, the momentum seeming to shift her brain against her skull.

Her very first. Her perfect work. Here.

Azrael. Bound to an upright restraint that Blake herself had designed. For maintenance. A cross design that held the carapaces' arms and legs out from their bodies, enabling access to every region of the humanoid structure and ensuring the design could be kept in optimum condition.

There was nothing optimum about the sight greeting her now.

Azrael was a shattered remnant of what Blake had passed to Kira. His smooth and unblemished skin, torn, stripped, and ruined. A great chunk of faux skin was missing from the right side of his face, exposing the cold and hard truth of what lay beneath.

They had ruined him. Bound him now with row upon row of inhibitor bars. Trapping him. Confining him. A metal plate curved over his forehead, holding his head in place. There was no chance he could turn to look at her, if he had even noticed she existed at all. Azrael did not fight. Did not move at all.

Blake's tired limbs betrayed her now, unable to keep her upright. She lay down on her side, certain not to let Azrael from her sight. Not giving a damn about the mess she placed herself upon. Not registering the chill of the fluid and floor. Staring at the many pairs of feet that wheeled the prisoner past. So many guards.

Such a precious cargo. Her precious cargo. Returned.

Is this bad? This is really bad, right? Perry's voice came from far, far away.

Blood and saline touched the corner of Blake's mouth, and still she didn't shift. Counting the pairs of feet. Ten pairs. Guiding her perfection into the cell two doors down. Placing her sublime work of art in the centre of a bare void.

Blake, hey. Stay with me. What do I do? Is Kira here too?

Tongue swollen and bruised, Blake could only manage a turn of her head. Her hair soaked up fluid with each movement. If Azrael was here, Kira could be only one place.

I'll find her. Perry's silhouette blurred Blake's view. *I'm going to find her, Blake. Maybe they have her here somewhere too. Do you hear me? Get up, Blake. For god's sake, tell me what to do.*

'Too late. We're too late.' The words dribbled from her. Barely intelligible.

Several of the guards stopped outside her cell. One of them tapping in the code to release the door. Voices rushed in, garbled, rapid, too much for her synapses to deal with. Blake raised her knees up hard against her chest, trying to make herself small enough to slip through the crack.

The viper had been right all along. Blake had broken them all. Kira was gone.

Eron - 62

Eron strode into the level eleven cavern and staggered beneath the weight of the air. It was pregnant with a heady mixture of static and pressure from the Tier, the press of it the greatest he had experienced. Eron struggled to conceal his discomfort. He did not acknowledge the nods directed his way by the handful of humans at work. The interest levelled at him had increased. Indeed, that applied to all the Syranians. A certain energy touched the Facility now. These workers would be unaware of detail but were not immune to the rise in fervour amongst their superiors.

As astounding and miraculous as Dumuzi's discovery might be, the brevity of the search left some difficulties in its wake.

Difficulties Eron negotiated as he moved across the vast space of the chamber. The arrival of the Four had been a chaotic event, one whose results were still clearly visible. Great chunks of rock had fallen from the ceiling after the Four had tried to shoulder their way to the surface, and most of that rubble now rested in three great piles dotted around the chamber, with the remainder being cleared from the chamber floor by a mini excavator. The elevator that Agar had tried to use as an escape hatch was beyond repair, its doors wide open, the innards dark. The main tech room was a mangled, unsalvageable wreck, and Tech Room Two had suffered fire damage. The remaining room, Tech Room Three, escaped unscathed, but was by far the smallest workspace, and valuable equipment had been lost in the destruction.

Eron reached the Tier's stonework edge. The dark, oily water bore not a single ripple on its surface, indifferent to the activity. Eron studied the upside-down reflection of the row of containment cells. Spiderwebs of cracks expanded along the glass walls of three of them, with the fourth cell at the far end the only one to appear to have escaped damage. Humans worked inside this one, removing sizeable pieces of rock that had cracked loose from the back wall.

Even the goddess could err in judgement, it seemed, though a curl of discomfort accompanied his thought. Allowing such a thought to take hold bordered on blasphemy, but the truth couldn't be denied. The goddess had underestimated the rebellion the Four would exhibit the moment they were thrust into this world. And it pleased Eron to know that even the divine, the greater powers that ruled ones such as him, that judged his own weakness with such fervour, could themselves be flawed.

Continuing to the tech room, Eron passed by the cranes that had held the carapaces. Three of them had been dumped in a twisted pile of steel and cables, something almost artistic in their intertwining. A pair of humans worked on the remaining crane, the sparks from their soldering iron sprayed blue arcs of light into the air, bright as any fireworks Eron had ever witnessed. Or was ever likely to witness. The days of furtive visits to the surface were long, long gone. What had possessed him to exhibit such curiosity about such vapid things? He had been weighed down by momentary insanity, surely. Extreme boredom. Restlessness. Whatever it was, the lure of it was dissolved now.

He reached the tech room. The solid white structure stuck out from the cavern wall like a giant shoebox. Inside, Blake's assistant, Weylen, leaned over a bulk that could be none other than Agar. The gallu was held down by multiple restraints on a stainless-steel table that took up a good portion of the confined space. She was, yet again, patching up the tears in his faux flesh. There was no sign of Blake Beckworth. *Have you heard anything about Blake?* That is what the assistant had asked him when she'd been sent to the penthouse to tend to Agar the first time. And he still had no answer to give about the Technician's whereabouts. Nor did he intend to pursue one. What point?

Eron fixed his gaze on Agar. Seeing the gallu this way, bound and contained – restricted – brought something akin to enjoyment. Cool amusement washed through Eron. As his mistress had done, Agar too had made an underestimation and assumed Azrael was, as the captain frequently pointed out, of no real consequence. A plaything to toy with. How wrong that estimation. Agar's shock had resonated through the mea stone when Azrael had landed his first blow. The memory caused Eron to smile even now.

A bespectacled human appeared at his side, hands in pockets, sweat on his wide brow. 'Sir, you need to come with me –'

Eron's hand whipped towards the man, taking a fast, sure grip around his throat. His tightening hold met the hardness of the man's oesophagus. Eron fixed the starch-white eyes he knew the humans abhorred so much on the trembling mass of skin and bone in his grasp.

'I do not *need* to do anything you tell me,' Eron said.

Even if the pasty-faced man had something to say, he could not get a word up his restricted throat. Each of Eron's pulses raced, each corner of his chest alive with their drumming. The veins in the man's face bulged, rising up against his skin. Eron's mouth parted at the sight. Tighten his grip a fraction and the human's windpipe would be crushed. A tilt and jerk of Eron's grip and a neck would be broken. His body ached to hear the sound. Eron raised his other hand to the man's face, fingers spreading wide to encompass the broadness of it. He pressed hard into the nubs of bone at the man's temple. Mucus ran from the human's mouth and nose. Tears from his eyes. One miniscule movement is all it would take to bring on the brittle break of bone.

Eron caught his unsteady breath and shoved the man away hard enough to send him crashing onto his back. An audience had gathered, keeping a cautious distance. A distance that grew when Eron levelled his gaze at them. The cavern was noticeably quiet, repairs halted. A woman, braver than the rest it seemed, darted forward to help the coughing, wheezing unfortunate to his feet.

Eron wiped his hands against his pant leg. A stench clung to the air. A woody bitterness. Not unlike that herb he despised so much, the clove. He frowned, attempting to decipher the scent.

'Back to your work.' Eron's voice rang high through the cavern, magnified and bounced into every crevice in the place. He strode forward, the human group scattering to allow him passage. The stench increased, reaching an abhorrent intensity. And all at once, the source revealed itself to him. The humans. It was their fear that clogged his nostrils. Agar had spoken of this on more than one occasion, though the gallu had not been so repulsed by the occurrence. Far from it. He relished it.

They raced from him, and the odour faded to a far more manageable level. Eron stepped into the tech room, and it was clear the three humans inside had seen what he'd done. The gut-churning smell returned, but understanding its significance, Eron breathed it in. Enjoying his newfound talent. Weylen's hands shook where she held them over Agar.

'Where is Azrael?' He stood over her, enjoying the way the shaking increased the closer he edged in. Understanding more intimately the enjoyment Agar drew from such behaviour.

'One of the containment cells on level nine. The ones down here were deemed too damaged.'

Eron cast a glance back towards the cells, but the tech room door had closed behind him, concealing the humans who worked to clear out the damaged space. Certainly it wasn't suitable for the likes of the gallu, hindered as he was, but it was clearly being readied for someone.

Weylen placed the instrument she was holding down on the stainless steel table. It clacked against the metal in a frantic beat before she let it go. 'I'm not to begin any testing on Azrael until Agar's integrity has been established. Captain's orders.'

'Then you best continue to do as you are told.'

All of the Four would be required to ensure that Inanna could not escape her Earthly prison before Tamas and his goddess were done. Having seen the fragility of the child – the fragile prison Inanna would be forced into – it would be a wonder if the human infant survived the cleansing ceremony Tamas undertook now, let alone possession by an unwilling goddess.

'Sir.' Weylen's voice was pitched high, and she gripped the edge of the table. 'Sir, I need Blake here. On my own like this, it's going to take too long.'

'Then you will work faster.' He breathed in her panic, the bitterness harsh and thrilling against the back of his throat.

'I thought . . . maybe . . . is there anything you can do . . . to help me?' It was quiet as a vacuum in the room, the two other hazard-suit-clad humans frozen. The air was so thick with their terror it was hard to breathe. Eron's fingers curled into the palms of his hands, pressing tightly enough to dig nails into flesh.

'Help you?' He could barely stand to look at her. The memory of lying with one of these insipid creatures made his stomachs contract. 'Do as you've been told and you may survive this.'

Weylen's lips parted but whatever she might have been readying to say never came. Her eyes widened a fraction, her attention on something behind him. Eron turned.

Seder strode across the cavern, his loose hair cascading around his shoulders, a sure sign the captain was nowhere nearby, or likely to be. Seder unbound his hair at the slightest opportunity, abhorring the tight style demanded by Nex.

'Eron, did you not receive my attempts to reach you?' He touched at the comms link behind his ear.

'If I had, I would have answered you.'

'Then you will not have heard.'

Eron frowned. 'About what?'

'The woman in New Weston,' Seder's impatience sped up his words, 'they lost communications there, and we've just received word as to why. She just won't die, Eron. Tamas thought her dead, but we've just been advised that she and the witch have destroyed the place.'

'Clara?'

'Kira.'

Hollow. That was the first thought that came to mind when Eron examined his reaction to Kira's name. No pang, no twist of pulses.

'I see. A concern no doubt, but we have Azrael contained.'

Eron couldn't make out Seder's expression entirely. The youngest of the god-soldiers had always been the most difficult to read. If he were to guess, as he did now, Eron would have determined amusement lurked in the creases.

'Eron, the Messenger tortured her in the belief her pain might bring in the gallu. When she became no longer necessary, Tamas sent word that she should be eliminated. Only, she was gone, and the utukku he set on her have been destroyed. Now she is free. The captain wishes to know why. He doesn't appreciate surprises; I'm sure you understand.'

Still nothing. The hollowness in his gut did not fill, despite Seder's words—the talk of torture and death—and Eron's own knowledge that he had been more than willing to place Kira in its midst. 'What are the captain's orders? Does he wish me to locate Kira?'

'Do you desire to do so, Eron?' Seder had never had a pleasant laugh.

'Caution, Seder. Do not test me.'

The Syranian tilted his head to one side, unblinking eyes watchful. 'Oh, I wouldn't dare, brother. We all sense the change in you. No one doubts your commitment now. I can assure you. In fact, I believe it is exactly why the captain has assigned you to this task. Your newfound ferocity may prove useful. You are to extract what information you can from the captured gallu, by any means, with my assistance. Find out whether this banal world has something worth fearing yet.' He bared too white teeth. 'Did you ever see anything worth fearing when you lay with her, brother? Or did your lust for Kira blind you so?'

Eron leaned in close to his brother. 'It is me you should fear, if you continue to taunt me, Seder.'

The smile slid from Seder's face, and a new scent, less bitter than the humans' but still unpleasant, drifted between them. He did not utter another word as Eron led him from the chamber.

Kira - 63

It turned out that Jared's sister's girlfriend's name was India. Which ticked all the right boxes so far as Kira was concerned. Something about people who were named after countries or cities just did it for her. It also helped that India let Kira sit in the cockpit on take-off and didn't even want anything in exchange. Not even a touchy-feel of the armadillo. Kinda weird, everyone wanted something. A free drink, a photo op, a fuck. Not today though. Which was sort of nice. Kira's energy just wasn't there. Fuck, she must be dying. Considering India had the ass of a professional booty-shaker, she was right up Kira's alley: cute little fox tattoo on her wrist; a jet-black pixie cut to die for; and sweet, perky boobs with nipples on high beam under the cool cabin air. Normally, Kira would have jumped in, balls deep. But hey, what the fuck was normal about anything, anymore? She had just swallowed a possessed stone. And she was wearing a suit of armour she couldn't take off. And man, had she tried. Dug her fingers in under the edge that wrapped around her belly and broke the only long fingernail she had. Armadillo fucker wouldn't budge.

'Kira?'

She jumped, and the seatbelt dug into her shoulders. 'Oh fuck, sorry. Did I fall asleep?'

India had a smile that could make panties drop. 'Yeah, you did. It's probably a bit more comfortable for snoozing out back. We've got some serious whisky on board too, if you need one . . . kind of looks like you do.'

Try a bottle. Or two. And that would just be scratching the surface. 'Sorry, yeah.' Kira struggled with the heavy-duty clasp that sat just above her crotch and locked her into her seat. 'Fuck, Jesus.' She smacked at the buckle that held her down. 'I can't get out.' Heat rushed into her face, her throat closing ever so slightly.

India touched her hand. Skin on skin. Resting her fingers there until Kira stopped struggling. 'Let me help you. Just take it easy. This won't take a second.'

Christ almighty. Kira let out her breath, not sure how long it had been since she'd taken one. She was losing her fucking marbles, freaking out over a goddamn buckle. India slid her hands down low, applied a little pressure, and the four-way buckle released. Kira leaned forward, elbows on her knees, and India's hand slid onto her thigh. Fuck. Not now. She closed her eyes, ready to put together a nice civil 'thanks but no thanks.'

'Let's get you back in the cabin.' India patted her leg and then undid her own belt. 'You look so wiped, Kira. It will be another hour or so till we reach New Weston. Make the most of it.'

Kira cleared her throat, adjusted her shirt. Mother of all fuckers. Her shirt. Kira's hand went to the puke shoulder. Did she stink? Oh for the love of all fucking gods. She was sitting next to the pixie queen, stinking of her own vomit, with bloodstains speckling her shirt. Only, she wasn't. Brain fart. She'd changed when she'd gotten on the plane into the only thing they had available: a soft cotton pyjama top. Button-up – all the way to her neck, hiding the rogue armadillo's spread nicely – black with white piping and the company logo, a tiny white jetliner with two puffy clouds on either side. Super comfy, velvety material. No wonder she'd fallen asleep. But the puke smell still lingered a little. Probably in her hair.

India unlocked the cockpit door but didn't open it straightaway. They stood there, in the cramped space on either side of the narrow door. Kira held her breath as if that somehow made the sick smell go away. She had to hand it to India. The chick hadn't batted an eyelid at the weird and wonderful passengers who boarded her plane. Vail looked as if he'd just gone a few rounds with a meat grinder; Greta was trying to pierce everyone in two with her stare; not to mention the bedraggled parrot and tanned-to-all-buggery witch. Kira stared down at the lettering that covered what she could see of the armadillo. Was she shaking? Nah. Got to be the vibrations of the plane.

'Kira, I know it's not any of my business . . .' India the Beautiful, hesitated. 'But is everything okay? Can I do anything to help?'

And her voice was so velvety, her words so achingly sincere, that Kira had to brace against the wall before she could speak.

'Well . . . no. Everything is not okay, and I'm not sure it's ever going to be okay.' She tried a smile but it hurt her cheeks, and her lips, and the inside of her mouth. Hell, everything hurt again, now that a goddess had stopped scribbling all over her.

India nodded as if she totally understood. And then she did something really dumb. She touched Kira. Just reached out those beautifully manicured hands and let fingertips brush Kira's cheek. 'I'm so sorry.'

And damn if it didn't sound like she was. It was the tipping point. And Kira hurtled over it. She grabbed the collar of India's starched pure-white blouse and pulled her in. Make it stop. That's what's India could do. Make all this stop for just a second. Like all those nights in the clubs and the copious amount of strangers in Kira's bed. Just. Make. It. Stop. Lips pressed together. India tasted like raspberry, and Kira's throat was so tight her head spun. Stop. Stop.

'Stop.' India pulled away. 'Please, Kira. I'm so sorry, but I can't do this. My girlfriend –'

Kira held up her hands, smirking as if her life depended on it. That fucking knot in her throat just wouldn't let up. 'My bad. Totally my bad. Been a weird day. Forget it happened. I owe you big-time for this flight. I won't forget it.'

And before India could land the soulful eyes on her again, Kira pulled open the cockpit door. She slipped into the cabin, which had about twelve plush leather seats in all, rows of two on either side of a narrow aisle.

An attendant was headed up that very aisle towards her, pushing a drinks cart. How very civilised. He plastered on a smile as fake as Kira's had just been. 'Can I get you something? A drink perhaps?'

'Perhaps? Oh buddy, we have some learning to do.' Kira dropped into the nearest seat across the aisle from Leona, who peered up at her with a frown. 'What's up, witchy?'

Nothing much apparently. Leona rolled her eyes and began tapping out a random rhythm on the Syranian bow resting in her lap.

Kira went with the whisky, and blamed India for putting the idea in her head.

'Here's to . . .' Kira saluted the ceiling, 'whatever . . . something fucking good . . .' She downed the double in one gulp and held up her glass for another. The attendant's tattooed eyebrows rose in amused approval, and he poured another double.

'Really?' Leona tut-tutted. 'Do you think that's wise?'

'Go fuck your broomstick, nana.' Kira flipped her the bird, and hated herself a second later. 'I'm . . . I'm sorry . . .' The words were lumpy and weird in her mouth. And far too quiet. The white-haired witch turned her gaze to the window.

Kira slumped in her seat, swirling the amber fluid around in her glass. She hated to admit it, but the booze wasn't sitting great in her gut. Someone slapped the top of her head. 'What the hell?' Kira cried.

Greta stood over her, all flames and indignant freckles. 'Pull yourself together. You're a Disciple of the Maiden now.' She snatched the glass from Kira's hand and replaced it with a water bottle.

'Bullshit I am. And you might want to rethink that name, 'cause Mrs Goddess of the Earth seems to prefer her original one.'

'Did she tell you that?' Greta glared.

'She didn't have to.' Kira knocked the water bottle against her arm. 'She bloody well wrote it all over me.' Had, in fact, branded Kira like a fucking cow. And the buzz was well and truly gone. 'You witches work out what the hell it's supposed to mean?'

'No,' Leona said. 'But you've been chosen for something –'

'I don't want to be a fucking chosen one. Tell your Maiden to work through someone else.'

Greta crouched down beside her chair, pressing a finger against Kira's metal arm. So goddamn rude. It was tempting to punch her in the face, but Kira held back. 'I would gladly take your place, but that is not my decision to make. Clearly. The Maiden is growing in strength, that much is evident, but the gods She faces are older, and far stronger. They are already ascended to a greater realm, but the Maiden is still anchored to this world, to this lesser realm. Her tools are limited. There is no way to know if She has power enough to drive back a deity like Inanna. Or Ereshkigal. Do you understand the gravity of this, the imbalance that the chaos of Inanna could bring if She is imprisoned here?'

Squeezing the life out of the water bottle, Kira squared up to Greta. 'I get it. How could I not? You guys look like you're going to shit yourselves every time you say Inanna's name. But what in all the holy fucks am I supposed to do about any of this? I just want to get to my sister, get her out of there –'

'Your sister is not priority –'

'Yes, she fucking is.' Kira's voice cracked like a prepubescent kid, but a satisfying spray of spit flew from her mouth and landed on Greta's cheek. If flame-head said one more word, fists were going to fly.

'Greta.' Vail's voice, super close, made both of them start. 'Take it easy. Kira needs some space. There's a lot going on, and half of it we don't even know about yet. Let's just all get some rest.'

The kid wavered on his feet, clutching at the seat back, his face an unsettling shade of not-so-great. Bradley clung to his shoulder, his bulbous eyes not leaving Kira's face.

'Best you listen to the boy.' Leona nodded. 'We all need some quiet time.'

With a grunt that said it was the last thing she wanted to do, Greta shoved past Vail and stomped down to the back row.

Vail pressed his hand to Kira's shoulder. 'It's okay, Kira. You should rest.'

'Pot, kettle is on line two.' She threw him a lopsided grin and was rewarded with one in return, but his pallor made her insides all swirly. Kids shouldn't be that shade of grey.

Leona shifted to the window seat and patted the empty one beside her. Vail dropped into it like the bag of bones he resembled, and she fussed over him, piling a couple of blankets on and shoving a pillow behind his head. All the while Bradley held on to his shoulder perch, eyes still on Kira.

She closed her eyes and turned away. Perhaps she needed another drink. Kira sighed. This day was truly fucked. Just the thought of alcohol made her gag. Time to think of puppies and rainbows.

They touched down two hours later on a small airstrip just east of Pryden, under a midmorning sky that was losing its battle with the thin cloud cover trying to snuff out its blueness. India disembarked first and stood at the bottom of the stairs. She stepped up to Kira as soon as her foot touched the tarmac.

'I hope the flight was okay.' Brown eyes were unabashed in meeting Kira's. 'I radioed ahead for a car. Nick is extremely discreet, I can vouch for him. We keep more than a few secrets of the rich and famous between us. He'll take you wherever you need to go.'

'Yeah, great,' Kira said, still groggy from the deep, dreamless sleep she'd fallen into. 'I can't thank you enough for all this. And I'm good for this.' She jerked her head at the jet, then towards the waiting black Lincoln Navigator parked alongside the small arrivals building. 'I'll make sure you get paid.'

India smiled. Damn the girl had a pretty mouth. 'I know. It's fine.' She turned as though to move back up the stairs, hesitating there. 'Kira.'

'Yep?' The others filed across the tarmac, headed for the car. Vail was a walking animal transport, Anzu on one shoulder, Bradley on the other.

'I can see things are pretty tough. Maybe when things settle down, you could come visit with Grace and I. We have a farm out near Breton, grow all our own stuff. It's so tranquil out there. No one would know you are there, not even Jared, I promise.' Another starburst smile, and it sucker punched Kira right in the soft spot beneath her ribcage.

Kira shrugged it off. 'Yeah. Sounds great.' Great? Nah, it sounded like fucking heaven. 'Might take you up on that.' Liar, liar, pants very much on fire. 'See you round.'

Very unlikely. Death by deity much more likely. Time to go. It was getting real dusty, real fast.

'Bye, Kira. It was nice meeting you.'

Kira walked away, waving a hand over her shoulder. Not looking back.

*

Nick the driver pulled up opposite a row of white townhouses on the outskirts of Pryden, near a building Kira knew as well as her own apartment on the Facility grounds. Actually, she probably knew this place better.

Number Seventy-five was Perry's second home when he wasn't camped out at the bar. She got Nick to pull up much farther down the row and made a vague suggestion that their destination was another street over but that they were happy to walk the rest of the way. Guy must think she was a lunatic, refusing to let him put the address in the GPS and then getting them purposely lost a couple of times. It had taken a lot of gesturing and U-turns to get here. Chances of him ever finding this place again, significantly reduced. At the very least, it distracted him from the conversation between Leona and Greta and Vail as they tried to work out what came next. They piled out of the car and Nick drove off.

Kira headed back up the road with her motley crew following behind. The sunlight filtering through the cloud cover was blood warming. Given the choice, she'd stand out here a little longer. But, as with most things recently, she didn't get a say.

'Okay,' she said. 'I know where a key is, but I'm going to knock first.' It was the middle of the day. Which meant Perry might be home. With or without someone.

Only Vail paid her any attention, giving her a nod before returning to the conversation with Leona and Greta. He wanted to send Anzu to look for Nina and Rossiter. Thought it was important that Nina knew about the graffiti scrawled all over Kira. But seeing as neither Leona nor Greta had met Nina, they were taking some convincing. The only thing everyone agreed on was that they needed to get into the Facility. Sooner rather than later.

Closing the ironwork front gate, Kira peered up at the second-floor balcony. The curtains were closed on the room she knew was Perry's, as well as on the room she always used alongside it. Same downstairs. A small part of her had been hoping they would turn up and Perry would be stretched out on the sofa, watching one of the old classics for the millionth time. Not a care in the world.

But the front door was locked, the townhouse very much empty. If Perry were in, the sliding doors on the ground level and the balcony would have been wide open. He was a fresh-air freak; windows were open whenever he was home regardless of the outside temperature. Good for the soul or some bullshit.

Kira lifted the false rock in the middle of the succulent-laden courtyard garden. Perry had bought the clandestine key holder after she'd lost a third set of his house keys. She rested them in her palm, the familiar metal contrasting with the most-definitely not-familiar etches in the armadillo.

'We going in or just admiring the view?' Leona shaded her eyes against a sudden burst of sunshine.

Kira swung the front door open. They all bundled into the narrow, sparsely decorated entranceway. A silver-rimmed mirror hung over a chocolate-coloured hall table, which in turn held Perry's favourite plant, an orchid, in a bright pink pot. His pride and joy had seen much better days. Kira ran her fingers over a stem that curved like an arthritic backbone, wilted flowers hanging low. Kind of odd. Perry loved that damn plant.

'Smells odd in here,' Leona sniffed.

'What's wrong with you?' Greta said.

Kira turned, ready to give her a crisp and juicy answer, only to realise Greta wasn't talking to her.

Vail leaned against the wall, fingers pressed to his temple. 'Nothing, just a little dizzy. Is it just me or is it really hot in here?' He tugged at his shirt collar. In the few unbruised areas on his cheeks, his skin blushed with a much healthier-looking peach.

'Odd aura in this place, that's for certain.' Leona pressed her hand to Vail's forehead. 'But it's hardly enough to churn your guts. Are you getting a fever?'

'Where is Anzu?' Greta frowned.

Great question. The bird was noticeably absent from his perch on Vail's shoulder, but answers could wait. Kira didn't like the way concern was adding another dozen wrinkles to Leona's face as she peered at Vail.

Leona waved down Vail's protest that he was fine. 'Where are the bedrooms, Kira?'

'Upstairs,' Kira said. 'I can take him.'

'I don't need to lie down.'

'Tell your face that,' Leona replied. 'And where has our feathered friend gone?'

'Anzu went to look for Nina,' Vail said.

'We didn't vote on that,' Greta said, glowering.

'He wasn't asking permission.' Vail might have been all sweaty and unsteady on his feet, but Kira gave him ten points for strong delivery.

'I think it is high time we ate something decent, shorten a few tempers. And get some wardings set up around this place.' Leona unzipped her tracksuit jacket, revealing a baby-pink T-shirt with several rainbow-coloured kittens printed on its front. The woman was nothing if not tasteful. 'Where's the kitchen, Kira?'

Kira pointed towards an archway halfway down the hall. 'Down that way, through the lounge room.'

'Righto.' Leona nodded. 'Greta, you come with me. Kira, time to shower, girl. Your hair still stinks of vomit.'

Kira grimaced. Christ almighty. No wonder India had backed off like she'd touched an electric fence. 'Good to know.' Kira's plan to call the pub went onto the back burner. Decontaminate first. Work out what she was going to say to Perry if she actually got hold of him, later. 'Let's go, buddy.'

She planted her hands on Vail's shoulders, catching her breath at the narrowness of them. The witch hesitated, fluttering hands getting ready to check Vail's temperature yet again. Kira manoeuvred herself into the space between them, pushing Vail towards the stairs. 'Off you go. Go fix us up some eye-of-newt stew or whatever it is you do.'

It was only when Bradley scampered down Vail's back and skittered across the floor to reach her that Leona stopped staring at Vail as if it were the last time she'd see him. Bradley squeaked at her, clawing his way up her stained velour tracksuit pants.

'I'm going, I'm going,' she muttered under her breath but stayed right where she was. 'Don't be trying to contact the bright one, Kira. Not till we have this place warded.'

Kira saluted, clicking her heels together at the same time. 'Roger that.' But as far as she could work out, Radio Azrael was busted. She'd tried thought-shouting just once on the plane, and a shooting pain in her temples had nearly popped her eyes from her skull.

'I'm not the bloody hired help,' Greta called from the kitchen amid the sound of drawers and cupboards being slammed open and shut. 'You coming in or what, Leona?'

Finally, the witch left the hallway, shouting at Greta to keep her pants on. And Greta fired right back about what she could do with her pants.

Kira jammed her thumb towards the kitchen. 'Geez, I'm so glad I don't have attitude like that chick.'

Vail gave her what she was looking for. A smile. Weak as all hell but there. 'You're pretty much a saint in comparison.'

'Yeah, and my halo is dirty as all fuck. Jesus, I need a shower more than I need oxygen right now.'

'Can I have one, too?' Vail asked. 'A shower I mean, not a halo.'

Oh adorable. The kid made a funny. Kira ruffled his hair. He wasn't kidding about needing a shower. Her fingers got embedded deep in his tangled black mop. 'Sure, you can have one with me if you like. Save some water.'

'Kira.' Vail groaned, but it morphed into a short laugh.

She grinned at his back, but it didn't last long. Smiling took energy she didn't have. Damn, she was bone tired. Body aching like she'd run a marathon and then done an obstacle course. She fucking hated obstacle courses. And Tamas. Goddamn what she would do to that little runt if she ever had a chance.

'Have you heard anything from Azrael?' Vail reached the landing. He turned to face her, scratching at the coin embedded in his face.

'Nope. And you heard the witch. Not allowed to talk to my boyfriend till she's sprayed the boy-germs juice.'

Vail was kind of cute when he smiled. He was one of those people that did it with his whole face. 'You're crazy.'

'Getting more so every day.' Kira paused on the landing, catching her breath. Man, torture took it out of a girl.

'I'm sure he's okay, Kira,' Vail said softly.

'Yeah. Maybe. They lost interest in me back there, Vail.' Kira folded her arms. The markings on the metal rubbed against her skin. 'Tamas bolted, and left the b-crew at the penthouse. Not exactly Fort Knox. I don't think they were expecting Az to come in, wings blazing and perfect lips pouting.' There. She'd said it. The thing that had been bugging her since Leona had bubble-blasted them out of the place. And if they weren't expecting Az, it could mean they already had him. Jesus, Vail was right. It was stuffy as all hell in here. 'Come on, let's get you horizontal.'

Vail nodded, still scratching.

From downstairs came the clatter of kitchen utensils and Leona singing badly in a language Kira didn't recognise. Kira turned into the first door on the right: Perry's room. It had a glass panel in the ceiling, which meant the room was always filled with natural light. The bed cover was a bright multicoloured patchwork he'd bought in Bali years earlier. There were orchids here, of course, two potted plants on either side of a decorative statue of some Indian god resting on a small carved wooden table. The multi armed deity sat with her legs crossed in front of a small pond. Flicking a switch on her back would activate a little trickle of water that flowed over a pile of sapphire-blue stones and into the bowl. It was the worst possible ornament to wake up to when you had been too drunk to take a toilet break before falling asleep. It was switched off now. The water had almost completely evaporated. Perry hadn't been home in a while.

Vail paused before entering, leaning against the doorframe so he could twist to reach one of the coins in the small of his back.

'Does Perry have a cat or dog or something?' He winced.

'Nope. You okay?'

'I don't know, the minute I walked in the house I felt so weird,' Vail said. 'But to be honest, I'm not sure when I last felt remotely normal.'

'You and me both, my friend.' Kira patted the bed. 'Check this out, he's got a waterbed. Have a lie down.'

She flopped back onto the mattress, surprised to find she could fling both her arms overhead with relative ease. All the new metal moving as smoothly as any real limb. No nasty pinching at her neck. One positive in a sea of shitty negatives. She'd take it.

Beneath her, the water slapped against its confines, and she rocked up and down. Vail joined her a moment later, and the waves got larger.

'I thought these were like an extinct species.' He laughed.

They rolled onto their sides, facing one another. Kira's nearly empty stomach lurched with the mix of whisky and water that was the only thing filling it.

'God, I'm hungry. I wish Caleb were here.'

Vail made a face, scratching at one of the coins on his leg. 'Bet you do. Apparently, his cooking made you see god.'

'Cheeky little shit.' Kira smiled, and this time it stuck. 'You're just jealous. I could show you what he taught me if you like.'

Even as the words slid out of her mouth, they went soggy and rotten. Gross. It was like offering to blow your brother. Not cool. 'Okay, on that note, I'm going to go have a shower. Alone.'

Vail's hand slipped into hers, and she froze. Awkward. 'Hey Vail, I was just talking crap –'

He rolled his eyes. 'You don't think I get your crap by now? You're not that good an actress, Kira.' Vail yawned, mouth stretching wide. He grimaced and grabbed at the coin on his face.

'Doing okay?' Kira propped up on one elbow, watching him closely.

'Yeah, I'm just so tired. I need to sleep, but I . . . can you just . . . maybe stay here till I fall asleep?'

Kira had to clear her throat before she could answer. 'Scared of the monsters under the bed?' She lay back down and they both rocked. 'Believe me, the only frightening thing under this bed is the two-inch layer of dust and the pile of big-dick magazines.'

Vail's eyes fluttered closed. 'You are so disgusting.' He shuffled in closer, his head against her shoulder.

'That much is often true.' She took his hand in hers, metal fingers closing gently.

A ghost of a smile brushed Vail's lips. 'Don't leave, okay? We need to talk about stuff . . . about Gaia . . .'

'Nah. Talking is overrated.' Kira settled onto her back. 'But don't blame me if I pee the bed. Because I have to tell you, the old bladder is bursting at the seams right now.'

Vail didn't reply, his breathing already dipping into the regular in and out of sleep.

The room was warm and quiet, and the waft of something not entirely terrible drifted up the stairs. Kira let her eyes close, Vail's breath soft against her cheek. She'd give him a few more minutes, make sure he was dead asleep, then she'd go shower and see just how much of her had been lost beneath her shiny new suit of armour.

Blake - 64

Blake lay exactly where they had left her, back on the narrow cell bed, staring again at the ceiling – but this time with far less freedom than before. Restraints pinned down her wrists and ankles. They were all going to die. There was nothing more certain in her world. Muttering under their breath, the guards had lifted her from the pool of red they'd found her in, one slipping in the bloody mess. She had a faint recollection of them handling her far more gently than she would have expected. One of them had even wiped down her face, clearing it of her blood, tucking her hair back behind her ears and whispering, 'I'm sorry,' as they'd strapped her down.

As if her sister's death could be excused. A mistake that could be forgiven. Of course, no one had said it outright, not a single one had uttered Kira's name. No one had the balls. And not a single person would look at her directly. The three guards who remained, taking up position outside her cell, had their backs to her, and had been that way for the past twenty minutes. Not speaking. Casting the odd, furtive glance towards Azrael's cell.

These morons had no idea what sorry was. 'Not yet,' she whispered.

Blake turned her head. They had left her that freedom at least. The joints in her neck cracked and popped with the effort. Nothing about herself fit right anymore. Her bones were too big for her body, her skin stretched too tightly. This body was a cumbersome, infuriating weight. And her brain, that part that had never failed her, did so now, offering no solution to her current predicament. Blake lay there. A prisoner in the house she had built, watching her greatest achievement hang from his metal cross. The positioning of the bed and her place in it afforded her a prime view of Azrael. Motionless, but eyes wide open. A glorious shade of sea green she could make out even from this distance. Hours had been spent on finding that exact shade, one that truly captured the changeability of the ocean.

Blake continued her countdown. Opportunity would come. It had to come.

Then watch them all fall down. All going to burn.

'All going to burn.' Blake nodded to the viper. Not fighting the sting of it. 'All going to burn.'

Azrael would burn with them. Changing that was beyond her. The concrete and stone and iron and emptiness above pushed down at her. She intended to take everything from Tamas. But the truth was acrid. Blake had already lost everything in return: her knowledge, cultivated and tended to the expense of all else; her sister; her creation. Even Perry had abandoned her. If he had ever stood by her to begin with.

Lifting her head, Blake strained to catch a glimpse of the hand that held the Starpoints. Her fingertips were so numb it was impossible to tell if she dug at her skin as she intended. The IV and its stand had been removed from her cell. The same guard who'd apologised had removed the needle and done a very basic clean-up job. Certainly no medic. No Cym.

But why would they waste time on her? Someone who would no doubt be disposed of shortly. Azrael had been found. She was in no state to attend to any work necessary on the carapaces, even if need did arise.

Blake dropped her head back against the thin pillow, abandoning her attempt to dig her fingers in beneath the bandaging on her hand, breathing through the resulting wash of spasming muscles.

The guards shifted, backs straightening, shoulders pulling back, murmurs passing between them. They pressed against the glass of her cell. Whatever had caught their attention came from farther up the corridor. Blake craned her neck, and stared at a lopsided world.

Eron paced down the length of the short passageway.

It was the first time Blake had laid eyes on him since the catastrophic arrival of the Four. Since he'd shoved her clear of the falling crane. He had saved her life. She did not expect that of him again. But she would seek something else from him.

'Eron. Eron, listen to me.' Blake twisted her shoulders, trying to wrench her hand free of the restraint. The metal dug with cruel accuracy into the tender skin around the splinter at her wrist, and she choked back a cry. 'Please, Eron. Is she gone?'

He wouldn't even need to say it. A yes or a no were irrelevant. His expression would tell her all she needed to know.

And Blake needed to know.

But Eron was listening to no one. Didn't glance at the guards as he passed them, would have walked right over the top of them if they weren't pressing back against her cell wall. That Eron was striking could be debated by no one. And at the epicentre of that attractiveness was his silken movement. The way he held himself. A dancer poised before a routine. Blake watched him move now.

All the lightness had gone, a driven, leaden footfall in its place. His disconcerting eyes – pits of endless white – held only one focus. Azrael.

Eron reached the cell door, and the glass slid open. Azrael remained still, no physical indication that he sensed the arrival. Eron turned, and for a brief moment Blake thought he was about to look at her. But his gaze travelled back up the corridor where another Syranian moved into the space. Seder.

The youngest of the god-soldiers. A vapid and uninteresting specimen who seemed incapable of speaking, or breathing, unless Captain Nex directed it. Blake and Seder had shared barely a handful of words over the years, most of those being messages relayed to or from the captain. Seder, if nothing else, was an adequate personal assistant.

He, like Eron, paid no mind to Blake in her cell.

Seder joined Eron alongside Azrael. Their difference in height was exaggerated by the lowered angle Blake viewed them from. Eron towered not only over Seder, but over Azrael. Her masterpiece appeared far more diminutive than he was. Eron moved up close, lowering his face so that he and Azrael were eye to eye. He placed a finger at the base of Azrael's throat and traced a line down his chest, coming to rest just above the material of the ripped black pants Azrael wore.

The Syranian had never frightened Blake. She'd never held any concerns for Kira's safety when the truth of her involvement with Eron became evident. As disinterested as she was in such things, Blake wasn't blind to the body language between her sister and the alien. No harm was intended by either side. And Eron's effeminate disposition induced a certain ease.

But Blake failed to find that ease now. He postured over Azrael, menace emanating from the lock of his body and the set of his mouth. This was not the graceful, anxious Syranian who had crouched over her on level eleven.

Eron spoke to Seder, who handed him something. A knife of sorts perhaps, though not one Blake recognised from either human or alien inventory. The blade of this one curved almost entirely in a rounded O shape.

'Get away from him, Eron.' She kicked her feet, fighting against the bands that dug into her ankles. 'Get away from him.' But she was as invisible as Perry had complained of being. Damn it, Perry had to come back. He had to be real. 'Eron, I said get away from him.'

She said it no louder than before, but Eron's head tilted. A bird of prey's jerky movement towards a sound. Blake had spent years around the Syranians and their white-eyed stares. In all that time she'd never shrunk from it. Not until this moment. Eron's eyes pinned her down, burrowed into her, and straight through her. He lifted the finger that still rested against Azrael's body and pressed it against his lips.

The bastard was shushing her.

His eyes didn't leave her as his free hand drove the circular blade into Azrael's back.

Azrael's body jerked against his restraints, his mouth widening until it threatened to split the skin at his cheeks. No sound reached her, and she was grateful for it.

'Shit,' Blake whispered. 'Oh shit.'

Eron struck again, his face a contorted, ugly mess beneath his rage. There was a brief pause, and Eron grabbed a handful of Azrael's hair, yanking his head back so they were again face to face. The Syranian spoke, or rather, yelled at his captive. A few inches between his mouth and Azrael's. The answer he sought wasn't forthcoming. Azrael's lips closed. Eron launched another assault, driving the blade deep into Azrael's back again, holding it embedded there, twisting it into whatever lay beneath the careful engineering and high-density Telteriun.

On and on it went. The silent agony. At least a dozen more blows before Blake could watch no longer. The power to stop Azrael's torment literally lay in her hands. Hand. So desperately close, but for all their usefulness, the Starpoints might as well have been on Syrana itself. Perry was not the only one to desert her. Even the viper lay low, leaving her alone to witness the brutality.

Blake was so intent on keeping her eyes averted that she didn't realise the guards had entered her cell until one of them touched her shoulder.

'Get off me.' Her cry came at far greater decibels than the light touch warranted.

'Just take it easy,' came the ludicrous advice.

A few metres away, her greatest achievement was being undone. She could not, would not, take it easy. Blake lashed out with the only weapon still available to her – biting at the limbs that moved around her.

'Fuck's sake, Blake. Don't make this harder on yourself.' The directive came from her right, so that's where she went with her teeth.

'She's fucking insane,' someone else whispered.

'This whole bloody place is,' the 'take it easy' verbaliser decided. 'Blake, Blake, listen to me.'

The slap to her cheek was not particularly brutal, but it accomplished its task. Blake slumped against the bedding, her chest heaving. A figure leaned over her, and she blinked to draw focus. A broad face with a trimmed black beard and searching amber eyes.

'Blake, are you with me?'

The man's voice held no aggression, nothing to suggest he was about to set on her the way Eron did with Azrael. There was substance in his expression. Light in his eyes. Though Blake was not *with* anyone, she nodded.

'Good. My name's Boyd. Okay. We've met a couple of times, don't know if you remember.' He paused, and she couldn't give him the answer he was looking for. The silence was brief. 'I've come to relocate you to level eleven. Boss wants you closer.' He threw the neighbouring cell a veiled glance. 'And I think the view is a hell of a lot better down there. Now just work with me, Blake. Okay?'

He was moving her to the heart of the Facility. The very core she craved. In a thud of quick-tempered heartbeats, Blake hedged her inadequate social skills on reading this man correctly. If she were to make an assumption – and she did – he was no enemy. 'Kira. My sister. I want to know. Have they killed her?'

The words came from her as the inanest would. She might as well have just enquired whether she could have milk with her coffee.

'Sir, we should get moving.' The voice came from her feet, but Blake's eyes didn't leave Boyd's.

He answered with a curt nod. 'One moment.'

'My sister,' Blake said. 'Is she dead?'

'Undo her ankles.' Boyd ushered the two guards at her shoulders away and scooped his arms beneath her, lifting her off the bed. Only once she was resting against him did he answer, voice lowered, words uttered close to her ear: 'They don't know where she is, but they know she is alive. Kira is alive.'

The viper, for all its vitriol, was no oracle after all. Its fangs were not half as sharp as they appeared.

Did you hear that? You were wrong. Her challenge went unanswered. No hiss from the blackness.

'Set me down.' Blake reached for the edge of the doorway, grasping it hard. A sudden buoyancy pushing her up and over the pain that came with using her injured hand. 'I will walk. Set me down.'

There was no doubt a simple twist of his body would have seen her handhold broken. But it did not come. Boyd lowered her, setting her feet on the ground and waiting until she steadied herself against the glass before he stepped back.

Two guards settled in front, another three behind her. An excessive security detail, in Blake's opinion, considering it took every shred of her willpower to even stand right now. But no one valued her opinion anymore it seemed.

Boyd stayed at her side. 'Very well then. Let's go.'

'Wait, sir.' One of the guards in front, a woman with a harsh crew cut and down-turned lips gestured up the corridor. A couple of workers, clad in the dark khaki of the general maintenance team, approached. The gofers of the Facility, assigned a variety of what appeared on the surface to be menial tasks but which ensured the smooth running of the entire complex.

Her security team shuffled her back inside the cell, allowing the passage of the two approaching workers. They passed by, one of them carrying a toolbox, the other a singular rectangle of metal. Telteriun. The dull nonreflective surface was unmistakable.

'What are they doing?'

But no one answered her. She was jostled out of the cell, leaning hard against Boyd, grateful that he did not attempt to support her. At the end of the corridor, a left-hand turn allowed her one last glance down towards the cells. She drew in a sharp breath, feigning a misstep that caused her escort to stumble and step on her bare toes. Painful, but it caused the delay in movement she hoped for.

Perry had not abandoned her. He stood right by Azrael's side. A wavering, unsettled image that moved in and out of visual lucidity. Blake opened her mouth, his name on her lips, only to find a new horror rush another's name from her.

'Azrael.' She struggled against Boyd's attempts to move her on. 'No. Azrael.'

Eron took possession of the piece of metal that had just been marched into the cell. He raised it over Azrael's eyes. Seder stepped forward, holding one of the drills the engineering team had designed especially to work with the incredible tensile strength of the alien metal. Perry turned and found her. His repulsion was evident even though his image struggled to hold form.

Beside him, Azrael strained and screamed and writhed as Eron and Seder drilled the plate into place. Across his eyes. Plunging Azrael into darkness.

Kira - 65

Kira shifted from dead asleep to sitting bolt upright, eyes wide open in two seconds flat. Fast movement in a waterbed is never a great idea, especially when you should have gone to pee hours ago. The resulting wave nearly toppled her off the side of the bed. Kira grasped the bedcovers, clinging there, waiting for the motion to stop, in the mattress and in her guts. A low ache niggled at a spot near her belly button. Maybe that fucking stone was going *Aliens* on her. About to burst out and face-suck anyone nearby. Beside her, Vail slept on, muttering in his sleep. Well, less muttering, more whimpering. He shifted his head from one side to the other, but his eyes remained clenched tight. His breathing was all messed up, sharp intakes then deep gulps.

'Hey.' Kira nudged him. 'You okay, buddy?'

He curled up into a tighter ball, knees practically touching his chin. Bursts of half-finished words jumped from his mouth. Kira leaned in closer, trying to make it out. Whatever was bugging him in his dream, he wasn't happy about it. Vail groaned, the deepest sound she'd heard his yet-to-crack vocal cords try to make. Turning to look for water, Kira noticed a plate on the wicker bedside table. The contents were probably meant to be macaroni and cheese, but the pasta was overcooked and falling apart, and the cheese was an unnatural McDonald's shade of yellow and, according to her fingertip, stone, stone cold. Still, her stomach rumbled, almost as loudly as the weird vibrating crying noise Vail was making.

'Hey, Vail. Wake up, kid.' Kira grabbed his shoulder, brushing the skin at his neck. 'Holy shit.' She pressed her flesh hand to his uninjured cheek. The frozen mac and cheese was nothing compared to this. If the kid got any icier, her skin would stick to his. 'Vail, come on, man.'

Enough Mrs Nice Guy. Kira wobbled onto her knees and grabbed his shoulders. 'Wakey, wakey.'

His head lolled from side to side but his eyes stayed shut, and the noises just kept on coming. Cries like machine-gun fire, if that machine gun was being wielded by a fairy, or a gnome. Teeny tiny rat-tat-tat sounds. Maybe it was the light, but those lips of his looked closer to violet than pink.

'Fuck, fuck. Jesus.'

Where was Nina when you needed her? This whole holding him together with coins was her brilliant idea. Kira swung out of bed, making sure to really rock the mattress and thump the water up against Vail's back. Knock him back into consciousness. She got a little too carried away. Vail jerked to the right, his arm swinging over his body as though it were being pulled on a string, and the kid rolled straight out of the bed face first onto the shaggy beige rug covering the cherrywood floor.

Kira winced. The thump was impressive. Racing to his side, she dropped to her knees and rolled him onto his back. 'You stupid son of a narcoleptic bitch. Come on, Vail. Wake up.'

The kid had just slept through a faceplant. Definitely high up there on the something-is-fucking-wrong scale. Kira cradled his limp pile of underdeveloped muscle and bone. Whoever had delivered the mush plate had closed the door and drawn the curtains on their way out. She had no clue what time it was. Suffice to say it was no longer the middle of the day. A crack at the centre of the blackout curtains – Perry did too many night shifts – let in a weak silver light, streetlight kind of silver. Guess no word had come in from Anzu about Nina. And judging by the heavy silence, Greta and Leona were snoozing, too. Either that or they'd died after eating the mac and cheese. Either way, time to call for backup. Kira opened her mouth, and Vail's arm lifted, slapping her across the face and knocking the call back down her throat.

'Christ almighty, Vail.' Kira tried to grip his arms, but he was a crazed octopus that seemed intent on landing a tentacle or three on her jaw. 'Vail, fuck's sake. It's me, Kira. Vail, come on.'

His body stiffened, spine locked rigid, and he jerked upright. The top of his head slammed her chin, and copper filled her mouth as her teeth dug into her tongue. For a kid who looked like a breeze could topple him over, he was doing okay with the sucker punches. Vail lurched out of her arms, flipping onto all fours. His eyes flew open. Holy sweet Jesus. The kid needed an optometrist, stat. A thin film of white covered his eyeballs. Not as thick as the starchy whiteness of the Syranians', a hint of Vail's deep brown iris was still visible beneath, but this was all kinds of wrong.

'Okay, everyone just stay calm.' Kira eyed the door. 'Just, just hang on, Vail. I'm going to get some help.'

The kid had other ideas. Whipping around like a ballerina on crack, he lunged at her, grabbing hold of her collar and gripping the soft material as if he wanted to squish the atoms out of the cotton. The momentum sent them both tumbling, Kira landing on her back, Vail square on top of her.

'No,' Vail said.

At least, that's what she assumed the weird *mewohoo* was that came out of his mouth.

'Vail, not cool, dude. Very not cool.' What in all things holy was going on? They lay there, Vail hunched on all fours over her, saliva running from the corners of his mouth. If some of it dripped on her, fists would fly. And Jesus what was with that ache in her belly? Burning, as though a whole jalapeno covered in Tabasco had lodged in her lower intestine.

'K . . . Ki . . . K . . .'

'My name is Kira. Correct. Time to wake up, buddy.'

Vail gagged, a scrawny but oversized pussycat coughing up a fur ball. He dropped his head low, his mop of black hair covering his fucked-up eyes.

'Throw up on me and we're done.' Kira shoved at his shoulders.

Vail's head lifted and those disconcerting eyeballs bore into her. 'Kira. Me. Perry. I'm here.'

Kira pressed back against the floor. How the hell had this kid done that? Note-perfect mimic of Perry's to-die-for accent. 'What the fuck? Vail, stop this shit right now.'

Vail sat on his haunches, which also meant sitting on her knees. Goddamn uncomfortable, but Kira didn't dare move. Vail stared down at his hands, a frown bunching around the bruises and coin on his face. He shook his head. 'Not Vail. Oh man, you hear me, don't you? I see . . . look on your face, holy shit, you . . . hear me, Kira?'

'Get the fuck off me now.' Kira shoved Vail, whipping her legs clear as he landed on his butt, a shocked gasp escaping him. The kid had never fucking met Perry. Had she even talked about Perry to Vail at all, let alone mention he was from Sri Lanka?

'Kira, listen . . . please. Don't freak out.' At some point Vail's hair had gone skyward, no more flat-to-the-skull goodness. Severe bedhead had taken its place.

'Oh, you've missed that boat, my friend.'

Vail, crouched on all fours, started towards her. But she wasn't in any immediate danger; he was moving at the pace of a stoned turtle. Kinda looked like one, too. 'Please, listen . . . Kira . . . don't know how long I can hold this.'

Fucksticks and jelly. That damn accent. The deepness. Vail usually sounded like a six-year-old touching a hot plate. Oh shit. Right. Let's roll with the insanity. Vail was being held together with currency and voodoo. The armadillo had gone rogue. Bradley had gone full dragon. Why not add a possession to the mix?

'Perry? Is that . . .' She threw her hands towards Vail. 'I mean . . . how?'

Stupid-ass question. Who gave a fuck? It was happening.

'The Facility. I'm . . . at the Facility.' Vail's snow-storm gaze dropped. 'Not sure I'm doing . . . good, to be honest . . . think I'm sick. But . . . not important . . . now. K, some serious shit going on . . . in here. That guy you came to . . . pub with, the . . . beautiful one, he's here . . . messed up – got to go.'

'No, Perry. Stay with me.' Kira dug her fingers into the shaggy rug. 'Azrael? You've seen him?'

Not the plan. Not the goddamn plan. The fucking angel was supposed to be flying free.

'Guy took to airport? Yes . . . he here, too . . . but talking about . . . other guy . . . fuck, what name? Really bad at karaoke.'

Maybe the armadillo had gotten into her lungs, because Jesus it was hard to breathe. 'Eron.'

Crazy-haired Vail nodded. Hard enough to shake a tooth loose. 'Eron. Why you never . . . tell me . . . what he was, K? Got to . . . go . . . go . . .'

Kira hobbled right up to Vail on her knees and grasped his sickly face in her hands. 'You're not going anywhere, Perry. You've seen Azrael and Eron?'

Vail tried to nod, but Kira held too tightly. The film across his eyes shifted, swirling. 'Eron hurt Az . . . now you . . . run.'

'What?' Kira leaned so close Vail's breath warmed her lips. The kid smelled an awful lot like bad eggs.

'Eron insane . . . coming for you. Blake said "weapon".'

Every nerve ending burst into flame. And Kira had to force the words out. 'Blake? You've seen Blake? Jesus. She's alive? She's okay?'

'Weapon . . . trace . . . you . . .' White foam filled the corners of Vail's mouth, and his body shook in her hands. 'Coming . . . run.'

A thin line of blood seeped from Vail's right nostril. This had to end. He was coming apart, but she'd be damned if she was ready to let go. 'Blake, just tell me, is she okay?'

'Hurting. All. Bad place.'

Christ almighty. 'Tell Blake I'm coming for her. For you both.' The metal over her chest hugged two sizes too small, her shallow breathing giving her head-spins. 'Tell her, Perry. Please. Both of you, hang on. All of you.' Eron hurt Az. All the fucks. 'Give me details. Who is coming? How long have we got?'

'Eron . . . grimalkin.' Vail wasn't so much forming words as spitting sounds. 'Dude nuts. Stab Az.'

Vail's blood ran across her thumb, the only warm thing about the entire room. 'Driving?' she barked.

'Huh?' Vail's eyelids fluttered. The starch-white layer across his eyes was now more like a sheer layer of chiffon. Kira let her hands fall from his face.

'Is he driving or flying?'

'Driving.' Vail wretched and a cascade of foamy white goo gushed out of his mouth like sloppy snow on the beige rug. He nosedived towards it, and Kira caught him before he landed faceplant number two.

'Fuck, Vail. Vail, buddy.' She gathered him up, giving no shits about the wetness, the muck, the blood. Kira tilted his head. Eyes so deep brown she'd thought them black the first time they met, stared right at her. Focused in on her.

'Me, sorry, Kira.' He coughed, and she clutched him tightly, just in case he rattled something loose.

'Sorry? Why the hell are you sorry? I shouldn't have let that keep going.' Kira wrapped her arms around him. Probably too hard but she didn't give a fuck in that second. 'Are you all right? Oh Christ, Vail.'

'That was intense.' His voice was muffled against her chest.

The room stank to high heaven, but she would have stayed there forever if he needed it.

'Kira?'

'Yeah?'

'You're crushing me.'

Dropping him like the proverbial hot potato, Kira finally took a breath. Her lungs sucked in every last drop, the armadillo expanding till she thought she'd bust a seam. Guts settled.

'What just –'

Vail shook his head. 'We've got to go, Kira.'

Sure. Yep. But, seriously, what the fuck just happened? 'How did Perry do that? Astral projection or something?' See? She could roll with this. Even knew some of the cuckoo lingo.

Vail's pools of black fixed on her, and she didn't like the downturn of his mouth. Not one little bit. 'I'm sorry, Kira. I don't think it's like that. It's a little more –'

Kira pulled herself to her feet, waving her hands in front of her. 'No. Stop. Just . . . just let me go with astral projection.' Dead orchids in the hallway, the waterless fountain. The emptiness that clung to this place. Never mind that Vail seemed to have enough empty space for someone to just jump on inside him. She would ignore it all. Store it away for some other time when the world wasn't imploding around her. 'Astral projection,' she whispered.

She held out her hand and pulled Vail to his feet. Grabbing the edge of the sheet, she wiped the blood from his top lip. Gentle as all hell. The kid's skin was rice-paper thin.

'Ready?'

Vail's smile was strong enough, but his old stick legs weren't up to the job. Kira scooped him up, cradling him in her arms, and headed to the door. Sure, he was light, but this was insanely easy. She might as well have just lifted a dust mite. Not the first time she'd gone a bit Hercules. She'd thrown that asshole who'd set the grimalkin on her like he was a blow-up doll. Whatever. Add it all to the list of things not to think about right now.

'Leona,' she shouted, and Vail cringed. 'Where the fuck are you?'

She manoeuvred them down the stairs, managing to slam Vail's feet against the balustrade only twice.

'Leona, for fuck's sake. Greta. Where the hell are you?' Kira set Vail down on the bottom step, where he proceeded to start coughing up a lung.

Leona staggered out of the lounge room, every strand on her head reaching for orbit. Bradley perched on her shoulder. 'Why the hell are you yelling like a banshee, woman?' Then she spotted Vail, and her legs couldn't carry her fast enough to get to him. 'What in the Maiden's great name is going on?'

Bradley said presumably the same thing in Lizard-ese, chittering as though he were the one possessed. His head bobbed madly. Vail's coughing attack eased, his eyes watering from the effort. It was getting hard to look at him. Like just the weight of a stare might crack him.

'We've got a problem,' Kira said. 'A tall, silver-haired one. We need to leave.'

Eron hurt Az. That's what Perry the Astral Projection Wonder had said. If Eron had hurt Blake too, Kira would . . . what the hell would she do? There had to be something. For crying out loud, she had a goddess's tramp stamp all over her, and a portable suit of armour. If that didn't count for something, then kill her now. At the very least they had the Syranian bow. One weapon. War was practically won.

'Vail, what happened to you, boy?' Leona's hands were all over the kid, pressing, tugging, fussing.

'I'm okay, Leona.'

'You don't look it.' Greta of the positive energy strode into the hallway, wearing only the chequered long-sleeved shirt she'd arrived in and lavender panties.

'Vail got possessed by Perry, and Perry told us that Eron is coming. They know where we are.' Pretty straightforward when said out loud, Kira had to admit.

Greta wrinkled everything. 'Who is Perry?'

'Damn it, I knew that limo driver was off. Kept looking at me weird,' Leona said.

'Yeah, I don't think the looks were because of . . .' Kira froze, mid-insult. Nick the driver hadn't called it in. If he had, the Facility would have been all over this place hours ago.

Weapon. Perry had said it. Loud and clear, pushing the words out of Vail's mouth. Weapon. Trace you.

'Where's the bow?' Kira grabbed Leona's arm, stopping the Vail fuss-fest. 'The bow, you had it in the plane.'

'Dining room, on the table.' Leona glared down at Kira's hand. 'Quite the grip there, girl. Want to let my blood flow?'

Vail gasped. 'The bow. That's how they've found us.'

'Bingo.' It figured that the Syranians would keep track of their extraterrestrial armoury, but it must have taken them a while to realise it was missing from the penthouse. Kira raced into the dining room. A fledgling plan was waving its arms in her head. *Look at me, I'm so terrible I might just work.* The slender metalwork sat like an elaborate centrepiece on Perry's pine table.

'What are you going to do with it?' Greta followed her, rubbing at her eyes. The movement lifted her shirt, revealing an impressively flat stomach.

'Seriously, I really don't need to see your lady garden.' Kira picked up the bow. Slight problem, no clue how to use it. Worry about that later. 'Greta, you need to get them out of here. Do what you have to do, but Team Asswipe is headed here from the Facility, and I don't want them anywhere near Vail. Or Leona . . . or you, I guess. I don't really know you . . .'

Butt-fuck crazy plan darted like a fairy around Kira's head, bold and insanely beautiful. *Do it. Do it.* She was on the right track. The certainty slow-burned deep down, warm as her favourite mulled wine.

Greta raised an eyebrow. 'Where exactly are you and your bow going, Kira?'

Terrible plan did the Mexican wave. All by itself. *Do it.* She craved the idea like it was vegetable lasagne. Christ, she loved vegetable lasagne.

'Eron is looking for me.' Kira slapped her hand against her chest, too hard against the metal, making her palm smart like a motherfucker. 'So, I'm going to make sure he finds me. You said I need to get inside the Facility –'

'Not like this, you idiot.'

'Finds you? Are you insane?' Leona stood in the doorway, bracing Vail against the doorframe.

'Highly likely,' Kira replied. 'Look at the kid. He's hardly ready to go on the run. We need to give Anzu more time to track Nina.'

'They tried to kill you once, you stupid girl.' Leona huffed. 'This isn't a plan, this is suicide.'

Again, highly likely. 'Well, we'll find out if your Maiden has scribbled all over me because she has plans, or just wants to be a graffiti artist, won't we? Either this will work and I'll be inside the Facility, or it won't and I'll be . . .'

Dead? Had Eron gone that batshit? The guy who had taken convincing to go down on her, 'cause he might hurt her. Would he put her on ice now? Had her world gone that inside out and upside down? Please be no. Please be no.

'Wait.' Vail's voice sandpapered its way out. 'Perry said Eron was there. At the Facility.'

Kira nodded. The kid was stewing over something. And that something made him frown.

'So he's not in New Weston anymore. Neither is Tamas. You guys said –' Another coughing fit stopped the reveal. 'You guys said he left the penthouse.'

'Oh shit.' Leona's lips set in a grim line. 'Have they found what they were looking for?'

Like the world's lamest bunch of mimes, they all stood there in silence. Letting it sink in. Kira's crazy plan fairy refused to go stationery. If she didn't move, like right now, her head was going to explode. *Go, go, go.* Lasagne. Eat me. *Go, go, go.*

Forget *going* insane, her marbles had been well and truly lost already.

Bradley emerged from the wild curls of Leona's hair and launched into a cacophony of chirps and squeaks. The pitch was tinnitus inducing, painful enough to have everyone wincing.

Ears ringing, Kira pointed at the black-and-orange lump on Leona's shoulder. 'What was that all about?'

Vail glanced at Leona and Greta. Neither said a word. Leona gave Vail a grim smile and nodded.

'You should go,' Vail said. 'She said you should go.'

Kira sighed. 'She.' No point in making it a question. But Vail clarified anyway.

'Bradley said the Maiden likes your plan.'

'Fuck.'

Kira - 66

'Just you and me, kid.'

Kira held the door open until Bradley scampered through into the garage. Apparently this trip was not entirely solo. The lizard wanted in. And who was she to tell a reptile what to do? Kira closed the door on the flurry of activity going on up the hallway. Greta was hell-bent on joining the party too, which, considering that Kira had only ever been a bitch to her, was kind of a nice gesture. But the gut-niggling, lasagne craving instinct, or whatever it was, told Kira that Greta should stay with the others. The girl was nothing if not fierce. Anyone tried something with the witch and the kid, Kira had no doubt Greta would fight like fucking Godzilla to protect them.

Just before the door clicked closed, Kira got a last glimpse of Vail. As the evacuation plans were hurled back and forth around him by Leona and Greta, he stood silent. Watching her. Giving her a soft smile, and a thumbs up as the door clicked closed. So fucking corny. Why did her eyes sting?

Kira blinked, and adjusted her grip on the bow. The Telteriun metal luke-warm against her skin.

'Okay, ready to meet my fuck buddy?' She asked Bradley who had climbed aboard her shoe, clinging to the laces. Licking an eyeball. 'Right. I'll take that as a yes. So, how do we do this?' She scratched her temple with the tip of the bow. 'Oh, you've got to be kidding me.'

Her choices for chariot of doom were severely limited. Perry's sunshine-yellow SUV was nowhere to be seen. Her choices were a bicycle with flat tyres, skateboard, or crimson-red electric moped. He'd bought it last summer, bitching after only two rides that it was faster to walk. Wonderful. But red chariot it had to be. Kira shoved the bow into the top of her jeans, glancing the tip against the metal that now covered her ribs. Static electricity cracked and buzzed through her skin, sending a not unpleasant hum all the way down into her crotch.

'Oh.' Kira said. 'Okay. I can live with that.'

Hitting the remote, she waited while the world's slowest retracting garage door groaned and shuddered as it lumbered up. Kira wheeled the moped's front tyre right up against it, flicking the key – which Perry hid ever so cleverly in the ignition – to start the pathetic whir of the electrics.

'Got a good grip down there?'

Apparently not. Bradley zigzagged his way up her jeans, diving in under the pyjama shirt she still wore. Possibly should have changed into something more befitting the occasion, but hey, the end of days waited for no one. Bradley vanished for a second, not a hint of him touching the metal over her chest, before a rounded head poked out from between her boobs.

'Best seat in the house. Let's go.' Kira declared.

A dark world awaited them. Well, dark save for the row of streetlights illuminating the narrow alleyway the garage opened out onto. It was paved with cobblestones, and the rough surface jackhammered her on the seat till she thought the whole vinyl thing was going to disappear into her ass. Kira floored it, focused on the main road about one hundred metres ahead. Smooth, smooth asphalt. The crimson moped would probably wake the dead, but Perry was a barefaced liar. This thing could move.

'Remind me to tell Perry that if he can walk this fast, he needs to sign up for the Olympics,' she said.

Because she would have that kind of trivial conversation with Perry again one day. Both wasted on terrible cocktails and cold pizza, Kira probably lying on the bar. Just like the old days. It would happen. It would goddamn fucking happen. Kira turned right onto the main road. The air had that damp but fresh smell it got before rain. Way off in the distance, behind the reaching silhouette of a water tower, lightning danced across the sky. The streets were empty, and not a single light shone in the houses around her. What time was it anyway? Better question, where the fuck was she going? So far as planning ahead, she kind of sucked at it. Had gotten caught up in all the 'hell yeah, let's go' shit and not given much thought to details. Jesus, if this Maiden Gaia chick was trying to use her, she was probably regretting it about now. The moped hit a pothole and jerked Kira from her pity party. The lizard barely shifted, sticking to her – to the metal – like a giant piece of lint.

'Could have warned me.'

Bradley chirruped right back at her, a cluster of sharp bursts that might have been 'fuck you' in Lizard-ese. Fair enough. Kira pushed the bike harder, the resistant whine of the shoe-box engine protesting every rev of the throttle. She knew exactly where she was headed. There was a park on the other side of town that would do just nicely. Perry had dragged her there multiple times after lock-in. The bar had been closed for hours, but they, and the hangers-on that still hung on, would stagger out into the predawn light and Perry would tell them how amazing the sunrise looked from the children's jungle gym in Merville Park. Perry had a serious hard-on for sunrises, but Kira had to admit, some mornings, Pryden could sunrise the fuck out of most places she knew.

The crimson bullet hauled ass across town. Christ almighty, the temptation to just keep going, blow this fucking popsicle stand, had never been stronger. Grip the handles any tighter and they were going to snap off in her hands. Kira stretched her jaw, the muscles ached from clenching. If she'd ever been more shit-scared in her life, she didn't remember it. What the fuck was she doing out here all alone save for a shape-shifting lizard, half a suit of body armour, and a nod from an invisible entity? Kira seesawed from scanning the streets to scanning the sky. Grimalkin, drones, whatever was going to be thrown at her, were bound to come soon. And if the suspense didn't lift, pant-shitting was going to become a real aspect of her day.

Ten, fifteen minutes, hell, an hour later – who knew? – the park finally loomed up ahead. She passed maybe two cars the whole way. Streets dead as dodos. The bike shuddered over the rise of the gutter and puttered towards the arch marking the park entrance. The moped ran straight over a massive sign painted on the pavement that made it very clear no motorbikes were allowed on the hallowed park grounds. Might disturb the squirrels or something.

So far as parks went, Merville was stock standard. Trees, grass, benches, pathways that all led to a central water feature, a seminaked girl with an urn at her shoulder sending a stream of water cascading into a green mould-infested pool. Kira switched off the motor, and the whine of an engine under duress was replaced by the trickle of water. Sucking in her breath, Kira pulled the bow out from under her shirt, managing to pop the very bottom button in the process. The static tingled through her limbs.

'Right. Let's get this shit over with. If you have ears, Slimy, you might want to cover them.'

Pink tongue met eyeballs. Nothing more. Either Bradley didn't have ears, in which case he didn't hear the instructions, or he didn't wish to cover them.

Kira raised the bow in her flesh hand, holding the device horizontal to the ground like the class-A bitch in the penthouse had done. A lifetime ago, Eron had mumbled something about how to use this thing. They'd sneaked into the storeroom where it was kept under lock and key, but she'd been too busy trying to get his pants off to listen. Right now, all she wanted to do was activate it, figuring that would send a stronger signal. Right?

No clue.

'And I'm guessing Eron won't be in the mood to give me any tips now.' She sighed. 'Shit. I don't know how to use this fucking thing.'

Christ almighty, so far as heroes went, she wasn't getting on a best-ever list anytime soon. Her fingers found three small grooves in the centre of the device. She tightened her hold. Ruby points of light brightened at each tip, and the bow elongated. Both ends sliding out to double the device's length. Sweet mother of baby Jesus. Something was happening. Good, good. On track. She gripper harder.

Boom. The bow jerked in her hands, three narrow beams of sapphire light streaking free, throwing her wildly off balance. Kira lurched backwards and the laser light tore at the tree canopy above her, leaves and debris raining down.

'Jesus.'

But, as usual, he wasn't listening. Or if he was in the park, he was running for his life. Dropping onto her ass, Kira's attempt to lower the target zone cost the unfortunate urn-bearing girl in the fountain her entire head. The whole thing exploded, sending marble chips high into the air, creating a small dust cloud that rained down into the water. Seriously freaking, Kira gripped the bow as if she wanted to strangle the life out of it. The triple beam tore through the trunk of a thick oak tree just beyond the fountain.

'Motherfu –'

A stabbing pain tore through Kira's fingers, the shock of it jerking them open. The bow slid from her grasp, clattering onto the concrete and skidding away. Its ruby points dulled. Bradley splayed himself against the back of her flesh hand, his tail wrapped around her wrist.

'You bit me.' Blood trickled from puncture marks on her knuckles. 'Thank you.'

Chirrup, head nod, more eye licking.

'So that probably got the attention of NASA, let alone anyone nearby.' She dragged herself to her feet, picking up the bow and being careful not to put her fingers anywhere near the grooves.

Tiny tongues of flame licked at the truck of the tree she'd nearly felled, a ribbon of dancing orange light crisscrossing the trunk, following the line of impact. 'I kinda want to do that again, though.'

Hell of a buzz.

Bradley's bulbous head moved from side to side, wide mouth uncharacteristically clamped shut.

'Party pooper, you suck.' Kira flexed her hand, causing Bradley to back his scaly butt up her arm. He squawked and somehow got his lidless eyes to bulge even more. 'You glaring at me? Seriously?'

One nod, then another. Oh, good times. Nothing to see here. Just chatting with my lizard.

The cicadas, deciding the coast was now clear and they weren't going to get fried out of the trees, launched back into their incessant hissing. A moment later, distant thuds silenced them again. Many thuds. Bradley chittered, guttural and deep as the shadows surrounding them.

'Yeah, I hear it,' Kira hissed. 'Here we go.'

Movement came from within the deeper pockets of the park, shrubbery rustling. Grimalkin emerged out of the shadows, skulking around the perimeter of the fountain. Four of them, taking their places around her, legs bent as if they were readying to pounce – which they most likely were. The orange light from the still-glowing fire line on the tree trunk danced over their smooth silver bodies. Kira's gaze darted to the bow. It would take two steps to get to it. But this wasn't about defending herself. Still, standing here, so vulnerable, didn't sit well. Bradley suddenly dropped from his perch on her arm, hitting the concrete and disappearing beneath some of the rubble around the fountain.

'Where are you –'

The words died in the air. A figure emerged from behind the smouldering oak. Slender limbs, narrow waist, a delicacy that always – even now when fear pushed at her bladder – took Kira's breath away. Eron wore his silver-white hair tied tightly back against his skull, the weak lamplight softening its harshness with a golden tinge. Jesus, those lips, cheekbones. Divine. Beside him, she was like a mud figure a five-year-old had put together. Lumpy and coarse. So not beautiful. Her guts went all light and fluffy, a hundred butterflies emerging out of the lining of her stomach. Pathetic. She wanted to slap her own face.

He raised his hand towards the bow, and it lifted from the ground, rushing back to him. Long fingers closed over its length. And the two of them just stood there. Staring at each other. Eron hadn't even bothered to wear his contacts. As if he'd been in such a hurry to hunt her ass down there'd been no time to stop and put them in. Wide, depthless pools of white bore into her. If he'd thrown her into a snowbank, she wouldn't have felt colder under his gaze. Never, ever had there been so much . . . nothing . . . in the way he looked at her. Her saliva wouldn't go down her damn throat, pooling at the back of her mouth, leaving the rest of her parched and dry.

'You will come with me,' Eron said. Sending shards of frozen disdain into the air between them. 'And you will not make it difficult, Kira.'

The barbed way he spoke her name trampled all over her crazy butterflies, squashing them flat. Son of all the bitches, in all the worlds.

'Eron, this is insane. What you guys are doing, it's fucked up.' Could he even hear her? She could barely hear herself.

Cicadas. A whole damn plague of them shrilling out a chorus. But nothing from Eron. No movement, no sound. As robotic as the faceless, sleek metal cats surrounding him. He didn't blink; there was barely even a visible rise and fall of his chest. A cool shiver traipsed up the back of her neck. She couldn't remember when she'd last felt a chill, with the damn armadillo deciding it was a heat pack these days.

'Nothing to say? You're good with all this?' Kira waved at him, wishing she could land a hard palm against that sculpted face and knock sense into him. 'Don't have an issue with Tamas torturing me, 'cause you knew about that, right?'

The stillness made her skin itch. Yeah. He knew. And it cramped her guts that she had no clue if he gave a shit. Fuck. Tamas and Blake *had* been making monsters.

'Eron . . .' The name stung the inside of her mouth, and Kira had no clue where she was going with the rest of the sentence. Her head was goop. 'This is . . .'

'You should not have interfered, Kira.' The cold seeped into his flattened words.

Goddamn it was hard to stand there, under that gaze. Like staring into a void. What had she really thought might happen here? He'd rush into her arms, tell her all was good? Yes. Yes, she fucking had. There. Admission done and dusted. And her reward for getting all fucked up over a guy? Her beautiful scared-to-hurt-her-pussy lover had drowned somewhere beneath the snowcloud eyes when she wasn't looking.

'I'm pretty sure you guys are the ones interfering,' hoarse as a sex-line operator, Kira pushed on, 'trying to bring on the apocalypse and all that –'

'You are piteous, Kira. I abhor what I did with you, it disgusts me. You disgust me.'

'That's so not true.'

But it so was. For a guy who cried at TV commercials, Eron sure knew how to give a death stare. Right now, Kira was alone on the planet, 'cause the Eron she'd fucked sure as hell wasn't here with her.

'Enough, Kira. Do as you are told, or we will kill Blake. It's that simple.'

Her solo planet stopped on its axis, everything froze.

'You fucking asshole.'

'You stupid bitch.'

Kira rushed at him, the butterflies replaced by nails that pinched and stabbed at her insides. She balled up her metal fist, readying herself to land the mother of all bitch slaps across that chiselled face. Eron lifted a hand, flicking his fingers towards her as though she were nothing more than a bug. Her feet left the ground, and she was thrown backwards, slamming against the edge of the water fountain. The armadillo took the brunt of it. The vibration of impact rang through her body and knocked the air from her lungs. But it stirred something else. Deeper. Hotter. The chill vanished. Kira scrambled onto her knees. Eron strode towards her, sliding the bow into a holster at his shoulder, moving with a pace that said he had all the time in the world to throw her around again. Bastard. Gorgeous, pathetic bastard.

He was going to kill her. No. Worse. He *wanted* to kill her.

Kira ground her teeth, heard something crack inside her mouth. Pressure flooded into the back of her skull, a tumour that was growing. Just looking at him made her eyeballs feel as if they were going to pop from her head. Kira shook her metal arm. Now would be a great time for this fucking thing to go bonkers again. Just like it had when the Facility fuckwits had tried to bring her in.

The grimalkin formed a semicircle and edged forward.

'Stand down,' Eron directed. 'I'll deal with this.'

This? Like she was a shit stain on the sidewalk. He reached for her and Kira swung. He blocked her blow and grabbed for her flesh hand. Before the cry had finished leaving her, he wrenched her arm behind her back, shoving her chest up hard against the solid concrete balustrade around the fountain. She stared down into the dank water, Eron's reflection floating alongside her own. The guy was goddamn empty, no more solid than the image of him floating atop the water. He shoved his knee into the centre of her back, pulling on her metal arm with a force that would have dislodged bone and tendon.

'Fuck. Eron, you're hurting me.'

'Stop resisting,' he said. 'And it will cease.'

And it was the plan. Get dragged into the Facility. Which is exactly what Eron intended to do. So why the fuck did she want to go all kinds of postal? Claw at this stranger manhandling her until she shredded enough skin to find Eron again?

He snapped something around her wrists, then jerked her to her feet, slamming her butt down on the balustrade. The grimalkin huddled around them, a fortress of steel and wiring blocking her in. Eron grabbed her shirt, two fists clenching so much material she was shifted forward towards him.

'You have brought this on yourself, Kira. Taking what did not belong to you.'

He was less than spitting distance away, so that's what she did. A great, glorious glob of phlegm flew from her mouth and landed just below his left eye. She braced, ready for a punch in the guts, a head-butt, maybe a kick in the girl parts.

Eron blinked, his stubby black eyelashes fluttering up and down. He cupped his hand to her cheek, the long reach of his fingers resting against her temple. His gaze moved over her face, and all at once, there he was. Her thirsty boy. Eron drank her in, same way he always did, before all this shit. Tracing every curve of her face, the bulge of her lips, the tip of her nose, even that little divot between the two that probably had a name but she was screwed if she knew or cared what it was.

'Kira.' A breath that barely formed the word, but it was thunderous in her head, easing the pressure there.

'Hey, Eron.' 'Soppy,' 'ridiculous,' 'pitiful,' all the entries for pathetic in the thesaurus were crossing her mind right now. Being away from this guy so long had bruised a spot inside her, creating a purple-grey mess of broken blood vessels. 'Are you –'

Eron pulled her face towards his and gently landed his lips on hers. It melted her. Always did. She'd taught him everything he knew, and her protégé had learned fast and become a champion at suck-face. All her parts ached and spilled. Delicate flickers of his tongue brushed against her own. Kira leaned into the kiss, disappearing into it. She opened her mouth wider, pressing into him, the familiar honey-sweet taste of him. He sighed into her mouth, warm breath moving against the back of her throat. Eron slipped an arm around her waist, raising her up and pressing her body against his.

Then he bit her.

Came down so hard on her bottom lip the skin popped and warm blood filled her mouth. Kira's cry rushed straight into his mouth, and he let her drop back down onto the hardness of the ledge.

'Did you think I would waver that easily? You are not desirable, do not fool yourself.' Eron wiped his mouth with the sleeve of his jacket, and a smile, cruel and tight, sat across the same plump lips she'd sucked on a second earlier. The glimmer of light in the white pools of his eyes snuffed out. She was looking into a dark, shadowed house. And her flashlight was all out of batteries.

Kira went all rag doll as Eron manhandled her to her feet. A full on out-of-body experience took hold. She was remotely aware that he was being rough, holding her way too tightly. Her own blood was salty in her mouth and warm against the curve of her chin.

Eron was broken.

The Facility had broken him.

Christ. Had they broken Blake too?

'No!' Kira pushed the thought into one screamed word. And the switch finally flipped. The heat roared through her, as intense and all-consuming as an orgasm, slam-dunking everything in its way. She arched her back against the rush. Sweet bliss. Feeling nothing, feeling everything. Eyes wide open.

She tilted forward and rammed her head into Eron's chest, barely registering the hardness of the body armour he wore. He grunted, staggering back. Kira grimaced with the effort of trying to snap the bindings around her wrists. They held fast. The grimalkin stalked in towards her, and Kira threw herself back over the waist-high border around the fountain. She landed on her side, the dank water splashing into her face, soaking every piece of fabric she wore. If she stood, the water would be barely knee high, but now it tried to fill her nostrils. Kira flipped onto her back, giving another god-almighty heave against the bindings. They snapped free. Eron hurdled the barrier with far more grace than she had, touching down alongside her. Kira drew back her metal hand and let loose. The punch found the side of his head. Bone crunched. It might have been his skull or the crack of a joint as the jerk of impact whiplashed his head to one side. Either way, it was immensely satisfying.

'Who's piteous now, fucker?'

Kira landed an uppercut on his chin. His head snapped back, and now it was Eron's turn to go down in the water, arms flailing, face a comedy of surprise. Sweet Jesus, what a buzz. Her clothes had to be on fire, she was all flame and roaring heat. A grimalkin launched itself at her, sailing over the barrier. She dropped to her knees, leaning back in a move that would make a limbo champion proud, and reaching for the legs sailing over her. She caught hold of the back right and swung the whole mechanical thing at the headless seminaked girl. The grimalkin flew from her grip, the effort no more than if she'd just hurled a Frisbee, collecting Eron on its way. Throwing both he and the metal cat towards the central statue.

'Sorry, lover!' Kira called out.

Stone shattered and water sprayed. Seminaked girl lost her torso, and Eron flopped down as if all his bones had turned to water. Kira raced at the barrier, lifting one foot to its upper edge and hurtling out of the watery confines. She soared – goddamn soared – through the air. A soaking-wet wingless bird. Every neuron was humming, every nerve ending drowning in adrenalin.

The nearest grimalkin propelled a spiderweb thin net from an opening along its spine. The ghostly veil rose up and over her. She should let it find her. Encase her. Bundle her up and deliver her to the Facility. As per the plan.

Fuck the plan. She wanted to disintegrate everything within reach. Tear each wire from the sockets inside these butt-fuck ugly pieces of shit. Kira raised her metal hand and pierced the shroud descending on her. It sliced cleanly; her fingers were hot knives through butter. And as it drifted down around her, Kira ran at the metal cat that had launched it.

Her fists met the square panel where a head and eyes and nostrils and a mouth should have been. Metal cracked eggshell-like under the pressure, and her hand was inside the cat. She grabbed a fistful of wires and yanked it free. It made a dislocated sound, something like the squeal of a microphone too close to its receiver. She let out a whoop. The heavens opened up, splatting down giant blobs of rain. Bradley appeared at her feet and darted in front of her, causing her to stumble. He was barking like a miniscule rabid canine.

'Change of plan!' she shouted. 'I'm not done.'

Tamas - 67

Tamas pushed through the doorway of Tech Room Three before it slid wide enough to accommodate him. He cursed at the impact against his hip, at the need for this journey down here at all. Being torn away from his contemplations in the shrine seemed to literally boil his blood. He wore only a thin T-shirt and jeans – the least amount of clothing he'd ever stepped out of his room in – and still sweat beaded on his lips.

'Why is this not done?' he said. 'You've been here for hours.'

The technician, Weylen, dropped the tool she held. It bounced off Agar's prone body, hitting the exposed metal, the surface of the table, and finally, the floor. Raucous in the otherwise quiet room. Her companions – a pock-faced man and a gaunt, purple-haired woman – stepped back from the wide bench that held Agar's carapace. The gallu was inhibited but conscious, strapped down onto the stainless steel bench at his wrists and ankles by tungsten-steel alloy cuffs. Eyes fixed on the roof above where he lay. A formidable bulk when he was upright, Agar was no less spectacular when horizontal.

'Sir . . . I . . . testing the carapace's integrity is highly complicated work.' Weylen's dark brown skin concealed any flush or paling that might have occurred, but her voice, high and constricted, betrayed her. 'I've repeatedly requested assistance. Blake is –'

Tamas groaned. 'Forget her. Do what you've been instructed to do. Or did you not understand your orders? Are you that big a fool?'

He was half the height of the others in the room, but they all shrank from him. It was a truly beautiful sight, ruined only by their utter ineptitude to carry out their task. Agar must be prepared. It was as simple as that. The carapace must be reconstructed to full capacity. The cleansing was approaching its completion, and the Four would now be set to the next task as sentinels who would guard the Tier as the soul of Inanna was wrenched into this realm. And into the body that awaited her.

Weylen's bottom lip trembled, but she dared to speak again. 'Blake is out there. Right there.' She glanced at her colleagues, whose eyes dropped to the floor. There would be no support there. 'Sir, I know you had her brought down to level eleven, and I thought that maybe . . .' He wasn't certain if she was trying to swallow or stop herself from throwing up. Both, Tamas suspected. 'I thought maybe it was to assist me. I've spoken to her . . . several times . . . but it is not enough –'

Tamas ran at her, the speed of his movement coming as a surprise. One moment he was by the door, the next he had scooped up the tool that had fled from Weylen's grasp and pressed it against her chest, pinning her against the bench. His body flooded with adrenaline. 'Be quiet. Just shut the hell up.'

She pressed her lips closed so tightly they paled. Her trembling grew so violent it shifted the tool Tamas held against her. The piece resembled a drill bit, but with the tip curved into a hook. The hint of urine was on the air, and her terror was palpable, but she didn't utter a sound. Behind them, though, it was a very different story. Someone was losing their shit, crying out to their god. Over and over. That imaginary friend of theirs that always seemed to have somewhere better to be.

'I said shut up,' Tamas raged. 'Shut the hell up.'

Pin-drop silence. So heavy the tinnitus buzzed loud and clear in his ears. But he could get used to this; the crazy heart rate, body vibrating with the thrill of causing someone to actually piss themselves.

'Sir.'

Weylen's lips didn't move. Nor her gaze. Fixed on him. Wide and frightened. Her back arched over Agar's body as Tamas continued to apply pressure to the hook at the base of her throat.

'Sir, is everything all right?'

Someone was insistent on ruining his moment. Tamas dropped his hand and turned to glare at the intruder. A familiar face. Cultivated black beard, serious set to full lips. His name slipped from Tamas's mind. The guard supposed to replace Reuben. As though that were possible.

'If it wasn't, I would have called you.' Tamas flung the tool away. It shot across the room, embedding deep in the wall alongside the purple-haired assistant. She screamed and dropped to her knees. So, she was the god-caller. Stupid woman. She worshipped a powerless being.

Tamas smiled, curling his fist and relishing the crack of his knuckles and the sharp cut of fear on the woman's face. To see her, one would think he'd just taken aim and fired a shot. He took a deep breath and brought himself back to the moment. Down off his cloud. There would be plenty of time for pleasure. When all was said and done, they would all stare at him the way she did. No one would ever smirk again if he stuttered – unless they wanted to have their tongues ripped from their heads. Moving his attention to the bearded man, Tamas asked, 'What was your name again?'

'Boyd . . . sir.'

Boyd didn't enjoy being forgotten, a minute lift of his eyebrow betraying his irritation. Tamas's smile broadened. 'Boyd. Right. Come with me. I'd like to show Weylen here just how useful the Technician is these days.'

He led the guard out of the tech room, setting a path for the containment chamber that had been cleared to accommodate the ailing Technician. Random workers scattered as he approached, scampering like rats. With every stride Tamas grew larger and larger until the chamber felt barely grand enough to accommodate him. Not once did he turn down his gaze, not like he might have before; desperate to sink into his own shadow. That pathetic piece of shit he'd been slipped further and further away with every second that passed.

He'd be damned if he would cower behind Blake any longer.

Using her as some kind of human shield. Protection against the boogeyman that lurked beyond the Facility walls. For crying out loud, had he lost as much of his sanity as Blake had? Whatever force aided Kira, there was no chance it could breach the Lucentshield. Chances were it had been Enkidu behind her sudden superpowers. The foolish gallu had chosen that pathetic cow as his hand puppet. For all the good it did him. Now Enkidu was Tamas's prisoner. A shredded ruin. Terrified of the dark, and with no way out of it unless Tamas showed him the way.

He had Enkidu. He had Dumuzi. And soon, Eron would bring in Kira. Alive or dead, or in between, Tamas didn't mind. Though he knew his preference. Bottom line, he didn't need to keep Blake protected like a ridiculous talisman.

Punching in the release code, Tamas stepped into Blake's cell. She reeked. Of what, he couldn't pinpoint. Suffice it to say, it was repulsive enough to cause him to cover his mouth. She huddled in the far corner, raising herself onto her knees as he entered.

'Blake. Happy to see me?' He beamed. 'Get up. Come on, come on.'

Her confusion was quite the amusing thing to watch. She strained to one side, trying to peer around him towards the open door. 'What's going on, Tamas?'

'Who you looking for? Anyone in particular? Kira maybe?' The name seared the roof of his mouth, but he held his smile in place. 'She'll be here soon enough. Though, in how many pieces, I'm really not sure.'

'If you hurt her —'

'You'll what, Blake? What the hell will you do?'

Tamas's laugh chopped the air between them. But it was hollow. Blake's expression cut into him. The woman was beaten, bruised, and fading away, but if looks could kill, Tamas would be a hundred feet under. Such passion for that slut she called a sister.

Blake's ferocity pricked at his bubble, deflating his fervour. Baring a truth.

They feared him, everyone around him, but not one would endure for him. Threaten those who might seek to harm him. Fight for him. Not a single one.

'Get up. Now.' Tamas lunged at her, digging his fingers into her armpit and hauling her to her feet. The force of it nearly sent them both toppling. Tamas gasped and quickly swallowed the sound, smoothing his surprise. 'Walk. Or I will drag you.'

He flexed his fingers, thoughts dancing. The strength that had just touched him, the ease with which he'd lifted Blake to her feet – it was beginning. The goddess might not fight for him but she would provide. As promised. His veins flowed with a renewed vigour. The power of the Abgal blood – the great sages of the gods – seeping like a virus through his cells. He didn't need anyone to endure for him. He could be his own saviour.

Blake fell twice on the way across the chamber. And twice he stood over her, waiting for her to rise. Head tilted, he regarded her effort. Watched the sweat build, sheeny on her skin. He could probably lift her with his pinky finger alone, if he wanted to.

Amber eyes glinted up at him both times she got to her feet. Swaying, she cast a baleful glare at him, but remained utterly silent.

They reached Tech Room Three. The stairs, short flight though it was, might as well have been Mount Everest for Blake.

She uttered only one muted cry, just as she reached the top step. And stumbled. Set to crash and burn. Again.

Weylen rushed through the doorway and threw herself onto her knees, catching Blake before she hit the concrete.

Tamas sighed. 'Well, that's disappointing.' And enough time had been wasted indulging himself. Tamas took Blake by the arm once again, hauling her out of Weylen's grasp. There it was again. The unexpected and glorious strength. She was a bag of feathers, barely causing his muscles to strain. An exhausted bag of feathers. Blake didn't struggle as he dragged her across the room. Weylen followed, making whispered requests for him to let Blake go. Not to hurt her. Tamas ignored her, dragging Blake across the pristine white floor and dropping her at Agar's feet.

'There you go, Weylen. You have the assistance you supposedly can't do without.' He crouched beside Blake. Amber glinted with steel, her damned ferocity still evident. Tamas touched a finger to her chin. Unreasonably warm considering the chill of the chamber and the thinness of the clothing she wore. 'I'm fairly sure that you would not want your sister to hurt the way you do. So it would be best, for Kira's sake, if you do what you are told. Want to know a little secret? We know where she is. And I've sent Eron to bring her in.' Tamas pressed his fingernail against her skin. 'I'm not sure if you remember what you saw up on level nine, but Eron has developed some anger management issues. Poor old Azrael didn't really do anything to deserve his beating. I just can't imagine what

Eron might do to someone who does.' He jumped to his feet, dusting off his hands. 'Right then, let's get working, shall we?'

125

Eron - 68

Eron fought his way through the blur, a windstorm of rage shaking him from semiconsciousness. High-pitched static rang in his comms device. The break in communications would send back-up his way before long. He was drenched, lying in the water. Its dank odour assaulted his nostrils. A grimalkin pinned him down. He pushed its now useless bulk from his waist and then gripped what remained of the statue to haul himself to his knees. Bruises that would heal niggled at his back. The level of pain emanating from his right arm suggested a fracture.

Injuries levelled at him by *her*. A human. Coarse and sickly things that they were, snapping as easily as the branches of the trees circling the water fountain. His directive was clear. Restrain Kira, bring her in. If that could not be done, destroy her.

Destroy her.

The taste of her remained upon his lip. The tang of her blood imprinted upon him. Eron slammed his fist against the legs of the statue, the impact snaking long, searching cracks through both the grey rock. The mea stone hummed, and the echo of the abyss called to him. The sweetness of that darkness within beckoned. Agar may not be by his side, but the pull of his presence had barely lessened. Touching at Eron's core, it widened the black hole there, dragging him ever down.

Kira was oblivious to his return to consciousness. A perfect opportunity to fell her. No small part of his sensibility shouted at him to do so. But instead, he watched. Kira raised her booted foot and slammed it down on the grimalkin's head, using a force that should not be hers. Could not possibly be hers. The metalwork collapsed in on itself, as completely as if it were an egg she stood upon. Wires mixed with the dirt like colourful worms. Eron's incredulity locked him into the space he knelt upon. Disbelief constricted his throat. Kira. That wreckage of a creature, broken and reassembled, now braced herself at the approach of the last remaining grimalkin.

You disgust me. His own acidic words.

Kira stood with her back to him. Her wet shirt clung to her curves. Eron frowned, peering at the odd pattern on her back. The metalwork moulded itself to the curve of her ribs, the slice of her shoulder blade – Syranian metal, where before there had been none. He knew that unequivocally. More times than he cared to remember – fought to forget – Eron had traced his fingers along her skin, followed the gentle undulation of her spine, set his lips upon the smoothness and softness of flesh at the base of her neck. An odd pang gripped him. A sudden compulsion to tear away that shield she wore and dig his fingers deep into the flesh beneath. Sink into the quiet bliss of memory and hide there.

Kira shifted, and for a moment he thought she was about to turn to face him. She crouched down, and Eron rushed to rise to follow her movement.

'Oh good boy, B!' Kira cried, jumping to her feet before Eron was fully on his own.

His focus had been grossly misplaced. Kira's body was not the main concern.

She held the zuary.

Eron's hand darted to the sheath he had slid the Syranian weapon into and found only an empty casement. Kira took aim and fired, setting off three penetrating darts of sapphire light at the same moment the grimalkin ejected a solitary pulse of crimson firepower towards her. Kira threw herself to one side – her speed defying normal human parameters – and the pulse flew uselessly over her shoulder. Tamas's metal cat was not so lucky. Direct impact. The heat of the implosion bloomed with rushing fingers towards Eron. He shielded his face, squinting into the glow. Over as quickly as it had begun, the illumination faded to reveal a charred, melted crush of metal that mixed sparks with the rain.

Now she saw him. And he, her.

Dark curls, soaked through, plastered themselves to her forehead. Only one button remained intact on her top, exposing most of what lay beneath the material. The metal had indeed expanded itself across her torso, covering even her breasts. Eron curled his hand into a fist as they stared at one another. The pulses at each corner of his torso raced, and from a pit within his core, the darkness—feral and hungry—rose anew, rushing up to swallow him. Revulsion spread through him, and his skin around above the mea stone. The swamping bloodlust drew his gaze to Kira's neck. Her veins were raised blue-grey lines that taunted him, whispering of the heat flowing within.

'Who did you whore yourself to for this, Kira?' Eron said.

'Oh baby, the pot is calling the kettle black, black, black.' Kira held the zuary at an angle, not quite raised but at the ready to do so. 'Believe me, if I was putting out for a price, I sure as hell wouldn't take this deal. Now you, on the other hand. What the fuck is your story? You cried when the kid found his parents in Home Alone. But now you're king of the torture chamber.'

She spoke loudly, with overzealous emphasis on her words, the curses in particular, but he caught the tremor of something more delicate beneath. More fearful. Now as his tongue caressed his lips, no taste of Kira remained. A bitter, more pungent sensation registered. And a picture bloomed in his mind.

Kira, bound alongside Azrael, in the level nine cell. Their screams mingling in one great crescendo. The Technician forced to endure the sight.

Eron's pulses were erratic and frantic. The mea stone dug itself deeper, sinking into bone. And the abyss clawed higher.

Take what you desire, Eron.

Agar's connection startled and confused Eron all at once. Impossible. The gallu lay miles away, behind the confines of the Lucentshield, deep beneath the Earth.

Let us take what you desire, Eron. End this.

Eron hissed into the back of his teeth. This could not be Agar's own voice, yet the brush of it against his senses triggered the cluster of glands at the base of Eron's spine, stirring his sex and unleashing the coils of a bleak and terrible lust to destroy, to wound, to break.

To take what he desired.

'I understand my place, Kira.' Eron's eyes would not leave the curve of her neck, fixed there as though they had a life of their own. Perhaps they did. 'And I serve a power you cannot imagine. Certainly cannot defeat.'

'Big talk, little man.'

He grabbed the haleon from the compact pouch at his waist. Eron pressed it to his palm and the device reacted, spreading itself across his skin, reaching to loop around each of his fingers. Enough hesitation, foolish melancholy. Heat gushed from the mea stone, mimicking the lick of his own internal anger. Eron fired off a shot. His movements were quicksilver, but they were not fast enough.

Kira shot out of the way, her image blurring before his eyes. Eron's attack ignited the tree behind her. She retaliated, launching ribbons of blue light towards him. The back and forth continued under a torrent of curses, Syranian and English melding together in the onslaught. A park bench bore the brunt of one attack, the entire structure melting as though it were little more than ice.

But for all her newfound talents, she was no soldier, no skilled warrior or master of her weapon. A blast from the haleon dislodged the zuary from her grasp, the impact throwing her onto the ground and wrenching a scream from her lips.

Eron's breath shuddered up his throat. She was slow to get to her feet, exhaustion starting to find her. Her left eye closed against the flow of blood from a cut above it. The sight of it fed him, bloated him. A choked cry fell from his lips. His flesh afire, his soul mimicking the world around him as it too melted and collapsed into itself.

'I will end this, Kira. None of us can run from what awaits.'

The fool he was, he'd thought *perhaps*. Perhaps he could. Escape. Survive. Endure. But there was no part of him capable of running now. Agar's thirst saturated him.

'You cannot be allowed to live.' Eron's words cracked in time with the flames around him. 'End this, Kira.'

She raised startled eyes to meet his. A wreck of humanity, flesh hand cradled to her chest, blood streaking her face, hair whipped wild by her efforts to survive. And survive she had.

'What are you talking about?' Her eyes darted again to the zuary, too far from her to risk dashing for it, then to shadows beyond the flames surrounding them. Looking for more enemies perhaps. But her enemy stood right in front of her. Ravenous darkness seeping into ever widening hollows within. It would not be long before Eron became a vessel for the bloodlust and blackness entirely.

'I thought perhaps, alone, I could find a way through. But this must end, Kira,' he whispered, lips wet with rain. The liquid cooling his flesh, the guttural rumble of thunder above urging him on. Finish this. Arms shaking, he raised the haleon. Muscles at his shoulders cramped. 'I cannot . . . let you . . . live.'

Why had he ever desired to? The recall slipped away, a stone rolling across the mouth of a cave. Shutting away the truth forever. Leaving in its place a craving of such magnitude, to resist now seemed ludicrous. The light scratched at his senses. He desired only darkness. And it beckoned him.

Prove yourself truly worthy, Eron. Destroy our enemy.

Agar's voice, or his own? In truth, the answer no longer mattered. Neither he nor Kira were as they had once been.

Eron raised his hand, a narrow band on his middle finger instigating remote protocols on the zuary. The slender weapon lifted from its muddy confine behind Kira, and the ruby ignition points flared bright. He lifted his other hand, the one brandishing the haleon.

'Jesus, Eron.' Kira didn't move. That ridiculous, impossible girl, did not move. Did not run for her life. Pinned between two power sources that – at his behest – were poised to tear her apart.

Could have torn her apart some time ago.

End this, Eron. Agar – his own mind – roared within him, taking hold of nerve and sinew. Any shadow of the bare thread of resistance Eron had offered now obliterated beneath the onslaught.

His fingers curved, moving in unison to ignite both weapons. Kira's eyes, sparkling with tears, did not leave him. And it struck him that there was no odour. No biting tinge on the air that marked human fear. Eron's cry rose from the very depths of the abyss, screaming through his innards. Kira's image blurred before him, and the world erupted in a blaze of sky-blue light as he fired both weapons on her. Her name slipped from his lips.

But it was not over.

A shock wave of radiant, pristine white light engulfed the sapphire energy from the weapons. Blinded, Eron raised his hands. Terrible pain barrelled through his chest.

An agonised screech reached him in the brightness. Not his own voice. Hers.

Kira. Calling his name. The sound growing ever louder. A shadow moving closer.

That reckless, stupid, beautiful girl running to him.

Kira - 69

Kira now knew that the world stopped rotating on its axis when someone held a gun on you. Guns. Plural. She wanted to scream. Her throat was full of it, but nothing made it past the back of her throat. Blood ran into her eyes and burned like long-held tears.

'Eron –'

Eron fired. And the weapon – whose name she'd forgotten and simplicity she had once thought quite beautiful – released a burst of sapphire light, illuminating her entire world. She *was* blue. The colour itself. Her lover had just shattered her into tiny pieces of cobalt. There was nothing else.

Until there was.

Her arms were in front of her face, and she had no clue when she'd raised them. Blows hammered down on the armadillo like a carpet bombing raid. The layers of metal shuddered, shifted, and the impact wave slewed through her whole body, making her eyes bulge and her teeth strain from the gums. Her belly was tight and swollen, cramps smashing her abs as if the mea stone were using her insides as a punching bag. The rush stole the air from her lungs. Fuck. She was exploding in slow motion.

The change in pace hit hard. A gear shift that nearly tore her metal heart out of her chest. It launched her out into the cosmos. Kira atoms everywhere. Holy fuck. Heat and cold fluctuating so quickly she was both and neither at the same time. The sapphire world sucked away from her, as if someone with the world's biggest Dyson were doing a cleanup. Then, dazzling, eye-watering brightness. Diamond light. Shimmering, vibrant, impossibly white.

A great mass of it shot away from her, racing the distance to where Eron stood and slamming like a wrecking ball into his chest. His body bucked, willowy arms grabbing at the empty air. The force of the strike hurled him into the fountain.

'Oh Christ, Eron.' Kira forced jelly legs to move. 'Eron, Eron.'

A coppery brown fluid streamed from his body, light against the dark mouldy water. Now she was screaming. No doubt about it. Had to. Had to make him hear her. Had to make him get out of the fucking filthy water. The armadillo clicked and grated, as though bits of it were loosened, grinding plate against plate. Kira hurdled the fountain's low wall, landing knee deep in the grimy water. Wading through the faintly fluorescent liquid streaming away from Eron. Not his blood. Not his blood.

His eyes were almost completely closed, a thin curve of white visible. The silver strands of his hair formed a spidery halo around his head, shifting as her movement rippled the water.

And his chest . . . oh dear god . . .

'Fuck. Fuck, Eron. Please.' Kira wasn't sure how the words made it past her clenched teeth. 'Shit, shit.'

Her arms shimmered, stained with his blood.

Not his blood. Not his blood.

Not a hole in his chest. Her vision was all fucked up, the cut on her head determined to stream blood into her left eye.

Rock him. That would make it better. Back and forth, back and forth. Humming against his ear. He said she had a lovely voice. Fucking beautiful liar. Told her she was funny, that her bullshit stories were interesting, that he could have eaten kimchi every day. Lied through his achingly soft lips.

'Open your eyes, Eron. Right fucking now.' Kira pushed her face up against his ear and sucked in a breath. Couldn't smell him. That salt-kissed-sunny-day-at-the-beach thing he had going on despite the fact that he'd never stepped foot on a beach. Jesus, she'd never taken him to the beach. 'I need to take you there. Let's go. Now. Fuck all this. Screw them all. Leave. Come with me, Eron.'

She strained to lift him, but the water sucked at him like syrup, dragging them both down. 'Come on, Eron. For fuck's sake, you dumb bastard. Get up.' Kira pounded her fist against his shoulder.

Don't look lower.

There was nothing there to see. A black hole.

Another one she had made.

Kira clung to him, rocking back and forth. Shaking. Gagging. Sinking. Fracturing into pieces. A moan hung on the air, slowly rising. Gathering weight. A sound tsunami that was about to drag her out so deep there was no coming back. All the while the armadillo, with its rattling joints, registered the heat in Eron's blood. Told her it was warm. She held her hand over his mouth. Right up close. For once in its fucking life let the arm do something useful. Detect the heat of his breath.

'No.' The word was tiny, absolutely minute, and ready to become something monstrous. Kira clenched her teeth, her eyes, her breath. Everything needed to stop. All of this. All of her.

A rough squawk speared into her black hole, catapulting her back into damp misery. Bradley perched on the edge of the fountain's stone wall. Padded feet set wide, a gridiron player readying for a play. Kira straightened, Eron's arm hitting her leg and, for a super-cruel moment, making her think he'd actually moved.

'You're too fucking late, asshole. You piece of scaly shit, you could have done something. Where's the fucking dragon now? Huh?'

The triangular head sank low and moved from side to side.

'What does that fucking mean? I can't speak goddamn lizard. You're sorry?'

She might not speak reptile but the reptile spoke human. Head lifted. Up and down. Yes.

'Yeah, well sorry won't fix this.'

It didn't three years ago. Sure as fuck wouldn't now. What godawful thing had she done in some previous life? Because fate had a massive hard-on for taking a hold of everything she did and shitting all over it.

Another squawk tore through her pocket of hell. Anzu stood just beyond the fountain's edge, stalking about on his emu legs, silhouetted by the dim orange glow still coming from the smouldering trees. And another flash of colour.

Red and blue.

Fine. Let the cops come.

Anzu spread his wings, cawing, tilting his head towards his own back. Bradley skittered into her line of sight. Barked. Lifted a padded foot and gestured towards the feathered beast.

Perhaps she was dead. Stuck in a nightmare where she had to watch these two play out charades for eternity.

'Fuck off. I'm not leaving him.' Couldn't let go if she wanted to. And she didn't. His weight was all that was keeping her from crumbling like a fucking sandcastle. Christ, his hair needed to stop drifting in the water. Making her think some part of him was alive. 'Just piss off. I'm done.'

'No. You are not.' Greta ran out of the shadows, auburn hair matching the orange glow on the tree trunks. 'This is just beginning. I can only keep them away for so long. You need to let me take him, Kira.'

'Oh you have no idea how much that isn't going to happen.' She pressed Eron in closer. He seemed to shift against her, and her eyes darted to his face. Paler than snow. Lids closed. Fucking idiot, she was. For trying to pretend that history didn't love repeating itself all over her ass. That she wouldn't destroy things she loved.

'Kira, please. I know this is hard –'

'You don't know a fucking thing.'

Behind Greta, the torchlights of the police danced across the lawn, but not one beam shifted towards the fountain.

'Kira, there's a lot of cops out there, and I've only got so many workings to go around. I can't keep us hidden for long.' She jerked her head towards the mangled grimalkin. 'And I'm guessing your Facility buddies are noticing this about now. They can't find you, Kira. Not now.'

So much talking. And so much assuming that Kira would give two shits about any of it. All around her there was movement, but here, right here, in the freezing water and warm blood, it was all statue still.

Eron's arm suddenly jerked down beneath the surface of the water.

'Eron.' Kira laughed, lifting her face from his. 'Eron you're . . .' Bradley emerged from beneath the water, clawing his way up Eron's arm. Laughter turned to a growl, and Kira swiped at the reptile. 'Get the fuck off him.'

Greta splashed down on Eron's far side. Her sharp features were distorted by the light reflecting off the water. 'Kira, you're not going to like what we have to do.' She paused, tongue tracing her lower lip. Since when did ballsy bitch get the uncomfortables? Now, she had all of Kira's attention.

'What the hell is going on?'

Greta lifted Eron's arm from the water, Bradley still clinging to the swell of muscle above the elbow. 'Try to understand, Kira.'

Understand fucking what? She leaned forward, pulling her hand from beneath Eron's shoulders, aiming for the beady-eyed bastard who slithered a pink tongue across bulbous black lips. The bastard who could have gone full fucking dragon and stopped this mess.

Bradley scampered headfirst down Eron's arm – down to where the mea stone was a dark, hard bruise against Eron's skin.

'Now,' Greta hissed and clamped her hands on either side of the stone.

The impossibly bad day got worse.

Bradley's mouth opened. And opened. Jaws grotesquely wide. Toothless gums filled with pointed, jagged barbs. Black as the lizard's body. He drove his head down and clamped a gaping maw squarely over the mea stone.

'Stop!' Kira cried.

Eron's eyes opened. Pristine white. His body jerked, just as it had when she tore him apart. And he took a breath. A strangled wheeze that seemed to draw up the length of his body.

'Kira.'

'Eron, Eron. Holy shit.' Kira's laughter twisted around a cry. 'Eron, it's going to be okay.'

Lips curved upward, and she melted. That smile. Fuck, that smile. 'It is now,' he whispered.

She brushed back the hair that clung to his cheeks, touching his nose, his lips, his chin, as though she were reading braille on speed. 'I'm so sorry.'

The strangled wheezing sound came with each breath he took. 'As am I. Kira, you must go. Let them take you.'

'Me? Eron, you're in shock, okay. We need to get you some help.'

He was limp as a doll. A doll whose chest didn't move when it should have. No rise of breath. 'The others will be here soon. I misdirected them, I wanted to . . .'

White eyes grew distant. Kira pressed her hand to his cheek. 'Hey, stay with me. You wanted to what?'

It took a few rattling attempts for the words to break free. 'It is not important now. You are strong. You have always been. And that is what will matter the most.'

Sensors within her metal registered falling heat levels. Something the goosebumps on her flesh already told her.

'What are you talking about? Jesus, Eron. Look what I've done . . .' Because she couldn't. That would be the end of her. 'I hurt you –'

He reached for her. Despite the fact that the move etched his face with lines, breaking him apart, he reached for her. Long, glorious fingers against her cheek. Goddamn it, he was a winter frost.

'Kira, you have saved me.' The smile only clung to one corner of his mouth, and his eyelids fluttered, but his hand didn't shift.

'No, no. No, you fucking don't, Eron. Don't leave me.' Jesus Christ. She wanted to puke, to scream, to do some goddamn thing, but there was barely space to force words out. There was a cliff up ahead, Kira sensed it, a giant motherfucker of a thing and she was barrelling right for it.

Frostbite fingers pressed against her cheek, and he dragged his eyes open. 'Kira, I'm sorry.' Copper trickled from the corner of his left eye. And the cliff edge moved closer. 'Those words, those I spoke . . . you were right. They were lies. Not my own. I do not, nor have I ever, despised you . . . or anything that happened between us. Do you understand?'

She pressed her forehead to his. 'Don't leave me.' 'Cause she had a lot to say and hadn't said a word of it. Never had. Not to his face.

Eron shifted – grunting with the strain of tilting his chin the tiniest fraction – so his lips could brush hers. 'It's all I can do for you. Forgive me for not having your strength. This is all I can offer.' Eron's head lolled to one side, moving his gaze towards where Bradley still sucker-fished his skin. The coppery sheen of Eron's blood ran from where reptile met alien. 'Let it be done. Protect her.'

There wasn't time. To do anything. Except stare down off the cliff edge as Eron pushed them both over.

Bradley lifted his bulbous head, ripping the mea stone from Eron's arm. Dark blood spilled down over the tiny paw-print tattoo at his wrist.

Lids closed over twin pools of pure white, and he was gone. Leaving Kira to fall alone.

Tamas - 70

Weylen hugged Blake in an embrace that went on far longer than Tamas had time for. The pock-faced man and purple-haired woman had noted his irritation and pressed themselves into a corner of the small room.

'Now, now, Weylen,' Tamas said. 'You wouldn't have lied to me about needing assistance now, would you?' He didn't even need to approach her to cause her visible discomfort. Just staring at the woman had her shrinking back. 'I don't like liars. And I wouldn't want to find out you made things difficult in a ridiculous attempt to have Blake released.'

His words were jabs of electricity; each one had Weylen recoiling.

'She hasn't lied,' Blake said. 'Tamas you can see for yourself there is extensive damage done. And what difference does it make whether I'm in that cage, or in this one?' Blake scratched at the bandages on her left hand. The material was soiled and starting to come undone near her wrist. He suspected if he held it close to his nose, the stench would be quite rank. 'There is nowhere to go.'

Tamas reluctantly gave up his dagger throwing at Weylen and turned to Blake. 'Good girl. You get it. There is nowhere to go. Or run. I guess you should have thought of that before you decided to steal my property, really, shouldn't you? Would have saved a heck of a lot of trouble. For everyone.'

Blake regarded him. Her distant, indecipherable expression was one he was familiar with, but still, it kneaded at his good mood. Blake Beckworth had always been the master of vapidness. To look at her gave you no indication whatsoever of what she was thinking. No matter the circumstance. When he'd told her about her father's death, and Kira's injuries, her resultant expression had been no different to that she wore when he'd informed her the Facility had sealed another multimillion dollar military contract, thanks to one of her quadruped robots. Blake's face was more of a mask than those she created for the gallu. And it did not shift now. Even when everyone else around them was pissing their pants in fear.

'Do you want this done, or –' Blake gagged on her words, an ugly gurgle leaving her. Her head jerked back, body convulsing with a spasm that dropped her to her knees. Her audience gasped.

'Blake.' Weylen dove for her – yet again – only this time she missed her target. Blake toppled forward, falling onto her face. The spasms sent her limbs in all directions, her bandaged hand slamming against the leg of the workbench. She flopped about, wild as a fish just pulled from the ocean.

Tamas tilted his head. 'This is unfortunate.'

'Get a medic!' Weylen cried. 'Someone help me.'

Taking a step towards the door, Tamas did neither, unable to tear his gaze from the jerking, unnatural twists of Blake's body. Weylen rolled Blake onto her back, and the purple-haired assistant stuttered out some instructions to set her on her side and check she wasn't choking on her tongue. White froth seeped from Blake's mouth. Tamas moved to cover his own mouth, repulsion coiling through him.

Just as rapidly as the fit had begun, it was over. Blake gulped at the air, half-open eyes searching the air in front of her.

'Blake? Can you hear me?' Weylen pressed Blake down as she tried to rise. 'Take it easy. You need a doctor.'

'No. A doctor cannot help her,' Tamas said. Nothing could. 'Get her on her feet.'

'Are you insane?' Weylen cried.

But Blake appeared to agree with Tamas, clutching at her companion and attempting to drag herself to her feet. 'Tamas,' she gasped, 'there's something –'

Agar shifted, chest heaving skywards, limbs straining against the restraints. A chesty caw catapulted from his mouth, harsh as a crow. His hips thrust upwards. If the creature had had actual blood flow, Tamas didn't doubt his veins would bulge now. Agar strained like a weightlifter trying to bench-press a mountain, and the caw morphed into a wail that would have impressed a banshee.

Tamas pressed his hands to his ears. 'Why is he not inhibited?'

'He is!' the bearded man shouted, frowning at a monitor at Agar's head. 'These levels should contain him.'

'Well, they are clearly not,' Weylen snapped. 'Increase the levels.' She fussed over Blake, the Technician's pallor a faded grey, propping her up against the storage units that lined the room.

Agar bucked and gyrated with the abandon of a wild horse. The force of it against the restraints would have snapped human bones, but his Telteriun skeleton held firm. The faux skin did not handle the abuse so readily. The tears that already existed grew larger, ripping back to reveal far more of the dull metal beneath.

'Can he overload the restraints?' Tamas shouted.

Tungsten-steel alloy was among the strongest metal on Earth, but the cuffs at Agar's ankles were making a disturbing grinding sound. Weylen stood up, hurling directives at her teammates.

'Evacuate, now.' She pushed the bearded man away from the monitor. 'Get Blake out of here, now.'

Agar bellowed, and his right arm snapped the restraint. The chunk of metal zipped through the air, slicing off the face of the bearded man and continuing on until it slammed into Weylen's temple. The force jettisoned her sideways. She was dead before she touched the floor, the side of her skull torn open, seeping blood and bone fragments.

'Weylen!' Blake screamed, struggling to rise. The purple-haired woman staggered, eyes rolling back in her head, and fell to the bloodied floor in a dead faint.

Tamas cursed and ran to the comms link by the door. He thumped the heel of his hand against the panel. Normally, a green light would illuminate the round surface, giving the go-ahead to relay a message. The panel was unlit. A circle of matte-white plastic. He pressed his ear against it. Not even static emanated from the speaker. Some imbecile had neglected to inform him that the system overload caused by the Fours' arrival had not been fully rectified.

'Shit.' He activated the door release, shouting at the handful of guards who raced across the chamber. 'Get the captain on comms! We need the Syranians down here, get them all here!'

The room behind him filled with screams and screeches. He spun around. Agar had hauled himself off the table, bound to it by only one paltry restraint now, one at his left wrist. Giant reaching tubes of metal plumed out of Agar's back, tilting him off balance. Agar staggered, throwing out his free arm to steady himself, catching a nearby cart, spilling its entire load of drills and blades onto the concrete floor with a crash that could have woken the dead. Tamas had no clear line of sight to the far side of the examination table where Blake cowered. But if she had not moved out of range of the wings that lifted up and down, then she was as dead and dissected as the bearded man whose brains and guts now stained the floor. Tamas held fast in the doorway, his focus on the solitary restraint that held the gallu.

This should have been impossible.

Impossible.

The tungsten-alloy cuffs, the supposedly unbreakable bindings, were failing. And though Agar swayed like a storm-tossed sailor, as least still partially inebriated by the inhibitors, his range of movement should have been unattainable. The gallu shouldn't have been able to blink an artificial eyelid with the volume of inhibitor being pumped into him. Muttering some of the choicest Syranian swear words he knew, Tamas edged around the table, keeping a wary eye on Agar's wings. With the gallu too fuzzy-headed to actually coordinate them, the long, slithering strips of metal were like a dozen disorientated vipers, but Tamas kept on.

The gallu would not defy the Messenger.

Tamas could not allow it.

The ground was covered with blood. An agonised moan rose from a far corner of the room. Agar attempted to straighten, and his foot slid from beneath him and sent him crashing onto one knee. The massive bulk of Telteriun sent cracks rippling out through the floor. With the gallu lowered, Tamas had a clear view of the woman with the mauve hair. Perhaps she had been alive when she'd hit the ground, but the same could definitely not be said now. Her guts spilled from an enormous gash across her midriff, one that had almost sliced her in two. But her demise was in Blake's favour.

The Technician lay on her back, just beyond the sliced-and-diced assistant, in a widening pool of blood. She had no visible slashes on her body; the other woman had provided a human shield against the wayward thrust of Agar's wings. Blake's face was smeared with the bodily fluid she lay in. She blinked her eyes, but the rest of her lay perfectly still. Agar hauled himself back to his feet.

'Sir, permission to fire?'

A solitary guard rested on bended knee at the door, machine gun aimed at the gallu.

'No, you idiot!' Tamas shouted. Fire on Telteriun in these close quarters and everyone would be peppered with holes. And Agar would still stand. 'I told you to get the Syranians. Where is Eron?'

'The comms system is down, sir. We can't get a line. I've sent word on foot.'

Tamas was surrounded by fools. Fists balled tightly, he stepped up to Agar, leaving only the bench as a meagre barrier between them. 'Enough. You will kneel to your Messenger.' The words flew from him, bold and booming. All the while his heart threatened to explode with its rapid pace. But they could not lose control of the strongest of the Four. Not now. 'I am the mortal hand of your goddess. You will kneel to Ereshkigal's Messenger.'

Agar's stare penetrated clean through him, but Tamas leaned forward. Breath held. The gallu's strike came as swiftly as Tamas suspected it would. Free arm swinging. And Tamas was ready. Ready as he would ever be to test the strength of the Abgal blood in his veins. His open palm met Agar's fist.

The hammerblow sent a shudder down to Tamas's very core. He rocked back on his heels, but righted himself immediately. No skin split, no bone broken. The gallu's face showed no surprise, but his actions spoke louder. Agar edged back, head cocked.

'You will kneel.' Tamas braced, waiting for the next blow. Agar would not be subdued easily.

This time the gallu aimed at Tamas's head, broad arm rushing up in a quicksilver swing. Raising his hands, cupping them, Tamas took the full force of the blow. His body shook, but he did not backstep, absorbing the energy of the strike. Letting it fuel him. He tightened his grip on Agar's hand, and in total silence the two of them strained against one another. Neither gaining an inch. The bench cut into Tamas's pelvis, but he ignored the pain.

Agar's wings rose, fanning out on either side of the gallu. Tamas didn't falter. Didn't shift his gaze from where it locked on Agar's dull eyes.

'Kneel.'

The gallu would not strike down the Messenger. The wings were a ruse, a threat that would not be carried out. Intended to intimidate. Tamas understood he was being tested. He set his teeth hard against one another, bearing down, forcing more from his overstrained body.

And Agar's counterforce faltered. Weakened. The barest of retreats, but there it was. Buoyed, Tamas pushed back harder still. His body screamed a protest, one he ignored for now. But he was not made of Telteriun, If this continued for much longer, Tamas's skeleton would fill with fissures and everything would crumble.

'No.' He hissed, digging into reserves that until now had been hidden to him. Locked away until the goddess had finally turned Her key.

The gallu sank down to his knees.

It was done. Tamas released him, fighting the urge to clutch at the bench for support. The fast retreat of adrenaline left him boneless but he would not dull the magnitude of the moment with a slouch.

'He has fallen.' Agar's voice rumbled in the silence.

'Who?' Tamas said. 'Who has fallen?'

Agar raised his head. Beyond him, Blake watched them from her thin mattress of blood.

'Eron,' Agar replied. 'The Bind has been broken. I sense him not. He does not live.'

Tamas's heaving breath was thunderous in his ears. Now he did lean against the solidness of the bench. For once his tinnitus was drowned out, but he would have rathered it remained. He could not catch his breath. Agar's words echoed, knocking the air clean out of his lungs. 'Eron is dead?'

A god-soldier of Lahar. Sent to retrieve an incomplete human girl. Dead?

Remaining on his knees, glinting, ever-hungry eyes narrowed, Agar nodded.

Finding oxygen at last, Tamas said, 'Get up. You will come with me.' He didn't wait to ensure that Agar followed orders, no doubt in his mind he would. Instead, Tamas turned his attention to the guard still at the door. 'Get a medic here now. If the Technician dies, I will kill you all myself.'

Kira - 71

Kira clutched a greater handful of Anzu's jet-black coat – a hybrid of feathers and fur, softer than silk – pulling herself forward and trying to bury herself in the thick mane-like ruffle that ran down the creature's neck. A monster sitting on a monster. How fucking poetic. Anzu bayed, shaking his shoulders.

'Too tight, Kira.' Greta relaxed her own grip on Kira's waist, placing a firm hand on the armadillo.

'Fuck off.'

Any other time Greta probably would have shoved her off the back of the giant flying bird-lion they were perched on. But this was not another time. It was here and bloody now. Eron's coppery life coated her clothes, damp and cool and sticky. Greta was uncharacteristically silent but held the pressure on Kira's hand until she relented, and made things more comfortable for Anzu. She and Greta were hedged in behind where Anzu's wings met his shoulders. His wings brushed the tip of Kira's knees with each lift and lower. They'd been airborne awhile. Kira's numb ass and the ache in her inner thighs told her that. The desert stretched out beneath them like an onyx carpet, city lights lost somewhere in the darkness.

Kira didn't recall climbing on board. She had a vague recollection of whispering, close to her ear, a lot of pleading, and a fuck load of effort on Greta's part trying to wrench Eron from Kira's arms. The lizard seemed to have vanished the moment he'd ripped the stone from Eron. Good thing too. When she saw him again, Kira would tear Bradley's reptilian guts out.

Protect her, Eron had said.

Nah, it was the lizard who needed protecting. Eron would still be here if that fuckfaced thing hadn't torn a piece out of him. Kira squeezed her eyes shut, bringing down a dark wall against the image of Eron.

The crater-wide hole in his chest.

Nothing to do with the fucking lizard.

Everything to do with her.

Her eyelids failed her. Big-time. The image of Eron's broken body seeped in around the barrier and, like a horror show, played out over and over. Kira gagged, huddling forward. Bone cold, her own body shaking so hard her teeth were getting ready to dislodge from her gums. She kept letting out pitiful whimpers, like a puppy caught in a drain. So lame. So fucking lame. There was a scream down in the depths, clogging her up. Bloating her guts, but only one word made it out.

'No . . . no . . . no . . . no.' Stupid, useless word that it was. And it wouldn't stop crawling out of her. She unclenched her fists, letting them hang to either side of Anzu's neck.

'Kira? Hang on.' Greta pressed up harder against her back, arms wrapped around her waist. A spot of warmth in the ice land. 'Just hold on.'

'I don't want to.'

Greta lifted one arm so that it lay across Kira's chest, her hand gripping Kira's metal shoulder. 'I know. Believe me, I know. We're all losing out.'

Kira's weight would have been considerable, considering the armadillo had extended its claim over her body – but Greta held fast. Held her upright. And she was the only thing keeping Kira in place on Anzu's back. Stopping her from free falling down to the ground. Way, way down. If Kira shifted just right, fell so that she landed on her head, then no amount of alien metal would prevent her brains from carpeting the landscape. And she wouldn't have to feel a damn thing anymore. All she had to do was get out of Greta's grasp. The woman would get tired eventually. Then, sweet merciful

Jesus, that swan dive into oblivion could happen. And this would be over. The blindsiding agony. A mini woodchipper slowly moving through her. Pulverising everything in its way. Making a hole in her, just like she'd made in Eron.

Anzu tilted his head back, the wind catching at the fur-feathers, parting them like a goddamn Black Sea. Bradley peered at her from the flattened mass. Every part of her shredded insides shifted, made their way to the base of her throat. The piece of reptilian stone-stealing shit seemed bigger than she remembered, but maybe that was just because he was all she could see. Nothing else mattered anyway. Bradley edged down the length of Anzu's neck, moving into striking distance. Kira balled a fist, shifted forward.

'Kira, stop. What are you doing?' Greta grunted, tightening her hold.

What was she doing? She was going to take the lizard in her metal hand and squeeze until he popped. Dig her fingers in and tear out his innards until she found the piece of Eron he'd stolen. Bradley kept coming, black-hole orbs watching her.

Dumb shit.

Let it be done. Eron had wasted his last words on this dumb shit. *Protect her.*

She should have told him to shut the hell up and listen to her. Just three fucking words should have come out of her repulsive, foul mouth. One of them a four letter word she used so rarely, she probably would have choked on it.

Christ almighty, what a time to become a fucking mute.

Heat brushed against her flesh hand and she sat bolt upright. When had she taken her eyes off the slinking reptile?

Bradley was draped across her hand, covering it entirely. And there was no getting around it, the lizard *was* bigger, doubled in size. Which meant he was the size of an adult shoe as opposed to a baby bootee. And that larger head tilted back and forth as Bradley rubbed his jaw against her hand. Slow and steady, contact sending a subtle, not-terrible shiver running through her. Her fury slithered down somewhere out of reach, back into the clogged-up mess inside her.

He knew.

The words floated around her, like a wind rustling through tree leaves. But they were in the fucking desert, not the Amazon. No trees to rustle.

He knew your mind, Kira.

Those trees sure knew how to make a girl's eyes ache. Bradley kept on with his swaying, a hypnotic rhythm to his movement. Each touch of scale to skin slowing down her gut-shredding woodchipper, dulling the blades. There were frogs that did this shit, right? Lick their backs and you got real high, real fast. Bradley was doing something, releasing something into her. Rustling trees in her head. And she didn't pull away.

His sacrifice is made, and for that the Maiden is grateful. With these two stones, her reach now broadens. Our time begins. Your time begins, Kira. I will remain at your side. You are not alone.

Insides went loop-de-loop. Bile simmered at the back of her throat. She raised her flesh hand, trying to dislodge her passenger, but something caught at her shoulder. On a day where things couldn't get any worse, things got worse. 'Oh Jesus.'

In the midst of all the shit and chaos, the armadillo had spread farther, now layering her left shoulder and bicep.

'What's wrong?' Greta said.

A question that would take days to answer if she answered it entirely, but for now, Kira focused on the immediate threat. 'I'm going to throw up.'

'We're almost there, can you hold it?'

'No.'

Anzu apparently didn't think much of vomit-coated feathers, because he descended at a rate that would have made her hurl chunks, even if it wasn't already on the cards. Her vomit hit the ground before they did, though. Greta snatched her hands clear, and Kira hurtled off Anzu, her knees touching down in rough dirt. It poured out of her. A volume of spew that seemed impossible considering it hadn't been that long since Tamas's torture technique had brought on the projectiles. Burned like fucking acid, too, leaving her just a bit rawer than she already was. The insane thought that it might have been a good thing if the armadillo had coated her insides crossed her mind as she dry-retched, body spent.

She was a metallic husk. Despite Bradley's hoodoo, the woodchipper in her guts had done quite the number.

'Let's get inside.' Greta stood over her.

Kira wiped her mouth on her sleeve, the black cotton soaking up whatever the hell stained her lips. 'Inside?'

From where she crouched, it looked a hell of a lot like they had landed in the middle of butt-fuck nowhere. A stunning almost full moon threw down silver light, deepening the fire-red dirt to a rich crimson. Bloody crimson. Save for rocky outcrops here and there, barely a cactus or two broke up the monotony. And the scenery was looking all too familiar.

'Where are we?' Kira croaked.

'We're only a kilometre or so from the Facility. Can you stand?' Greta didn't give her time to find out, looping her arm around Kira and straining to get her to her feet. 'This way, come on.'

Kira's pyjama top had not done well in the death match. She was down to one button holding it all together, not that it mattered. With the armadillo covering most of her upper torso, it wasn't like her tits were hanging out. Not that she would have given a fuck either way.

Greta limped her through a narrow opening in the nearest of the rocky outcrops and into a circle of rock that mimicked a rustic amphitheatre. The whole space was no bigger than an Olympic-sized pool, so the Winnebago parked on the far side under a ledge of rock was easy to spot. It was one of those vans that had beds over the driver cabin. Kira's dad had had one of those, a lifetime ago. Blake and Kira had fought over who got to sleep over the cabin, both wanting the space to themselves. Dad had other ideas. Forced them to share. No doubt regretted it when, at three in the morning, Blake kicked out in her sleep and got Kira in the ribs. Screaming and fighting ensued. Christ, that family holiday in the camper might as well have been a thousand years ago, not ten. Kira would have taken that kick in the ribs again at the drop of a hat.

'Who's in the van?'

'Everyone of importance.' Greta set a fast pace across the expanse of the rocky enclave. 'Leona managed to secure the vehicle in Pryden to enable our escape.'

The witch had stolen a Winnebago. Of course she had. Because nothing said 'clandestine' like a large brown-and-tan recreational vehicle. But where Leona was, so was Vail. And just thinking about the kid did that stingy thing to Kira's eyes again. Fuck, she wanted a rewind. Back to where they were both rocking and rolling on that ridiculous waterbed. Giggling like teenagers on their first sleepover. Kira stepped up the pace, faltering when a crack of branches sounded behind her. She turned. Not twigs. Bones. Anzu the soaring shagpile was gone, the black parrot in its

place. He glided past her – the breeze lifting her tangled hair –
before he came to rest on the flat roof of the camper.

The curtains were drawn, and only the tiniest hint of light
made it as far as the red soil outside. Greta opened the door, and a
cascade of brightness flowed out. Inside, Leona huddled over a
dented pot on the camper stove. The pale orange curtains behind
her did nothing to flatter her bleached hair and Oompa Loompa
tan. Leona straightened and their eyes met. The old witch sucked in
a breath, pressing her lips together so tightly she gave herself a few
more wrinkles. A nearly impossible feat.

'I'm sorry, love,' she finally said. 'I'm so, so sorry.'

Kira held up her hand, waved it. Nope. This wasn't going to
work. Not if she was going to hold herself together. And the cracks
were already making that a mammoth task. Didn't matter a damn
that she was practically all metal now. The armadillo had seams,
joins and bits that would fall apart if Leona didn't stop giving her
the piteous eye. Luckily, the witch was more clued in than she
looked. Giving Kira a sharp-chinned nod, she returned to her
hissing pot. When she lifted the lid, the interior of the camper was
flooded with a stench that brought a very different kind of tear to
Kira's eye.

'Where's Vail?' Kira said, grateful her stomach was already
empty. Whatever Leona was cooking smelled rancid.

'There.' Leona pointed a shaking finger towards the back of the camper. 'Stupid boy insisted on trying to summon your friend Perry again.'

Vail lay on a double bed that took up the entirety of the space. He'd reached a new level of paleness. Kira could make out some veining on his forehead, his blunt fringe damp and pushed back from his face, the coin nearly lost beneath the swell of the skin around it.

Kira's legs wouldn't slide into first gear. She stood there like a dirty, bloody, stinking statue. 'What's wrong with him?'

'He passed out on the way here, and I can't wake him,' Leona said. 'She keeps telling me he can't be woken, but I think she's full of the same stuff as her blown-up tits.'

'She?' Kira glanced at Greta, who'd seated herself at the fake marble table in behind the driver's cabin. The redhead didn't get a chance to answer.

'I understand you are extremely anxious, Leona. And we're still getting acquainted, so I will let that comment slide.' Nina stepped out of what Kira assumed was the bathroom cubicle, halfway down the length of the van. She took the handful of steps to reach Kira's side in the slow, feline way she had. The leather pants she'd poured herself into creaked as she moved, and her crocheted top – a smattering of sequins glinting – slipped from one shoulder. A brooch perched on the swell of her right breast, a fox head that glittered with clear and burnt yellow stones. The whole fucking world might be toppling down, but Nina still pranced about as if she were in a high-end cosmetics commercial. She laid manicured fingers to either side of Kira's cheeks and brought her forehead to meet Kira's own. 'Oh my little sweetheart, you have certainly seen better days. Let me add my condolences to your list, Kira. It is a terrible thing that befell you. I hope I can give you some comfort when I say that this was inevitable—'

'Jesus,' Kira hissed.

'No, listen. The Four are beasts, and they hunger for destruction, for disassembly and chaos. Your lover's intimacy with them doomed him from the very beginning. The Four feed on a spirit until there is nothing left but a reflection of their own souls. And they are dark, dark creatures. What happened, was not your fault. Don't beat yourself up too much.'

'Sure, no problem. I'll just get over it . . .' Kira dragged the barbs up her throat, better out than in. Surely. 'I just . . . I just killed him. No biggie.'

Rancid words that carved a crater as they moved. Kira breathed in Nina's scent, trying to find a foothold in a reality that was eating her alive. Breathe. Keep breathing. A scent like a candy store.

'If it is any consolation, death can be a beautiful freedom.' Nina's hand traced the length of Kira's metal arm, from wrist to collarbone. A touch almost as soothing as the lizard's. But seriously? Her pep talk sucked ass.

'It isn't and it wasn't. Beautiful.' It was nightmares for the rest of whatever miserable life Kira had left. Her dad and Eron could team up now. A horror-dream marathon that was going to make her nights as unbearable as her days. Good, good times. Nina's hand found the curve of jawbone, and Kira leaned into her. Bone tired. She closed her eyes.

But there they were. Daddy-O and lover boy. Side by broken side. Eyes open, Kira stepped away.

Nina sighed, but she was doing the Leona thing. Soulful eyes that just oozed pity. 'You alone did not take his life, Kira. You walk with the gods now, and with that, great burdens come. We are handmaidens, you and I. And we must do the best with what we have been gifted.'

'A gift?' Kira laughed, the sound cracking a few more fissures. 'What kind of fucking gift is this?'

'A difficult one,' Nina said, the soulful eyes on full beam. 'A very difficult one.'

'Give the girl some breathing space.' Leona glowered. 'And for all the gods' sakes, let her get cleaned up. Kira, I'm going to get you a clean shirt. And if we are lucky we can get the dodgy shower in this jalopy to work. You smell disgusting.'

This coming from the chef who was apparently cooking sewerage. Being bossed around was better than sinkhole sympathy, but Kira wasn't following orders. 'I'm not changing my shirt. It just needs some buttons.' Sure. Right. What it needed was lighter fluid and a match. But putrid as it was, the stained and torn cotton was all she had left of him. So, fuck it. The blood stayed all over her.

Leona screwed up her lips and exhaled loudly, but the protest Kira expected didn't come. 'All right. I'll see if I can find some pins or something once I'm done with the broth.'

'Here, take this for now.' Nina unpinned the fox brooch and tossed it to Kira, the stones glittering wildly as it moved. 'Try not to lose it, orange sapphires are ridiculously hard to find.'

Not exactly the fix Kira was hoping for, but it would do for now. She pinned the brooch just below the solitary button that still held fast, the fox upside down so its diamond coloured eyes stared right up at her.

'Where have you been?'

She might have been addressing Nina, but Kira's focus went again to Vail. Why was he lying so fucking still?

'Well, here. Trying to find a back door into that Facility of yours.' Nina regarded her flawless nails. 'But I think all the Shifting has weakened me. I'm not ready to admit defeat just yet, but whatever protections they have around that place they are rather . . . prickly, shall we say? Then I sensed the arrival of the little wizard, and decided to take a break and join them.'

'Could have told you you wouldn't be able to get in. Been there, tried that.' Leona ladled the reek-broth, lumpy and brown, into a bowl.

Nina perched herself on the short, narrow bench beside the cook top, continuing as though Leona hadn't uttered a word. 'I've had no direct contact with Inanna in nearly two thousand years. I'm what many would call a "has-been".' Her smile was sharp. 'Whatever protects that place is a formidable obstacle. At least for people like us. People like you, Kira.'

The clang of Leona's ladle against the pot rang like a tinny death knell. Kira decided that she'd had enough of chitchat about 'people like her.' What she wanted was to be with the one person in the cramped camper who didn't make her feel like a freak.

Kira climbed up on the bed alongside Vail. He was propped up against several pillows, Bradley on the uppermost one, right beside his ear. The reptile's onyx-and-orange colouring accentuated by the lily-white of Vail's skin. The kid clutched the stone deity she'd last seen in Perry's bedroom. The multi-armed goddess rested on his belly, both hands cradling her carved, crossed legs. He was breathing, though Kira's eyes were starting to water by the time she'd held them open, unblinking, long enough to decide. This wasn't how it was supposed to be. That goofy grin should have been a damn supernova at the sight of her.

'That's how I found them,' Nina said softly. 'When they got close, I felt him. I suppose, after what I did, we have a connection.'

'Why won't he wake up?' Kira said.

'I believe he's lost his way, in a place he does not understand,' Nina said. 'If anyone had bothered to ask me, I would have informed them that trying to encourage a possession was, quite simply, a stupid idea. The boy barely clung to the land of the living as it was. When he was injured so gravely, I did what I could at the time, and to be honest it worked far better than I had imagined. But he was foolish to strain himself. What was he thinking?'

Leona shoved past Nina with far more elbow involved than was strictly necessary. Poo-brown goop sloshed over the sides of the bowl she held. 'He was thinking that he had to do whatever it takes to stop what's going on in that fortress out there. So you might want to shut those overmade-up lips. Handmaiden or not, you keep talking about my boy in the past tense, and I'll get personal.'

'Yeah, I'm going with the witch on this one.' Kira wiped Vail's hair back from his face. 'He'll find a way back. Won't you, Vail? You hear me, buddy? Don't make me come in there. Get back here. Quit fucking around. You're not leaving me. Not today. I'm so not in the fucking mood.'

Not another one. Not today. Not if she wanted to stay remotely sane. Vail had to come back. Leona threw her a lopsided but grateful smile, and a faded red dishcloth, as she lowered herself to the ground, raising a spoon of the stink-fest broth to Vail's lips. If the stench didn't wake him, Kira wasn't sure anything would. She held the cloth at the ready, presuming it was for wiping up dribble. Vail wasn't exactly waiting open-mouthed for a feed.

'I understand the child is important to you.' Nina hesitated. 'But there are greater things to consider . . . while. . . we wait for him to return.' She added the caveat in a rush, and Kira had no doubt Nina didn't believe a word of it. 'Obviously, we need to be inside the Facility, not out here on family vacation. But the shield around the complex is designed specifically to keep out our kind, preternaturals, supermundanes, even you, witch.' Daggers flew and Nina flipped them away with a toss of her curls. 'Don't get all demon-eyed with me. I'm just pointing out that it will detect even the smallest degree of supernatural ability. Only humans,' she glanced at Kira, 'true humans, are oblivious to its presence. And unaffected by it. And there is . . . well, was, only one among us who qualifies.'

Penny dropped with a huge thud. 'Rossiter,' Kira said. Shit. Rossiter. She hadn't given the big man two thoughts since the split. 'Wait, you said *was* . . .'

'Don't panic,' Nina said. 'Rossiter is alive. He was with me but went inside before we realised that I wouldn't be able to follow.'

'Kira,' Leona hissed, nodding at the streak of broth that had escaped down the side of Vail's neck.

'Rossiter is inside the Facility?' The Samoan-Canadian brick wall was in the nest of vipers on his own. Just terrific. Kira mopped up dribble dutifully. And when Vail was clean, she took one of his hands from where it clutched the statue and cupped his frail fingers with her flesh hand, frightened she'd grip too tightly with metal. Break him even more. The kid was less than skin and bone.

Nina nodded. 'Rossiter believed he could get in with little fuss through some secondary entrance. Said someone owed him a favour or two. I can only assume he made it. I haven't seen him since.'

Kira focused on Vail. The coin lodged in his cheek had a swell of flesh around it that was difficult to look at. He was so still. As if he had never been capable of moving at all.

'How long has he been like this?' All at once, every bruise on her body – and there were a lot of them – ached in unison. Kira lay down beside the kid, sighing as her head touched the pillow.

'Coming up on an hour now.' Leona dumped the spoon in her goo, apparently giving up on trying to get it down Vail's throat.

'So, say Rossiter is in, then what?' Greta asked. 'How the hell is he going to shut down the barrier? Not like they won't be guarding the shit out of it at the moment. They're going to know about Eron and the fact that we've removed the mea stone.'

Vail's hand tightened around her own, and his eyes flew open. Leona dropped her bowl of mush, and Bradley whirled in circles.

'Oh!' Nina's world-class eyebrow lifted. 'That's rather unexpected.'

'Jesus, Vail. Buddy. Can you hear me?' Kira rocked onto her knees, the movement of the mattress making his body shift. He stared up at the ceiling. And a new feature was all too apparent. A haze of white covered both eyes, not quite Syranian levels – she could still make out the darkness of his irises beneath – but unhealthy looking all the same. Vail winced, exhaling softly.

'Don't you ever, ever do that to me again.' Leona grabbed his other hand, and the statue resting on his belly rolled onto the bed covers.

'I'm sorry, Leona. I'm sorry . . . but . . .' Vail blinked, fluttering those long lashes as if he were trying to score a date. 'Where's Kira?'

'Right here, dude. Tell me you're not blind.'

He rolled his head towards her. Jackpot. That goofy smile turned up the corners of his mouth, a miniature sun. 'Kira, I'm so happy you are okay.' The sun set with whiplash speed. 'But I'm so –
'

'Don't say it.'

The kid's fingers tightened on hers, and his tired eyes glinted. *Oh shit. Don't cry it, either.* If he started, it would set her off too, and that flood would be unstoppable. Vail swallowed. Hard work apparently; he used his whole head, chin bobbing, Adam's apple straining.

'We need to hurry, Kira. Something…it's already started. I know a way in. . . but . . . it's not real nice.'

'Nothing about this day is. Spit it out.'

Vail started to speak, and the words choked his airways. He coughed till Kira expected a lung to pop out of his mouth. But he waved off Leona's concerned tut-tuts and flutterings. And never once did he loosen his grip on Kira's hand. Voice hoarse, his cloudy eyes locked on her.

'Perry told me how we can get in. And we don't have much time. I'm so sorry, Kira, but Eron is our key to getting you into the Facility.'

Tamas - 72

Tamas's breath raced from him. The sharp pull of the goddess had quickened his steps on his journey from level eleven.

The cleansing nears completion.

Her summons pushed his lungs to bursting. Urgency lay upon all things now. It filled him, a disconcerting sensation beneath his skin. Tamas rushed into the Orientation Room, glancing at the mobile inhibitor units that caged the four gallu; Diresh, the only female carapace, Tek, Sora, and Agar were placed at intervals along the south wall, like exhibits in a museum. Kept close to their alien handlers. Tamas strode past the assembled Syranians, all grim faced. One fewer in number and so much rawer for it, their air of arrogance whisper thin. For all their bravado and swagger and looking down of noses, one of them had fallen. Eron's death resonated through everything now. Even, Tamas suspected, through the rapidity of the cleansing process. It had been far from done when he left the Shrine to deal with Weylen, yet here now the goddess declared it almost complete.

The Waters frothed and bubbled within their panes of glass, streams of pale mauve light wove amongst the emerald. At Tamas's feet, white froth so thick it gave the appearance of snowfall.

The child lay cradled in a natural indentation at the top of the ancient stump. All but his face – the colour of sun-kissed sand – submerged in a pool of the Waters. Blue eyes wide open, staring hard at the carvings of the gods' totems in the ceiling above. Angry red welts still evident at his temples, the puncture of the wolf's fangs through thin skin some hours ago. A clear fluid seeped from the tiny marks, but the child had not uttered a cry since Ereshkigal's wolf had struck.

Do not fail me now, Messenger.

Her voice staggered him, his already strained lungs gasping for more air. Jaw locked to hold in any murmur of distress, Tamas straightened. He would not be bowed. Not by the goddess. And not by the unexpectedness of Eron's death. Tamas tilted his chin, lifting his eyes to the goddess's wolf, a flat and inanimate carving in the glass above. He smiled. 'It will be done, my lady. There will be no failure.'

Not on his part. *He* had forced one of the Four to yield, brought Agar to his knees no less. Tamas had tasted the power that awaited him, and was instantly, irrevocably addicted. Nothing would separate him from knowing its full magnitude.

He was stronger than Eron. And would not allow himself to be bettered by whatever power had felled the godsoldier. Tamas would not fail his god as Eron had done. His smile ripped the skin at the corners of his mouth. Let whoever it was that had made the foolish choice to work through Kira, come and show themselves.

The child gave up its hold on silence and widened toothless jaws, letting loose with a cry that tore through every inch of the shrine. All at once the glow from the Waters dulled.

It is done. Dumuzi is bared.

The Waters' manic patterns slowed, their twisting and churning easing, settling back into a gentle flow.

It was done. Just like that. Tamas was unsure what he'd expected at the end of the cleansing, but it was more than this. A child's tantrum. A cacophony of wails and screeches.

Tamas stepped up to the ancient wood, gazing down on the infant.

On Dumuzi. The demi-god exposed.

The child's cheeks bloated with the effort of crying, his face reddened, and fat tears slid from tightly shut eyes to slip into the Waters. His arms and legs thrashed in the fluid, sending sprays of it onto Tamas's feet. He took a step back, noting that his bone-coloured loafers were splotched with blood. Blake's blood, likely. Perhaps by now the captain had spilled yet more. The Syrana leader's rage was palpable when he'd finally arrived down on level eleven. The medic tending Blake had shaken like the proverbial leaf as she tried to work beneath the alien's interrogation of the Technician. Nex was fixated on the removal of the mea stone from Eron's arm. As though it were a far greater loss than that of his soldier. In all likelyhood it was, but that was the captain's concern to deal with.

It was childish, Tamas knew, but a thrill of delight urged a smile from him once again. He'd failed to convey to the captain the nature of the goddess's summons. So while Lahar's minion wasted his breath on a near-insane human, Tamas basked in this moment.

I will return to you soon. Await me. The goddess tore the smile from his lips, and for all his newfound assuredness, Tamas wavered beneath Her weight. *Dumuzi remains here until then. Prepare yourself. The time is short until my sister walks your world.*

Like a blade withdrawing from between his ribs, the goddess left him. A vicious cramp of muscle in his gut doubled him over. And the child's cry lifted unbearably high. Taking short breaths against the pain, Tamas pulled back his shoulders and moved to the entranceway.

The Syranians all bowed low; Cym, Bel, Seder, Parator, and the now fully healed Gren. The sight smoothed away Tamas's aches and pains. The aliens' loss had dulled the self-righteous light that normally illuminated them. They called themselves god-soldiers but strutted about as though they were gods themselves. Eron's death had settled them in their place.

Tamas walked the short flight of stairs down to their level. For long years the Syranians had stood over him, their presence towering and imposing. But he was greater now.

'Send word to the captain, he must return here immediately.'

Bel nodded and raised his fingers to the comms link at his ear. His lips moved but the child's wretched screams rendered his words inaudible to Tamas. The high-pitched wail was truly irritating, reaching under his skin. Dumuzi was not taking kindly to his awakening.

'. . . not working . . .' Bel said.

'What?' Tamas moved closer, squinting to make out the movement of dark lips.

'Interference in the comms link,' Bel returned. 'I'm not certain I reached him.'

Drawing himself up, Tamas inched his face closer to Bel's. 'Then find a way to be certain. Send a guard. Get it done. But do not leave the Orientation Room.'

The communications system outage left him with a vague sense of unease. One he admonished himself for. Even if they were working to repair it, the unwrapping of a demigod had probably created energy levels that would rival those at the Meldings. Tamas spun on his heels as Bel headed to the main doors. If someone didn't shut the kid up, Tamas was going to tear his ears from his head.

'Cym,' Tamas cried, 'come with me.'

Cym's company had always been endurable. An aura of calm surrounded the medic. And amid the raucous noise, that calm was welcome. The ceaseless cries of the child rattled Tamas's core.

The Syranian followed him into the Shrine with impressive speed and bowed low. 'Messenger?'

'Do something about that.' He waved a hand at the semisubmerged infant. A good quantity of the Waters had spilled out of the shallow cradle since Tamas had turned his back.

'About . . . Dumuzi?'

'Yes. Dumuzi. Make it stop.' Tamas had never held a baby in his life. He had no inclination to start now. Especially not when this particular child seemed intent on shattering his eardrums with the razor pitch of his infantile voice.

True to form, Cym's reaction to Tamas's words was suitably controlled. But he could not hide his confusion entirely, a subtle twitch of his mouth betraying him.

'Just do it, Cym.' Tamas pressed his forefingers to his ears. His skull vibrated and his eardrums thudded. The pressure behind his eyes intensified.

Silence thudded down on the Shrine, heavy as a soaked blanket, but far more soothing. Cym cradled the child in slender arms, rocking it from side to side. A fragile, naked bundle, arms and legs kicking in uncoordinated jerks, its wide blue eyes fixed on the Syranian. In the beautiful quiet, Tamas could think straight again. Dumuzi was as vulnerable as the child he resided in. And equally alone. A pawn, yet again, in a timeless game of spite between the two goddesses. It struck Tamas then, that he and Dumuzi did not play such dissimilar parts in this all consuming story.

Tamas winced, his gaze darting towards the gods overhead. But what interest did they have in his fleeting, pathetic moment of empathy? Lahar's Precon beast bored a hole right through him with its three misshapen eyes. Ereshkigal's wolf sent a baleful glare in the opposite direction. Disinterested, as She'd always been, in his humanity.

Shaking himself off, Tamas rubbed his face. Hard hands against rough skin. He couldn't recall when he'd last shaved, or brushed his hair or teeth. Done anything remotely mundane. And if all went as it should, there would be no need to do such things ever again. That is what should hold his focus here. Nothing else.

With a long exhale, Tamas left Cym with the child and moved into the greater Orientation Room to await the captain's arrival.

Blake - 73

The captain was far taller than Blake recalled. The Syranian leader stood over her, the lengths of his two braids almost brushing against her chest. She lay on the uncomfortably hard surface of the bench in the only cell on level eleven that had escaped destruction.

'Tell me who is out there, Blake. Tell me what you know before I rip your tongue out.'

The air of contempt that Nex had always exhibited was a full-blown wave now. It buffeted her, pressing at her legs. Blake frowned and lifted her head, not just trying to fathom what the captain was demanding of her — who was out there, in a world she'd not seen in a lifetime — but where she was at all. Then she realised that the pressure at her legs had nothing to do with the captain's disdain. A nurse tended her. She wore a familiar lavender hijab. This was the woman who had seen to her after Tamas had embedded the splinter, the woman whose timely intervention had stopped the discovery of the Starpoints in Blake's hand. Now she dressed the gash that ran the length of Blake's right thigh, running from pelvis to kneecap. The irony didn't escape her. It was not Agar's wayward wing sweeps that had wounded her, but the blade of one of the tools she and Weylen had developed to work on the Telteriun. The tool launched off a nearby cabinet, caught up in the maelstrom of Agar's frenzy, and found Blake's thigh. Embedding itself there with pointed teeth.

Blake stared at the swaying silver-white braids as Captain Nex continued to demand answers of her that she did not have.

'She has not done this on her own. We both know she is incapable of such a thing.'

She? Capable of what thing? Blake's thoughts swam, her skin still tingling. Did he speak of Weylen? Though it pained her, Blake frowned. Hadn't Weylen been with them? In the tech room?

'I don't know, I don't know,' she whispered, but his rising temper told her the captain heard her well enough. Something terrible had happened. The memory flitted in her head, refusing to settle.

Nex spun on his heels and paced his razor features away from her. The only thing blunt about the man was his speech. It had always been that way, but now his words held tips as jagged as the blade that had cut her. With some distance between her and the captain, the wayward memory finally sought rest. Blake held her breath.

Eron was dead. Agar had said it. Tamas had hardly believed it. The captain raged at it.

One of Nex's god-soldiers had fallen. And the breaking of the bond between Syranian and gallu had been a violent, palpable thing.

Igniting Agar into a frenzy.

Burning. They could all burn now.

'I know, I know.' With a groan, Blake rolled her head against the hardness of the surface she lay on. It wasn't the viper she needed to hear from right now, but she'd seen no sign of Perry since he appeared—albeit hazily— at Azrael's side. Disappearing from that horrendous place without uttering a word. She wasn't even certain he'd seen her at all, his image too distorted to make out.

'You know what?' Captain Nex appeared above her once again. 'It would be in your interest, Technician, to release your secrets.'

A laugh hiccupped out of her. The only secret she knew with certainty festered beneath her skin. And Nex would know when she released it. That had to be soon. Blake's body was failing her, betraying her every bit as much as her mind. Shattered flesh and a crumbling consciousness made discerning reality ever more difficult. The bone jarring fit that overcame her in the tech room would not stop replaying itself in her head. The attack had come moments before Agar went beserk, an event triggered by Eron's death. The jolt to her system came as though she'd thrown her body into a tub of live wires. External, rather than an internal malfunction. Was it a delusional mind that taunted her with the possibility that she had sensed that event somehow? The shattering of the bond between Eron and Agar so powerful it had sent her compromised nervous system into free fall? Blake rocked her head, back and forth, back and forth.

Toxins and infection filled her body. Nothing more. Nothing less. Nothing greater.

The viper was right. *They could all burn now.*

Blake was here on level eleven. Exactly where she'd hoped to be. Alongside the Tier, with all its 'holy' water and destructive force. The time was now. Ignite the Starpoints, and the captain would be right at her side when they all went to hell.

But so would the medic whose hands moved gently against her leg, trimming the tear made in Blake's black linen pants so she had room to work on the leg wound. She reaffixed the bandage until satisfied it would hold, making ultimately futile attempts to convince the captain that Blake needed more than a patch up. The medic's face, framed by the delicate material of her hijab, might have been familiar, but the woman's name escaped Blake. She wasn't certain of any of the names of those who dotted the chamber. A skeleton crew of humans rushed about like ants desperate to stay out from under Syranian heels. Weylen would be one of them. She was certainly somewhere here, too.

A memory fluttered, just out of reach. Goosebumps rose hard and pointed along Blake's skin. Weylen.

She was here somewhere. She was always nearby. A coppery tang touched at Blake's lips.

'Your amusement is ill-considered,' Nex said.

Blake stared up at the alien looming over her. She wasn't smiling. Was she? She couldn't begin to work out how to do so. So many shadows. She could see so many shadows in the captain's white eyes. Squinting, Blake regarded him. Whatever had destroyed Eron, had created those shadows.

'You . . . are afraid.' The three words limped out of her mouth, but were arrowed sharply enough to hit a mark. Captain Nex knelt beside her, placed his hand around her throat and held firmly enough to allow only the merest trace of air to slide through.

Oh, how the great and mighty leader fears what he does not know. It was as close to gleeful as she'd ever heard the viper.

'The Lesser should be dead,' Nex said, voice low and full of venom. 'More times over than is possible. When that crash took your father, it took her too. And my sole regret is that I allowed that to be reversed. But trust me, it will come to pass. What she has done will end her. I have no fear of that.' His breath condensed against Blake's face. Unadulterated hatred widened his eyes. 'What has begun here cannot be contained. Dumuzi is being readied for the ceremony. A new age is about to begin in your feeble world, a goddess of war will trample your borders, your pathetic lives. That cannot be stopped now. By any force. And when Lahar's role here is done, he will punish the one who destroyed his anointed soldier. Kira, and whoever works through her, will endure a level of suffering unlike any they've ever known.'

'Kira?' Blake forced the word up her constricted throat. Kira was the 'she' that the captain had spoken of earlier? A thin veil coated Blake's vision, shimmering at the edges.

Kira had killed Eron? Light-headed, Blake fought to focus. Impossible. In so many ways. But the simplest was the most powerful. Kira loved him. Even Blake had seen that.

'It may have been Kira's hand that felled him, but it was not her power. Kira has no such power of her own.' Captain Nex spat her name. He let Blake go. Her head met the hard surface with an audible crack, but nothing could hinder her delight in breathing again. Each breath rich and warm in her starved lungs. The veil drew back, her vision clearing, though the edges of the cell still seemed to shimmer. The world still clamped in on her.

This is the time. Time for the fire to light.

The prize the Syranians sought was here. And Kira was free. Blake stared up at the jagged rock beside her. The back wall of the cell was the ageless bedrock of the cavern itself. A solid mass that had seen a thousand lifetimes come and go, and it cared nothing for any of them.

The captain had said it, but he had to be wrong; *it was Kira's hand that felled him.* So few things were impossible. That Kira would kill Eron, was one of them.

She's done it before. Destroyed one she loves.

Blake lifted her arm and dashed her fist against the rock. The impact shoved the splinter deeper into her flesh, and nerve pain, hot as a poker, radiated all the way into her skull and blazed behind her eyes. She bit down on a cry and hit the wall again.

'Blake, no.' The nurse jumped to her feet, grabbing hold of Blake's arms. Her strength was impressive, but then again, Blake's resistance was piteous. 'Please stop.'

Captain Nex regarded them, but Blake couldn't make out his expression. Her vision was a watery mess. A flutter in her periphery turned her head. The silhouette was remotely familiar. She blinked, over and over, desperate to confirm Perry's silhouette. But the figure that had appeared was not the one she sought.

'Captain, I'm so . . . sorry to interrupt.' A slight man stood in the doorway, hands clenched in a restless fist. 'Mr Cressly has requested you return to level ten, immediately. They are ready to proceed, and he wants all Syranians in attendance for the escort.'

'Very well.' The captain headed for the door but stopped short of leaving, and turned to Blake. 'Enjoy the spectacle you are about to see, Technician. The Lesser was once kept alive to ensure your compliance with our plans, now the role is reversed. But once this ceremony is complete, there will be no need for the existence of either of you. And that is a spectacle I myself will welcome.'

The captain departed, and Blake stared after him. With slow, relentless purpose, the viper uncoiled and rose high, filling her.

They bring the spectacle to you, Technician. All those who should burn. All those will be brought to you.

Blake nodded. Up and down, up and down. Long, considered movements that lulled her.

'Blake?' The medic leaned close. 'Blake, is there anything I can do? What do I do?'

Blake stared at a spot above her shoulder, continuing to nod. If she stopped that small movement, she would freeze. Solid as the stone around her.

'Blake, let me help you. Weylen . . .'

Now Blake's gaze dropped, head held still, finding the woman's face. Tears rimmed her lids. Threatening to spill.

'Weylen what?' Blake croaked.

'She was my friend, too. And their monster killed her. I want to help you. Tell me what to do.'

'Killed her?' Her mouth swam with the coppery tang. And its dank scent filled her nostrils. Blood. So much. The goosebumps pierced her skin, and set the memory free from where she'd buried it.

Weylen was dead. Head smashed in.

At the hands of a monster you created, destroyer of worlds.

'Tell me how to help you, Blake.' Tears ran in vibrant trails down the woman's cheeks.

'Help me?' Blake took hold of the woman's wrist, hard enough to cause a grimace. 'Run. Get as far from here as you can. Survive.'

Kira - 74

Kira scooped her arm around Vail's back, taking most of his weight as he grunted his way into a sitting position on the bed. The sensors in the armadillo registered five pressure points. Five fucking ribs. Jesus, Vail didn't need the shit Leona was trying to spoon into him, he needed a burger. Several.

'Hit me with it,' she said. 'What did Perry say?'

Yeah, what did the ghost of my best buddy tell you, wizard? Christ. Don't even go there. Those thoughts were full of thorns. Perry was fine. Totes.

'I'm sorry, Kira.' Even with the egg-white eyes, Vail still managed to do doe-eyed well. Too well. Kira busied herself with a loose thread on the bed covers and Vail continued. 'They have organised a team to retrieve Eron's body . . .' He grimaced as if the name had burnt his tongue. Kira took a breath and then took his hand.

'You're good. Go on.' *The sky is falling, everything is fucked, but go on. Doesn't hurt a bit.*

'He gave us some time . . . there's something you should know, Kira. Eron went out with a small team, but he split off from them. And he didn't call it in when he located you.'

'Why would he keep something like that under wraps?' Greta sniffed. Like, actually sniffed. *Allergies or something.*

Leona readied another spoonful of brown crap. 'That seems obvious to me.' She too sniffed. *What was with the air in this camper?*

'Want to share?' *Let's keep talking about Kira's dead lover, why don't we? Prick a few more holes undone.*

The shit-coloured gunk on Leona's spoon seemed to intrigue her. 'He didn't want them to find you, Kira.'

'So he could kill her himself?' Greta dove in there, blunt tongue thrashing open a couple more holes. The only one keeping silent was Nina, her deep-browns thoughtful.

I misdirected them, I wanted to . . . Kira blinked, the thread wrapped around her finger blurring. *What? What did you want, Eron? 'Cause it sure as hell had seemed like it was her guts as a necklace.*

Leona shook her head. 'A battle was fought, and lost. That is what Bradley believes. An internal struggle that Eron could not hope to win. Kira, sometimes all the good intentions in the world are not enough.'

Nina's laughter fluttered, bitter and sharp. 'Never enough. Not against the Four. If the reptile is correct, if your lover found a way to you even after walking alongside Agar all this time and did not tear your heart out the moment he saw you as they wished, then he has my respect. The Four are pestilence of the highest order, and no one is immune. You saw what just a passing glance was doing to the people in New Weston, the riots and the sudden outbreaks. The Four are hell on Earth. I've always hated those bastards.'

'Righto, I think she gets your drift.' Leona scowled. 'Can't you see the girl is suffering?'

Suffering? Kira couldn't feel a thing. Not the mattress beneath her, or even Vail's hand, still in hers.

'I'm trying to help her,' Nina said. 'Whatever existed between them, was not there in the end. It had been stolen, eroded. Her lover was gone, well before she...' She had the decency to let it go.

But Nina was wrong. God, she was so wrong. Kira's lover wasn't gone. Eron was there. Right at the end. Sparkling bright.

This is all I can offer. That's what he'd said, dying all over her. Like he hadn't just given everything.

Bradley chittered from his perch on Vail's shoulder. For whatever reason, the lizard was staying out of her head. Maybe it was as fucked up in there as it felt. A reptile could drown in all the hurt. But Bradley had said all she needed to hear, back at the fountain.

He knew your mind.

Eron knew he'd found a way under Kira's skin. Made her feel all the feels. Even the ones she'd made a career out of avoiding. And hell, he'd tried to fight off a fucking horseman of the apocalypse for her. Chances were, she knew his mind too. The glorious idiot had loved her right back.

There was nothing to forgive, not where he was concerned. But fucking hell someone was going to pay for taking him away from her.

Kira picked up the statue, holding it upside down, drumming her fingers against the little god's butt. 'You know what, you've all got to stop with the sad eyes. We don't have time for that shit. I want into that Facility. I want my sister, and I want Az out of there. Your Maiden can stick her hand up my ass and use me like a puppet. So long as I get to fuck over every single one of those a-holes in there.'

Jesus. Lizards could smile. It looked disgusting, like they were shitting bricks and dislocating their jaws at the same time, but there it was. Bradley bared fangs like a pro. Even Greta broke the stony mask she usually wore, one corner of her mouth lifting.

'When this is all said and done, I really think you should consider your language.' Leona grunted, rising to her feet and dumping the bowl in the tiny sink.

When all this is said and done? Kira clung to the statue a little tighter. She was talking the talk, but if someone asked her to move right now, she'd end up on her face. Guts were flip-flopping all over the place in this tiny space. Van was too bloody small. And the thermostat was busted. One hundred degrees and climbing.

Nina's languid smile lifted her cheeks, and with eyelids lowered she let her gaze rake the length of Kira's body. 'Well, I can vouch that Gaia, your Maiden, will enjoy every moment of sticking her hand up that lovely ass.'

'Oh man, so gross.' Vail clutched a pillow to his chest, warding himself against the filth. Theatre-school-drama level. Leona's tut-tutting went into overdrive. Greta's momentary smile vanished beneath stone again.

Yeah, sure. The anal-sex thing was supposed to stay in the bedroom, but it breathed a bit of life into the mood. Kira let the statue drop onto the bed, face down, pudgy butt up. She'd been storing up questions, deciding it was better for her sanity to keep them on her mind-shelf rather than spit them out there and get an answer that would hollow her out completely. Now, they shot out of her mouth before she could reel them in.

'Does Perry have any updates on Az or Blake? I mean, last time he . . .' She shrugged her shoulders against the last time. When she'd asked Perry-Vail about her sister and the metal angel, there had been way too much use of a single word. Hurt.

Eron hurt Az.

Blake. Hurt. Bad place.

Real reassuring conversation.

'He doesn't know where Blake is now.' Vail rubbed at his eyes. 'She's been moved. I don't know . . . He said something about her being behind a wall? It gets kinda fuzzy sometimes . . .'

'They won't kill her,' Greta declared. 'Not if they think Kira's got anything to do with what happened to Eron, which they must do. If they kill Blake, they've got nothing to bargain with.'

It was the day for real reassuring conversations. Kira picked up her stone buddy, needing something to play with.

'And Az?' Just how much had Eron hurt the wild man? The infuriatingly incapable-of-taking-orders wild man who was supposed to have run as far away as he could. Spread those pretty wings and fly the coop, just like Blake had wanted. God, Kira was going to kick his sculpted ass when she saw him.

'They . . . he's . . .' Vail swallowed as if he'd just downed a handful of pins. 'He's there. They've . . . Kira they've put him in the dark.'

The multi-armed deity didn't stand a chance. Metal fingers dug in so hard the statue shattered, shards falling onto the bed covers. Oh those alien assholes had just made a huge mistake.

'Vail, you gonna finish telling us how we use Eron to get us into the Facility?' Kira's voice sank low, down into a pit.

He shuffled beneath the covers, edging up higher against the pillow. His crinkled face said it was a damn hard move. Kira would have helped him, but moving right now, even just an inch, felt like it would ignite a spark she couldn't douse. Az was in the dark. And they were wasting time. Leona stepped in, fluffing up the pillow as Vail began to speak.

'Like I said, Eron gave us time. There's a convoy with his body headed back to the Facility now, but it took a little longer to locate him because he went off on his own like that. Apparently, the cops got to the scene before the Facility did. It got complicated. But they're headed back now. Anzu is keeping watch. He's going to give us the heads-up the minute the convoy is close enough. Kira and Nina, that's your way in. Bradley will go with you –'

'Why just them?' Greta said.

'You've seen the size of Anzu?' Nina clicked her tongue. 'There's a maximum passenger load. VIP passengers only.'

'Listen, please.' Vail tried to get control of his audience. Mildly amusing, considering he always spoke as though he were trying to coax a kitten out of a drain. 'They will have to lower the Lucentshield –'

Greta's frown deepened. 'The what?'

'That barrier that Nina bounced off –'

'I didn't actually bounce –'

'No matter how many times I hear it, that name doesn't get any better,' Kira said. 'Lucentshield. Was the naming guy high?' She didn't expect an answer, and she didn't get one. But talking shit helped to stifle the spark. Someone must have hit the snowflake button on the cooling system, because all at once it wasn't the middle of the sun in Winnebago town.

'But Eron doesn't have the mea stone anymore. Are you sure they will have to lower it?' Greta poured herself a glass of water, the tap water browner than Kira was comfortable with.

'What Perry is hearing indicates yes. There's orders in place to lower the barrier when the convey arrives.'

'The lad was a god-soldier of Lahar, he's a preternatural if ever there was one.' Leona washed out the bowl, grabbing a tea towel to dry it. Calm as you like, as though they had all just popped in for a cup of tea and gossip.

Sliding off the bed, Kira shook her legs, trying to shift the pins and needles in her feet. 'Perry told you all this? Without possessing your ass this time? How are you guys communicating?'

The question made him squirm, enough that Leona screwed up her nose and asked, 'Do you need to go to the toilet?'

'No.' Vail blushed. 'I don't need to go to the toilet. It's just, well it's kind of . . .'

'He's discovered they don't need the physical realm to communicate.' Nina spoke softly. And with deceptive gentleness. 'Because your friend Perry is dead, and Vail is . . .'

The bowl slipped from Leona's iron grasp and clattered into the sink. 'Vail is doing just fine. Now let's get on with what must be done.'

Kira was on team witch. Move along. No conversations about death here.

'I'm fine, I'm good,' Vail insisted but his face defied him. Seemed to go paler with every word. 'And so is Perry . . . considering . . . but he is frightened . . . said it's intense in there. Whatever is happening in there, it's happening really soon. We can't miss this chance –'

'What's happening is the end of your world as you know it, if they are readying to replace Dumuzi's soul with Inanna's.' Nina leaned towards a mirror fixed on a narrow cupboard door, tilting her head, adjusting her hair. Getting all spruced up for the end of the world. 'My mistress's temper is – how shall I put this? Catastrophic?'

'Okay, time out,' Kira snapped. 'I mean, seriously, what the fuck do I do once I'm in there?' She raised her arms, and her sleeves slipped down to reveal the dull matte of the metal. 'This is great and all, the full body armour. Real fun times, but does anyone have a play by play here? Aside from their demons and monsters, they've got good old guns and ammo and all the shit down there. I'm just a chick with her pet lizard.' A huge downplay of the truth, sure, but Kira was on a freaking-out roll. 'One bullet to the head and I don't think even your Maiden can fix that one –'

'Then don't let them shoot you in the head.' Greta stood up, adjusted her jeans.

Kira lifted her gaze from the bloodstains on Greta's pants. Fairly certain that same blood clung to her, too. 'Thank you. So much. Why the fuck are you even here?'

'Because they killed someone I gave a shit about too, Kira. And all I can do is babysit your ass. Think I'm loving this? No one is having a good time here.' She paused, biting on her bottom lip for a moment before continuing. 'I saw what happened . . . when . . . when Eron fired that last shot. I know you tried to do nothing. I know you didn't want to hurt him. But he wanted to hurt you, and the Maiden didn't let that happen. She saved you. I wish she'd saved William too, but he wasn't part of the plan. He was pretty sure you were though. The big guns get to pick and chose, and the Maiden chose you. For better or for worse. William would have wanted me to be here. Do what I can. So you've got me, like it or not, till this is done.'

Pin-drop time. Quiet as a Winnebago tomb. Bradley was an onyx headstone on Vail's pillow, but Kira felt his beady gaze on her.

'I'm sorry this has fallen on you, Kira,' Leona whispered. 'But the Maiden has chosen well. Keep your faith, She will guide you. And you'll do what needs to be done. You are strong. Your guts were already metal, long before any of this.'

The comment definitely dipped its toes in the corny pool, but Kira would take it.

All of it.

For a moment the whole insane gang stood in silence. The desert was impossibly quiet at night. Kira had forgotten that. She used to despise it. It made her feel like she was alone on a distant planet. Made all her freaky bits so much freakier. But now, standing amongst the strangest bunch of people she'd ever known, it was okay. Actually, this stinking, crowded, decor-disaster camper van felt a lot like home.

A heavy hit on the camper roof rocked the whole vehicle.

'Shit.' Kira threw herself over Vail. The fucking sky was falling.

'It's okay, Kira. It's Anzu. The convoy is coming.'

She straightened but stayed straddled over the kid. The white haze over his eyes had thickened and the sight of it made her breath snag. 'Time to go then.'

Vail's smile tried really hard to be bright and beamy, but the rest of his face didn't play fair. 'Yeah, time to go.'

Bradley scurried off Vail's pillow and made his way up her metal arm, settling in on her shoulder, right up close to her neck. She was too busy trying to side-eye the lizard to notice Vail move until his scrawny arms were around her neck.

'I'll be with you, Kira. You won't be alone.'

Sure. Kid couldn't march to the toilet, three steps away, let alone march into battle. But the sentiment threatened to unravel all the strings and coils and bruised bits that kept Kira in one piece.

Her lungs couldn't get more compressed if she'd worn all her favourite leather corsets at once. Vail clung to her, and her to him, the two holding one another together until someone tugged at their arms, pulling and coaxing until they both let go. Kira didn't put up a fight as Nina guided her out of the camper, leaning into her, breathing deep into the rich honey scent that clung to Inanna's handmaiden. They stepped out into a cool and empty night. Nina pushed her against the side of the van, and her warm lips found Kira's own. There was nothing pretty or sensual about the kiss. It was all violent tongues and banging of teeth. Grasping, clinging, clawing. And it was perfect. Tension flowed with the saliva and searching hands found wetness and heat. They consumed one another. Until all that was left was a hot sticky mess, and a buzz that held something other than sheer terror.

They pulled apart, chests heaving as if they had tried to mount the Himalayas and not each other.

'One for the road, as they say.' Nina touched Kira's cheek. 'Do you feel a little better?'

'As good as it's going to get.' She leaned into the touch, watching her own saliva gleam on Nina's lips. Pretending, just for a second, that they were back on Santorini.

'It's the best I can do while keeping your clothes on.' Nina let her hand drop. 'Good luck, my lovely girl.'

'You too. I hope you . . . I hope you find what you're looking for.' Which was death, basically. But saying that out loud would just ruin the post mouth-orgasm glow.

'Thank you. And the same to you, both of you.'

Nina walked away and Kira frowned, adjusting her shirt. Both of you?

Bradley shifted, edging out from under her hair, and settling on her shoulder. Front row to the mouth fuck.

'Invasion of privacy much? You enjoy that, slimy perv?'

The purr rumbled through the lizard and into the metal beneath him.

'Yeah, I thought so. Let's go clean up Blake's mess.'

Tamas - 75

Tamas stood before the small crowd gathered around the low stone rim of the Tier. Stalagmites dotted the immediate area around the stonework, damp structures that had multiplied in number over the past few days. A semicircle of alien and divine guardians found their places between the towers of mineral deposits: Parator, hands braced behind his back, alongside the beak-faced gallu, Tek; Bel with the ghost-skinned female carapace containing Diresh; Seder, hair braided and sculpted into an elaborate high style, flanked by the slightest of the gallu, Sora; Gren just behind them. Though his recovery was complete, the captain had not seen fit to Bind him with Agar. The Syranian leader had taken on that burden himself, the gallu at his side. The ever-scowling Agar did not dwarf the captain's ample height, but the carapace's girth and solidness enabled him a dominating presence nonetheless. Agar had maintained silence since Eron's death, but there was nothing respectful in his voicelessness. Agar viewed them all with an air that reminded Tamas of Ereshkigal's wolf. A glint in the eye that spoke of a dark hunger. Once, it might have set Tamas trembling. Not now. He held the gaze when it landed on him. And bared his teeth with a sneer to match Agar's own. He was rewarded with a wavering in Agar's resolve. The gallu turned his gaze downwards, and Tamas grinned before moving his attention elsewhere.

None of the Syranians moved with quite the ease and purpose they had before the news of Eron's death. And Tamas welcomed the mild pleasure it brought him. Witnessing the alien demeanours' lose their haughty sheen provided brief respite from the tension.

Captain Nex held a naked Dumuzi in the crook of his right arm. The child's legs hung to either side of the Syranian's forearm, their rich golden hue contrasting with Nex's alabaster skin. Dumuzi might well have been a small coat slung there, only showing muted signs of life when the captain moved. Tamas's moment of sympathy for the demigod had vaporised, rather rapidly, as he'd waited in the Orientation Room for the captain. The child had soiled itself, shitting all over Cym, who, to his credit, had not flinched. Tamas had though. Dry-retching at the stench, an odour ten times greater than the child it had escaped from.

'Cym does not join us?' Tamas said.

'He awaits Eron's return,' the captain replied. As though Eron were about to turn up in a taxi and come racing down to join them.

'Why?' Tamas folded his arms. The captain hadn't bothered to consult with him on this. 'That doesn't seem wise. I would have thought the presence of all god-soldiers would be required at this time.'

Captain Nex shifted the child from one arm to the other, handling it like the lifeless coat it resembled. 'Well, you are entitled to your opinion, of course, Messenger. But opinions do not assist us in understanding our enemy. You are amply guarded down here. As is Dumuzi. But the threat does not come from within. It is without. Beyond the Lucentshield. Cym will ensure that Eron's body was not compromised and that he returns devoid of any corruption.'

'Nothing of that nature could get past the Lucentshield.'

Nex shifted his head, moving his braid out of reach of the child who suddenly raised a grasping hand to toy with it. 'Nothing of that nature should have gotten past a god-soldier. Yet Eron is dead.' His voice rose with each word, lifting in volume enough to cause the child's face to wrinkle, his wide blue eyes shimmering.

Tamas may have had to tilt his chin to meet the captain's angered stare, but he'd never felt taller. He wasn't sure if the captain's fury was born from indignation that a god-soldier could be destroyed or genuine grief at the loss, but the rage drained his sublime face of any hint of colour, and hollowed out his enviable cheeks.

'Do try to calm down, Captain,' Tamas said. Smooth as any silk. 'You're upsetting the child. Do what you think you must, I'm sure you know what you are doing.'

That the captain wished to strike him for his condescending tone, Tamas had no doubt. He was also certain the blow would never come. This was not the captain's moment. It was Tamas's, and they both knew it. Let Cym wait for a corpse. Eron had proved himself fallible long before he paid for that weakness with his life.

Whatever might be out there, was exactly that. Out there. Too far from the Tier to cause a problem now. And if Kira was being used as their puppet – the idea pushed a smile to Tamas's lips – then let her try to break through the Lucentshield.

Tamas adjusted the cuffs of the midnight-blue linen shirt he wore, a shade that set off his eyes nicely in his humble opinion. The shirt was his choice. He'd had it brought to him in the Orientation Room, still warm from being pressed. There would be two deaths today: Dumuzi's ancient existence, and Tamas's mortal life. It was only right that he dressed for the occasion.

He sought out Blake. Right where he had arranged her to be. The lighting within the cell was dull, another technical issue being remedied, and Blake was a hazy shadow against the glass. She had dragged herself to the front of the cell, legs bent and unsteady as she pressed against the glass. Was she watching him? He had to bite back the urge to have someone shine a light into her face. See what expression greeted him. Admiration, surely. Awe, perhaps. She'd watched him force a demon to kneel. Surely she wore something other than contempt now she could see how much greater, grander he was? Silly bitch could have been right here with him. Not in there, with her own blood stiffening her clothes.

A cough at his side drew him back to the Tier and his audience, uncertain of how much time he'd just spent staring at a walking-dead woman. A ghost of a life past.

'Is there a problem, Messenger?' The captain served his enquiry with a generous dose of hostility.

'No. Of course not. It is all just as it should be. Let it begin.'

Turning his back on them, Tamas sent up a silent prayer to his goddess. Let it be Kira who stalked them out there, and send her right in. He'd force her to kneel, too. Right before he made her another ghost of his past.

He stepped up onto the edge of the Tier, then sank his bare feet into the Waters, finding the ridge that ran the circumference of the structure. Considering what was about to commence, there was a definitive lack of pomp. No grand declaration, no roar of an adoring crowd or chanting of devoted subjects. Not even the prick of the goddess in his skull. Just a bunch of brooding aliens and hulking, sour-faced carapaces.

The mustard-coloured trousers Tamas wore – one of the few gifts from his mother he'd ever received, and only because she'd found his personal choices repulsive – soaked up the dark Waters, the stain rising fast up the material. As the Tier reacted to his presence, the Waters shifted from dank and oily to lighter iridescent shades of emerald. The liquid pressed the linen to his thighs, encasing him like the wrappings on a mummy. Within seconds his body shook under the bitterness of the temperature. Beneath clenched teeth, Tamas sucked in the air, his breath emerging in white clouds. *Focus. Don't let your goddamn teeth chatter*, he admonished himself. When he'd gathered enough control, certain he could hold his arms steady, he raised them.

Captain Nex stepped up onto the edge of the Tier and lifted the wriggling child to the roof of the chamber. 'The will of Lahar be done.'

His voice echoed up into the shadows that clung to the rock. Up there too, the stalactites were more numerous than Tamas recalled. Daggered formations clustered high above the Tier. Dumuzi was in Tamas's arms a moment later, a warm mass that instantly stilled his shivering. The first, and final time, Tamas would cradle that most vulnerable human form of all. A newborn child.

'The will of Ereshkigal be done.'

Kira - 76

Anzu wasn't loving the strong headwind, which meant Kira wasn't loving the ride. Rollercoasters had never been her thing. A tilt right, then a sudden dip, stomach-droppingly fast. Anzu was making a beeline for the three Hummers tearing a dusty crack through the desert. Not that Kira could get a clear look at them. Nina's hair was determined to get down her throat, slapping at her face, whipping against her lips. The only escape from it was to keep her head low, cheek pressed to Nina's back, arms wrapped tightly around her waist.

'You all right back there?' Nina called over her shoulder, sending her loose curls on a new directional attack.

'Great.' Kira spat black strands. Eyes watering. Cold as shit up here. And she had not dressed appropriately for Operation We-are-so-fucked. Blue jeans did nothing against the chill, and the ratty pyjama top, with its fox head clasp, flapped in the breeze like a sub-par cape.

'I think there is a storm front moving in….oh!' Nina released a startled cry as Anzu rolled left.

'Wonderful. Fucking double great.' Kira must have been making it hard for Nina to breathe with her arms gripping bear-trap tight around her waist, but she didn't protest. Probably too busy trying not to fall to her death. As was Kira. 'Are we actually going to make it in time?'

The bright lights that shone down on the outermost border fence of the Facility were getting uncomfortably close. There were three rings of fences, with five hundred metres between the outermost and innermost. Anzu still had a ways to go before he'd draw level with the Hummers shotgunning along the long strip of black that led to the Facility, drawing up fast on the first border fence. Nina's call on the storm front was on point. A heavy swirl of blacker-than-the-already-black sky loomed up ahead beyond the Facility, hanging low and dark over the desert. Shudders of lightning cross-stitched the black cloud quilt. Real dramatic stuff. Because this whole thing was way too relaxed so far. But one thing was going their way: the clouds had gone full bouncer on the moon, shutting it the hell out of this club. Confiscating all the light.

'He'll make it.' Nina had taken way too long to reply to Kira's question, which meant her answer was likely a big chunky piece of lie pie.

But the great flying lion-bird sure as hell was making a good go of it, notching the speed up and shifting just enough that Nina's hair whipped over her left shoulder and gave Kira a momentary clear view of the convoy.

Funeral convoy. Eron was in one of those fucking ugly things. With a fucking ugly hole in his body.

The procession slid past her favourite cactus in all the world. Nature's permanent bad boy, its prickly finger ever raised to the world. A world that lit up as a sheet of lightning burst across the sky, and in that millisecond of brilliance, Kira caught sight of Bradley on her shoulder, head strained forward as he took in the view. The lizard with a piece of Eron in its gut. Kira dry-retched, but the only thing coming out of her stomach was gas, a belch that stank of the foul potion Leona had insisted they drink before leaving; all of them, including Anzu, who had been the least pleased of all. The potion tasted like sweaty balls smeared with anchovy, but the tan queen said it would help hide them from prying eyes while they were up in the air. Keep them off radars. Somehow. Whatever. Kira had given up on questioning shit like that.

Nina turned her head, and got a mouthful of her own voluptuous curls in reward. 'They're at the first gate,' she said through the hairy assault.

No shit. Christ almighty, it had been a long time since Kira had hurtled through that same gate, pissed out of her mind, running to answer Blake's call. She should never, ever have taken that call. Should have stayed right where she was. Impaled on Liam's cock, playing with his dimpled ass. Getting yelled at by Perry 'cause she'd bailed out of working the bar, yet again.

Crap. Just thinking Perry's name made her head ache.

The Hummers moved off the main road and took a dirt road to their right.

'Oh, you're fucking kidding me,' Kira muttered against Nina's back.

The convoy was headed for the Reesen Entrance. Last time she'd used it, Eron had been with her. Very much alive, and very much tanked out of his alien skull. She sagged. Right down to her core. Bradley pressed his body against the length of her neck and purred in behind her ear, sending fuzzy vibes through the metal again. It didn't help this time. The grief was more fortified than the Telteriun encasing her. Nothing would break up that fucker. It was double-layered now. And it was getting harder to believe she could carry the weight. Pity the Maiden hadn't bothered to take away the pain as part of the deal.

'Is there a problem?' Nina threw over her shoulder.

'No problem.' Nothing better than following a dead lover's corpse into a potential gateway to hell. 'All good.'

Anzu rose higher, and Kira slipped back much closer to his admirable tail feathers than was comfortable. This was the badly-thought-through plan. Stay high. Come in right up at the highest point of the shield. Strike from on high? Who knew. As soon as Anzu straightened out, Kira thrust her hips forward, pressing up against Nina's backside. They were a fucking long way up. Definitely skull smashing height, but there was shit to do before any plummeting to certain death could be reconsidered.

'So the shield is only at that final border fence, the one with the blueish lights?' Nina said.

Bradley leapt from Kira's shoulder, hopping onto Nina's and disappearing under her curls. Taking his mildly comforting vibes with him. Wonderful. 'Cause Kira wasn't feeling shit enough.

'According to spirit detectives Vail and Perry, yep.' Kira spat out yet another strand of Nina's hair. 'You getting any mojo vibes or anything yet? Can you see the shield?'

'No.' Nina's stomach tightened beneath Kira's hands, a reaction to Anzu's sudden downward shift. 'I can't see it, not even a flicker, which is really quite annoying. But Mr Blaine assures me the Lucentshield is quite the sight.'

'Mr Who?'

Nina wiggled her butt, trying to edge back after the downward rush pushed her forward onto the bony protrusion of Anzu's front haunches. Kira pressed her lips closed tightly, trying to ignore the sudden heat in her lady garden. On the list of things she never thought would bug her, Kira had to admit the constant low-level horniness when she was around Nina was a pain in the ass.

'Mr Blaine is a shedu, loyal to me for many years. You met him, I believe,' Nina said. 'At the penthouse.'

Kira's nails dug into the material at Nina's waist. 'Penthouse?' Where Tamas had dug a gazillion holes in her, turned her into a human colander with the help of his supernatural spirit buddies.

'Kira are you okay…oh gods, sorry. Not that penthouse. Leona told me what Tamas did to you.' Nina looped an arm back, pressing a hand to Kira's hip. 'No, Mr Blaine is a shedu. They are about as vicious as bathmats on the best of days. After centuries in a godless world they are practically sloths. Nothing like the utukku that hurt you.'

Hurt was too tiny a word. Kira swallowed down on the memory.

Nina returned her hand to grip at Anzu's mane. 'I meant the penthouse at the hotel in Beleiro. Vail ended up throwing Mr Blaine's human host out of a window, I believe.'

The convoy slowed, approaching the second gate. Anzu's wings swept faster and faster through the air. Curls of panic began to rise up through the witch juice, and Kira grasped at the discussion as if it were a life raft.

'That was you? You sent the zombie waitresses? They died. Did you know that? You got those girls killed.'

Scarred Vail for life.

Nina clucked her tongue. 'That was hardly my intention. I was just curious about who was shining like the sun all of a sudden. It's been a dull world for a very long time.'

Way too much death and carnage for one day, Kira didn't need the image of that girl soaring through the air in her head, too. She pressed her forehead against Nina's back. An odd sensation shifted up the length of her arm. A vibration, followed by a distinct series of thumps, as though someone were using her limb as a xylophone. 'Did you feel that?'

'No, I . . . oh . . . ' Nina hunched forward, pulling Kira with her.

'You okay? Is it the shield?' Kira asked. Bradley jumped Nina-ship, finding his place back on Kira's shoulder and barking his reptilian heart out. 'Jesus, how many times have I told you dude, I don't speak –'

'Not the shield,' Nina gasped. 'So much . . . power. It is beginning.'

'The whole bringing a bitch-ass goddess to Earth thing, you mean?'

Kira's phantom musician played out a frantic tune along the length of her arm.

'Yes. Fuck.' First time Kira had heard Nina swear. Might have given her a high-five any other time. But hearing it now gave Kira a super intense rush of the bad-feels.

'The shield, is it down? What does ghost man say?'

Nina still hunched forward, fistfuls of Anzu's feathers in each hand, hanging on for dear life. 'He said no.'

The convoy pulled away from the second gate. Headed towards the final barrier, the Reesen Entrance. Not more than a couple hundred metres ahead. Leona's witchy potion might be distorting them on any radar system, but it wasn't an invisibility elixir. Not as far as Kira knew. And Anzu was getting mighty close to the outer buildings of the Facility now. If anyone bothered to look up, they were busted.

The vehicles were less than twenty metres away from the gate, down to a slow crawl. The high steel gates began to roll back on their tracks, and the metal spikes protruding from the roadway slid back into the dirt. Giving the vehicles an obstacle free path.

'Nina,' Kira said. 'Talk to me.'

'The Lucentshield is still active,' Nina said.

Bradley chirruped his opinion, but Kira ignored him. A guy stepped out of the guard house on the left of the entrance, waving to the incoming drivers as though it were a delivery of soda. Not an annihilated alien.

'Maybe we got it wrong, they're not going to lower it.' Kira relaxed her hold on Nina, edging to one side to take a look at an invisible barrier. Stupid idea on so many levels. Anzu suddenly dropped like a stone. 'Jesus. Shit, warning. Warning is good.'

The xylophone player on her arm beat out a manic soundtrack to their descent.

'It's down. It's down, but we're too high.' Nina braced herself low against Anzu's back, her face buried in the lion's mane of crimson-and-black feathers. 'They didn't lower the shield . . . they raised it, bottom up. Hold on, Kira.'

'Brilliant idea.'

Kira curved her body over Nina, desperate hands scrambling to grip something. Anything. Finding the pliable softness of Nina's tits. It would have to do; she'd apologise later. No chance in hell Kira was letting go now. Anzu soared hard to the right, skimming round in an arcing half circle, dropping all the while. Fuck. Ground zero was coming in like a supersonic jet. Anzu straightened and shot forward, drawing level with the last of the vehicles, his great wings thrashing the air. Only the blind couldn't see them now. And no one down there had a guide dog.

She assumed. It was actually fucking hard to see. The chilled air made tears run, blurring the world. Beneath her skin, and the metal, her body alternated between heat-lamp warm and razor-sharp goosebumps. She'd had sunburn like this once. Left her fried like a tomato and shaking like a leaf.

'Go, go. Now!' Nina shouted.

A burst of gunfire erupted in the air around them.

'Fuck.' Kira raised the armadillo, covering her head.

Anzu bayed, nothing short of blood-curdling, and lowered his head. His muscles bunched, tensing against the inside of Kira's thighs. The first vehicle shot through the opening. But Anzu had them close enough to make out the driver's face in the final vehicle. Staring in horror at the gigantic winged bird-lion thing headed his way. The guy reached for his weapon, producing it with a speed that was admirable considering what bore down on him. Anzu's claws made contact with the windscreen, and the windscreen's mundane life was over in a spray of glinting hard confetti. The driver swerved and the vehicle ploughed into the antiramming pole just outside the gate.

'Shield is closing on us. Hold on!' Nina shouted, planting her hand over Kira's. 'This will hurt.'

'What?'

Kira screamed. A hundred needles raked their way down the back of her eyeballs. A fireball consumed her. Ate at her. She snatched her hands from Nina's grasp, now hands-free on the beast. She barely registered her slide from Anzu's back. Her skull was about to implode. If they were forty feet in the air, it didn't matter. She just had to get away from this.

'Kira, no!' Nina's voice evaporated.

Impact was hard as fucking hell and rolled her like a bowling ball let loose by King Kong. Gravel tore at Kira's jeans, finding her face too, and hammering at the armadillo. The world flipped over and over and over till up and down disappeared entirely. And her head. Fuck, her head. If her eyeballs weren't bleeding right now, it would be a goddamn miracle.

Kira tumbleweeded. Her skull hit the ground once, twice, a third time for good measure. And all the while her scream kept on coming. Her mouth was warm with blood. Things were getting real hazy, stuck-in-a-fog kind of hazy.

She came to a dead stop on her back. The world still a spinning blur.

'Kira, get up.' When had they gone underwater? Nina sounded as if she were twenty feet under. 'Move!' Nina screamed and bubbled. 'You're too close. The shield is coming down.Move!'

Move. Was she fucking kidding? Kira could barely draw breath, let alone hop up and shuffle along. Spinning, sweating, and shivering, Kira was all the S things, all at once. A figure appeared over her.

She blinked and squinted, trying to clear the haze. A rush of hot air swept over her. An enormous oven door thrown open, trying to bake them all alive.

The figure hunched, covering her. Fuck's sake, why couldn't she see straight?

A second later, she was back on the gravel train, shooting across the ground. No maddened tumbling this time, though. This time she was sliding with all the ferocity of a sled on snow, moving away from the supernova-bright wave that curled down towards the ground. About to break all over whoever had just shoved her out of harm's way.

'Kira, I've got you.' Nina dropped to her knees, digging her hands into Kira's armpits, trying to get her to her feet. 'We need to go now.'

But Kira struggled against her, refusing to let her eyes drop from the scene playing out. She didn't need Nina's spirit sidekick to tell her what the Lucentshield was doing now.

The wave hurtled down, bright as a nuclear blast, casting light on a figure standing just inside the final fence. The same silhouette she was certain had just thrown her out of harm's way.

They lifted a hand, tilting their blurry head. And it was all Kira needed. She let out a pathetic whimper, the only sound in a world gone silent.

And watched as Perry shattered into a gazillion fragments beneath a tidal wave of light.

Kira - 77

Nina burst Kira's shock-bubble with rough hands and pinching nails. Dragging her to her feet. Their surroundings were lit up like a sports stadium at night. All the electricity in the world seemed to be right here, in this place, making the whole damn thing glow. The quadrangle was surrounded on three sides by imposing warehouses.

'Help me here, Kira. Just a little.' Nina's words were muffled. Kira's ears rang at rock-concert levels. 'You're bloody heavy.'

Undoubtedly true, considering she was three quarters Telteriun now, but Kira's legs wouldn't follow any orders. Her bleeding knees stayed bent.

'Are you hurt?' Nina's hands wandered up and down Kira's ribs, brushing the metal over her breasts. 'Are you injured?'

Injured? She was bleeding from enough cuts and grazes to start her own vampire ready-meal outlet. A walking gravel rash. The worst of it down the side of her right leg. In her gut something burned like balls of acid. Nothing was broken. Bonus. And her clothes were still on. A positive. But who gave a shit anyway? Perry had just blown apart in front of her.

'Where is he?' Kira twisted, trying to find a way out of Nina's pincer grip. 'Where is Perry?'

'Gone. He and Mr Blaine both. But they gave us this chance, we cannot waste it. Kira, we have to move. Right now.'

The ear-buzzing edged down a notch. And it didn't take a rocket scientist to work out this was a bad place for a chat. Anzu stood off to the right, every feather on his body bristling, inflating him to double the size he actually was, wings stretched wide. Through the up and down sweep, Kira caught a glimpse of the flaming vehicle at the gate. A giant metallic bonfire now. She hoped like hell Eron's body hadn't been in that one. It would be the cherry on a shit cake if she'd just managed to get him cremated. At last, her knees locked into place and she was up, kind of. A human Leaning Tower of Pisa that used Nina as a scaffold.

'Where did they go?' Kira bounced off Nina's side as the woman navigated them both through the chaos. 'What just happened to Perry?'

Even through her cottonwool ears, Kira could make out the shouting – lots of shouting from a bunch of people streaming out of the windowless building on the west side of the quadrangle. Assholes with guns. And where there were assholes, there were grimalkin.

'That Lucentshield was about to fry your pretty brains, my dear.' Nina pulled Kira down in a crouch, gunfire rat-tat-tatting around them. 'Your friend made a choice. He saved your life.'

Kira's knees shifted back to screw-you mode, and she stumbled. Nina didn't miss a stride, hauling her up and keeping on, keeping on. Anzu bellowed, and his cry tore a hole in the atmosphere. Kira had always hated this place, and right now it was hell itself.

'Is Perry still alive?' Kira was shouting, her throat told her so, but her ears didn't compute. 'I mean . . . alive as in . . .'

Ghosting it up. Hanging out in spook central? She'd take undead over cadaver, any day. Jesus. Please don't let that have been the end. Kira clung to Nina's arm, as much to stay on her feet as to have something to grip hold of. The zings coming from the various grazes on her body were packing quite the punch.

'Just keep moving, Kira.'

They reached a squat grey building that sat just forward of a larger green steel warehouse. The warehouse had lighting fit for the Yankee Stadium, but the smaller building, not so much. Nina shoved Kira into a shadowed area up against a wide venting grid that ran the length of one of the walls. The whole unit vibrated and rumbled. The grates said a trembling hello to the grazes on Kira's back. With a hiss and a curse, she sat forward. They had taken refuge beside a transformer. How did she know that? Because she'd fucked an electrician several times. In a spot just like this, on the other side of the Facility, and he'd told her what it was as she'd gagged on his cock. Man, those days. Shit, she missed them. Doing pointless, wonderful things, like forgetting who she'd just banged before her pants were even back on. Never stopping too long.

Stopping was bad.

Reality sniffed you out like a beagle tracking cocaine. Clogged up your brainsack with shitty, shitty memories. Car. Tree. Dead dad.

Water fountain. Pretty park. Dead alien.

Now, Perry. He was the straw and she was all camel.

Kira stretched out her shredded leg, biting down on her lip. And where the hell was the slimy reptile when you needed him? 'Is Bradley with you?'

Nina kept up watch at the edge of the transformer but shook her head. 'No. I haven't seen him since we came through the gate.'

Picking flecks of gravel from a pulpy graze along her calf, Kira said, 'Great. So, what's the plan, fearless leader? 'Cause this sucks so far.'

Nina turned away from her spying efforts. 'Why did you throw yourself off Anzu? You are going to have to listen to me if we are getting through this.'

'I did not throw myself.'

'Well you sure as hell didn't hang on.'

'Did you not feel that shit back there? I like my brain inside my skull, thanks very much.' Just the memory of it caused her head to ache.

Nina sat back on her heels. Her hair was tangled, she had a smudge of dirt on her chin, and her crocheted top was more ripped threads than intricate needlework. Kira had time to take all this in because Nina just stared at her. Anzu was screeching blue murder, but Nina just kept staring. Until, finally: 'You felt it.'

Not a question, so Kira said nothing. Nina shuffled forward on her knees and took Kira's hands in her own. Her mouth opened, first a little, then a whole lot, a gasp moving between parted lips. Her eyelids lowered, covering her chocolate irises almost entirely.

'Not a great time for a power nap,' Kira said. Chances of not being found behind this pathetic barrier had to be next to nil.

Nina laid her fingers against Kira's cheek. 'I have not felt less like sleeping in two thousand years. We are truly going to do this.'

'Jesus, you went into this thinking we weren't?'

Nina's lips jerked. Maybe a smile. Maybe she was having a fit. 'It was hard to be sure. I know things have happened to you . . .' Her gaze flitted down to Kira's belly, then ricocheted back to her face. 'But witches are prone to exaggeration.' She tugged at the collar of the pyjama top Kira wore. The fox brooch had held on valiantly, though the same couldn't be said for chunks of the cotton material. 'But now I'm seeing things with my own eyes. And I believe I may once again dance with the gods.'

A burst of gunfire tore up the gravel not more than a few metres from where they crouched. Nina pressed Kira to the ground, covering her body with her own. Kira kissed the dirt. Actually kissed it, spitting and struggling to lift her head.

'Keep down.'

'I'm three-quarters metal, with a fucking holy stone in my gut and a trigger-happy goddess up my ass.' Kira coughed, and dust stung her eyes. 'I should be the one on top.'

She elbowed Nina, who eased up enough that Kira could raise her head. And catch sight of a figure by the green steel warehouse. A figure that seemed oblivious to the chaos on the other side of the quad.

Watching them instead.

'Oh shit,' Kira and Nina whispered in near-perfect unison.

With the blaze of lights in the quadrangle, there was no mistaking Cym. Just staring at them. No way he couldn't have spotted them. Nothing interrupted his line of sight. But the dude didn't start shouting, or running, or aiming any bullets their way. Didn't even raise his weapon. Just stood there while the rest of the quadrangle dealt with the rampaging Anzu. Maybe he didn't know what the hell to do with a weapon. The guy was a medic, right? Kira'd never had much to do with Cym, but Blake had. Two weirdos working side by side in their little laboratory, building monsters. Maybe Cym the weirdo was blind as a bat. Too much squinting at tiny screens.

'What is he waiting for?' Nina hissed.

Fuck, maybe Leona's potion *had* made them invisible. Kira did her best deer-in-headlights impression. The stand-off was creeping her out. Why the fuck wasn't the guy doing anything? He had Eron's murderer in his sights. Surely he gave a shit? If she were Cym, she'd be tearing her guts out and wearing her intestines as accessories. Hell, if this saving-the-world shit wasn't happening, she would hand him the knife herself and bid them all Happy Kira Death Day.

'He sees us,' Nina whispered. 'He has to see us.' The weirdness of the situation seemed to have thrown her off too. They should be running, or Shifting, or something. Anything.

A fresh swell of voices rose through the quad, and Anzu's hoarse cries grew more frantic. And more distant. Kira would bet the zero dollars she had on her that Anzu was sky bound, and with any luck, Bradley was buried somewhere in the feathers. In one piece. Damn it, she missed that fucking lizard. Nina grabbed her hand, attempting to do god-knows what, but Kira resisted. Not ready to take eyes off Cym. The Syranian balled up his fists, and Kira held her breath. Fuck. He was going to call them out.

Cym shook his head and turned, breaking into a jog that took him and his extraterrestrial ass out of sight around the far side of the warehouse. But his voice rang out loud and clear.

'Follow after it,' Cym bellowed. 'Bring that creature down.'

Nothing about the two chicks hiding behind the transformer.

Kira expelled a stale breath. 'What the fuck just happened?'

'Opportunity,' Nina said. 'Kira, this is it. We are going to Shift inside. And I have an idea . . . it should work –'

'Should? Oh god –'

'Listen to me.' Nina grabbed her shirt collar and hauled her in close. 'I want you to focus on Azrael when I begin the Shift. I will concentrate on the Messenger, but I want _you_ to go to Azrael –'

'Az? How am I supposed to –'

Nina tapped her finger against Kira's temple. 'You can find him. There is a connection between you. I've seen it. You've felt it. I know you have, it's in the way you look at him. And this place, it's a tinderbox of power, Kira. Set it on fire. Use your power. I believe you can control your own Shift.'

'Hell of a time to mention a new superpower.'

Nina's breath was warm against Kira's lips, and those rich eyes of brown sparkled. 'You must feel the strength of this place. Feed on it. Take control. I said once you were a handmaiden just like me, but I was wrong. I don't think you are like me. I don't think you are like anyone else who exists. You are trapped in your own skin, and yet bursting out of it. So desperately human, and utterly divine. Take hold of both. Your pain fuels you. Make it your servant here, and let the Maiden guide you. Go. Find your metal angel, and we will tear this house down.'

If Nina had been practising her pep talks, this was the gold-medal performance. It gave Kira the proper feels. Actual goosebumps and all. Bra-fucking-vo. Kira wrapped her hands around Nina's wrists, finding a firm hold. A hum filled her body, and it had nothing to do with the transformer. This was just like the moment she'd swallowed the stone, a rock-a-bye-baby melody soothing her. Eron had said once the mea stone enabled him to carry out the will of his god. Well, if the Maiden was using the stone right now, She seemed to be telling Kira to chill the fuck out. Stay calm.

If you're going down, go down swinging, right? Kira had been going down a long damn time. Sinking under the weight of just being. Never out from behind that steering wheel. Always careening towards that tree.

Time for the big bang. But she was getting Az and Blake out of here first.

She closed her eyes, shutting out the gunfire, the bright lights, the aches and hollows of her own body.

'Let's do this.'

Tamas - 78

Tamas accepted the child from Captain Nex, wrapping his arms around the limp – and thankfully –clean body, cradling it tightly against his chest. Standing behind Nex, Agar's fervour was visible, the gallu's wild hunger imprinted on his unsettling face. He might as well have licked his lips. Tamas sought out the next step with a pointed toe, easing down farther into the brightening depths. Crystal clear, all the darkness swept away, and the Waters flowed in thick, lazy currents around his body. Pleasantly tepid. Rising up over his calves, his knees, his thighs, as Tamas followed the short flights of wide concrete steps that led him to a platform jutting into the centre of the Tier. The Waters played at his clothes, alternately pressing them hard against his body and tugging them away from his skin. There were multiple currents; several danced around him, all shifting in different directions, as though invisible schools of fish moved about. The Waters covered his belly and lapped at the baby's back by the time he reached the platform. The child's tiny eyes widened, and spittle bubbled from a puckered mouth, but Dumuzi did not utter a sound. The Waters left his skin a shade of blue, evidently the warmth extended to Tamas was not shared by the demigod.

'Don't fret, it will all be over soon,' Tamas muttered, as much to himself as the child.

Tamas cleared his throat and closed his eyes, soaking in the silence that pressed down on the huge chamber. Not even the growing clusters of stalactites dared to drip. The sensation of the Waters against his body, the hardness of the concrete panel beneath his feet, even the weight of the child in his arms, drifted to a place more distant. Emptying him out. Giving Her room. His ears did not ring. His head did not ache. So far, the Final Meld was nothing like the last, when the Fours' arrival seemed to tear apart the very atoms that made Tamas whole. This time, Tamas stood quietly and calmly. Unfazed whether anyone watched him. No desire to cast one last glance towards the cells. Let Blake rot there, let Kira come. Fuck them both. They were far too late to this party. The only thing that bothered him at all was that he'd let Kira unsettle him.

Warmth built in Tamas's feet, flowing up his legs. Utuabzu's blood – the blood of the demigod sage – ignited in Tamas's system. It burned far brighter than before, rising up his thighs, swelling his veins, pumping through his organs. Stiffening his cock, and sending a sweet pressure through his groin that made him shudder.

No. This was nothing like before.

Tamas groaned and opened his mouth.

Ereshkigal's words fell fast and thick from his tongue. Ancient tongue-warping words choked him as they made their way up his throat. He spoke the goddess's words as though he'd been reciting them all his life, not just finding them now, flowing off his tongue, controlling the curve and tilt of his lips. As they continued to fall, Tamas grew light-headed, dry-mouthed, thrown off-centre by the sensations moving through him. He blinked, eyes stinging against the increasing brightness. He was no longer certain he still held Dumuzi at all. The child was nothing but air in his arms.

The Waters exploded in a shockingly vibrant spray of green, drenching him. Dampening the roar of blood through his body. Tamas ground his teeth against the sudden bitter chill, conscious all at once that he did indeed still cradle the child. The goddess was coming. Her approach niggled at the back of his skull and reignited the hiss of tinnitus in his ears. Tamas braced his feet and set his shoulders. Ready.

The Waters churned in a great funnel around them. Twin tongues of liquid were siphoned off from the main body. They contorted and twisted until distinct shapes formed. Lahar's totem, the diminutive but ferocious Precon from Syrana, and Ereshkigal's great wolf tore free of the funnel. The goddess rammed into Tamas's senses, but he didn't falter. Nor did his grip on the child waver. Holding fast, Tamas met the goddess head on. This time She was not just a whisper in his mind, an unpleasant heaviness on his bones. This time She sank deeper and found Her way into every inch, melting away his humanity. The Waters collapsed back into the Tier, leaving the deities pacing around its circumference.

The Syranians all knelt. Supplicant not only to the gods, but to Tamas himself. He stood upright, firm on his feet, worthy of his bloodline. The captain could not have bowed deeper if he'd tried. Even Agar had lowered to his knees, though he did not drop his head. His fierce gaze was set on his mistress's wolf.

The gods opened their mouths, each letting out a cry so feral it shook the chamber. Small fragments of rock and dust rained down. Behind Seder, a stalactite fell, crashing to the ground close enough to cause the Syranian to jump. Tamas tilted his head back and revelled under the deafening roar. Unseen fingers traced a path down his spine, found a gripping point, and tugged. The sensation strengthened until it seemed set to rip his spine from his body. Gut him like a fresh catch. Tamas leaned into it, praying that perhaps it was the goddess Herself finally freeing him from his mortal shell.

At his feet, the Waters swirled, rotating in a vast circle around him. Faster and faster until it pressed so hard against the

Tier walls Tamas and Dumuzi were left standing on a water-less platform. The child lay silently in his arms, nothing more than a damp sack of flesh. A shift in the air bore down on him. Gigantic hands gripped both shoulders and forced him to his knees, cracking them against the concrete, forcing a cry from his lips.

The ease of the Meld altered in the blink of an eye. Where he'd burned with pleasure before, now acid crawled through him. The simple movement of his tongue against the roof of his mouth, the light touch of air in his nostrils, even the curve of his fingers where they held Dumuzi, all brought pain. A crescendo was coming.

Ereshkigal's wolf bayed, right at his ear, and the sound ricocheted against him with a force that knocked the breath from his body.

Take it.

The wolf extended one shimmering, fluid paw. Arching claws, as long as the child itself, hung in the air close to Tamas's face.

Take it.

With the power of the Waters surrounding him, and the goddess literally breathing down his neck, Tamas sat at the eye of a monstrous storm. His bones tried to lift from his body, tear themselves free of his skin, but still he held fast. No longer so unconcerned with who watched him. He hoped they all saw. He hoped every single one of those bastards on their knees saw that his hand did not shake as he raised it. That his fingers didn't tremble as he reached for one of the wolf's liquid claws; as wide as the blades that Blake had constructed to make up the ridiculous wings on the carapaces, though much shorter in length.

'My lady. Your will be done.'

He closed his fingers around her offering. The claw morphed under his touch with an audible crack, hardening into a piece of ice that burned his skin. Smooth as marble, the ice sparkled at the sharp tip, particles within glistening as brightly as diamonds. Tamas drew his weight down, wrenching at the ice. A snap, brittle as the break of bone, shuddered through his hand, and the claw broke free from the wolf's paw.

Strike.

Ereshkigal's wolf and Lahar's Precon beast dissolved, the fluid that had created them rejoining the Waters.

Strike. A single word with consequences whose magnitude struck Tamas even now, huddled here as he was at the eye of a divine storm. Tamas placed the frozen blade between his teeth, mouth stretching to accommodate its girth, and used his now free hand to grasp the child by the ankles. He hoisted Dumuzi in the air, dangling the child upside down. The motion lifted Tamas's head and gave him a perfect view of his audience.

Blake's decision to give the carapaces wings was one Tamas had considered puerile, until now. The Four stood around the Tier's stone edging, each with wings extended into giant pluming structures of metal that formed a shield around him. Wingtip to wingtip they stood, their shells veined with light as the fissures vented the strain of the radiance, the essence that gave these creatures life. Breathtaking.

Tamas, basking in the glow, rested the claw-blade against the child's fragile ribcage. With the barest pressure, he would puncture skin, and the needle-point tip would pierce the gem-sized heart beating within. With the strike of this blade, Tamas would free Dumuzi from his immortal prison. And a new prisoner would shift beneath the flesh. Inanna, a goddess of war, a divine queen of lust, forced into the confines of a human that still shat its pants.

Ereshkigal's pleasure roiled through him. So often Her presence was devoid of emotion, Her mood indecipherable to him.

Not now.

Tamas pulled back his arm, muscles tense and bunching. Fingers vice tight around the blade. His moment arrived.

A blow hammered at his wrist. Unprepared, he lost grip on the claw-blade. Another impact followed, hard against his chest.

'No!' Tamas screamed, Dumuzi slipping from his grasp. The momentum pushed him back as the child dropped towards the Waters. Metal blades flashed, dangerously close to Tamas's face. Diresh lunged over him, reaching for the child, wings sweeping low. The gallu found her target, grabbing hold of a kicking, tiny leg. Tamas hit the Waters, hard as concrete against his spine, erupting upwards in a giant emerald curtain. He sank down, and someone moved with him. Their presence was a pinprick against his senses. The Waters enveloped them both, drawing them into their depths.

Pitch-black depths. The sheen of emerald had been extinguished. An abyss yawned beneath him, beside him, blotting out every source of light. Tamas blinked into the nothingness, lashing out with his now empty hands, searching for the one who had fallen with him. But his attacker found him first. And aimed a blow at his gut. But the strike was far weaker than before. Tamas roared into the syrupy blackness, bubbling the Waters with the sound. The goddess was a void, an empty space in his mind. The Messenger drowned alone. Tamas lashed out, arms and legs thrashing.

This could not be happening. He could not be failing.

An orb of light appeared above him. Sunshine-yellow radiating down, piercing the gloom. A surge of movement swept him up against the Tier wall. Strong hands gripped his shoulders, hauling him up and out of the pit between worlds. Tamas's head broke the surface, and his rescuer flung him with the minimum of care onto the hard surface of the chamber floor. The gallu Tek stood above him. Every aspect of the carapace was sharp. From nose to cheek, to the flint in his eyes.

'On your feet, Messenger.'

'Where is Dumuzi?' Tamas lurched to his feet. 'Who attacked us?'

Diresh held the child. The infant damp but none the worse for wear, toying with a button on the gallu's uniform. Agar had possession of the claw, pinching it between two chunky fingers and dangling it as though it were a token prize out of a Christmas cracker. Each of the Four regarded him; a dripping, shaking mess.

'This is what felled you, Messenger.' The captain moved from the far side of the Tier, brandishing a small captive. A black-and-orange reptile wriggled, bulging pink tongue moving whip-fast against the creature's eyeballs.

'A lizard?' Tamas shook his head, and his body shook with it. 'It was far more than that.'

Ridiculous. Something much more substantial than a reptile had just body-slammed him into the Waters. A far greater force had laid him low in front of his goddess, in front of each of these judgemental, presumptuous beings. It was impossible to stop shaking.

The captain regarded him in silence for one, two heart beats. 'It was observed striking you, Messenger. Before you lost your footing, and the child. And fell.' He dashed the lizard against a nearby stalagmite, twice for good measure, and tossed the broken lifeless body away.

The gallu lifted their heads in unison towards the chamber's main doors. Tek and Sora placing themselves in front of Diresh and Dumuzi, while Agar took his place ahead of them all. A figure ran in through the doors. Cym. Rushing at speed towards them, followed by two human guards.

Gren stepped forward, a frown crossing his dark features, but the captain stayed him with a look.

'Captain, the Lucentshield has been breached.' Cym was breathless. 'The same beast that fought Agar's control and escaped Eron.' It was there, though only barely, the hitch as Cym spoke his dead brother's name. 'I believe it took advantage of the shield being lowered to return Eron's body. It forced its way through with the vehicles.'

'And you've destroyed it?'

Cym matched the captain in stature, but Nex loomed large over his soldier as he shot the question.

'No, sir. We've lost track of it. But it cannot escape. The shield is fully operational. Is the Meld complete?'

Agar released a growl. And his needling eyes found Tamas. The remainder of the Four followed suit. Every pair of eyes, Syranian and gallu alike, rested on him. Accused him with their naked hostility.

Tamas strode towards Agar, holding eye contact until he stood right up close to the creature whose smirk did not lessen.

'Give me the blade.'

Agar obliged and Tamas turned his back on the gallu, moving to where Diresh held the infant. She edged the child from the crook of her arm, shifting his head onto one palm, her other cupping his buttocks. An offering lifted to the sacrificial altar.

'Hold him still.' Tamas did not hesitate. No delusions of grandeur this time.

He struck.

And did not miss.

Was not made a fool of by anyone or anything.

The blade's tip sliced through delicate flesh and soft bone. And the ground shuddered beneath their feet. Now, after such long silence, Dumuzi made himself heard. A desperate sound that flew upwards and infiltrated every crack, every pore, in the ancient cave.

Kira - 79

Shifting was not something Kira imagined she'd ever get used to. Which was a big call for someone who had done a shit load of drugs and knew how to handle an inside-out, upside-down world. A mushroom trip had once left her huddled on some random bed for an hour, terrified of the patterns on the curtains. The gold and red threads had morphed into dancing tigers with sharp teeth and claws, snarling at her if she so much as thought about trying to move. Scared her shitless. Almost literally.

Kinda like now.

She was lost in a blizzard, whiter than white. Nina had held both her hands, but there was no sign of the handmaiden now. No sign of jack shit. And the silence. Fuck, it was as if concrete filled her ears. There was no world beyond her own body. Nothing. Zip. And beneath her skin, it was not pretty at all. She sat at the top of a long, long slope of panic. And if the bleached-out existence didn't stop in a second, she might just claw her own flesh open to break free.

Focus on Az. Focus on the bright one, on that connection Nina seemed so damn sure they had. Didn't seem like Kira had anything much at all right now, save for the scream banging at her ribs. Wanting out. Way out.

'Nina.'

The word was a hiss of air escaping under pressure. And no one replied. Which was far less surprising than Kira would have preferred. The sense of aloneness surfed her along. Goddamn it, focus on Az. The hot mess with wings.

He'd found her when Tamas had been torturing the fuck out of her. It had better work in reverse, or Kira was never getting the hell out of this snowbank. She would freeze to death in here.

'Jesus.' No, not the Christ. Fuck's sake. Focus. 'Az. Azrael.'

Come on, buddy. Find her tiny, tiny self before she melted away to less than a speck.

She repeated his name over and over, in her head and with her hissing mouth. Picturing those eyes of the deepest green. If you were going to die in a colour, it should be that sea green. Not this. Find him. Keep calling his name.

'Az. Please. Az.'

Kira.

The snowstorm faded, and a wall of dull grey appeared. An actual wall.

'Oh crap.' Kira threw up her arms, body-slamming solid concrete a second later. 'Fuck!'

The armadillo took most of the impact, but any thought of double-checking for broken bones drowned beneath the god-awful terror swamping her. Oh this was uncomfortably familiar. Monsters-under-the-bed-when-you-are-five kind of shit. Her fingers shook so hard she wouldn't have been able to hold a cigarette. Though Christ, she needed one. No. Check that. Azrael needed one.

They had him trussed up in a glass cell. She didn't recognise the level. Sure as hell wasn't level eleven, but it was right where she should be.

Sons of fucking bitches. Perry, the ghostly harbinger of bad news, had been right. It wasn't pretty. Az was strapped up like a submissive waiting for his dom, upright on an X-shaped contraption that splayed his arms and legs. So much of his skin was shredded or missing altogether, and his hair had been torn from the right side of his head, leaving a bare patch of faux skin.

'Jesus, Az.' She pushed off from the wall, stumbling like a punch-drunk boxer. 'Az, I'm here, buddy.'

He raised his head at the sound of her voice. A rectangular slice of metal had been bolted across his eyes. Blinded. Just as Vail had said.

'I'm going to kill them.' She'd never meant anything so much in her short, dysfunctional life. Azrael's fear was an out-of-control wrecking ball, hitting Kira right smack in the brain with every step she took. She leaned her body into his terror, fighting its attempts to set off her own. Sweat trickled into the grazes and cuts on her skin, triggering sharp bolts of pain. She might have looked like shit, but it was nothing compared to Az.

Across his lower back were two deep gashes. Piercing the metal he was made of. Some kind of oily grey fluid seeped from the edges of each wound, and she could just make out a faint golden glow emanating from the holes.

'Kira. You are here.' His whisper was a brick dragged over concrete.

'I'm right here, buddy.' She didn't know whether to cry or scream or punch the wall. Didn't know whether to touch him. The guy had been done over. No doubt about it. Most of his faux skin was gone from his torso, shreds of it from his arms, and half his face was missing. But nothing was so horrendous as the blindfold. That was just pure evil. 'Az, I'm going to get you out of here. Okay.' She pushed up on tiptoes and cradled her hands around his face. He flinched. 'It's just me, Az. Only me.'

The dude was shaking so hard the rest of the faux skin would probably just fall off. Kira swallowed. Az's fear was thick and rich, stinking up the air in this place. She tried again, reaching to touch him with a light-as-a-feather brush against his shoulder. Az bucked his hips, straining his arms against the bindings. His mouth opened in a silent scream.

Shit. Where was their fucking connection now, that orgasmic buzz of metal on metal?

'Az, please. It's okay. I'm going to get you out of here.' That's what you did right? Kept talking to people when they were trapped? Kept them calm. 'Hang in there.'

Hard to keep calm. Not just because Az was electrocuting the air with his panic, but because Kira wanted to smash this damn place into pieces. Find the cunt who had done this to him. To Eron.

Perry told them that Eron had hurt Az. But this shit, this cruelty, was so beyond the Eron she'd known. She'd seen for herself what they'd done to him. He'd been every bit as tortured as Az.

She glanced around. Christ. Here she was, standing in the middle of a secured cell after appearing out of thin air. The Facility had made a good chunk of its fortune out of surveillance equipment. Eyes would be watching Az's prison. They were always watching. She needed to move her ass.

Kira ran her hands over the back of the restraint, feeling along the surface for a hint of a release button. Because it would be that easy. 'Shit. Help me out here, Az.' Her trembling fingertips brushed his.

This time he didn't try to snap a Telteriun wrist to get away from her. It was worse. He whimpered. A short sound that repeated. Growing longer each time. Lifting into a moan soaked with desperation. She knew the sound. Primitive, guttural notes that grief had dislodged from her over and over in those first few weeks after the crash. Let loose into her pillow many a time, so no one would notice she was dying inside. Az was sinking deep.

Heat rushed to Kira's cheeks and fired up an almighty furnace in her guts.

'Fuck this shit.' She grasped the cuff at his right wrist, two-inch-thick Telteriun, and heaved her body weight against it.

The cuff snapped free in her hands.

Unprepared, Kira flew backwards, colliding with the single other piece of furniture in the room – a black stool – and sent it hurtling back against the glass. Her butt met the concrete floor with a none-too-comfortable thud, but bigger things were happening. Kira gaped at her metal arm.

Jesus. She was glowing. Like, actually glowing. A human firefly. A subtle burnt-amber glow between the layers of the metal.

'Kira.' Az slumped forward, free arm dangling.

She scrambled to her feet. No, she bounced. A move that took no effort. Her body crackled. She was kindling and the energy – whatever the hell it was – was fire.

'Round two, we got this, Az.' Kira took a deep breath and hauled against the cuff at his right wrist. It didn't give quite as easily. She clenched her jaw, hauling back again and again. Sweat ran down her forehead. It was a sauna in here. Or in her. Hard to tell. 'Come on!' She might not have shit herself earlier, but was in danger of doing so now with the pressure she was putting her body under. Kira strained against the metal, the muscles in her flesh arm screaming at her to give it up. No fucking way.

The cuff snapped clear. Azrael slumped forward, and Kira was there, ready to take his weight. Ready to have it squash her flat, considering he was all Telteriun.

Didn't happen. Az was heavy, no doubt about it, but Kira kept her footing and held steady despite the giant humanoid she nursed. But she had next to no chance of being able to reach the remaining cuffs at his ankles.

'You need to lie back, Az. I'm not going to leave you here.' Kira shoved against him. 'Jesus, dude. Sit back.'

He was totally unresponsive. A sack of mush. As a last resort, Kira landed a punch to his belly, certain it hurt her flesh hand far more than it did him. But it had the desired effect, knocking a little comprehension into the big guy. Az dropped his weight back against the panels of the restraint.

'Good boy, now we just need to –'

Kira spun around. The door into the cell opened, and a freckle-faced girl raced in, semiautomatic waving in the air. She was screeching at Kira to step away from the asset.

Oh man. Kira was so done with being shouted at and threatened and ordered around. This chick had no idea.

'Stop pointing fucking guns at me!' Kira screeched right back at her. Her metal arm lifted, and it was Eron all over again. All golden light and bad things for the person threatening her. Energy ripped from Kira's fingertips, piercing the space between her and the girl. 'No . . . shit . . .'

Freckles lifted off her feet, cartwheeling the short distance to the glass. Hitting it upside down, halfway through a turn. Dropping head first to the ground. No gaping black holes through her body, but a broken neck wasn't pretty, either.

Kira snatched her hand back against her chest. Oh god.

But Az didn't give her time to hurl her guts over the new body on her list.

'Kira. Have you left me?' He clawed at the band covering his eyes. 'Kira?' Choked, guttural sounds pulsed out of him as he repeated her name.

'No. Az, I'm right here. I'm okay.'

What strips of the faux skin were left on his face came away with his frantic attempts to de-blind himself. Trying to gain a grip on his flailing hands, Kira dodged from wayward jerks of his arms.

He landed a nice slap to the forehead before she was in, pressing herself against his body.

'I'm not leaving you. Take a breath.'

'Don't let them take me, Kira.' Az rocked against the remaining cuffs, moving his bulk back and forth against her. 'I cannot return to Kur. I cannot endure this.'

His fear was old, ingrained so deep it had made itself a part of him. The monster under Az's bed was ferocious.

'They are not taking you.' Kira placed both hands on the blindfold, tried to ease her fingertips into the narrow crevice between metal and what remained of his skin. 'Please. Help me.'

Az's hand settled over hers. Metal against metal. Contact bloomed with tingly, toe-curling goodness. Much more like the good old days.

'On my three,' Kira said. 'One, two –'

In one, beautifully synchronised move, they wrenched the blindfold free. Azrael cried out, and his arm found her waist, sweeping her off the floor.

He pressed his mouth to her ear. 'Thank you.'

The door was wide open, and the silence in the hallway beyond it was unsettling. Time to get moving. Haul ass out of here while they had the chance. But they dangled instead. Kira's breathing was the noisiest thing in the room. 'That goddess really hurt you. Didn't She?'

Azrael set her down. 'Yes, She did.'

Kira crouched at his feet. Flexing her fingers, she found a hold on the cuff at his ankle. 'I'm really sorry.'

'As am I.'

Glancing up, Kira met piercing pools of jade set in a face that was now half metal, half flawless skin.

'I'm sorry, Kira, that you too have endured great suffering.'

'Thanks, but I can't do this right now.' Kira lowered her head, zooming in on the cuffs. The rage and the fear and the adrenaline were pumping her full of life. And if she wanted to get up off this floor, she'd need to stay pumped. No time for sob stories. A heave, a yank, and a snap. Another cuff succumbed to the armadillo's charms. There was no telling how long she could keep this shit up. And she hadn't even begun to search for Blake.

'You need to go, Az. Get the hell out of here.' She rose to stand, steadying herself against his shoulder as the world swam.

'I will not leave alone.' So solemn and rumbling. Movie-trailer voice-over material right there.

'Hey, I've got all kinds of shit going on now. I can handle myself.' To prove the point, she snapped the final cuff around his ankle as if it were an oversized wafer. She straightened, and Az's hands landed gently on her shoulders. Her metal covered shoulders. Boom. There is was. The woozy bus crashed straight into her. She clutched his waist to steady herself, finding mostly metal. 'Look, we can chat later, okay. You should go. I get it if you want to get out of here. I really get it.' She sucked at her bottom lip, eyelids fluttering at the flowy, gooey thing that had them both wrapped up and toasty warm. 'But I've got to stay.'

He touched his fingers to the back of her neck, and goosebumps popped up along her spine. 'They hurt you too, Kira. And you did not run. I will not run, either.'

'Kinda wishing I had right now.' Azrael shifted his right hand, sliding it down over her breast. Kira's eyes widened, and a blow-torch hit the lady garden. 'Hardly seems the time.'

But he ignored her, cupping his hand against her ribs, tracing the extended metal. Her body hummed. 'Kira, what has happened?' He pushed back her top. The armadillo coating over her ribs held a faint glow, accentuating the markings.

He traced his fingers over the symbols. And mini-fireworks set off in all the creases and folds of her body.

'Can you read it?' Kira coughed, trying to get rid of the huskiness.

He frowned, a super-weird look considering only one eyebrow remained intact. 'It is a declaration. A young god declaring to the old that a new age has commenced. She abandons Her ancient name, a moniker from a time when She was subservient to those greater gods. Gaia is no more, and the Maiden takes Her place, claiming this world as Her realm.' He edged Kira's shirt up higher. 'The Maiden declares war on any who trespass. And announces the one who carries this declaration . . . as Her Messenger.'

His words landed on her, soft as baby-bird feathers. Their bodies rocked in towards one another. Now was the perfect time for a freak out. Kira wanted to be a messenger about as much as she wanted root canal work. But it was hard to recall when she'd felt less likely to lose her shit. Her body hummed with purpose, as if Azrael uttering the word – Messenger – had released a whole truck load of endorphins. If Kira punched a wall right now, she was certain she could bring the whole damn Facility down, with Az punching right alongside her and taking out the whole cursed place. Burying it where no one would ever find it. All the king's horses, and all the king's men wouldn't be able to put the Facility together again once she was done. And it didn't scare her. If the Maiden was working some voodoo, brainwashing her, then bring it on. It would make a welcome change.

'Blake.' Kira edged out of Az's grasp. Her astral self dive-bombed back into her body, her skin and bones lead heavy. 'I have to get her out of here.'

'Well . . . yes . . . you . . . do.'

Az and Kira moved as one, spinning towards the voice. A dark-skinned woman stood there. The right sleeve and shoulder of her lab coat was covered in a chocolate-coloured stain. A spotted scarf sat tied haphazardly around her head.

'Weylen?' Kira said.

Weylen was as close to a friend as Blake had ever had. The assistant had tried more than a few times to get Blake and Kira to share a meal or shop together. Whatever the hell normal sisters did. So much for that shit now.

'Not . . . not . . . her.' Was Weylen drunk? Her lips moved as much from side to side as up and down. A cow chewing a cud of words. 'Kira . . . me . . . it's Vail.'

Weylen lifted her arm. The wild up and down movement might have been her lashing out at a swarm of bees, or an attempt at a wave.

'Vail, seriously?' Vigorous head nodding. Up and down, wobbling a little left, a little right. If he kept it up, Weylen's head would snap clean off. 'Why are you in Weylen?'

Why did that question just roll off Kira's tongue as though she spouted crap like that every day?

'Told you. You not alone. Come. Might be…too late.' Weylen-Vail's head didn't fall off, but her scarf did.

'Christ.' Kira recoiled, hand to mouth.

Weylen's right temple was crushed like an eggshell, the hair around it coated in dried blood.

'That's gotta hurt,' Kira said.

'Will explain.' Weylen reached for the fallen piece of fabric. One swipe, two swipes, three. Her fingers never quite able to curl at the right time.

'Oh for fuck's sake.' Kira snatched up the scarf. 'Start explaining right now –'

'Get key card.' Weylen's head wobbled towards the woman slumped beside the door. 'Let's go. Shortcut up here.'

Considering the lack of coordination with the scarf pickup, Vail manoeuvred Weylen's body out into the passageway with impressive speed. But fuck, it was all kinds of nasty, the disjointed way she moved. They raced into the hall. Kira checked to ensure Az was following. But of course he was. Right behind her. Any closer, she would have felt his breath on her neck.

A violent shudder ran through the floor beneath them. Kira cried out, thrown forward against Weylen. The weight of her armadillo coated body sending them crashing down onto the concrete. And right behind, Azrael, still half-baked from his time in hell-ville, barelling down on both of them.

Blake - 80

Blake edged towards the jagged rock in the far corner of the cell, taking care to place as little pressure on her slashed thigh as possible. The bandage applied by the medic was now coloured a vibrant merlot. The woman in the lavender hijab, Zara – according to the ID that had spilled out of her kit in her haste to pack up her belongings – had taken some convincing to heed Blake's warning to get the hell away from the Facility. In the end, Blake had swung at her. More than once. The past few days had seen Blake engage in more physical violence than she'd ever instigated in her entire life. For all it was worth. The blows she aimed at Zara were pathetic, to say the least, barely glancing off the women's shoulder. And in the end, Zara's concern had been for Blake, and not herself. She'd promised to back off if Blake promised to calm down.

She thought you mad, deathbringer.

'Yes, but she left. Now, quiet. I need to focus.'

Blake swiped at her brow, brushing back the hair plastered there. She could hardly blame Zara for thinking Blake mad. Barefooted, her clothing in strips, bloodied and swinging punches, it was hardly Blake's finest moment. She sized up the distance between her and the sharp edge of rock she aimed for. If she'd had more sense – more clarity of mind – she would have demanded Zara leave the med kit behind, with its scalpel and miniature scissors. All able slicers of flesh. But the roughness of the chamber wall would have to suffice. Dark spots blotted her vision, and yet another wave of dizziness overtook her. Inhaling, deep and slow, Blake moved her focus outward. Beyond the confines of her glass prison, to the muted world beyond.

To where Tamas had just disappeared in behind a great funnel of emerald-green Waters that rose up out of the Tier.

The Waters that her body craved, shaking ferociously with the nearness of the liquid. Mouth parched, and her skin slack with dehydration, Blake stared into the churning, sparkling mass and imagined those flickering droplets landing on her tongue, sinking into her veins. Her tired, misfiring brain registered strange sights. Portions of the Waters morphing into life, shaping into the creatures that had glared down on her in the shrine: the giant wolf;

and the other foul beast carved into the glass, the Precon. That monster held some semblance to a rat, one that had grown to the size of a horse, with three eyes all of varying size and shape, and limbs that contorted at odd angles, giving the appearance of broken bones. Blake's tortured vision had her seeing both these beasts stalk around the rim of the Tier, moving in and out of the great tower of Waters, the base of which was partly obscured by the flash of extended wings as the carapaces brandished the appendages that Blake herself had given them.

Vanity overtook you. To embellish your creations with such nuances.

Blake rocked away from the viper's presence in her skull. Her knee slipped from beneath her, pushing her weight onto her injured thigh. Blake screamed against the back of clenched teeth. She planted her hands on the ground, searching for distraction before the pain ate her alive. Finding it there, beyond the glass.

The Waters' brilliant light pulsed, a flash that lived only a moment, and the funnel collapsed, sending a wave thudding against the stonework and spilling over onto the concrete floor. A flurry of unrest rippled through the assembled group, and the gallu, Diresh, the female carapace, launched herself into the now flattened Waters, emerging a second later clutching something to her chest. Captain Nex's face told Blake this was not part of the plan. The Syranian leader's fury animated his features enough for them to be evident to her, halfway across the massive chamber. He brandished an item in his hands, thrusting it at Tamas, who didn't baulk when the object almost struck his face. Tamas fronted the captain with a brazen step forward, a move that Tamas of old would have struggled to enact, but the Messenger – as he called himself – was no longer content to be a supplicant. Blake did not recall when she'd lost sight of the boy whose need for validation had driven her to distraction in their university days, but he was long gone. The man who had threatened to kill her sister, then threatened to kill everyone around him if Blake died, was not one she recognised. And that he would carry out his threat, she had no doubt.

The captain slammed the object onto the ground. Several times. Before tossing it away. Turning his back before the object had finished flying through the air. Blake's eyes followed it though.

'What the hell?' Blake muttered, trying to blink back the annoying black dots that had taken up residence in her vision. It appeared the item that had brought on the captain's ire just scampered beneath the rubble. Or had it? Perhaps it was just another of the shadows plaguing her retinas. With body and mind deconstructing, she did not trust her own eyes anymore.

Nex and Tamas gestured in an animated, clearly heated exchange. But their argument was silenced by a new arrival.

Cym raced across the expanse of the chamber, not sparing Blake a glance. An urgency in his pace stripped the Syranian of his usual graceful stride. He reached his captain, but with his back to the cells, any hint of Cym's message was lost to her. Not that any message mattered. The important fact was that they were all here, each of the carapaces, Tamas, and every single one of the Syranians.

Save for Eron.

Blake pressed her fingers against her eyes, unwilling to allow further thought of his demise to plague her. She could not be distracted. Her moment to act could not have been clearer.

Let it be done. Watch them all burn.

'Quiet. Be quiet.'

A clear head was what was required. Not one soaking in delusion's brine. Think straight. Blake reached for the jut of rock, pressed her palm down on its tip, the angry infected flesh activating a thousand pain receptors. Throwing all the weight she could summon behind it, she drew her arm downwards, letting the pointed stone tear her skin. Stars exploded, filling her vision, but she kept up the pressure. Dragging the nub of stone through the stitching, cutting the strands. Opening her skin wide. Blood roared in her ears and flowed down her arm, the warmth of it flattening the goosebumps that had made a home beneath her skin. Not a sound escaped her. Blake watched the act of self-harm from a distance. The pain that surely should have been there was numbed into something more irritating than breathtaking. Her flesh now open, she dug her finger into her palm, scooping out the stones that nestled in angry folds. A foul odour drifted from the yellow-tinged edges of the wound, and it took immense effort not to expel the bile that burned at her throat.

Why could she not steady her hands? As she worked the stones free, each tremor sent fresh waves of unpleasantness through her body, the numbness now evaporated. Her pain sensors sharp and heightened, once again. Her heart raced at a pace that hollowed her chest, and the slickness of blood made grasping the smooth Starpoints problematic. Near damn impossible. The amethyst crystals slid from her, hitting the floor and bouncing.

'No.' Blake lunged, seeing stars as she leaned too heavily on her leg. Bracing on all fours, sucking in gulps of air, Blake edged back towards the front of the cell. Breathing hard, she sought out the group by the Tier. No one observed her.

Tamas turned on his heels and gestured at Agar. The brutish appearance Blake had given the gallu had never been more evident. His expression brimmed with a lust that parted his lips in a grotesque smile. The gallu handed Tamas something that caught the light and flashed brilliantly for a moment. Tamas snatched it away and stepped up to where Diresh stood. The gallu shifted and raised her arms, cradling the package she held. She turned at an angle that finally allowed Blake to see what she carried. What Blake had spotted momentarily in Captain Nex's arms earlier, but had been unable to discern.

A child. Naked and still. Tiny head hanging back at an angle that could have only brought discomfort.

Blake drew back from the glass. A baby? This was what they had hunted? She was hardly an expert, but the infant was so small it couldn't have been more than a few months old.

Does it matter at all? Would your intentions have been altered had you known?

Clutching at her temples, blood warm against one side of her face, Blake shook her head. 'I don't . . . I don't . . .'

You do. You do know. Everything dies anyway. What would this child matter? Death already took what you love. Because you were too busy to care. Kira is not to blame, at all. Is she, Blake?

'Get out, go away.' Spit flew from her mouth, peppering the glass.

Blake.

Her head jerked at the new voice. Faint, but far more welcome than the viper.

'Perry?'

By the Tier, Tamas raised his hands over the infant, a gleaming piece of something held tightly between clenched hands.

'Oh god –' Blake whispered, sensing his next move.

A downward strike plunged the item straight into the baby's chest. Blake's cry rose. A dry, coarse sound that was repelled by the glass. There was no way it could have reached him, but Tamas turned. Looked straight at her.

A tremendous shudder ran through the ground, rattling the glass walls in their frames and jerking Blake onto hands and knees.

Dust rained down on her, particles shaken loose as the entire chamber rumbled with life.

'No, no.' Blake's pitiful protest drowned beneath the thunderous shifting of earth. She reached for the Starpoints, but the violence of the quake that gripped the chamber stole them from her. The twin gems rolled into the back corner of the cell. Cracks serpentined across the rock wall and several small chunks broke free. One of them large enough to provide the sledgehammer she would need to activate the stones.

. . . ake . . . lis . . . me . . .

A quick sweep of the cell showed no sign of Perry. If that was indeed who plagued her. The timbre of his voice differed from what she remembered. It now pitched and hummed, like someone speaking into a fan.

'Not now.' Blake settled onto her side, and barrel-rolled herself towards the back of the cell, the quickest way to get her damaged limbs to work together in the unsteady environment. As each rotation brought the concrete against her thigh, she clenched her teeth and refused to allow a cry to pass. The hard touch of rock poked at her back, stopping her dead. Within reaching distance lay the amethyst stones. She clasped them with her uninjured hand, and grabbed the largest shard of broken rock with the other. Dizzy with the pain, Blake struggled to shift into a seated position. Heavy strikes were needed to ignite the Starpoints. She'd need leverage room to get the most power behind her blows, but her limbs were lead and her quickened breath left her light-headed. The still-trembling earth shifted beneath her. Jaw tight, lungs as full as she could manage, Blake lifted the rock over the Starpoints, bracing to bring them down as hard as her shattered body would allow.

Blake.

A boombox in her head, undeniably Perry, louder even than the alarm system that erupted in the chamber beyond her cell. Her arms dropped, the stone touching at the dirt beside the Starpoints. Blake scanned her confines, and did a double take when she reached the front right corner. Perry's image was more suggestion than substance, minute specks, particles only slightly bigger than the dust that filled the air.

Blake. Kira is here.

Blake gasped. A subtle tremor ran through the cell as a new sound erupted in the chamber. The whine of Syranian weaponry, releasing bolts of bright blue, sending sprays of shattered concrete into the air over towards the tech rooms.

'Shit.' Blake dragged herself onto her knees, desperately searching the chamber. 'Kira? I don't see her. Where is she?' Damn it. The girl was utterly incapable of doing what she was told. 'Why is she here?'

Getting shot at, blasted to kingdom come. But where the hell was she? Parator and Seder were running towards the ruined tech rooms, firing off shots, making a greater wreckage of the already decimated area, but Blake glimpsed only a fleeting shadow ahead of them. Impossible to tell if it was Kira. The gallu tightened their circle around Tamas and the child, blocking them from view entirely. The captain and the remaining Syranians, including Cym, formed a second barrier, weapons raised.

'I don't see her, Perry. What are you talking about?' Blake braced against the glass, every atom ached. And her heart was incapable of going any faster.

*She is coming. For you. For all…*Perry was barely conceivable. The slightest of images, even when Blake squinted. No sign of his lower body existed now. And what remained of his torso gradually shrank, like a chalk drawing being wiped clear. *I'm sorry . . . I can't hold on . . . I'm scared, Blake.*

'Where is Kira, Perry?' Blake shouted, ignoring the clear ring of fear in his voice. Offering no consolation. 'I don't see her. Perry? Damn it, Perry. Come back.'

The empty air gave her no answer. She rubbed at her eyes. Damned eyes. Had Perry ever been here at all? Or was she just delaying an awful, inevitable moment with hallucinations? Igniting the Starpoints would be catastrophic. Creating war machines was very different to becoming one herself. Blake gave up rubbing her eyes and closed them instead. Seeking refuge. Some semblance of clarity.

'You must be Blake Beckworth.'

Blake's eyes flew open. A tall woman, with hair spilling in waves around her shoulders and leather pants hugging her curves tightly, stood just inside the open cell door, flanked by two far more recognisable faces: Tamas's bodyguard, Boyd, the black-bearded man who had whispered to her that Kira was alive; and the female medic Zara, the one Blake had told to run and never come back. Clearly, she hadn't listened. She'd returned, and this time a sizeable firearm hung from her shoulder. Both of them paid Blake no attention, fixated on the woman between them.

'Who are you?' Blake demanded.

A civilian, surely. No one Blake associated with in the Facility paid quite so much attention to her make-up. Remarkable eyes too, a lush brown that seemed to draw you in, and eyelashes that curled up to touch at the base of her eyebrows.

'Me? Complicated question. Short answer, I'm the handmaiden of the goddess Inanna, immortal, very tired of being in this world, and a rather close friend of your sister's.' She smiled, two sparkling rows of dental symmetry revealed. 'My name is Ninshadur, but everyone, including Kira, just calls me Nina. Feel free to do the same.'

Kira - 81

Az had pulled off an impressive four-point landing when the earth tremor shook them all off their feet. Hands and feet planted around them, his body held just above Kira's, butt up in the air as if he'd decided to pull off some yoga moves while the Facility shook itself to pieces. He offered a hand to Kira, to help her to her feet but she waved him off.

'I'm good. It's Vail's body-buddy I'm worried about.' Kira sat back on her haunches. Her hand was shaking. 'Vail, tell me that didn't break any more pieces off this chick.'

Weylen's head flopped a little too hard to the right as Vail adjusted the headscarf. 'All still in one piece,' he said.

Kira took hold of Weylen's wrist and pulled them both back onto their feet. Weylen's soles left the ground, and a gasp left her blue lips. 'Geez, Kira,' Vail cried. 'Take it easy.'

'Sorry, sorry. My bad.' Kira danced on her toes, quickstepping her weight from one foot to the other. 'Holy crap, are you guys not feeling this?'

A buzzing beneath her skin. Not a Nina or Az kind of thing, one that left her bones like jelly, this was ten cups of coffee on an empty stomach.

'I am feeling it, and I fear we are too late.' Azrael clearly didn't share her high. He led them down the long corridor, the gashes in his back faintly glowing, like warpaint marking a shredded-up warrior. 'Hurry, Kira.'

'Too late?' Kira hesitated. 'That's what it was? The tremor . . . Inanna is here?'

'The heightening of energy would indicate so, yes.'

Her caffeine levels dropped. 'Shit.' After all this fucking effort, that was it? Just, yep, goddess of war is here. Night, night. End of days starts, now.

'Vail, hurry the meatsuit up, dude!' Kira shouted at the figure in the gloom behind her. The kid made trying to navigate a dead body look like really hard, really uncoordinated work.

'Do...do...ing...my...b–'

'Do better. Az could carry you—'

'N…n…no. Too, too much energy. I…might…g, g, get kicked..out.'

'Why are you even still in her anyway?'

'Thou . . . thought . . . it . . . might . . .' Weylen stumbled and Vail ghost-lifted her arm to brace against the wall. A very broken arm. Vail had lied through his ass about his meatsuit not taking any damage in the fall when the quake hit. Her left arm had snapped at the forearm. And was now useless. The woman toppled forward.

Kira dove in, wrapping an arm around Weylen's waist to stop yet another faceplant, and managing to grab the broken arm in the process. The pointed bone hadn't pierced the skin but it was damn close. 'Oh Jesus, Christ, fuck.'

No amount of Maiden mojo could cover the sensation of bone and goop against her hand, and her stomach contents agreed. They raced up her throat, hot and nasty at the back of her mouth.

'Kira . . . you . . . k?' Vail managed to brace Weylen's shoulder against the wall, the angle of the lean way too wide to appear even remotely natural.

Kira turned away, blinking against the Morse-code-manic flickering of the emergency strip lighting along the floor. 'Az, wait for us.'

He'd not stopped when they had and was some distance up ahead.

'There is no time, Kira. Come.'

The jittery emergency lighting didn't exactly lend itself to super-fast movement, but at least the ground had stopped shaking. Thank fuck for whatever it was that was hyping up her system right now. Any other time, a quake hitting when Kira was a kilometre underground would have sent her batshit crazy. Granted, her panties were a little damp, but show her someone who hadn't loosened a sphincter back there and she'd show you a bald-faced liar. Or Az. So long as the lights were on, the dude was cruising. Mostly. A shadow of the panic from earlier still clung to him, a lingering niggle. But it didn't stop him charging down the hallway right now like a general leading his army.

Vail edged Weylen past her, waving his meatsuit's working hand, but the limp wrist movement was a tad too reminiscent of the other limb's fish-flop style. 'Go . . . K . . . keep up . . . faster. Rossiter has . . . back.'

The corridor was empty. Way too empty and way too silent. Definitely no sign of the human tree trunk.

'Rossiter?' Kira said. 'What about him?'

An aftershock rolled down the hallway, and Kira tightened her sphincter. Vail braced Weylen like a newbie skater on the ice. 'The comms sy . . . sys . . . system . . . is down . . . you . . . c . . . c . . . an . . . thank . . . h . . . im . . . for . . . th . . . th . . .'

'Stop talking, you're gonna bite your fucking tongue off.' Kira pulled at the metal against her throat. So damn tight. 'We need to get a hell of a lot deeper in this place. We need to move faster.'

'Wh . . . what . . . I . . . said.'

'Then get out of the meatbag.'

'No . . . not . . . yet . . .'

The stampeding general stopped dead farther up ahead, turning towards an adjoining corridor. 'Az? We all good?' The coffee buzz was giving Kira the shits now. Making her itch where the armadillo met skin.

'We must go this way,' he said.

'Then that way we shall go.' Kira jogged up the hallway. Like, actually jogged. She'd despised running since the day she was born, but now had to force herself to stop at the door Az waited at. If she'd let them, her legs could have sprinted through this place for days. Seeing the closed door, Kira fumbled for the security pass she'd swiped from the freckle-faced girl. The one with the broken neck. Kira blew out a breath. Danced her feet, trampling the memory away. She pressed the pass to the scanner. A big juicy 'fuck off' flashed up on screen, and an obnoxious beep made her jump. Kira scanned again and the answer was a resounding nope.

'Me . . . me . . . this . . . why . . . still . . . here . . .' With each agonisingly drawn-out word, Vail lumbered Weylen up the hall, one hand lifted. 'Help . . . finger . . .'

Help his finger? What the fuck? Then it dawned.

'Oh, ten points you delicious nerd-wizard.' Kira took Weylen's hand, the one attached to the arm that didn't threaten to fall off any second. 'Christ, you smell bad.'

She guided Weylen's index finger to touch the scanner.

Nope. Fuck you. Have a nice day.

'Shit.'

'I shall break down the door.' Az shifted side on, bracing himself.

'Wa . . . wai . . . wait . . .' Weylen dipped forward, head-butting the door.

'What the hell are you doing?' Kira grabbed a waist that had way more squish factor than it should do.

'E . . . eyes . . .' Weylen's head banged against the door again. Catching on, Kira slid in behind her, taking hold of her upper arms, bracing her knee against a butt with even greater squish factor than the waist.

'Oh god,' Kira gagged. 'Make it quick. Az, get her eyes near the scanner.'

The panel was only slightly lower than Weylen's head, so it didn't take long. But a few seconds was a lifetime more than Kira needed. The door slid open onto a darkened hallway.

'Woo . . . woo . . . hoo.' Weylen wobbled like a tower of flesh jelly with Vail's self-congratulations.

'Yeah, all right,' Kira said. 'I'll give you that one.'

The Facility was big on biometric authentication, and nowhere bigger than down on the lower levels. Having a high-security-clearance corpse on your team *was* helpful. It also meant that it was going to take three years to get to level eleven if Vail couldn't speed the walking dead up. And if the security team had half a brain between them, someone was going to notice the access activity.

'Let's keep it moving, people.'

Kira headed into the hallway. Nowhere near as many lights here. In fact, it was bare minimum in terms of emergency lighting, just a couple of red dots along the floor that didn't pierce the darkness up ahead. Vail navigated Weylen through the doorway with a speed that was promising. But Az stayed where he was, framed by the light.

'Az?' But Kira got it. Couldn't miss it. Mixing in with all of her own jangling nerves was the low curdle of Az's fear. This place was too dark, and he was still too raw. 'Az, it's okay. Please. I'm right here.'

They so didn't have time for this shit. Blake didn't have time for this shit.

'You need to move.' Kira raised her metal arm. She needed to glow. Again. Of course she did. It was what every girl dreamed of. Becoming a human torch. 'Come on, come on. You want my help in this, Mrs Maiden then fucking help me out.' She closed her eyes, going back to that hellhole she'd found Az in. She'd been mad. Really fucked off. But there had to be a more controlled way to use this thing. Turning into a berserker every time she wanted to do something seemed like a surefire way to give herself an aneurysm. The image of Santa Claus darted into her head. Well, at least the witchy equivalent of him: William, the kaftan-clad guy from the farmhouse. The guy who exuded a calm that Kira could only ever dream of. No wonder those fireflies had done his bidding, lighting his way with the most beautiful torch she'd ever seen. He was walking Zen music. She drifted back to that moment. Felt the coolness of the grass, and the softness of William's voice on the air.

'Kira?'

Her eyes fluttered open. Weylen watched her, as wide-eyed as Vail could make her. Kira's arm was raised, and the armadillo filled the hallway with subtle firefly-yellow light. So freekin pretty.

'Thank you, Santa,' she whispered, a ludicrously large smile on her face. 'Az, look. You gotta love this right? Stick with me, you'll be all good.'

Please be good. Please be good.

In a rush, the damn, debilitating fear swept from his face, and their connection. Allowing her to exhale. Her two-tonne scaredy-cat stepped into her light. 'Kira, I'm sor –'

'Yeah, yeah. I know. Let's just find an elevator and find my sister. I want to show her this new party trick, she'll shit bricks.'

'We need to keep going down,' Weylen declared.

'Of course we do. Because saving the world in the sunshine and fresh air is just so yesterday.' Kira bounced along, still partly zinging with the buzz, partly high on the fact that she could glow on command. Simple enough thing, but the simple things were going to stop her from heading where Az had just been. Swallowed whole by sheer panic.

Up ahead, two men emerged from an emergency access stairwell and stepped out into the corridor. Kira's perky party came to a grinding halt. 'Balls.'

One of the men hollered something at them. Something about staying where they were and putting hands in the air. Kira obliged.

Almost.

She flicked them a double bird. And the trigger-happy hired guns took it as an act of war. They opened fire. Kira dove at Weylen, pulling the woman to her knees and throwing herself over her. Azrael rushed past them, wings unfurling in whiplash speed, setting up a barrier that spread the width of the corridor. The spray of bullets collided with Azrael's body, rain on a tin roof. Rat-tat-tatting. His body shuddered with the blows, but he held his ground. Kira risked an upward glance. Azrael rushed forward, feet barely brushing the concrete, his wings angled back in the narrow space, finding room to move. Shouts carried over the sound of gunfire, morphing into cries high with terror as Azrael bore down on them.

It was never going to be pretty. Kira should have buried her face in Weylen's dead hair, but Az was on the poor bastards before she had a chance to avert further nightmares. Slicing, dicing, creating human sushi. The blood on the white walls either side of him, a grotesque artwork. Weylen made a choking sound, and Kira shifted her weight.

'Tell me you didn't see that, Vail.'

'I . . . th . . . po . . . se . . .'

'Forget I asked.' Kira dragged Weylen to her feet. Dead people really were ice cold. 'Just keep your eyes on me, okay. We need to keep moving, we can take those stairs.'

Oh Jesus, just the thought of Vail trying to negotiate his meatsuit down endless flights drained her buzz further. This was the worst rescue in history. Tamas probably had Inanna checked into a fancy hotel in the Maldives by now. They'd be rubbing each other with coconut oil, sipping martinis, and starting wars.

'Come, Kira.' Az waved them forward as if stepping through body parts was on par with stepping through a field of daisies. His wings concertinaed back into their hidey-holes with the hush of a knife on a whetstone. He was patterned with blood. It ran down off his shoulders, streaking his bare chest.

Churning up some almighty bad memories for Kira.

'Go,' she said. 'We're right behind you.' Her foot sloshed in a crimson puddle, and her sneakers left unpleasant marks as she and Weylen staggered down the hall. Fuck. Enough with the blood. She shook her head, trying to dislodge the picture that clung to the inside of her skull: Eron's face, her dad's face, becoming one god-awful combination. When Weylen suddenly stopped, Kira had lost track of how far they had gone. 'What? What is it?'

'A problem,' Az said.

'The elevator.' Weylen slumped against her.

What was left of it anyway. A tangle of metal and concrete surrounded a gaping hole. Steelwork, the skeleton of the underground complex, poked like red bones all around the hole – the hole that had once been filled with the cage of the elevator. A shudder rocked the corridor, dislodging rubble and sending it tumbling into the blackness.

'Shit.' Now Kira leaned against Weylen. 'We've screwed this up so bad.' Fucking dusty air, making her eyes sting.

A door slammed somewhere farther down the hall. Everyone leapt into defence mode, none quicker than Azrael. He edged in front of Kira and Weylen before either of them had a chance to do much more than shuffle their feet. His posturing had them a lot closer to the edge of the pit than Kira felt comfortable with. If the wings came out, chances were she and Weylen would end up like the rubble. Tumbling into an abyss.

'Kira, it's me. Nobody shoot.'

'Rossiter?' Kira frowned, trying to edged around Az's body barrier.

'Kira, show caution,' Az said.

The approaching man drew closer, his shoulders the width of a cruise ship, yellow light bathing his bald head in a golden halo.

'Fuck, it is Rossiter.' She shoved Weylen against Az and bolted as fast as her goddess-infused legs would carry her, which, it turned out, was pretty damn fast. She crashed into the brick shithouse, wrapping arms and legs around him. Going full sloth.

'You're heavy.' He grunted, staggering backwards. 'And you're glowing.'

'Nice to see you, too.'

He wrapped her up in a muscle burrito that she could have melted into forever.

'Kira, I heard what happened,' he mumbled into her hair. 'Nina told me, before I came in here.'

She clung a bit tighter. *Don't say it, Big Man, don't be saying Eron's name.* Don't say sorry, 'cause there were enough cracks in this place already. He set her down, releasing his grip and letting silence do his talking. She liked to think he'd heard her thoughts – mind-reading didn't seem like a big deal this week – but it was more likely that he just knew her too damn well. Knew her better than her own dad ever would. He'd nursed her, in his own boot-camp kinda way, through a whole tonne of bad shit.

'Ross . . . Ross, hey . . . me. Vail.' Weylen raised the broken arm, the bone had pierced skin. And it flipped a calcium bird to the air.

Rossiter's eyes bugged and he took a step back. 'Sweet Jesus.'

'Fuck's sake, Vail.' Kira moved in between them, trying to block the view.

'Why is the kid in a dead woman?' Rossiter held up two meaty palms. 'You know what, don't answer that.'

'No problem.' Kira shrugged. 'Vail said you've been screwing with the comms system?'

'How did he know . . .' Rossiter shrugged off his own question. 'Yeah. Couldn't think of much else to do while I waited for someone to show. Figured I might as well make life as difficult as possible. But there were only so many favours I could call in before people started getting edgy. After your arrival – impressive by the way – I had to go underground. Been trying to find a trace of you since, and gotta say those are some horrific breadcrumbs you've left back there.'

'A threat had to be extinguished.' Azrael stepped out of the shadows that hugged the perimeter of the armadillo's light.

'Well, mission accomplished, buddy,' Rossiter said. 'But those guys will be missed soon enough, if not already. You better do what you intend to do here.'

Kira didn't miss the glance he cast her as he spoke. The brick shithouse was worried about her. Welcome to the club.

'We need to reach the Tier in order to do that, ' Azrael replied. 'If we are not already too late.'

Rossiter adjusted his hold on the gun. 'You're not. Not yet. Last I could verify, Tamas and his tin men –' He hesitated, searching Az's face for sign of insult, but the metal didn't give anything away, even if Az had given a shit. 'They are all still in the

chamber.' He shifted his focus to Kira. 'So is Blake, Kira. I couldn't
—'

'How do we get to that chamber?' Az was in full commander mode. No time for chitchat.

Kira gave Rossiter a nod. A go-ahead to focus on Az instead of her. So, Blake was in the lion's den. Okay. Bright side, they knew where she was.

The big man cleared his throat. 'Well, you could backtrack. Almost back to where you came from, the holding cells . . . there's an elevator just down the southern corridor —'

Weylen's shoulders slumped, and the scarf covering the head wound slipped. 'We went left, I should have taken us right.'

'Pretty much.' Rossiter's gaze narrowed in on Weylen's exposed and broken skull. If the sight made him woozy he gave nothing away. 'But chances are you would have run into a whole lot more trouble that way, too. Even more so now. That elevator takes you to the main entrance of level eleven. Your best shot, by my calculations, is right there.' Rossiter pointed over their shoulders. 'That's your way in. The damaged shaft. One of those. . . gallu, you call them, right? . . . went berserk the day they . . . activated them, or whatever the hell they did down there. And that hole right there, that will take you straight into the level eleven chamber.' He peered at Kira from beneath heavy knitted brows. 'We're on level nine, it's a ways down, but I'm guessing at least two of you could survive the trip.'

'You guess right.' Kira tried a smile, but lead lips made it impossible.

Rossiter exhaled, his frown softening. 'Damn, I wish this wasn't happening to you, K –'

A sharp snap rang out and Rossiter jerked, mouth wide, his bulk collapsing towards her.

'Rossiter!' Kira screamed. 'No!'

His dead weight hit the floor. And she had a clear line of sight to the asshole who'd shot him. A scrawny fucker with semi-automatic still raised. Multiple fuckers actually. Headed their way. Her glow-bug arm raised, and the sun shot from her fingertips. The force of it tilted her to one side, off balance, sending the energy tearing down the length of the concrete walls. She wasn't the only one screaming now. Fuckers scattered, diving to the ground. She thrust her hand forward, fingers of fire, rays of her sun reaching for everyone who tried to outrun it.

Burn you motherfuckers, just fucking burn. Little pissants were running. Scattering like cockroaches.

'Kira. Stop.'

A hand pressed down on her metal arm, and the sunlight extinguished. The last licks of it played against Azrael's metal cheek. Kira's breath hitched, and her fingers curled into tight fists. Rossiter lay at her feet. Perfectly still. Weylen knelt beside him, and Vail told her all she needed to know through Weylen's anguished eyes. But there was nothing. No stomach roil, no lump in her throat. No tsunami of hellish grief. Absolutely nothing, save for certainty of what she would do next.

'I need to go now, Vail.'

Vail-Weylen gave her a grim nod. 'I know. I'll find you.'

Kira took one last look at Rossiter. Storing up the memory. Putting it in a little corner where it could fester with all the other shitty recalls. Fuel for the fire.

'Get me down there, Az.'

There was only one thing left they could take from her. And the fucking sky would fall before she'd let them destroy Blake, too.

Blake - 82

Blake registered the woman's words – her name was Nina, handmaiden of a goddess, and a friend of Kira's – but Blake couldn't find any words in return. The chaos seemed to hold its breath. Or perhaps that was just Blake herself. She traced a path from the woman's feet: black high-heeled leather boots, polished to within an inch of their life; a tattered, crocheted top that barely concealed the lace of a bra beneath, and sequins that glinted as she breathed, generous breasts pushing at the material. Nina, Ninshadur, whoever she was, was ludicrously out of place in the surroundings, but Blake could not drag her eyes away from her. She touched a hand to her own intensely knotted hair, dropping her arm as she caught sight of the opening in her palm, and its odour touched at her nostrils. Blake was a foul, deconstructed version of herself, barefoot and clothing in tatters. She'd *become* the void that tormented her. But this woman . . . she was a blazing sun. The urge to touch her, stirred a twist of muscle deep in Blake's core.

Blake shook herself. What in god's name was wrong with her?

God's name? The gods have no time for one who denies their existence.

'Blake, I need you to pay attention,' Nina said. 'I apologise, being this close to the Waters, my talents are rather amplified. I'm afraid you will be finding me quite irresistible right now. Pliable to my every word. Putty in my hands, as they say. Though you are much more attractive than putty, I have to say.' Nina laughed with throaty gusto, but she was distracted, her eyes darting between the gallu and Blake.

Blake glared at her, failing to find the situation remotely amusing. 'Yes . . . I mean . . . no.' As if she were not trembling hard enough already. 'Where is my sister?'

'She's alive and inside the Facility, that much we know. But she is taking her sweet time. She needs to be here now, with her pretty little angel.' Nina tossed her hair over her shoulder, sending another glance towards the centre of the chamber.

'Here? No, she can't be here.' Blake slumped against the rock. Shudders still ran through the chamber, though shallower than before.

'Actually, Blake, it is you who is in the wrong place. Kira is right where she must be, but she will falter if she knows you remain here. My, friends, will take you to safety. But you must go, now.'

Her *friends* didn't appear to be capable of more than staring with slack jaws at Nina. Boyd had actual dribble at one corner of his mouth.

'No. I can fix this.' Blake gestured to the Starpoints and found herself desperate to make Nina understand. 'These are explosives. I can blow up the Facility. Destroy everything.' She pressed bloodied fingers to her mouth, as though that might stop the nonsensical desire to impress Nina. Putty in her hands.

'Fix this? With some little bombs?' Nina's smile was gentle, but her eyes danced with amusement. 'Oh sweetie. Good try, but no prizes for you. It will take a bit more than a few tonnes of rock to break my mistress's connection to this world.' She picked up the Starpoints, turning them over in her palm. 'Pretty though.'

'I don't understand, who is your –' Blake squinted, peering past Nina. The shadow she had spotted earlier, running ahead of Parator and Seder, now dashed across the chamber, barely a few feet from where the gallu protected Tamas and the child. Blake stared at Nina, then her eyes returned to the figure.

The very same woman moved in two places at once. Nina, standing right in front of her, also dodged through the stalagmites that provided a natural obstacle course across the chamber floor. Parator and Seder were in pursuit, releasing round after round of fire that created dust and debris but never managed to hit the target. Nina ran with a sway of hips that eased her around the stalagmites gracefully. Waves of hair flew out behind her, and generous breasts rose and fell with each footfall. Blake glanced away, appalled at where her mind had chosen to rest its attention.

'It is a diversion.' Nina waved off the show behind her and slid the Starpoints into a tight-pressed hip pocket. 'Just in case I'd lost my touch and wasn't concealing my presence here quite as cleverly as I intended.' Her perfect smile flashed, and she clapped her hands. 'I know Inanna is terribly annoyed right now about being trapped inside that wrinkled bundle of unintelligible flesh, but I have to say, it's good to be back. Even if it's only temporary.'

Blake waded through the information overload and came out with just one concrete kernel of understanding. 'Holograms. Those other versions of you.'

Nina shrugged. 'Sure. We'll go with that. You're the smart one, or so your sister says. I have my own opinion, which I'll reserve for now.'

Blake was aware the woman's comment should have irritated her, but the annoyance wouldn't quite stick. 'Did you . . . did you make Perry appear? Was he a hologram too?'

'Perry? Kira's friend? You've seen him?' A tilt of a slender neck, hair brushing across the swell of breasts. Blake chewed at her lip and glanced away. In reality, she had no idea who this woman was. Blake should keep her mouth shut.

And you should not have let her steal your pretty pellets. Does she not know who you are, destroyer of worlds?

'Yes. Perry was right here.' The words took on lives of their own, jumping off her dry tongue. Anything to stifle the viper. 'I've been seeing him for a while now. He appeared, just a moment ago, told me Kira was here, at the Facility.'

That seemed to interest Nina, her almond eyes widening. Rendering them no less transfixing. 'Truly, you could see him? And just now? My, my, the boy survived the incident with the Lucentshield, and Blake is seeing spirits. Enthralling. I have to say, you Beckworth girls are quite the revelation.'

'But he's dead. I've seen his body.' Blake didn't fight the cascade of desperate words. 'He is brain dead, on level three —'

Right where you put him. Threw the boy into the pit, didn't you?

'No!' Blake banged her knuckles against her forehead. 'No, I didn't.'

'Enough of that, Blake.' Nina dropped to her knees in a sweep of impossibly sweet fragrance. She took hold of Blake's wrists, turning the one that held the splinter. 'Ah, now I see some of your problem. Ereshkigal always did love to impale things. Did it to her own sister once, strung up Inanna on hooks in her throne room. All over a terrible misunderstanding that I had to try to sort out. But the gods love nothing more than holding a grudge. And so, here we are. Now, let's get rid of that, shall we? This will sting a little, but I don't have time for subtlety. I'm expecting a couple of deliveries, very soon. And I need you out of the way.' Blake leaned back, but the cavern wall stopped her from putting any decent distance between her and the woman.

'Get away from me.'

'What, you'd rather have that damn splinter embedded in you? Do you not value your sanity? How you are still able to function at all, I have no idea,' Nina said. 'Come now. I'm sure you're not half as frigid as Kira liked to imply.'

'She did not –'

Nina's hand slipped around the curve of Blake's neck and pulled their faces close. Close enough for lips to touch. Blake managed a startled cry, but the sound sank into the warm, damp folds of the mouth pressed against hers. The cry dwindled into a sigh. And all the pained atoms in Blake's body relaxed. A coolness spilled into the heat, and lungs filled. She did not so much lean as collapse into the embrace, her body no longer capable of holding itself upright. And Nina was every bit as soft as she appeared. Blake's groan mortified her. But she pressed harder against the mouth that worked against her own, filling her with a strange, blissful release. If this was what Kira found as she moved from partner to partner, then perhaps Blake should not have discounted sex so readily. The years since anything, anyone, had moved this way against her were too numerous to count.

'Rather hungry, aren't we?' Nina mumbled against her mouth, her tongue diving deeper.

Blake dove with her. Her shortness of breath was no longer brought on by the bite of infection or addiction, her heart rate not sped up to accommodate fear. All of that was removed, stripped back to leave Blake Beckworth – a human no different to any other – her body alive and burning in places she'd long ignored.

'Here we go,' Nina whispered.

The wave crashed down, drenching Blake's body, making her nerves dance and buck and writhe beneath her skin. The orgasm lifted her way up high, out of this cave. Out of this place entirely.

And the agony rushed in behind it, swallowing it whole.

You deserve this, the viper bit into her. *And more.*

The scream that left Blake's lips was a hybrid of ecstasy and anguish, quickly stifled by a hand over her mouth.

'I'm sorry,' Nina whispered against her ear. 'I'd hoped to remove all pain, but the goddess buried it deep. How long has that been in your body?' She uncovered Blake's mouth.

'A few days . . .' Hours? Forever? The time spent chained to the base of the tree in the shrine might have been long lifetimes ago.

'And you're still standing,' Nina said, 'with sanity relatively intact? Remarkable. This is quite a substantial serving of toxin. And it had run deep. You must have pissed off Her Royal Highness greatly.'

Nina brushed her fingers over the skin on Blake's wrist that only a moment before had been furiously red, bulging with the swell of the splinter beneath it. Not anymore. The puncture was still visible, but all the redness was gone. Along with the splinter itself. And the indomitable ache. But it had no dislodged her venomous passenger.

Gone. As you should be. Out of the way.

The splinter sat in Nina's hand, pinched between long ruby-red fingernails. The sliver of wood was longer than Blake had imagined, at least the length of Nina's index finger, but no thicker than the needle that had been used to sew up Blake's palm. A palm whose heat did not burn quite so painfully.

'Keep it.' Nina offered the sliver to Blake. ' A weapon that may prove handy, when you are removing yourself from this place. Stick this in any human, and well, you understand how that feels. Or it's a souvenir if you manage to get out of here unhindered.'

Blake hesitated, still reeling. Nina sighed and tucked the splinter into the shallow pocket on Blake's tattered blouse, before rising to her feet. She turned to the medic who had remained barely a step away the entire time. When Nina touched her shoulder, Zara moved even closer, eyes bright.

'Yes, Nina?' Longing filled the lavender-framed face. 'What can I do for you?'

'Zara, we need to get Blake to safety, there is nothing else more important in your world.' She ran a finger over the woman's cheek and down the side of her neck, reaching the strap attached to the firearm Zara bore, a semi-automatic normally in the possession of the guards. Zara gave her an overly enthusiastic nod, and Nina's attention shifted to Boyd. 'No one stops you. No one gets in your way. Are we clear?' Nina's hand went much lower on the bearded man. Down below his thick waist. Far too close to Blake's eye level.

'I'm not going.' Blake used the bloodstained rock to lever herself up, and Zara rushed in to assist her. 'Leave me alone, I'm not going anywhere.' But perhaps she could have if she'd truly wanted to. Movement was easier, less bone-jarring, and though her body still shook and her heart raced, strength existed where there had been none before. 'I can help.'

Nina turned on her, the deep brown in her eyes lifting to an intense amber. The handmaiden didn't approve of her putty resisting her. 'Help by leaving. And that is not a request. Boyd, get her out of here.'

The man jumped to do her bidding, draping Blake's arm over his shoulders, grip tight around her wrist. She dragged the top of her feet against the ground, seeking to find a delay, no matter how infinitesimal, but only managing to add fresh grazes to her bare feet and tug at the gash on her thigh.

'No. Nina, don't do this.' Blake fought off Zara's attempts to take hold of her other arm. 'Please, let me stay. I need to be here for Kira.'

No one wants you here. Get out of the way. They see you now. They see how you destroy. Blake bit down on the tip of her tongue. Pressed the snake back into its pit.

'Damn it, just do as I'm telling you.' Nina's frustration set off colour in her cheeks. 'You're not helping, you are hindering. Kira doesn't need you here, Blake. But I need her. We all do.'

Blake shrank back against Boyd, trying to find a way out from beneath Nina's flinty glare. No one wants you here. Just as the viper had told her.

The air in the cell stirred, as though the air-con had suddenly burst to life with a surge of heat. But the blast came from directly above, where no vent existed. And Nina's hair did not shift from where it hung in graceful waves around her face. The woman's expression shifted, though. Her frown vanished. She touched a hand to her belly, and a curse left her lips.

'What was that?' Blake said. 'What's happening?'

Because something was. The air deadened, thick humidity sweeping down over the cell with all the press of a storm front. Out in the main chamber, the gallu were on the move. Blake couldn't catch a glimpse of Tamas as they moved in tight formation, guiding he and the dead child towards the fire-gutted shell of Tech Room Two.

'Too soon, too soon.' Nina pulled at her neckline, her smooth demeanour ruffled. 'If the Four remove Inanna from this place, things will get terribly ugly. Has she no concept of the element of surprise? Kira has revealed herself too soon.'

With a surprising amount of strength, Nina shoved Blake towards the cell door.

'Revealed herself?' Blake gripped the door way with her uninjured hand, all at once dizzy again. 'What are you talking about? Where is she?'

Blake's gaze darted, frantic as a moth around a flame. Seeking some hint of her sister in the chamber.

'Oh for goodness sake,' Nina shoved her again. 'Why will you not just follow my direction mindlessly like these other two? You are quite frustrating, Blake Beckworth. Go, go now. They are coming for you—'

Blake frowned. 'I thought you had hidden us—'

'Hidden myself, I can't do everything for everybody,' Nina snapped. 'If you wish to help your sister, remove yourself from here. Now, I'll ask nicely – move.'

A dozen thoughts duelled with one another in Blake's head. Aching head. She needed more time. Time to think straight. Time to decide if this stranger, with all her confusing words and directives, even stood before her at all. Or whether Blake had simply, completely, lost her mind. She dug her fingers into her palm. The agony was real enough.

And the woman had not wavered or vanished into thin air.

What was also apparently real, was Gren. Headed straight for her. The Syrana raced across the chamber floor. A pack of grimalkin at his heels, leading the robots through the maze of stalagmites.

'Blake, go.' Nina shouted, heeding her own advice. Disappearing in a few long strides.

You are a hindrance. The hiss found every crack and crevice in Blake's mind and cemented itself in each. *No one wants you here.*

She let go of the door frame, and didn't protest when Boyd dragged her roughly from the cell.

Kira - 83

Kira sprinted at the gutted elevator shaft and jumped. She hung in the air for a fraction of a second, more than enough time for Azrael. They connected in mid-air, falling into one another as if they'd been practising this move a thousand times. His arms scooped beneath her, cradling her against his chest. Wings surrounded her in a metal blanket, the tips spearing down into the pick-up-sticks assortment of iron rods, torn steel, and fractured concrete. They dropped into the pit like a wrecking ball, the blades of Az's wings making light of anything the tunnel put in their way. The squeal of metal through metal, metal through rock, metal through whatever the hell went into an elevator shaft was fucking horrendous. Kira's ears would ring for days. Or maybe just a few more seconds. Before they were julienned and spat out at the other end, all prepped for one hell of a shitty salad.

Kira pressed her cheek against Az's chest, her skin meeting a patch of faux skin that still hung on to his metal shell for dear life. She cradled her arms against her own chest, hands bunched under her chin. No more rays of sunshine, burning bright. The armadillo was back to its dull old self. So the Maiden needed good old rage to fire this thing off, huh?

You've been chosen, and the Maiden has chosen well. That's what Leona had said. But not because Kira had guts of steel – also what Leona had said – the tan queen was dead wrong about that. Her guts weren't steel. They were molten fucking lava. And *that's* why the Maiden had chosen her. Kira was bubbling away with enough anger and self-loathing to fuel a nuclear power plant.

Mix in a few more losses – Perry, Eron, Rossiter – and hey, presto. Handmaiden of the apocalypse.

Jesus, Blake had better be alive. 'Cause the world was so fucked if that stupid cow had let herself get killed. Kira groaned, way too low to make it above the freight-train-through-scrapyard cacophony, but Az's hold tightened, and she felt a touch to her head. Considering where his hands were, she could only assume he had just kissed her. But even their usual touchy-feely thing wasn't doing it for her right now.

They continued their jerky, jolting way down. Ground zero couldn't be too far off. Not the way they were travelling, like a meteorite through the centre of the Earth. Two floors down, that's what the big man had told them. Right before he left her, too. Kira's molten lava insides bubbled and popped.

Az jerked hard right, their fall suffering a momentary adjustment that would have given any normal-boned person whiplash. Kira's lucky day. No one normal for miles.

We must focus on the Four. Ninshadur will handle the child.

There he was, like a whisper at the back of her head. Az's voice better than any meditation guide she'd ever . . . wait . . . a child?

Are you fucking kidding me? They've got a kid down there?

Dumuzi's soul was located in infancy. A newborn —

Stop. Just. No. When was someone going to tell me this?

Why does it matter?

Her thoughts tripped and fell into a vat of 'well you got me there.' *So, the goddess of war is in a baby. She's a nappy-crapper now?*

Inanna must be held in the same body that Dumuzi is removed from. A soul for a soul.

Inanna the banana is a fucking nappy-crapper. Az, let me have this one tiny moment, okay.

Light seeped through the slivers between metal wing blades.

'Hold on, Kira.'

As if she would have done anything else. As if she had a choice about anything at all. Azrael balled himself up, then there was a rumble and more screeching before Azrael's feet slammed into the ground. Kira's head banged against his chest, and she blinked madly, coughing dust. Az drove forward and they were lifting off again. His wings extended, dragging at the air as he lifted them high. No prizes for guessing they had been spotted; that tumble down the shaft could have been heard on the moon. Gunfire erupted around them, an off-note herald of their arrival.

'Hold fast to my underbelly. It will allow me to utilise my hands.'

'Don't bloody drop me.'

'I would never drop you.'

He kept his arm beneath her shoulders but let her legs go.

'Fuck, this feels like dropping.' Kira clawed at his shoulders, legs kicking wildly.

'I said I would never drop you.'

His hand planted against her butt. Kira blew out her cheeks, readying to puff and strain to lift her legs. But they rose up as though she were made of carbon, and not half-Telteriun. She looped her limbs around Az's waist, like they were an act in a Cirque Du Soleil show. A water show apparently, the jean material on her right leg felt soaked through, clinging hard to her body. Weird. But hardly the time for a wardrobe check. And it could be sweat, because hot fucking damn it was toasty in here.

They'd flown into a sauna. An emerald sauna. The Tier at the centre of the chamber put on a light show that Disney would have been proud of. Kira pressed in tightly against Az. Probably the adrenaline but this hanging thing was easier than she'd expected. Kira tilted her head to try to get a glimpse of something other than Az's armpit. Stalactites. Every-fucking-where. Jesus. Had *Caves-are-us* had a sale on dangly bits? Handy as hell, though. Made great targets for a hell of a lot of the bullets aimed their way.

Several rat-tat-tatted themselves into a bulbous length of rock just off to their left. Azrael manoeuvred a stomach-shifting barrel roll, wings slicing through a cluster of protruding mineral deposits.

'Jesus, Az!' Kira cried.

Dazzling, all-too-familiar pulses of sapphire-blue light replaced the emerald sheen of the place, blowing holes in the roof of the chamber no more than a metre away. Az went into another body roll. And as they spun, Kira was right back there – in the park, on her knees beside the fountain, watching those blue pulses race towards her, then sitting in the middle of an exploding star as the armadillo – the Maiden – got in on the game. And destroyed her universe.

Oh crap. Bad time for flashbacks. Really, really shitty. Kira fought to sledgehammer it back to the cesspool it came from. She tensed. What the hell was she doing, just hanging, literally the useless tit on a bull that everyone talked about? But the fact was, she was far from useless. Or a tit.

Az, get us near whoever is firing that fucking E.T. bow.

I don't understand –

Let them fire at me.

That is –

Just let them aim at me, don't shield me. I can—

Oh fuck it. The chat was taking way too long. Kira let go, arms and legs spreading, fingers loosening from where they dug into Az's shoulders.

'Kira!'

Az lunged for her, and she flipped. A human cannonball-slash-pancake, realising pretty quickly that the chamber was not nearly as high as she'd been hoping for. The ground was coming up to say hello way too fast. But so were the blue pulses. One big mother headed right for her.

'Shit!' Kira's scream rose falsetto high as she shielded her face with her arm.

The pulse collided with her limb, the shock of it like the Hulk himself had just landed a punch. A blinding, violent starburst of light followed; sapphire and pure goddamn beautiful white. The force sent her tumbling head over heels with no clue of what was up or down or sideways. 'Fuuuuck!'

Her trajectory came to a short, sharp stop. Upside down. The world all splotchy, her vision hazy from the brightness. Az's arm was wrapped firmly around her waist, pressing into a bladder that probably should have been emptied before they tried to save the world. But Az didn't stop to let her get to her feet. He rose up and over a metal jungle gym, twisted panels of yellow mixed in with cables and chunks of solid silver. She recognised the cranes that had been set up in the chamber when Blake had dragged her down here to check out Az. They'd seen better days. Az and the cranes.

As Azrael dropped them in behind the makeshift barrier, Kira blinked madly. Trying to make out the figure on the far side of the chamber.

'Blake. That's Blake.' She wriggled, caught Az in the head with her flailing legs, and slapped at his arm. 'Let me down, Az.' She was still gazing on a world full of shadows and glare, but she would have recognised that outline if her irises were melting.

Az obeyed orders this time, and her feet landed in a tangle of wires. Kira crouched there, waiting for the mother of all head spins to pass. She would have high-fived Ereshkigal Herself in that moment. Blake was alive.

'I saw her, Az. I saw Blake.' Her sister hadn't gone and died on her. This was the best fucking day ever. But she hadn't been alone. Two people either side of her. Were they hurting her? Christ, maybe Kira had done that herself? Too busy feeling like hot-shit setting off her little light show, she didn't consider who might get caught in the crossfire. Kira shook off the thought. Blake was alive.

All that was important. Kira bent her leg, bracing to stand. 'Oh, crap.'

Her jeans weren't soaked through, like she'd thought earlier. The *material* wasn't clinging to her skin. That would have been way too simple. A tear in her jeans over her right knee revealed the armadillo's latest extension. Metal now all the way down her right leg. Jesus Christ, where else had this thing gone? She pressed her hand to her crotch. No sign of metal pussy. And mild relief to know shitting herself was still an option, too. A quick squeeze of the butthole passed on that good news. Kira froze, staring at the hand resting on her crotch. The hand she had raised against the zuary pulse. Her flesh hand. *Former* flesh hand.

'Kira, are you hurt?' Azrael said.

She pushed up her sleeve. Metal from shoulder to the first row of knuckles. Kira wiggled her fingers. 'At least I can still bite my nails, right?'

Remember to breathe, K. Oxygen, always good. Passing out, very bad. She was motivational speaking the hell out of herself, but the panic sneaked its way in around the edges. A metal-munching termite.

Az laid his wings low. 'Kira, that act you just performed was remarkably foolish.'

'Yeah, well it worked. Didn't it?' Did it?

Az's lip lifted, quite the horrendous sight when only half of it was still fleshy. 'Well . . . yes . . .the impact caused considerable

brightness. There is confusion as to our whereabouts. But you must
_'

'Then mission accomplished. What now?' Before the termites got too hungry. 'I need to get Blake out of here.'

'You know as well as I that there is neither time nor necessity for such a move. Your sister will have to fend for herself.'

This sergeant-major Az was kind of an asshole. He didn't use a glowing arm to help her through her darkness, just a couple of slaps to the face.

The Four hold the child in their midst, Kira. He was a lot gentler in her head, though. *They must be separated from Inanna. The handmaiden does what she can —*

'Nina? She made it?' That backed the termites off a fraction. 'Where is she?'

His answer caught her off guard. Az shoved her, hard enough to send her toppling onto her side. His wings flowed from his back, Telteriun extending in elegant curves. And he lifted off.

'Az, what are you doing?'

He got no more than a metre or so off the ground before a mass cannonballed into his side. Limbs wrapping around him. A new set of wings cutting through the air.

One of Tamas's angels had broken rank.

Tamas - 84

Tamas watched from within his protective circle. His indignation muted and distant, his hand on the blade still embedded in the child—the goddess's—chest. Seder's zaury sent a shot, straight and true, at the girl falling from Enkidu's arms. Kira. So insufferably alive. And here.

Somewhere within, Tamas raged at her presence. The insult that was her very existence. But his human emotions were faint and so very far away. The blue pulse found its target. One that the power of the Syranian weapon should have annihilated with ease, but the assault was repulsed by a radiant energy burst. A glare so intense Tamas was forced to avert his gaze. By the time he could return his focus to the scene, eyes watering, both Azrael and the girl were gone. Seder had sustained a significant injury to his left shoulder but remained on his feet.

Annoyance niggled at Tamas, far off in the distance. A pesky echo of emotion that was at once familiar, and foreign. Barely able to penetrate into his altered world.

He jerked his head at Diresh.

'End this. Find Enkidu, bring them both down.'

Her heeding of his command was instant, and she lifted off before he'd finished speaking. Agar's eyes narrowed, displeasure in the twist of his mouth. Likely, he wanted to finish what he had started back when Eron's poor mastery of the mea stone had almost seen Enkidu extinguished prematurely from this world. But Agar would not dare defy Tamas. Certainly not now. Not as the blood of the great sages boiled within him. Tamas met the sharp edges of Agar's glare, holding it. Unblinking. His reward, the lowering of the gallu's head in deference.

'Well done.' Tamas smirked.

Satisfied that Diresh had things in hand, Tamas returned his attention to what was of true importance. The weight in his arms. He pulled the claw-blade from the infant's chest. There had been no need to leave it in place as long as he had, but he drew a certain satisfaction from seeing the icy weapon protrude from the tiny ribcage. Not a drop of blood spilled from the child. Not when he'd impaled it, and not now. Tamas slipped the blade into his trouser pocket, its press cold against his buttock. The child's wound had sealed before he was done, locking the new inhabitant within Her mortal coil.

The goddess of war lay in his arms, nose wet with snot and cheeks drenched with the tears that fell unceasingly. Inanna didn't make a sound. Not a gurgle or a hiccup. She stared up at him with eyes like two pieces of burning coal. Were Tamas anyone else, terror would have gouged a place inside him. But Ereshkigal's pleasure ran through him, unlocking the codes within his blood and purifying what time had tainted. The Abgal, the great sage Utuabzu, was rebirthing within him. Tamas's veins bristled with the goddess's reward. Once more, an Abgal would stand at a god's side.

Tamas watched Inanna from his safe place. Protected. Assured. Indifferent.

For those merely human, Inanna's stare would reach into their hearts, and wrap cold fingers around it.

She was ferocity and rampage and wrath. She was the bloodlust that sent men into battle. She was the strife that triggered all conflict.

And She was here.

In his possession. At his mercy. Despite the foolish, ridiculous attempts of Enkidu and his whore to make it otherwise.

Tamas smiled and pinched a damp cheek, squeezing skin between fingers until, finally, the baby's lip trembled. It began to cry.

With the hoarse sound ringing in his ears, Tamas fixed his gaze on the clamour beyond the ring of gallu and Syranians that surrounded him. Diresh had pinned Azrael to the roof of the chamber, and let loose with a flurry of maddened punches as she sought to claw her way into his shell. Ereshkigal would have Her precious Enkidu soon. Tamas would bring his goddess *everything* She sought.

Whatever Kira and Enkidu thought they might do here – with their parlour trick illusions darting about the chamber, trying for some pathetic distraction before their arrival – it was far too late. And they were far too few. Even if Kira had survived the onslaught from Seder, she would not survive what was to come.

Tamas thrust the child into Agar's arms. The imposing creature locked hungry eyes on the child. On the goddess. Perhaps he was indeed starving, after time spent in the mortal world, confined and controlled. But it would be over soon. Tamas knelt, and raised his hands, palms splayed to the high dome of solid rock above. And the words tumbled from him. Ancient, cumbersome, guttural sounds that had lain dormant for generations, passed on from descendant to descendant in silence. Until now.

With each syllable, the glow of the Tier heightened, peaks forming on the water as though a sea breeze whipped at the surface. The first hint of hairline fractures appeared in the rock above him, his vision sharp as any bird of prey. These new fractures were not born from the arrival of Inanna, when the quake had rocked the entire Facility. These fractures were Tamas's own making.

His tongue caressed each word that formed upon it, loosening it into the air in the gentlest of whispers. The veins along his arms swelled, pushing against the skin that held them bound. Laughter mixed with the words, Tamas's delight welling up and flowing with his commands. Shifting to rest on his heels, the tip of the claw-blade dug into his backside, but there could be no stopping what had been started. He edged his butt against his heel, seeking to nudge the blade into a more comfortable position, mildly irritated by the interruption. A twist and wiggle and the claw dropped from his pocket finding the concrete. Fine. So long as it didn't plague him. Tamas returned his full focus to the spiderweb of fractures spreading across the cavern roof.

Just as his own power had hibernated, so too had that of the creatures who had served the Abgul thousands of years ago. Long buried deep within the Earth, entombed until they could be awakened by the call of a new, great sage.

Whatever force attempted to interfere here, whether it be the Maiden the witch spoke of or Enkidu seeking revenge, it would be destroyed. And Kira Beckworth would die as she should have, years ago.

Kira - 85

Kira scrambled to her feet, neck craned to follow Az's flight path. The gallu that had bomb-dived him was like a rampaging Snow White, skin that actually *was* as white as snow, black hair cropped short against the head. A build almost as solid as the heavy-ass Kira'd seen with Eron. Az pushed his attacker out to arm's length, and Kira spotted a swell beneath the tight black clothing at Snow White's chest. Blake had made a girl monster. And this chick was not happy to see Az. The pair of them danced one hell of a violent dance, high up towards the chamber roof, dicing the stalactites as they went.

The two opponents couldn't been more contrasted. Az all pretty, pretty ballerina, to Snow White's bull in a china shop. Wingtips thrust in hypnotic, sweeping movements. And in the wing design lay the starkest contrast of all; Az had slender ribbons of metal, while Snowy had tubular, writhing tentacles. Both the styles though made god-awful sounds on contact. Like tin cans going through a woodchipper.

Something struck Kira's shoulder, pinging against the metal. She dove back down behind the collapsed cranes, fingers flying to the spot and finding a fresh hole in one of the last unscathed sections of her pyjama top. The armadillo suffered only the barest of dents in its surface. Jesus Christ. Bulletproof. Very good to know – because Kira's shooter wasn't done yet. Another three sharp raps came, two against her back, one grazing her arm. Kira grabbed a broken slab of concrete, lifting it as if it were polystyrene. Greta's caustic but on-point suggestion came to mind – *don't let them shoot you in the head*. Girl should be a life coach. And Kira should have used more deodorant this morning. She may be two-thirds metal, but she was sweating up a storm and had the stink to prove it.

She huddled under her chunky shield, searching for the person trying to put holes in her. 'Son of a bitch.

That Kira should run was a no-brainer. Basic survival 101. But where? She laid eyes on her shooter. Some weedy bastard coming at her from the back of the chamber. Human. Face covered in a balaclava. Gun raised, shouting at her to stay where she was. What a dick.

Kira bolted; she locked in on a pile of rubble about twenty metres away and ran her nonbeating heart out, seriously missing the wild man wings. A shape swooped down on her, and for a split second she thought the wings had returned. They had. Kind of. But Az's unwanted guest hadn't left the party yet. Overhead, two intertwined bodies thundered through a pocket of stalactites. Chunks of debris rained down. Big, big chunks.

'Jesus.' Kira threw herself to one side, narrowly missing becoming a Kira kebab. Her shooter wasn't so lucky. He made it onto the kebab menu.

'Get up, Kira. They must not leave the chamber.'

Kira blinked, sweat sending a salty sting into her eyeballs. Seeing double. Hell, triple. 'Nina?'

She'd been up close and personal with that body too many times not to know it instantly. But which body exactly had she been with? The one standing just to her right, or one of the three other Ninas who dashed about the chamber, manic as a crowd at the Boxing Day sales, guards in tow.

'They must not leave,' possibly-real Nina declared. 'Get the child to me. I am Inanna's Messenger. Only a Messenger can return her to her rightful realm. We have to get to the child.'

Nina moved away – drifting through the pile of rubble that Kira had been headed for. Definitely-not-real Nina. 'Wait. No dramatic exits, for crying out loud. Don't just leave me here.' She hunched down, making her way around the pile until she had line of sight across the chamber. The rest of Blake's merry band of demon-carrying metal men formed a pack around a solitary figure. Captain Asshat Nex and the Syranians flanked them, Cym included. That weird moment up on ground level came back to bug her. Cym sure as hell didn't seem to be in the turn-a-blind-eye mode now, though, brandishing a bow along with the rest of his space brothers. Kira would bet one of the Facility's ridiculous military contracts that the guy at the heart of this congregation, was Tamas.

With the kid.

So there it was. Ground zero. Target locked and loaded. She shook her hands. 'Come on, Mrs Maiden. Tell me what to do here. Do I go?' The kid-must-not-leave advice was all well and good from Nina, but what the fuck did it mean for Kira? Go in guns – arms – blazing? There was a shit load of firepower and supernatural Red Bull in that group. Did the Maiden want Kira to just kamikaze the whole thing? 'Come on, come on. Someone help me out here.'

Banging metal palms together, she waited on a sign. There had to be a sign. An almighty shudder ran through the chamber, and the water in the Tier brightened from dull forest green to an intense emerald. Something the Wizard of Oz would jizz over. Kira's rubble pile shook, losing height as the base widened with the vibrations. The world coming down on top of her, was not quite the sign she'd been searching for.

A squad of grimalkin drew Kira's gaze, a mini herd streaming out from a storage tunnel almost directly across the chamber from where she huddled. The headless cats skirted around the Tier, turning green as the light caught them. They moved into formation behind one of the aliens, Gren. He broke into a run – his light-as-air movement reminding her far too much of Eron – headed towards the main entrance. Gren was shouting something, but the calamity of Az and the other angel overhead wiped his words out of existence. She didn't need them anyway.

'No,' Kira said. 'No, no, no.'

Those people she'd seen flanking Blake, weren't trying to hurt her. They were doing what Kira should be doing. Getting Blake out of here. Rushing her so fast her feet dragged along the ground. But it must have been as clear to them as it was to Kira that they had no chance of reaching the exit before the grimalkin and Gren would reach them. The guy on Blake's left shoved her, pushing her onto the ground, before he and his partner, a short woman whose purple hijab was the only other spot of colour in the chamber aside from the water, turned round and lifted handguns.

Bad move. Gren was a shoot first-questions later kind of guy.

'Jesus, no.' Kira hadn't moved an inch before the pair was dropping dead to the ground. 'Oh god, Blake.'

But her sister was untouched. She got to her feet as unsteadily as Kira in a club at four in the morning, but still got to her goddamn feet. Kira took a shuddering breath. All the fucking superpower in the world and it wouldn't have been enough to help those poor bastards. To save Blake. Death was blindingly fast.

'Surrender, Kira.' Captain Nex's order lifted up and over the chaos. It rang clear and crystal across the chamber. 'Or I will kill her. It is that simple.'

Too busy making sure Blake didn't have holes in her, Kira had failed to notice the Captain of the Dickwads move from his protective duty at Tamas's side, and make his way to where Gren pointed alien weaponry at her sister. Kira could feel the bastard's smirk of satisfaction like a rash against her skin. Only saving grace of the moment was that he clearly didn't know where she was. Sending out his ultimatum to various sections of the chamber, looking up towards the roof like she was dangling there, a metal chandelier.

Kira, do not yield.

Az's thought was faint, strained. She was conscious he was overhead, still thrashing it out with his metal date, but she'd be damned if she'd let her eyes move from Blake. Her fingers curled into fists. Blake might look as if someone had put her through a wind tunnel and a meat grinder at the same time, but she was eyeballing the captain like a pro. Chin up, chest puffed. Never, ever looked so magnificent. The grimalkin settled into brace mode. Panels on their haunches slid open, and something that looked a lot like a stainless-steel umbrella lifted from each of the machines, levelling sights at her sister.

'Kira,' Blake shouted. 'Don't do it. Let me go.'

For fuck's sake. Everyone needed to stop telling Kira what to do. When did she get to have a single iota of choice in any of this shit? Blake was certified batshit if she thought Kira would just stand here and watch them blast a hole in her, too. Never going to fucking happen.

Blake's death stare shifted and dropped from her face entirely. All at once, the heat that had been burning Kira up since they'd dropped into the place sank beneath a cold wave.

'No,' Kira whispered. 'Don't you dare.'

Kira knew that look. That grim determination Blake plastered all over her mug when she got set on an idea.

'I'm sorry, K. I'm so sorry. For everything.' Blake raised her hand. A gun clasped between her fingers. And pressed the nozzle against her temple.

A vacuum sucked every drop of air and sound from Kira's world. She was moving, knew that she was, but the pounding of her feet on the ground didn't reach her. Nor did the scream that was scraping the insides of her throat away. Or the thunderous crash that must have come when Azrael and Diresh slammed into the ground, a fireball of golden energy landing barely a few feet in front of her. Cutting her off from Blake.

Kira didn't falter. Didn't miss a step. She was not losing this race. Blake wouldn't suffer because of her. Not again. Not a-fucking-gain. Maiden could wait. So could the world.

Get there.

Get there.

Kira launched herself over the glow of Az and Diresh. One of them was spilling way too much of that golden mojo. But that would have to wait. Everything would. Her feet left the ground, and the armadillo brightened. She soared – fucking soared – over the gallu death match. Trying to outrun death.

Blake - 86

Blake had handled a gun only twice in her life, and both times had been at Rossiter's insistence. He'd wanted her to learn to protect herself. The lessons had lasted all of five minutes, Blake unwilling to hold the weapon any longer than that. The feel of the metal against her skin had made her uneasy back then, even with an unloaded gun and an expert by her side. Now, it made her downright ill, and uncertain she wouldn't vomit before she had a chance to pull the trigger. The muzzle knocked against her temple, her hands shaking too violently to hold the damn thing still. She knew better than to pray to any god that Kira might be spared the sight of this. The gods weren't listening.

Remove yourself from here. You heard what the handmaiden said. Remove yourself. How else are you to do that now? End this. Help your sister.

The viper's vitriol had never lacked for truth. It was what caused the words to burn deep and scar themselves into her psyche. Blake *was* a hindrance. An exhausted, desperate hindrance. At the very least, this chosen path would end the viper's flagellation once and for all. Give her reprieve from constant, deepening damnation. The singular world she needed to destroy was her own. Blake held her breath and brought pressure down on the trigger, both her grip and her bowels threatening to loosen.

'Blake, stop!'

The body came at her as the bullet should have, rapid and sure. Cym aimed his weight at her arm, forcing the gun away, and sending them both tumbling into a gasping pile on the debris-strewn floor. Blake landed on her injured leg. Consciousness hung on by a mere thread, blackness stealing most of her vision. Cym's voice rained down on her, but faintly and from far away. He rattled off a Syranian curse that she recognised from the time he'd spent by her side in the tech rooms.

'*Brandis mer*, this is not the way, Blake.'

Cym shifted onto his knees. Unable to even consider moving, Blake lay against the hard, uneven ground. Beyond Cym, something moved down from the heights of the chamber. Blake watched as a wingless angel descended towards them, her body lit with a pale golden glow, her hair a shock of black against a ghostly face.

'Kira.' Shock vapourised the single word as it left Blake's lips.

Her sister's descent slowed. She lifted a hand towards where Captain Nex stood, bewilderment clouding his expression. The Earth must have slowed on its axis and gravity deepened, because the blinding pulse of light that flew from Kira's fingertips did so in slow motion. A ray of pure sunlight made its way across the space between Kira and the captain. Blake watched from her sideways world, shocked into stillness. The ever-present shake beneath her skin, gone. Her heart had ceased to beat. Lungs discontinued their rise and fall, as she followed her sister's path.

Captain Nex did not cower or attempt to defend himself. Either of those would have taken time. And that was one thing he was without. The pulse of sunlight met his chest and crackled the length of his limbs, streaks of lightning that singed his clothing and turned his silver hair to strands of inky black. The captain of the Syranians, the proclaimed Messenger of Lahar, died a very quick and simple death. And his god was nowhere to be seen. Nex dropped to his knees and toppled forward, landing flat on his face with his hands trapped underneath him. He made no attempt to rise, no attempt to do anything at all.

A cry rose higher and higher. Gren, screaming Cym's name. The Syrana medic was on his feet, his back now to Blake. Seeing the same thing she saw. Kira barrelling down on him, arms raised, pristine, white light balled around her hands.

'No.' Blake breathed. Struggling to co-ordinate herself, find a way to rise.

Kira needed to see she was alive. Or Cym was going to die.

But the world was racing too fast. Before Blake could do more than consider moving, energy shot from Kira's fingertips. Gren threw himself in front of Cym, crying out his lover's name. And Blake finally found her own voice.

'Kira, no!'

Her sister's hand jerked, sending the energy skyward, but it was not soon enough for Gren. The radiant light slammed into him, before everything grew too bright for human eyes. Blake curled up in a ball, eyes squeezed tight, as everything in existence was drenched in sunlight. And the sky began to fall. The thump and thud of great, heavy things crashing around her. Shaking the ground with their weight. A body pressed against hers, lying on top of her. Her eyes flew open. The person was too close to see clearly. But Blake didn't need any clarity to recognise her sister.

'Stay down,' Kira shouted, loud enough to make Blake cringe. 'What the fuck were you thinking, Blake?'

The rainfall of debris ceased, and Kira edged back. 'Don't you ever, ever do something so fucking stupid again. You stupid, stupid . . . '

She threw her arms around her, clinging so tightly Blake had to blink against dots of light. The embrace was uncomfortable, painful even, far too tight against a body that felt set to come apart at the seams. But Blake sank into it, willing it to engulf her altogether. She pressed her arms around her sister, and noted the hardness of metal at her back. Body armour. It must be.

'Kira . . .' Her hands traced the solid surface all the way down Kira's spine. And the very faintest of sheens struggled to push through the material of Kira's clothing. 'This is not how any of this should have been.'

'Nope. So let's stay right here.' Kira's breath warmed her ear. 'Pretend we're back in that crappy bedroom, the one with the disgusting orange wallpaper, and the creaky bunk beds.'

Blake abandoned her search and wrapped her arms tighter around Kira's shoulders. Hardness of metal on both sides there too. 'Your bed creaked because you treated it like a trampoline.'

'God, how cool would a trampoline bed be?'

A smile tugged at Blake's mouth, despite all that went on around them. 'It would be extremely cool.'

She'd all but forgotten that draughty two-bedroom apartment they'd shared with their father, Blake approaching her teens and perturbed about sharing with her younger sister. At least, to begin with. Then it had become all but impossible to sleep without drifting off to the sound of Kira's chatter. Which always continued long after their father told them to be quiet.

Blake allowed herself one more moment of the embrace, and let her sister go. Kira sat back, and Blake pushed herself onto her elbows. A short distance away, Cym was on hands and knees alongside Gren. A grimalkin lay not far from his body, legs jerking as it attempted to right itself. The rest of the robots had fared even worse. Only the hint of one or two visible beneath the rubble.

'I thought Cym had…'Kira hesitated. 'I thought you were dead. I couldn't think straight.'

She was not the only one. But for now the viper was silent. Sunk deep, or vanished, impossible to tell.

Cym was urging Gren to get up, to move, to open his eyes, none of which Gren did. Nor would he ever do so again. It did not take a medic to understand the graveness of the injury he'd sustained to his torso. One, Blake noted, her sister kept her eyes averted from.

'I thought you were dead,' Kira whispered again, strain coating each word.

Even if Blake could have found something to say, the opportunity was taken from her. A great rumbling flowed through the chamber. Far more intense than any of the tremors that had proceeded it.

'My god.' Blake ignored all the pain receptors that told her she leaned too heavily on her wounded leg. The Earth was slowly opening. A widening crack parted the chamber roof right over Tamas and his cluster of carapaces. 'What is happening?'

'Oh fuck,' Kira said. 'This just gets better.'

The shower of loosened rocks and dirt that fell over the group did so in the oddest of ways, not raining directly down but edging out almost at right angles and avoiding those standing beneath the enlarging crevice.

'I think the little fucker is tunnelling his way out of here,' Kira said.

'Kira, look out!' Nina appeared out of nowhere, running towards them from the direction of the containment cells, gesturing wildly. 'Behind, turn around, you fool.'

Blake and Kira did so in unison, and Blake's language was as vibrant and crass as her sister's. A creature of liquid rose from the Tier, its shape etched into Blake's mind after what had felt like an eternity beneath its malevolent glare in the shrine. The Precon bounded over the stone edging, the ratlike creature large as a draught horse, far bigger than what Blake had witnessed pacing the Tier earlier. The beast released a sound, a hundred pigs squealing in unison, and all at once Blake shuddered – as though the Waters within her fought to escape what approached.

An arm slipped beneath hers, and she was dragged backwards. Away from her sister. Blake reached for her, missing Kira by the barest of lengths, her fingers clutching at empty air.

'Kira –'

'I told you to leave here!' Nina shouted, her grip around Blake's chest bordered on breathtaking.

'I tried.'

In more ways than one.

The Precon zeroed in on them. The creature left wide puddles of gleaming emerald with each footfall. Nina shepherded Blake out of harm's way while Kira faced the approach. Pacing backward, taking slow, cautious steps. Not attempting to run. Merely bracing for what came at her.

'Kira. No, Kira, move.' Blake attempted to dig her heels in, forgetting entirely that she wore no shoes, and her resistance was short-lived.

'She does what she must. Make it easier for her, Blake. Let her go.'

Let her go? She had refused to do so three years ago, she would not start now. Blake renewed her struggle. Cym remained with Gren, despite Kira's shouts at him to do otherwise. The Syranian clutched his fallen brother – lover – to his chest, but reached for the zuary, straining his body over the distance that kept it just out of reach.

The Precon reared up on its deformed hind legs, the bend differing for each limb, one protruding outward while the other jutted back. It arrowed itself at Kira, who stood, maddeningly still, a dim glow haloing her body.

'Kira!' Blake screamed. Nina dragged them farther away, her strength belying her appearance.

Another shape rose up from behind the debris pile Kira had created, and rocketed towards the Precon. A second beast, an enormous reptile reminiscent of a Komodo dragon. If those dragons grew to rival the size of a lion. Glowing with the same sheen as Kira did, only far, far brighter, the creature threw itself against the Precon's side. The impact lifted the duo up and over the meagre pile of rock. Their rapid descent was headed directly for where Cym still clung to Gren. The creatures barrelled in on them, oblivious to anything, anyone in their path. They clawed at one another with all the ferocity of starved animals over a carcass. The Precon lashed out with a barbed, liquid tail. The lizard dodged, leaving the path clear to where Cym tried to get to his feet. Kira reached him, just before the Precon's strike did. Her shoulder took a glancing blow from the sweeping tail of luminous green liquid, and sparks radiated from the impact point. The momentum forced both Cym and Kira clear of the battle, one that continued without the slightest indication their presence had been noted at all. The lizard—the dragon—clamped wide jaws around the Precon's ratlike head, thrashing back and forth in vicious, jerky movements.

'Where did that come from?' Blake fought to catch her breath. 'The dragon?'

An ally of some kind? Or would the creature simply turn its attention on the rest of them once it was done with the Precon? And done it almost was. The screeches coming from the watery beast reached higher and higher. The Waters dulled, the emerald dipping to a danker shade of mould green. The creature's form bulged then deflated, bulged then deflated, as though the fluid struggled to retain its shape.

Nina's breath came equally as rapid, pushing against Blake's back as the woman held her fast. 'The witches called him Bradley, but their goddess was far closer than they knew. The true name of that being is the Maiden. You are witnessing the fast-tracked ascendance of a god. It should have taken millennia for Her to reach this point, but the Waters have changed everything. She's looking rather good right now, wouldn't you say? Putting on quite the show.'

A show that concluded a moment after Nina finished speaking. The dragon's jaws snapped together, a sound like the crack of thunder. The Precon bulged, expanding until it ruptured, exploding in a fountain of liquid that cascaded down and formed a wave deep enough to sweep over Cym and Kira, who had been able to get far from the maddened action. The dragon creature – a god if Nina was to be believed, and Blake was fast running out of reasoning that would allow otherwise – raised a diamond-shaped head and released a bellow that rippled the surface of the Waters. The glow of the beast lifted in curling tongues from its body. Eyes black as any desert night, focused on the liquid that flowed around its thick legs. Those same jaws that had just destroyed the Precon widened again. And a torrent of light – the shades of ember and flame – were breathed between jagged teeth, spilling across the surface of the Waters. The instant the fire touched the liquid, it was as though it leapt against Blake's skin. She buckled in Nina's grasp, letting loose an anguished cry.

And so the deathbringer shall burn, too.

The viper and the fireball tore through Blake's senses in unison.

The new god takes back what you stole.

She was burning alive, skin flaking from bone. Bone turning to ash, as the Waters that intertwined with her own DNA ignited.

'Blake? Blake, what's wrong?' Nina's words reached her, and each was a red-hot iron against her ears.

'Water.' Blake couldn't be certain the word had reached the air. She sank beneath the flames, seeing through a veil of red, a warmth running from her nostrils.

All at once, her face was covered in liquid. And the flames extinguished. The heat slunk away, far less intense, but a hint of it remaining. The Waters' hum played at her core. Her breath wheezed in her chest, her throat too tight to allow much oxygen to escape or enter. And her eyes slowly found focus. Blake wiped at her face, and her hand came away coated in clear slimy wetness.

She found herself under the watchful gaze of the creature who had just decimated the Precon. Eyes of jet black, set in a head equally as dark and contrasted by the bright orange spotting that marked smooth, scaled skin. It was equally as large in size as it had been when it had battled Lahar's beast but with no hint of the golden light that had enveloped it. In ordinary circumstances, Blake may have been fearful, terrified, most likely, but ordinary had long since disappeared from her world. She raised her chin, meeting the creature with an unblinking stare. A god, the viper had declared.

The beast ran a bulging pink tongue back and forth across smooth lips. The same viscous slime that covered Blake's face, dripped from its wide mouth. She had been slobbered on by a diety.

You carry a burden, Technician. A precious one. The voice was satin and velvet against Blake's own mind, caressing the very corners of it, in stark contrast to the viper's vitriol. *If you survive this, you will be the Waters' last vessel.*

Blake blinked. And the Maiden turned and left her, no explanation, no translation of Her words. A huge bulk, there one moment, gone in the next.

Kira stumbled in her rush to get to Blake's side. Cym was close behind her. Alive, and as close to well as could be expected.

Blake couldn't place it, what was different about her sister. There was the obvious – the presence of metal where Blake had never set it, the light emanating softly from the folds of her clothes – but it was over and above that. A largeness to her presence that had been absent before.

'Are you all right?' Kira demanded.

Blake's pause was infinitesimal. 'Yeah. I'm fine.'

'God, you're a shit liar.'

Blake was saved from having to try to prove Kira wrong by the arrival of Azrael. Touching down alongside the group, several long lengths of metal in his hand. Blake recognised the pieces at once. Impossible to forget after the hours she'd spent labouring over them. The wings she had designed for the Four.

Az landed right alongside her, swaying as he settled his feet on the ground. Kira frowned. He'd looked better. Way, way better. But he'd done it. Killed? Dismantled? Whatever it was technically, the outcome was the same. The female angel was down and out. Az brandished parts of her wings in his hands, twin blades that had been metal feathers a short while ago but now, two kick-ass swords. He glanced at Bradley – all ten tonnes of him that there were now – before bringing his focus back to Kira.

'The Messenger creates a pathway.' Az pointed one of the blades, as long and wide as his own arm, to where Tamas merrily tore the Earth a new asshole. Habit shoved a sarcastic reply onto her tongue, something along the lines of 'no shit, Sherlock', but Kira dug her teeth in, crushing the retort. Grow up, K. She wasn't a rich, lonely brat playing it up for the cameras anymore. Fucking everyone off with a sharp tongue so they couldn't get too close to her bruised bits. Hell, she didn't know what the fuck she was right now, but at least it wasn't that.

Kira rolled the sarcasm back down her throat. 'Any idea what we do about this pathway?'

Tamas was still surrounded by a tight cage of Telteriun wings, along with Parator, Seder and Bel, who hadn't followed Cym's lead and come over to Team Beckworth. Though Kira had to wonder if the medic was second guessing his decision to jump ship. Gren's death hadn't been pretty. She assumed. Kira refused to lay eyes on the new mess she'd made.

'I tried to get closer,' Nina said. 'But Ereshkigal protects them. All her energies are focused on that group.'

'If they get out . . .' Kira cleared a raw throat. 'The Lucentshield wouldn't hold them?'

Nina shook her head. 'Not someone such as Inanna, definitely not with three of the Four accompanying her.'

'I guess the chunky angels will need to rethink their band name,' Kira said. And no one gave her so much as an eye-roll, including Blake. Tough crowd. 'So do we just rush them? Everyone at once, maybe? Fuck, I'm not a general, and this ain't my army. Ideas, people.'

Bradley had not taken his saucer-sized eyeballs off her. She stared at her reflection in his glistening black orbs. Talk of Az looking like shit, Kira herself was a whole new level of bad-hair day. Her black curls were now a flattened, soaked mop against her head, but damn, she looked fierce. Held herself like a warrior, not some kid who had fucked up everything with a moment's distraction. If she'd seen herself in a club, she wouldn't have messed with herself.

This was a bad day, one of the worst as far as they went – Perry was gone, Rossiter was dead, Vail was fuck-knows where, and she'd probably just sliced a guy in half– but hell, she'd never felt less like she was about to drown. There were no holes where the panic could seep in. She was wrapped up nice and tight, and it didn't scare her. As if she should have been all armadillo all along. Kira ran her fingers down the length of her metal limb, feeling its bumps and grooves through the soaked fabric. The original metal arm. When Bradley had kicked the crap out of that god-awful rat-bastard, the energy coming off the lizard had almost floored her. Every move he'd made had seemed to echo through her, each contact punching her square in the guts. And she wanted more. Wanted to drink it in till she was wasted off her tits. Because the blows glanced off her, couldn't get through the barrier inside. Not really. Not down where things were truly broken and vulnerable. Those human bits, the ones that had made life hell the past few years, were sinking down deep. And she couldn't wave them off fast enough.

Patience, young one. It was the leaf-rustling whisper of Bradley. Sort of, but not quite. She knew it was the reptile, but there was a resonance, a depth and pitch that wasn't Bradley at all. As though the lizard were speaking to her from inside a cathedral.

The ground chose that moment to let them know what it thought of the situation, shuddering till it tore itself open; a thin crack barely a few feet from where they stood. Patience? The place was coming down on top of them. About to bury them alive, and they just stood there. Letting the baddies do their baddie thing.

The crevice in the roof above Tamas's gathering hadn't widened any farther, but it didn't need to. That space was more than enough for at least one, possibly two, of the gallu to shoot on up into the great wide yonder. And Tamas was still firing super-juice. He hadn't seemed to bat a goddess-hand-puppet eyelash when Bradley had brought down the water rat, or when Azrael had torn open his angel sister. Just concentrated on his hole. And where he wanted that hole to continue to, didn't take a genius to work out. Topside.

'Kira.' Blake leaned against Nina, who was biting on her lip as if she wanted to devour the thing. 'Those gallu, that energy source they are created from, it's toxic. Radioactive.'

She left it there, the warning hanging on the rattling, tremor-laden air, adding another shitty fact to their steaming pile. If Tamas got his tunnel to freedom completed, it was *Hello world, here's a goddess of war and a truckload of radiation. Have fun with that.*

Az's handywork, the demolished carapace, lay not far from where they stood. A giant's paperweight, good for nothing else. Even though she knew the thing wasn't real, at least not human-real, it sure as hell looked like a chick with her guts and ribcage wide open. Way too much dismembering was happening today. Kira pressed her fingers – metal fingers – into her sodden hair. Her warrior-goddess moment was losing its sheen. Like it or not, she was still human. And Telteriun shoulders or not, this load felt like the whole damn world. She hadn't saved Blake. She hadn't done jack shit in the scheme of things, except make a grand entrance. And get people killed.

Still getting people killed. Why the fuck were they still just standing there? When the hell was this Maiden chick making Her call? Kira couldn't shake the sense that She was still in cruise mode. Biding Her time. But what more did they need? Bradley was megalizard with dragon breath, Kira had sunrays for fingers, and Az had just proved he could open up the gallu like a giant tin of sardines.

Kira, catch.

Holy shit. Az's head jerked to find her. The bit of faux skin holding onto the right side of his mouth might have been trying to raise a smile. He'd heard the voice, too.

'Vail?' Kira searched for a sign of him. Or at least, whoever he was inhabiting right now. The kid was somewhere out there, still hanging in with them. Shit, her metal heart could have burst if it wasn't practically explosion proof. 'Vail, where are you?'

Her answer was a smack in the face. Right on her cheekbone. Practically the only place on her entire body that could still bruise. 'What the fuck?'

I did say catch, to be fair.

No one had sneaked up on their little stop-the-apocalypse party. The dead bodies around them were exactly that. Flat to the ground, not being waved about by a wizard-zombie boy.

Nina darted forward, snatching up the item that had struck Kira. 'Oh, you delightful boy,' she exclaimed, raising her hand. She held a curved piece of glass. Almost as broad as the blades Azrael held at its base, but only a quarter of their length, and curved to a fine, sharp tip. Sparkling. Like someone at Swarovski thought a giant claw would sell. 'Now I can do some damage.'

This. This was what they had been waiting for. Kira was as sure of it as she was of her own ability to devour three kebabs in fifteen minutes. If she was drunk enough. The certainty sat as heavily and uncomfortably as the kebabs themselves. Damn it, Vail. Show your crazy face, with your coins and bruises. Just a glimpse. A final hurrah. Something to smile at.

But Vail didn't play her game with her. Not even a thought fist bump.

'That is the blade Tamas used to destroy Dumuzi.' Cym spoke up for the first time, Gren's bow clutched in pale fingers. 'And bring Inanna to your world.'

Kira didn't get why the guy had gone full traitor, but he'd saved Blake's life. Bradley could have eaten him whole, but hadn't. So she was going with the lizard on this one. Besides, the guy had Eron's gentle vibe. So much so that her guts twinged to look at him.

'And it is the blade that will send Ereshkigal's Messenger to a place he is well-deserving of,' Nina declared, sounding far too perky for the moment.

Kira gave up her search for Vail. *Thanks, buddy.* She sent the thought out there, just in case. But the mind-silence was deafening.

'They're moving!' Blake cried, wrestling out of Nina's arms and looking way too much as though she wanted to run at Tamas's hell team all on her lonesome. She was right, though. Seder and Parator shifted from their positions, moving in closer towards the big ugly Brutus, Agar.

Locking and loading on Kira and her gang.

'We must move, now.' Azrael's wings spread from his back, a shield that blocked Kira's view of Tamas and his buddies.

'Blake, get out of here,' Kira demanded.

Blake shook her head, and tried to shoulder past Kira's raised hands. Good luck with that. If anyone knew that Telteriun made a pretty formidable roadblock, it was Blake. But ten points for trying. Kira easily shoved her at Cym, who placed a slender arm around Blake's chest.

'Both of you just get the hell out of here.' Kira slapped off Blake's attempts to cling to her. 'Blake, please. Stop.'

'Kira, I need to do something to help you.'

'Survive, B. That's what I want you to do. Live.'

'Yeah, well I wanted you to do the same.' Blake's voice pitched high. Her eyes bright.

'I know, B. I know.' Blake had gone to the ends of the Earth to keep Kira alive that day everything crashed and burned. The ends of the Earth and quite literally beyond. Whether Kira wanted it or not. Whether the goddamn universe wanted it or not.

Perhaps Blake was doing the mind-read thing now, too, because the words she rushed into the open space could have been torn out of Kira's own head. 'But I was wrong, wasn't I? Bringing you back, like that. I hurt you so much . . . I didn't fix you. Didn't fix anything. And I couldn't even look at you in the end because it wasn't right. I'd gotten what I'd wanted, and you were in so much pain. I know it wasn't right. And I'm so, so sorry.'

Jesus. There it was, brutal and undeniable. But an honesty so beautiful and rare it chipped away a piece of a mechanical heart.

'I know. And so am I. We both made a mess of things. And if I could take it back, if I could just keep my eyes on that fucking road, I would go back in a heartbeat. But it doesn't work that way.' No one outruns the reaper.

Kira didn't touch her sister. Didn't need those fissures messing up the armour.

Blake's reply might have taken forever, or a second. 'No. It doesn't work that way.'

'Goodbye, B. Love you. Always will.'

Blake's eyes shone like stars, but no tears fell. 'Goodbye, Kira. Love you. Always have.'

Come, Kira.

Bradley turned his broad head, tossing his stumpy nose in the air. The certainty kebab returned. He wanted her to ride the reptile train. Shit, *yes.* Azrael wrapped Nina in his arms, lifting them skywards.

Blake and Kira turned away from one another. And if Blake took a last look back at her, Kira would never know. She ran to Bradley, leaping onto his back, settling there, finding her grip. Finding her place. Going down swinging. No mistakes this time.

Tamas - 88

Tamas's laughter had long since dried up. And if this did not end soon, so would his veins. He shook his raised arms, the skin mottled by burst blood vessels beneath the surface, creating a labyrinth of crimson and grey. Every lick of the Abgul blood was sharp as razors within him, focused on the task at hand of creating the pathway for Agar to remove Inanna from this place. To open the skies to the gallu and set them beyond the reach of . . . damn it, he could barely even allow himself to *think* her name.

Kira.

Soaring like a blazing angel of death through the chamber, she was a stunning sight, Tamas would admit to himself, but he'd cut off his own tongue before he spoke the words aloud. That fractured human being got a halo, and what did Tamas get? Varicose veins, and a deep silence where the goddess had been. Agar seemed to grow impatient, shifting the child he cradled from broad arm to broad arm, as though Tamas should have been able to coax open the Earth far quicker than this. If the Four were so formidable, then why were they now three? One of their own lay like a gutted carcass across the chamber. Alone, Kira would not be enough. She'd never been a complete package to begin with. Just a slice of what was once whole. But she was not alone. Not alone at all. Enkidu walked with her, freed from the prison made for him. And that other entity, the Maiden. The one Tamas had dismissed so readily, such a short time ago. But he saw Her now.

Tamas had watched Her creature set fire to the Waters and destroy not only Captain Nex, the Messenger of Lahar, but the very corporeal representation of the Last Living god Himself; Lahar's Precon. Doing so with an ease that must have enraged His divine self. Tamas had faltered as the altercation reached a crescendo, his arms falling from their task as his foes had gained the upper hand. But the only indication he received from his goddess that She had noticed at all, was a sharp stab at his thoughts.

Continue. Do not fail me.

Her tone was laced with accusation, as though something She had long suspected may come to pass. As though his failure was an assured thing. Then She left him again, that hollow place in his being darkening with Her absence. No suggestion She was concerned about the enemy, only his ability to do as he was tasked. Tamas supposed an adult did not shudder in fear of a babe. And the Maiden was a newborn, certainly. Reliant on a hastily-gathered group of strangers.

Besides, Ereshkigal had already gotten what She wanted. Inanna was here.

He'd done that much. No one could deny Tamas that victory. Not even the gods. And Blake had witnessed it all. Could not have done otherwise. He had *made* her look at him. See him. He'd brought her to her knees, and she'd stayed there.

'Almost there, almost there.' Tamas took the encouragement upon himself. The gallu stood with their backs to the chamber, their eyes resting on him with impartial, steadfast gazes. Their expressions had not altered, even as Kira had brought down Captain Nex, even as Lahar's Precon had dissolved beneath the fire. Tamas would shed no tears for the harsh Syranian leader but he'd expected the gallu to show some sign they had recognised the attacks. If Tamas had to name their expressions, he'd have called it boredom, as though they no longer coveted any part in this at all. The game of aiding and abetting a goddess having grown old and tired. Well, it would be easy to show such disinterest if you were immortal. Whatever punishment might befall you, you simply suffered and forgot in the unfurling of the decades.

Tamas's senses received feedback on the progress of the energy, and in the past few moments the level of force required to carve a path through the dense layers of the Facility had decreased. And the impetus increased. Whatever was left of the barrier between this chamber and the outside world was weak enough for the gallu to breach. Some of Tamas's buoyancy returned.

'Agar, prepare yourself.' He allowed one arm to shift, gesturing to the three Syranians who surrounded the gallu. Parator, Seder, and Bel had not lowered their weapons since Tamas had begun. The captain had ordered them to hold their ground as he'd raced to his own demise. And they had done just that, with a grim resolve that did not shift, even as their brothers and captain fell. They had become hardened reflections of the gallu they shared a Bind with, seemingly untouched by the death that surrounded them.

'They approach!' Parator shouted. 'Your orders, sir.'

Tamas baulked, only just stopping himself from searching for the captain. Idiot. The god-soldier waited on Tamas's orders. 'Keep them back. Use everything you have, including yourselves.'

Agar lifted off his feet, the child cradled in such a way that Tamas couldn't glimpse the tiny body before the gallu was overhead. Tek followed after the bulkier carapace, his body held so that he faced out towards the centre of the chamber, keeping the approaching foursome in view.

Kira approached astride the mammoth reptile. It would have been ludicrous if it weren't such a threat. Her body pressed down low against the broad back, swaying with the sashaying motion of the creature as it ran. Enkidu swooped in overhead, brandishing the wing blades of Diresh like broadswords, a woman once again clinging to his underbelly, a far more voluptuous figure than Kira this time. Tamas recognised her as the woman whose image had multiplied itself around the chamber earlier.

'Fire! What are you waiting for?' Tamas bellowed, thrusting his arms forward and lifting the tangled wreck of cranes that lay over the far side of the Tier, hurling them at Kira and her mount.

The Syranians did as he ordered. The thrill of it was something Tamas could grow accustomed to. White and blue lasers pierced the rapidly closing distance between Tamas and those who sought to ruin this moment for him. Both firepower and metalwork hit their mark at the same time. Enkidu spiralled, moving to block the projectile aimed at Kira. His wing tips sliced through the cables, one of the wing blades batting away a rectangular chunk of yellow metal and sending it thundering towards Tamas. A flick of his fingers sent it off on a different, violent trajectory, and he grinned. Adrenaline saturated his body, and his pores soaked it up, leaving him dizzied with the rush. Sora moved as though to lift off, and Tamas stayed the gallu with no more than a narrowed eye.

'Not yet.'

Enkidu would have to do better than that. Tamas whipped his hand towards the thick cables Enkidu had just sent flying and worked just a single strand free. He sent it straight back at the wild man. The narrowness of the projectile kept it hidden until the last possible moment, and the wild man was too focused on the tunnel above Tamas. The cable landed on its target, finding Enkidu's head, winding around those indulgently beautiful eyes that Blake had given her very first carapace. The metal made a full circumference before Enkidu could raise a hand to stop it.

Such a beautifully simple thing, a fear of the dark. Enkidu's flightpath rose and fell, and he dropped one of the wing blades so he could grab at the metal blinding him. The woman's legs dangled, her grip loosened by the sudden instability of her vehicle. Tamas twisted his index finger in a rapid circle. The cable moved on his command, as everything now did, embedding itself in the wild man's face.

'Close your eyes, pretty boy.' Tamas's breath came in sharp, shallow intakes, the rush of strength barely contained by his human shell.

With a tightening of his fist, he imagined the metal liquifying and blanketing Enkidu's view of the world. And, in that world, Tamas's imaginings were king. The wild man crash-landed, skidding along on his front. He'd made a decided mess of his passenger if she had managed to hold on this long. With no sign of her elsewhere, Tamas held dual theories. She had been crushed or had never existed at all, just another of the apparitions this misguided group had used to give the illusion of greater numbers. Azrael's speed and bulk slammed him straight through the glass containment cell that had been Blake's front-row seat to activities earlier. What a pity she wasn't there now. How ironic if her own creation had killed her.

'Go.' Tamas gestured at Sora, the slightest of all Blake's carapaces – a lightweight boxer to Agar's and Tek's heavyweights. 'Bring him to me.'

The gallu's hawklike gaze swept the length of his body, and for one terrible moment, Tamas thought he would be refused. Sora swept his wings back, almost touching at his feet, and lifted away.

Tamas surveyed his domain. The bitch still clung to her beast, both their bodies smudged with light at the edges. The creature opened its jaws, widening them until it seemed impossible they wouldn't dislocate. Bel and Seder ran at the beast, firing off enough shots to keep the air full of radiant blue light. Kira deflected the onslaught, hands darting this way and that as though she were enacting a manic dance. But her whiplash speed was not fast enough. A bolt hit hard at her shoulder, threatening to spill her from her seat. The beast contorted, angling its body to move with her slip. And the torrent of fiery light it had been preparing to expel directly towards Tamas rushed out in a torrent just right of the intended target. Its force landed entirely on Parator. The Syranian's cry was a mere snippet of sound before he was incinerated. Bel and Seder maintained their positions, not even sparing their brother a glance – though they could not have missed the anguished cry – setting off round after round towards the beast that still hurtled towards them. Though they might not be succeeding in felling the creature, they *were* delaying it.

And time was all that Tamas required.

He lifted his head. Tek and Agar, with his precious cargo, had disappeared into the black hole Tamas had created for them. His smile cracked the corners of his mouth, his physical body drained by its labours, but his soul incandescent.

'They are too late,' he singsonged to himself. 'Far too late.' Was the goddess seeing this? Why was She not dancing through his mind, revelling in what he did here? 'Does this please you?' Tamas's euphoria raised his hands – in question and not destruction. Just a word. It was all he sought. 'Do you see what I do in your name?'

'You'll not get any praise if that is what you seek. Believe me.'

Tamas recoiled from the one who had so silently come upon him. Azrael's passenger, now just a body length away. Decidedly real. A woman of such beauty even the mask of contempt she wore did not mar her. It took the breath from his body, and he flushed warm and tingling with faintly familiar sensations. She used his split second of hesitation, stepping in close. Driving the claw-blade she held deep into his belly. Driving it through the fleshy knots that bound him to the goddess. Killing him with the singular thing that had given him true life.

'No,' Tamas sobbed. 'Eresh . . .' He called on the goddess, a lost child all at once, frightened and alone. And the hollow place inside him widened. 'Don't leave me.'

The woman's mask slipped, and he knew her for who she was. Inanna's handmaiden whispered soothing words, her eyes oddly gentle as she drew the blade up through his torso, ruining beyond all repair the fragile mortal shell that had borne him this far. She cradled his body as he slumped, still whispering to him, her voice as enticing as her body. He wanted to crawl inside her, hide away from what was befalling him.

'We are only ever small things in their eyes. Only ever servants to those so much greater. It is all we can ever be. You have served, now hush, little one.'

Tamas's cheek found rest against breasts of overwhelming softness, and he whimpered. 'But did She see me?'

The woman rocked him. And the Abgul blood he'd so treasured as a part of himself flowed. Leaving him, too.

'She sees you. She sees what you do in Her name, great sage. And now you are beholden to Her no longer. Find your peace, Tamas Cressly.'

He had words he still wished to utter, a smile he still wished to raise. But they all flowed away, just as the rest of him did. And Tamas Cressly was beholden to no one, anymore.

Kira - 89

Dragons – Komodo or otherwise – were excruciatingly uncomfortable to ride. Kira re-lost her virginity several times over on Bradley's back, his spine pushing up at her, trying to widen the clam till it felt as if she would split in two. It should have been comforting to know that she was still all fleshy down there, her favourite part of herself, but right now, as Bradley's swaying motion dug at her like a mole digging for China, metal would have been a blessing. Kira's grip was still solid, her fingertips digging into the tiny gap between scales. Scales that hadn't been evident at all when Bradley was just an itty-bitty thing scaring the crap out of her when he'd first appeared in Leona's shitbox.

It also didn't help that she'd twisted round, once or twice, trying to work out if Blake and Cym had gotten their asses out of here. Damn it, she'd tried hard not to do that. Look back. Wanted to remember that expression on Blake's face. Eyes like twin diamonds. Being so fucking brave because they both got it. These goodbyes were the big ones. These were the ones that they'd missed out on, three years ago.

No one got second chances like this. No one but the Beckworth sisters. So don't fuck it up by looking back.

Kira's reminiscing was interrupted by aliens trying to shoot her to smithereens. 'Christ!' She flailed her arms, swatting a thousand death-ray flies. Bouncing those beams off like a pro. Until she wasn't. The rebound off her shoulder rattled every part of her metal self, and she slipped hard right, her foot dragging along the ground. Uncomfortable, but nothing compared to what Parator felt. Bradley launched a fire spray that landed entirely on the Syranian. One moment the guy was there, the next . . .

Kira, are you harmed?

Bradley's leaves rustled in her brain, and something sweet and soothing as honey touched at her tastebuds. It was impossible to freak if you were eating honey, as it turned out.

I'm good. I'm good. She grunted, deflecting another pulse that came dangerously close to making a liar out of her. *What do we do? They've got the kid, they're up the tunnel.*

And we shall reverse that. Just as soon as the handmaiden is done. Much will be asked of you, Kira.

Much already had. But, details.

Kind of assumed that.

She'd known the minute Vail had shoved that stone down her throat. Kira dug her hands into Bradley's deep-ink scales. Don't think of the kid right now. She was holding it together nicely.

You share much in common with Vail. Okay. It was like that then. She and the reptile were brain-jacked together, big-time. *Neither of you exist wholly in one realm or another. The handmaiden and I hold the boy here, in this realm. But it is the godmetal that holds you. Just as your sister created those who would destroy, she also created you. And I have need of her handiwork.*

Blake *created* her? Don't let the girl's head get any bigger. And what was with the, *I?* Pass the pipe, dude. Bradley was talking like he *was* the fucking Maiden.

This Tier must be sealed. But that task will take everything from me. Reduce me to far less than I am now. Time will be needed to rise once again. A great amount of time. A gatekeeper is required to watch over the seal.

Shit. Balls. Shit. Kira pulled her hands from where they pressed against the lizard. Eyeball-licking Bradley, and the Maiden. One and the same. Kira was barebacking a god.

The holy-crap moment lost its lustre the second Azrael's panic almost threw her off Bradley's back. And it *was* Bradley. Screw a name-change this late in the game. Kira dug in her heels.

'Az. Something's wrong with him.' Shit. Kira clenched her thighs tight against Bradley's sides, rising up to try and get an idea of where Az was exactly.

He was down, and there was no sign of Nina. Az had crash-landed in the cell the aliens used to dump him in after their use-and-abuse sessions. Back when he dribbled rather than used his words, and she'd sit and talk shit to him until he stopped shaking so hard she thought his skin would fling right off. The glass that had separated them then was all gone now, but he looked just as wrecked as he used to. He rocked on his knees, fingers dragging against his eyes. Well, whatever it was that covered them anyway. They'd done it to him a-fucking-gain. Put him in the dark.

Calm him, Kira. Guide him. He does not need his sight to aid us. He must follow after those gallu.

Kira winced, hunching her shoulders against Az's distress. Man, he was working hard to hold it together. Working his wild heart out. But it wasn't quite enough. And one of those butt-ugly winged fuckers was getting ready to fly. Ten bucks said it was headed straight to Az.

He hates the dark. Bad memories.

It is his fear that blinds him, not the dark. His vision has been there all along. Bradley marked his words with another spray of death rays aimed at the chamber roof above the Syranians.

Hell of a time to go all cryptic on me, Brad. Your Highness? Majesty?

Bradley will suffice.

Okay, queen of the earth. You do you. Stick with the ridiculous name.

Bradley's onslaught dislodged a small mountain of rock. The entire pile coming down on Bel and Seder, silencing the high-pitched ping of their weapons.

Calm him, Kira. And he will see. His true sight.

Even as he laid waste to the chamber, his thoughts came in that same calm, whispering rustle, as though they were taking a meditation class and not trying to stop all hell from breaking loose. Bradley, the Zen master, wove his . . . Her . . . goddamn it . . . way around the few stalagmites that hadn't yet been decimated. Calm Azrael? That Kira could deal with. Been there, done that.

Az. Kira thought-fired. *I am right here, buddy. Just me. No bitch-ass goddess.*

Present company excepted. Different bitch-ass goddess. Christ, this was hard work.

Through a fuzzy head, Kira tracked the gallu headed for him, his lazy wing strokes dancing him across the short distance like a cat coming up on a broken mouse.

I am failing you, the mouse squeaked.

Quit the pity party for one and listen to me. I promise you, you are never going back there. She doesn't get to hurt you again. No more darkness. Never. Bradley's Zen mojo had washed off on her; Kira had never felt so damn calm and certain of what to say in her life. *But you can't bring the bitch with you. You've got to get over the fear, okay? Our scaly friend here says you can see.* There was a lull in the panicked waves washing against her. *That you've always been able to see. Open your eyes, buddy.*

The fear slipped down the mental drain. And the cat got the surprise of its goddamned life when the mouse roared up to meet it.

'Yeah, Az!' Kira whooped, punching the air, then scrambling to hold on a moment later as Bradley made an abrupt turn. He took them away from where Az raised a makeshift sword – one of the metal feather souvenirs from his fight with Diresh – and drove it home. Unhesitatingly. Landing a blind bulls-eye and ripping open another tin of gallu sardines.

The mea stones, Kira. We need all that remain.

A vertebrae high in her neck snagged as she twisted to try and keep her eyes on Az. A sharp reminder that not all her human bits had sunk into oblivion.

With those beautiful sea-greens lost beneath a layer of metal, Az's wings spread and he swept towards the gaping hole Tamas had created, finding it with the same precision he'd used to destroy the gallu. As she followed his path, Kira caught sight of dark curls and a generous, familiar ass. Nina crouched with Tamas cradled in her arms, right beneath the cracked earth. All Kira could make out was a skinny olive-coloured arm draped by his side – and a widening puddle of ink spreading around them. Nina laid him down and edged back from his body. She flicked her hair back over her shoulders and leaned forward, scooping her hands through the dark puddle she knelt in. Lifting her cupped hands to her lips.

Kira's eyes widened, and a faint sound left her. Blood guzzling was gross. Wasn't it? Maybe? Why the hell couldn't she find it repulsive?

'He's dead.' Kira played 'state the obvious'.

The handmaiden takes his divine blood for greater strength. Greater brightness. So that Inanna might see her once again.

Kira had thought there would be zero fucks given if Tamas bit the big one. But a fleck of pity found its way to the surface. Tamas's goddess hadn't saved him. He'd had the world's biggest hard-on for Her, and She'd abandoned his ass, standing back while he became a bloody sippy cup. The gods were just like life itself. Trampling all over the people who worshipped them.

Ereshkigal has abandoned this world, and Her Messenger. Bradley was right there, front row to her thoughts when she assumed she had the place to herself. *The goddess has no need of either anymore. She sought a distraction, something to turn Inanna's eye. A fate that may plague my world for thousands of years, to them is nothing more than a trivial play in a much larger game.*

My world.

'Our world,' Kira whispered.

Bradley brought them to a halt in front of the mini mountain that had come down on Bel and Seder. A hand stuck out from one edge of the pile. A foot from another.

Once the handmaiden removes Inanna from this realm, we must seal the Tier. Bradley closed his jaws around the hand, massive jaws engulfing it, and pulled. *To close off a gateway will take immense energy. These mea stones will magnify our strengths.*

Kira stared down at Bel's mangled face, a vague sense that once she would have thrown up everything at the sight. The Syranians could heal fast, but no one came back from a caved-in skull. Bradley opened his jaws, readying to clamp down on the grey stone embedded beneath dust and surrounded by deep bruises. Kira held up her hand.

'I've got this.' She knelt beside the dead alien, shutting the flashbacks behind an impenetrable wall. Kira's fingers sank through skin, through mush, and found their way to where the stone conjoined with bone. The mea stone slid from Bel's skin, hot-knife-through-butter easy. She lifted it to her lips, staring at the threads of something fleshy that dangled from one edge. Not even a flicker of revulsion, or nausea, or general WTF. Just clear sense of what she should do. Kira was buffered behind the armadillo, peeking out through a humanity hole that was getting fuzzy round the edges. She opened her mouth and placed the stone on her tongue. It dissolved like a slice of Jesus bread at Sunday service.

At least, she assumed the similarity. Kira had never actually got down on her knees for the guy whose name she regularly used in vain.

Mea stones tasted a bit like kimchi. Or perhaps that was Bel.

Bradley's head jerked up, his jagged teeth biting down on the mea stone he'd just removed with surprising tidiness from Seder's arm. A serpentine tongue flicked it towards her. Kira's hand lifted with the super-speed she'd gotten pretty used to now, and popped it on her tongue without raising a question. She didn't have any. Just got it. Bradley had said it was going to take immense energy to close the gateway. So, Kira was levelling up like a mofo. And the notion wasn't ruffling her feathers. Not a bit.

Bradley's head swayed towards a spot over her shoulder. *One falls.*

Not Az. Kira was gut-sure of that, didn't even need to take a peek. Her boy was still slam-jamming with Agar, somewhere in the guts of the Earth. Az's fury set off the glowbugs in her metal. A thunderous crash marked the predicted fall. Nina dove out of the way of chunks of Telteriun falling like massive raindrops, pieces of another of Blake's precious carapaces making a dartboard out of Tamas's body. From deep within her shell, Kira's thoughts touched on Blake – *please be out of here* – before drifting back down into the depths.

And so, one remained. The biggest, ugliest of all.

Kira gasped. A slow crawl of heat gyrated through her body. Az's bat signal coming in loud and clear.

He was bringing Agar right to them.

That body-fuzzing, mind-mushing buzz that existed between Kira and the wild man rang in the catch, sounding every alarm and setting every sensuous nerve alight. Kira's body hummed; the layers of the armadillo shifted, widening, making her bigger than she already was.

'They are coming!' Nina shouted.

No shit.

They were here. A river of rock and soil announcing their arrival. Expanded wings tore the tunnel wider at its entrance. Agar and Azrael emerged from the darkness, twin cannonballs that slammed into the ground and left a crater in their wake. The tips of their wings slashed at each other, at thin air, at anything that got in their path. If Agar was holding a kid, ten points to the guy for agility, but at the speed he moved, Kira couldn't make out anything in arms thick enough to replace ramming poles.

The surface of the Tier bubbled, steam rising off it. She was already running when Bradley's voice filled her head, already understanding where her place was.

Kira, get the child to the handmaiden.

The Zen master was feeling the heat. Tension jangled through their connection.

Kira followed Az's lead, grabbing at a length of the dismantled gallu's wings, rushing at the pair who shook the chamber with their fight club. Her feet never quite touched the earth; her surroundings blurred around her. But Azrael felt her coming. As she drew close, he lunged right and pulled Agar with him, giving Kira a clear shot at his back. Big target. No chance of missing that wide expanse of shoulder and length of spine. Kira hollered out a war cry and threw every ounce of her weight into the blow. She was so much more *substantial* now. Shedding your messed-up human self, was the ultimate health kick.

The blade sank through the Telteriun, and as the tip reached Agar's core, the gallu let out a screech that vibrated right through to Kira's fillings and shook every atom around them. He swung round to strike at her, and now Kira caught a glimpse of the child at the heart of everything.

Inanna locked eyes on her. Pale blue eyes set over a pudgy nose and gummy mouth. Underwhelming to look at, but Kira couldn't shift her gaze away. Her eyeballs on chains. Then that fat-cheeked face was rising, the kid lifting into the air. Agar's body bent backwards, his neck in the crux of Azrael's arm.

'Fuck.' Kira leapt for the kid, her push off the ground sending her way higher than she needed to be. She flipped herself forward – and wished someone had a damn phone to catch this. Kira did a full forward roll, grabbing hold of the baby midrotation and coming to land on her feet in a gymnastics move that could have made the Olympics. Azrael nailed the moment. Even with sightless, hidden eyes, he found the blade Kira had stuck in Agar's back. Driving it deeper, then hauling it down through the gallu's metal body.

Through chest and guts and gonads, ending the asshole who had ended Eron. Setting off a sunset that burned bright for a second, then died.

The kid – the goddess of war – opened Her toothless mouth and screamed. But not with sound. Nothing stirred the eardrums. This went to a different place. It made Kira's fingers itch, and skin she barely had, crawl. The cry compressed her chest until there was no room for anything but the rage that made the marrow in her bones boil.

'Let her go, Kira. Don't let her sink too deep.' Nina appeared at her side. She was grinning like a madwoman. And Kira wanted to strip those lips from that perfect fucking face and shove them down that perfect fucking neck.

'Piss off.' A venomous hiss. She'd fight till she was nothing but a pulpy mess if she had to. Bring it on. But don't touch the kid.

Nina leaned in closer, and the heady scent of lavender and sugar lay a velvet blanket over the whole shit show. She tugged the child free of Kira's clamped arms. And all the fight went with it.

'Oh my god,' Kira breathed. The itch was gone, the crazed drive to hurt and destroy, vanished. That was what Ereshkigal had tried to land them with. A 'roid-rage goddess. A match to the tinderbox this world already was.

'Inanna's influence would have destabilised this world beyond repair.' Azrael kept his distance – the two halves of Agar flanking him – while he made his understatement of the decade.

The only one who seemed unfazed was Nina. Sublime and radiant in her ecstasy. 'Thank you, beautiful.'

She landed a kiss – a hard peck – on Kira's lips, a glancing touch, but strong as the best of orgasms. 'We'll tell the Queen of Kur you said hello.' Nina giggled – schoolgirl-on-weed style – and offered up a fleeting glimpse of a couple of amethyst stones in her free hand. Kinda pretty, but each no bigger than an olive. If she wanted to piss off Ereshkigal with a pathetic offering, she was on the right track. Nina turned, pirouetted on the tips of her toes, and ran. Doing it in style in high-heeled boots, trying to keep her footing in a world that no longer held still. The tremors heightened, and the chamber floor by the main entrance split open, a chasm reaching beneath the enormous doors and stretching out into the corridor beyond.

Jesus. This was it.

The Tier was a cauldron, a giant emerald cauldron that smoked and bubbled like a hot spring. The lizard stood at its edge, his forked tongue darting at the Waters. Bradley took up three times the amount of space he had before he'd given her the order to grab the kid. And he shone bright as an afternoon sun.

So did Kira. The mea stones, fresh in her belly, darted round like crazed goldfish in a bowl.

Ready yourself, Kira.

It was all she had been doing. Maybe since the moment she'd woken up in a hospital bed with parts of her gone. She was good. Ready. But Az was still here.

She'd promised him, he was never going back. No more darkness.

And she could keep her promises now. But he was never going to go quietly. He'd bitch and moan about leaving her, and no one had time for that. Nina was almost at the Tier. When Kira moved to stand beside him, she noticed the oddest thing. Kira was taller than Az. Had to look down on him to meet his gaze. Bradley wasn't the only one taking up more space. The gaps between armadillo layers strained wider, she was more glow than Telteriun.

So. Damn. Awesome.

'I'm really sorry if this hurts, Az.'

She lifted her hands, her metal palms as broad as the wild man's head. Despite the covering over his eyes, he jerked away from her, seeing all too clearly what she intended. His defiance roiled through the connection.

'Kira, no.'

But he didn't get a say in this. He would take her place, play her role. The role where someone else bigger and brighter pulled the strings. Decided his fate. Her decision was final. And Kira was keeping her promise.

'Az, yes. You're done here, buddy.'

Kira took the last of the metal angels and threw him back into a world that would need him. Launched him up into the hole in the Facility's guts. The armadillo fell away. Or melted into her. Either way, she was no longer flesh or bone or metal.

Kira watched Nina take the last few steps towards the Tier.

Kira guided Azrael through the tunnel Tamas had forged.

Kira shared Bradley's transformation, his form—their form—shivering and contorting.

She was witness to all things at once. Eyes on all the prizes.

The energy that flowed from her, that *was* her, lifted Az back towards the light. Her name falling from his lips.

He'd remember her. Blake would remember her. For something good Kira had done. Something that didn't shatter a world, but saved it instead. What else was there?

Nina jumped. And the chamber erupted.

The Earth's molten core rose up, flooding the crevices and chasms and drenching the chamber in thick sulphuric clouds. And in the folding, snaking creases a figure formed. Someone else was keeping a promise they'd made.

Vail watched her from the dense air. Haircut still abysmal, eyes still puppy-dog adorable. *You won't be alone*, he'd promised her once. A long time ago. When Kira was in pieces. And damn if the kid hadn't found a way into the end of all things to make good on his promise. He mouthed just two words.

Blake. Safe.

So there it was. All the boxes ticked.

Kira's stupid-ass grin was the very last thing to go. Hanging there while she let everything else dissolve.

The lizard that had been Bradley, and the human that had been Kira Beckworth, lifted enormous, sweeping wings of fire and drove them down over the Waters.

Sealing the Tier.

And saving the motherfucking world.

Blake - 90

Blake groaned and swiped at the pair of legs that were placed far too close to her face. Of all places where there should be some peace and quiet, it was here. In her own bed. But her roommate had other ideas and had decided that the springy mattresses in this cramped room they called a bedroom was perfect for practising trampoline skills.

'Kira, for god's sake.' She slapped at the ankles before their owner hauled them out of reach, up onto the overhead bunk. 'I need to get some sleep. Just sit still.'

Something Blake could have done for the next year. Even the small effort of trying to slap her sister was exhausting. Her joints burned with a dull ache, and her head was too heavy to lift off the pillow. The air was stuffy in here. Hardly any oxygen at all.

'Can you open a window?'

Kira was closest to the latch, up on the top bunk, so it seemed right she should be tasked with the job. Blake stared up at the base of the mattress overhead. Its floral pattern was visible through the wooden slats. The flowers blurred into swirls of violet and baby pinks. She squeezed her eyes shut for a moment, opened them again. The action made her eyes burn.

'Kira? Did you hear me?'

Blake's nightgown clung to her, wet through, at the neck and under the armpits. Perhaps the heater was on. It shouldn't be, of course, it was far too mild outside and their father would be furious, but Kira felt the cold even when it wasn't actually there.

'Kira!'

A head dangled over the side of the top bunk, a tangle of onyx curls hanging from Kira's head like a crazed mop. She giggled and let her arms swing over the side, pretending she was going to topple off the bunk altogether.

'Stop it.' Blake tried to sit up, but the sweat that stuck her gown to her back in turn stuck her to the sheet. 'Stop messing around, K.'

Her sister's amber eyes were bright pinpoints of light, as though lit from behind, glistening as they did when she had a fever. The giggling rose to a higher pitch. Blake struggled against the sheets. Something was wrong. With Kira. She was always the first in the family to get the flu. Maybe it was a fever after all. Blake kicked out at the sheet lying over her body, but with every jerk of her leg the thin cotton rose higher, found another limb to tangle. Kira's giggling bubbled into a more frantic sound, her pale arms waving about. Sweat flicked into the air.

Arms of skin and bone. No metal.

Where was the metal? Metal? Blake shook her head. Maybe it wasn't Kira with the fever at all. Perhaps it was her. Why would Kira have a metal arm?

'Kira, just get away from the edge, for goodness sake.'

Liquid dripped from the overhead springs, the drops seemed to be trying to find Blake's eyes. She threw her head from side to side, and the sheet wrapped tighter against her. Finding her throat.

Kira wasn't giggling anymore. She was screaming. And murky water cascaded over the edge of the top bunk.

'Kira! Kira!'

Her sister tumbled from the bed, arms and legs working to reach for something solid. She reached for Blake. Their fingertips met, and then were parted, the current sweeping her away.

'No!'

Blake jerked upright, pushing frantically at the bedclothes. Scrambling out of the bed, wincing at the sharp sensation that came when her feet met the ground, Blake didn't make it more than two steps before she collided with a flimsy wall. The entire room rocked from side to side.

'Take it easy, Blake.' A young woman with a shock of red hair rose from a camper seat at the foot of the bed. 'Just another dream.'

She pushed open the window – a narrow pane above a much larger sheet of glass that didn't open – and tepid air moved into the cabin. 'Leona said you need to sweat if those tinctures she gave you are to work, but she's not here right now, so it's our secret, right?'

The smile offered was so faint it was barely visible at all. And Blake did not return it. Didn't have the energy. Her chest rose up and down like a piston, and the sweat that had coated her in the dream did so here, too. She sank back onto the bed, pressing her fingers into the corners of her eyes. Remembering where she was.

'Would you like some water?' Greta moved across the cabin, and the fall of water from a faucet filled the length of the camper.

'Turn it off,' Blake snapped. 'Turn it off.'

It was done before she finished asking the first time, but she kept repeating the words. Shouting them. Using them to stop from curling herself up in one of the corners of this rundown old camper and rotting there. The van door opened, and a metal man edged in, turned sideways to accommodate his bulk through the narrow entranceway. She fell silent.

'Blake?' Azrael approached with cautious steps. 'Are you well?'

'Great.' She shook. A low-level tremble that didn't show in her hands but hid beneath her skin. She ached. But not with a pain that any of Leona's disgusting medicines could fix.

Azrael had lost all but a small portion of the faux skin off his face – just a patch at his right cheek – and some charred strands of hair at the back of his head. Those sea-green eyes she had spent so much time agonising over, now lost beneath a melted panel of Telteriun. Her wonderous creation was a frightening sight. Not just because only small sections of what made him human remained, but because of the clothes that Leona had insisted on dressing him in. Clothes that belonged to the boy named Vail. A size too small for Azrael's frame, and the young Asian boy band adorning the front of the shirt, far too vibrant and youthful and . . . alive.

Blake was slowly patching those last few hours in the Facility together, but the bruises at the back of her head spoke of a head injury. Which would account for why so much was still blurry. Including the boy. It seemed that he had died. Though when, Blake couldn't work out. Greta had spoken of burying him. Leona had gone white with rage, declaring it too soon, and the conversation ended. Unresolved. They had driven on, taking the dilapidated camper across the desert. Putting distance between them and the Facility – what had been the Facility.

Leaving everything behind.

One day, maybe just a half, had passed. Blake had lost sense of the timing and didn't care to work it out. That would mean knowing how many hours and minutes it had been since she'd lost her sister.

Blake pushed herself off the lumpy mattress, the ache at her thigh a dull and distant pain. However long it had been, it had been long enough for Leona's stinking paste to work its magic. Beneath the careful wrapping of bandages, the deep cut was almost healed. Certain to scar, but in a super-fine line of soft pink. The wound on her hand was the same. Her feet stung with the cuts there, but nothing she couldn't bear. In fact, the only point that truly ailed her was the puncture where the splinter had lodged. Itchy rather than painful. But an itch that never faded was almost worse than an infected laceration. When Greta and Leona had discovered the splinter in Blake's clothing – as they'd dragged her out of her singed, smoky, and blood-drenched pants – they had exclaimed over it as if it were the rarest of gems.

'Why have we stopped?' Blake asked.

When she'd laid down to sleep, Leona and Greta had been discussing travelling to a place called a Rudiment. From what she could gather, it was a farm. With horses, Azrael had informed her as she'd drifted off. Greta apparently owned it now, after the death of someone close to her. But it was a long way away, and Leona didn't want to leave, not just yet. If Blake could have raised her head from the pillow to add her opinion, she would have agreed with the woman with the ruinous white hair and terrible fake tan.

'She'd agreed to go, but now she's changed her mind,' Greta said.

Azrael stood over her, but his focus was on the open window.

'Leona mourns the boy, as we mourn Kira.' His facial plates shifted, and grief found a way to etch itself into adamantine Telteriun. 'She is not ready to let him go.'

Blake dug teeth into the pliable, splitable flesh inside her cheeks. 'Where is she, now?'

Greta nodded at the door. 'Out there. There's no hurry. We'll go when you're both ready.'

'I'm fine,' Blake said.

To her credit, Greta didn't comment. Just nodded. Acknowledging the bulbous lie as it rang out between them. Blake left Azrael and Greta and stepped out into the desert night. A beautiful thing, even if everything else was grotesque. Tar-black sky, with stars bright as Kira's eyes had been in the dream. And in the level eleven chamber. Blake's feet dragged, the weight of their goodbye rendering her as heavy as any of the carapaces she'd obsessed over. Her toe met a hard surface, and she swore at it. No curse Kira would have been impressed with. Just a weak 'bloody hell'. Blake drew back her foot to kick at what had hindered her, throwing her aim wide as her eyes adjusted.

A desert tortoise. Young, if its small size was a measure of youth. And bold. The animal didn't shrink back into its shell at their collision. A nubby head stretched at the end of its long neck to peer up at her, and stumpy legs dragged it a step closer. The patterning on its rounded back was quite elaborate, the rust colour that was common to the species didn't sit in the usual blobs upon each scale. They flowed like ribbons through the darker pigments of the rest of the shell. Blake stepped over the creature and continued on. It was not difficult to find Leona in the dark. Her hair led the way, a ghostly beacon in the dim light. She stood, gazing back out the way they had come.

And in the distance, far far off, the Facility's glow was evident on the horizon.

Of course there was nothing left of the complex itself. No matter how impenetrable that place might have been once, no man-made structure could withstand a volcanic eruption of that magnitude.

'How are you feeling, Blake?'

The words out of the dark startled her, and Blake took a moment to compose herself. 'The medication seems to be helping. Thank you.'

Leona continued her desert gazing, her back still turned. 'You are welcome, but a little more than my tinctures and pastes is aiding you, girl. I don't believe everything was destroyed in that inferno.'

Night owls moved in to fill the silence. The wind added its own voice.

'I saw your boy. Vail.' Too blunt, too forthright, but Blake had neither energy nor inclination to meander around a truth. 'He told me his name. He led Cym and I up through the levels, remembered shortcuts that I was forgetting.' She took in a breath of the warm night air. The boy Greta spoke of burying, had saved Blake. But why had he not saved himself? Escaped, as they had done. 'It was hard to think straight. But it was him, wasn't it? He was young . . . blunt fringe, dark eyes, and a very lovely smile.' Lovely. The word didn't do it justice. His smile had been an oasis that both she and Cym clung to. And she could not recall when that smile had drifted away.

Leona had become a statue, no more wavering than any of the cacti that stood like sentinels around them. And, for whatever reason, Blake needed her to say something. Anything.

'I'm sorry,' she hesitated, 'that he didn't make it.'

'Don't say that, till we know for sure.' Leona whirled around, arms crossed tight against her chest. 'He might have made it. If anyone could, it's my Vail. And I'm not burying him until I'm sure.'

'I don't understand . . . you have his body? But how —'

'There's a lot you don't understand, young lady, but you'll need to learn. We need to be prepared.'

Blake took a step back, even though the woman had not come any closer. 'Prepared?'

'Think this is over? Despite all that they sacrificed? It should be. But that's not how it works. When has there ever been any peace?' Leona drew a long, dramatic breath that lifted her chest. And she held it there a good few seconds before she continued. 'Your sister, she hid a lot of things beneath that metal shell of hers. She was braver than I ever would have imagined. My Vail, too. When they were called on, they answered. Got the job done. Served the Maiden so beautifully it could make my heart burst. And it does. Breaks it. I see you know exactly what I'm meaning. So, we won't be letting them down. Not anytime soon.'

How the older woman managed to move from point A to point B at such a speed was lost on Blake. But there she was, the whites of her eyes glowing in the opaque night, up very close and personal.

'And I'll help you through this, girl. We'll help each other. I can fix your cuts and your bruises, but there is more inside you, I see it. And I know it doesn't sit right. It pains you. I'm not talking about this awful blister we share. Grief is one thing. There's another thing entirely within you. And we'll get to it, so you hold on. You hear me? '

It was too close. And far too personal. And Blake strained so hard to hold back what wanted to burst out of her, that her body jerked. Acid hit the back of her eyes. And the lump in her throat grew so large it pressed against her collarbones. But at least there was no taunt from the viper. No declaration that this was all the very least she deserved.

Since the dragon had drenched her, Blake had neither sensed, or heard, anything at all from her tormentor.

'Blake.' Her name was proceeded by a thump on the ground. 'You must see this. I've located it. You must see it.'

Cym, skin so white he glowed as Leona's eyes did, sat upon the back of the creature that had lifted both him and Blake from the collapsing grounds of the Facility, bearing them up high, and higher, beyond the reach of the molten rock that boiled from the Earth's guts and devoured everything. It was Leona's turn to take a step back as Cym approached. But Blake didn't shift. Nor was she about to. Of everyone here, Cym was the most alone. Worlds and death separated him from all he knew.

'See what?'

'Come, come.' He patted the back of the flying . . . bird? Lion?

It had been easy for Blake not to consider too deeply her escape from the Facility, when she'd been drifting in and out of consciousness. Now, here was one very large part of that escape, purring and cocking a burly head towards her, wings catching the heavy night breeze.

Avoiding the need to do any further contemplation, Blake swung her leg over the beast, and the cut on her thigh gave her no pause. She settled in behind the Syranian, wrapping her arms around his narrow waist.

'Just going to leave me here?' Leona huffed.

'I can assist you. Where are we going?' Azrael – and Greta – had made their way to the party unannounced, Greta childlike against Az's larger silhouette.

'This way, come.' Cym reached a hand towards Leona, and she abandoned all her caution, letting him settle her in front of him.

The beast lifted off, and Blake let out a surprised gasp.

She barely recalled the first journey. Had no inkling of how she had managed to hold fast to the silken feathers that coated the creature. Her physical body had been aboard, but every other part of her – heart, soul, and whatever came in between – had been down on level eleven.

Azrael brought Greta alongside, the girl a dark blob against his underside. The wings Blake had given him stretched wide, the Telteriun catching no light.

The journey was short. Or perhaps Blake had been paying too much attention to the stars that shrouded them. Either way, they were descending. And it was not so dark here, anymore.

Cym had taken them back towards the Facility. What the Facility had become. And all at once Blake felt as she had in the dream. Unable to breathe.

'What are we doing?' she may have whispered, or said nothing at all.

The Syranian drew himself off the creature's back, moving in that slow, measured way that he and Eron had shared. He lifted Leona high from her mount as though they were caught in a Brontë novel.

Azrael delivered Greta to their meeting place with a similar grace. And his wings settled into the cavity on his back in the precise way that Blake had designed.

'Eron spoke to me of Kira. Many times. He understood we both shared secrets, and he rightly believed himself safe confiding in me.' Cym took Blake's hand. They had landed on an outcrop of rock that sat above a shallow valley. At its north, the place Blake had regarded as home was on fire. 'He loved her, Blake. As purely as any I've known. And I saw what became of him. Agar eroded him. For Eron to become capable of . . . of trying . . . of wanting to kill Kira, then I saw that I too was capable of destroying what I loved. And that what I loved would be capable of destroying me.' His skin held a tinge of the fiery light thrown by the volcano. As did Blake's. 'But this is not a moment for sorrow. Look. Do you see it? Eron told me that Kira loved it, though we both could not understand why.'

He pointed down into the hollow of the valley, targeting a place not far below where they all stood. The long black length of a roadway marked the way to the Facility. But that wasn't what Cym was referring to.

It was a cactus plant. Tall and proud. Its resemblance to a hand giving a one-fingered salute to the world, unmistakable. She could not decide on tears or laughter, so Blake chose neither. She stepped forward, closer to the edge than was wise. And for the second time, her foot found some resistance.

For the second time, a desert tortoise blocked her way.

One with flowing rivers of rust along its back. A fearless head stretched towards her. Wide eyes fixed on her own.

Leona moved to her side. She considered the creature for a moment and then clucked her tongue. 'I'll let you name Her this time. I'm not sure She ever was a Bradley.'

Reviews are awesome!
I'd love to know what you think of Metal Angels.
If you have a moment, head to your favourite site and leave a
review :)
Amazon   *   Goodreads   *   Kobo   *   Bookbub

Want to keep up with all the good stuff yet to come?
Subscribe Now!

daniellekgirl.com

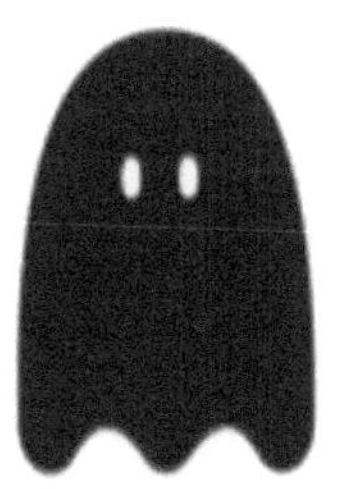

Fantasy   Sci-fi   Paranormal